Roderick Field

Jason Goodwin is the bestselling author of *The Janissary Tree*—winner of the 2007 Edgar® Award for Best Novel—and *The Snake Stone*, the first two books in his series of novels featuring Yashim. Goodwin studied Byzantine history at Cambridge and is the author of *Lords of the Horizons: A History of the Ottoman Empire*, among other award-winning nonfiction.

The
Bellini
Card

The Bellini Card

a novel

JASON GOODWIN

PICADOR

———

SARAH CRICHTON BOOKS
Farrar, Straus and Giroux
New York

www.picadorusa.com

Picador® is a U.S. registered trademark and is used by Farrar, Straus and Giroux
under license from Pan Books Limited.

For information on Picador Reading Group Guides, please contact Picador.
E-mail: readinggroupguides@picadorusa.com

Designed by Cassandra J. Pappas

ISBN 978-0-312-42935-5

Originally published in Great Britain by Faber and Faber, Ltd.

First published in the United States by Sarah Crichton Books,
an imprint of Farrar, Straus and Giroux

First Picador Edition: March 2010

D   10 9 8 7 6 5 4 3 2

For Bibby

Com'era, dov'era
[As it was, where it was]
—VENETIAN MOTTO

Never judge a painting or a woman by candlelight.
—VENETIAN PROVERB

The
Bellini
Card

1

HE sank slowly through the dark water, arms out, feet pointed: like a Christ, or a dervish, casting a benediction on the sea.

The stone at his feet hit the mud with a soft explosion, his knees buckled, and in a moment he was bowing gracefully with the tide. He had always been graceful, pliant, too, when fixing a price, a man who traded and left something in the deal for the other fellow.

Overhead, the killer turned his head from side to side, alert to the slightest motion in the darkness, feeling the rain on his face. He stood for a few minutes, waiting and watching, before he blinked, turned, and padded softly from the bridge, to be swallowed up by the night and the alleyways of the sleeping city.

The tide ebbed. The water sucked at the green weed that lined the walls, gurgled around old pilings, and slipped and receded from worn stone steps. It sank, nudging the trader closer to the sea on which, in her days of glory, the city had made her fortune. Beneath Byzantine domes, dilapidated palaces, and tethered boats the corpse was hustled noiselessly toward the sea, arms still flung wide in a gesture of vacant welcome.

Yet some obstruction, a block of stone or loop of rotten rope, must have checked his passage for a time, for when dawn broke, and the tide slackened, the trader was still yards away from the deep waters of the Riva dei Schiavoni into which he would have otherwise sunk without further trace.

2

THE sultan gave a high-pitched sneeze and patted his face with a silk handkerchief.

"The Queen of England has one," he said petulantly.

Resid Pasha bowed his head. King William was dead, like Sultan Mahmut. Now, he thought, England and the Ottoman Empire were being ruled by little girls.

"As the sultan says, may his days be lengthened."

"The Habsburgs have several galleries, I understand. In their dominions in Italy, whole palaces are stuffed with pictures." The sultan dabbed at his nose. "The Emperor of Austria knows what his grandfather's grandfather was like by looking at his picture, Resid Pasha."

The young pasha folded his slender hands in front of him. What the sultan said was true but perfectly ridiculous: the Habsburgs were notoriously ugly, notoriously alike. They married their close relations, and the chins got bigger every generation. Whereas an Ottoman prince had none but lovely and accomplished women to share his bed.

Resid Pasha tensed his shoulders. "The Austrian dogs always piss on the same spot," he said with a jocular grunt. "Who would want to see that?"

Even as he spoke, he knew he had made a mistake. Sultan Mahmut would have grinned at the remark, but Mahmut was dead.

The sultan frowned. "We are not speaking of dogs now."

"You are right, my padishah." Resid Pasha hung his head.

"I speak of the Conqueror," Abdülmecid said loftily. "Of the blood in these veins." He held out his wrists, and the young counselor bowed, abashed.

"If the picture exists, I wish for it," the sultan continued. "I want to see it. Do you desire, Resid Pasha, that the likeness of the Conqueror should be exposed to the infidel gaze, or that an unbeliever should possess it?"

Resid Pasha sighed. "And yet, my sultan, we do not know where the painting might be. If, indeed, it exists at all."

The young padishah sneezed again. While he examined his handkerchief, the pasha pressed on: "For more than three centuries, nobody ever saw or heard about this—picture. Today we have a rumor, nothing more. Let us be cautious, my padishah. What does it matter if we wait another month? Another year? Truth is like musk, whose grateful odor can never be concealed."

The sultan nodded, but not in agreement. "There is a faster way," he said, in a voice treacled with mucus.

"Send for Yashim."

3

CLOSE to the shoreline of the Golden Horn, on the Pera side, stood a fountain set up by an Ottoman princess as an act of generosity, on a spot where the boatmen used to linger and drop their fares. Hundreds of fountains existed in the streets and squares of Istanbul, but this one was particularly old and lovely, and Yashim had admired it many times as he passed. Sometimes, in hot weather, he would rinse his face in the trickle of clear water that splashed down onto the tiled basin.

It was those tiles that now stopped him on the street, where he stood unnoticed and aghast in the stream of traffic passing along the shore: muleteers with their trains, porters under enormous sacks, two fully veiled women attended by a black eunuch, a bashi-bazouk on horseback, his sash stuffed with pistols and swords. Neither Yashim nor the ruined fountain attracted anyone's attention: the crowd flowed around him, a man standing alone in a brown cloak, a white turban on his head, watching stricken as a trio of workmen in overalls and dirty turbans attacked the fountain with their sledgehammers.

It was not that Yashim lacked presence; his only lack was of something more definite. But he was used to passing unnoticed. It was as though his presence were a quality he could choose to display or to conceal, a quality that people would be unaware of until they found themselves mesmerized by his gray eyes, by his low, musical voice, or by the truths he spoke. Until then, though, he might be almost invisible.

The workmen did not look up as he approached. Only when he spoke did one of them glance around, surprised.

"It's the bridge, efendi. Once this has gone, then the tree, there'll be a way through here, see? Got to have a way through, efendi."

Yashim pursed his lips. A bridge linking Pera to the main city of Istanbul had been talked about for years, centuries, even. In the sultan's archives in Topkapi Palace Yashim had once seen a sepia design for such a bridge, executed by an Italian engineer who wrote his letters back-to-front, as if they were written in a mirror. Now, it seemed, a bridge was about to be built—the new sultan's gift to a grateful populace.

"Can't this fountain just be moved aside?"

The workman straightened his back and leaned on his sledgehammer. "What, this?" He shrugged. "Too old. New one'd be better." His eyes slid along the shore. "It's a shame about the tree."

The tree was a colossus and a welcome patch of shade and shelter on the Pera shore. It had stood for centuries; in days it would be gone.

Yashim winced as a sledgehammer cracked down hard into the basin of the fountain. A chunk of stone broke away, and Yashim put out a hand.

"Please. A tile or two . . ."

He carried them away carefully, feeling the old mortar dry and brittle in his palm. The boatman who took him gliding across the Horn by caïque spat on the water. "The bridge, it'll kill us," he said in Greek.

Yashim felt a shadow across the sun. He did not risk a reply.

Reaching home, he laid the tiles by the window and sat on the divan, contemplating the strong lines of the twining stems, the beautiful deep reds of the tulips, which had so often refreshed his eyes as the water of the fountain had refreshed his skin. Such flaming reds were unobtainable nowadays, he knew. Centuries ago the potters of İznik had fanned their talents to such heights that the river of knowledge had simply dried up. Blues there always were: lovely blues of Kayseri and İznik, but not the reds beloved of the heretics, who came from Iran and vanished in their turn.

Yashim remembered how he had loved such tiles, where they decorated the inner sanctum of the sultan's palace at Topkapi, a place forbidden to all ordinary men. In the harem itself, home to the sultan and his family alone, many women had admired those tiles, and many sultans, too.

Yashim had seen them only because he was not an ordinary man.

Yashim was a eunuch.

He was still gazing at the tiles, remembering others like them in the cool corridors of the sultan's harem, when a knock on the door announced the messenger.

4

RESID Pasha tapped his polished boot with a swizzle stick.

"The Sultan Mahmut, may he rest in peace, was pleased to order the construction of the bridge." He pointed his stick at the divan. "The old city and Pera have been too much apart. That is also the view of the padishah."

"Now Pera will come to Istanbul," Yashim said, "and we will know no peace."

Resid pursed his lips. "Or perhaps the other way around, Yashim efendi."

"Yes, my pasha," Yashim said doubtfully. He took a seat, cross-legged, on the divan. "Perhaps."

He tried to picture Pera subsiding into dignified silence, as the sober pashas and the minarets and the cypresses of old Istanbul spread their leisurely influence across the bridge, stilling the perpetual scrimmage of touts, tea boys, porters, bankers, shopkeepers, and sailors that milled through the Pera streets. Where would the cypresses find space to grow, between the Belgian hatters and the Greek peddlers, the steam presses and the foreign crowds? Old Ottoman gentlemen brought their families to Pera now and then, and led them in stately astonishment through crowds of every nationality and none, staring into the big glass windows of the shops on the Grande Rue, before embarking again for home.

"I understand that you know many languages," Yashim added pleasantly.

Yashim did not know Resid well. The young vizier belonged to another generation at the palace school, the generation that studied French and engineering; his training had taken him beyond the boundaries of the empire. Resid's mother was from the Crimea, an exile; his family were poor. He was in his midtwenties, maybe four or five years older than the sultan he served, but reputed to be a hard worker, pious without ostentation, quick thinking, and very sure of himself. Certainly he had advanced very rapidly under the eye of the old sultan, who insisted that he learn languages and had sent him on missions to Paris and Vienna, for Mahmut had lost confidence in the official dragomen, or interpreters, most of whom were local Greeks. No doubt he had considered him, too, a useful influence on his son.

The pasha shrugged. "Languages, of course. It saves time."

Yashim lowered his eyes. He spoke eight languages perfectly, including Georgian, and loved three: Greek, Ottoman, and French.

"The sultan has called for you, Yashim efendi. He is aware of the services you have rendered to his house. It was I who reminded him."

Yashim inclined his head politely. There had been times when old Mahmut would roar for Yashim and present him with some dilemma that suited Yashim's peculiar talents. Many things in the harem, and beyond, had required his attention, not all of them mere peccadilloes. Theft, unexplained deaths, threats of mutiny or betrayal that struck at the very stability or survival of the oldest ruling house in Europe—Yashim's job was to resolve the crisis. As unobtrusively as possible, of course. Yashim knew that the air of invisibility that surrounded him should also envelop the mysteries he was called upon to penetrate.

"And I would remind you, Yashim efendi, that the sultan is very young."

Yashim almost smiled. Resid Pasha's only visible affectation was a small mustache that he waxed with care, but his chin was smooth and soft. He wore the stambouline, that hideous approximation of Western dress that the old sultan had officially prescribed for all his subjects, Greek, Turk, Armenian, or Jew, and that people were still learning to adopt. Yashim, long ago, had decided not to bother.

"Sultan Mehmet was young four centuries ago, Resid Pasha, when he took this city from the Greeks."

"But one would say that Mehmet had more experience."

Is that what you have? Yashim wondered. At twenty-five—experience?

"Mehmet judged his interests very well," Resid continued. "He also overruled advice. But times have changed, I think."

Yashim nodded. It was well put.

"Each of us must strive to serve the sultan's best interests in our own way, Yashim. There will be occasions, I am sure, when you will be able to serve him with your special talent for peering into men's hearts and minds. Many others—it is natural and no shame to them at all—serve him by their mere alacrity."

His dark eyes searched out Yashim's.

"I understand," Yashim murmured.

The young vizier seemed unconvinced. "We Ottomans have many generations of understanding the ways of princes, Yashim. They give us—the sultan is pleased to give us his orders. And we say, the sultan has said this, or this. It shall be done. Among these orders, though, we have recognized a class of—what? Watery commands. Written on water, Yashim."

Yashim did not stir a hair.

What is written on the water cannot be read.

"I believe the sultan will receive you this afternoon." Resid raised his hand in a vague gesture of dismissal. "You will have many opportunities to show—alacrity," he added. "I can see that it shall be so."

Yashim stood and bowed, one hand to his chest.

The elevation of the new sultan, like the rising of a planet, was creating new alignments, shifts in the weight and composition of the cabals and cliques that had always flourished in the palace around the person of the all-powerful sultan. Resid had been singled out for advancement by Mahmut; now Abdülmecid had confirmed his father's choice.

Was Resid's friendship—his protection—an offer Yashim could afford to refuse?

Outside the vizier's office, Yashim turned and walked a long way down a carpeted corridor, toward a pair of double doors flanked by motionless guards and a row of pink upholstered straight-backed chairs.

The guards did not blink. What did the sultan want, Yashim wondered, that Resid so palpably did not?

He took a chair and prepared to wait—but almost immediately the doors flew open and a white-gloved attendant ushered him into the presence.

5

YASHIM had not seen the sultan for some years before his elevation to the throne. He remembered the skinny boy with feverish eyes who had stood pale and alert at his father's side. He expected him to have grown and filled out, the way children do to their elders' constant and naïve astonishment, yet the young man seated on a French chair with his legs under a table did not, at a glance, appear to have changed at all. He was almost preternaturally thin and bony, with awkward shoulders and long wrists concealed—but not made elegant—by the arts of European tailors.

Yashim bowed deeply and approached the sultan. Only his brows, he noticed, had developed: heavy brows above bleary, anxious eyes.

The sultan screwed up his face and opened his mouth as if to scream, then whisked a handkerchief from the desk and sneezed into it loudly and unhappily.

Yashim blinked. In the Balkans, people said you sneezed whenever you told a lie.

"Our gracious parent always spoke highly of you, Yashim." Yashim wondered if the compliment was hollow. Mahmut had been a tough old beast. "As our esteemed grandmother continues to do."

Yashim cast his eyes down. The valide, Mahmut's French-born mother, was his oldest friend in the harem.

"My padishah is gracious," he said.

"Hmm." The sultan gave a little grunt. It was the same grunt as the old sultan's, though higher pitched.

"Our ears have received a report that concerns the honor and memory of our house," the sultan began, a little stiffly. Mahmut would have spoken the same words as if they came from his belly, not his head.

"Does Bellini mean anything to you?"

With a sultan one does not gape like a fish. The room, Yashim now noticed, was papered in the European fashion.

"No, my padishah. I regret—"

"Bellini was a painter." The sultan waved a bony hand. "It was a long time ago, in the age of the Conqueror."

Yashim cocked his head. He remembered now the man who had once designed a bridge across the Golden Horn: Leonardo. Leonardo da Vinci. A Florentine.

"From Italy, my padishah?"

"Bellini was the greatest painter of his age in Europe. The Conqueror summoned him to Istanbul. He made some drawings and paintings. Of—well, people. With colors from life." The color seemed to have risen in the young sultan's face as well. "He was a master of *portraiture*." He pronounced the word well, with a French accent, Yashim noticed.

Yashim thought of the tulips he had rescued from the sledgehammer: they were very pure. But to paint people? No wonder the young man was embarrassed.

"The Conqueror desired that it should be so," Abdülmecid added, his blush subsiding as he spoke. "Bellini rested at the Conqueror's court for two years. I am told that he decorated parts of the Topkapi Palace—fresco, it is called—with scenes that the sultan Bayezid later removed."

Yashim nodded. Mehmet the Conqueror's successor, Bayezid, was a very pious man. If this Bellini painted people, Sultan Bayezid would have been shocked. He would not have wanted such blasphemy in his palace.

The young sultan laid his bony hand on the papers on his desk.

"Bellini painted a portrait of the Conqueror," he said.

Yashim blinked. A portrait? Mehmet the Conqueror had been only twenty-one years old when he plucked the Red Apple of Constantinople from the Christians in 1453. An Islamic hero, who became heir to the Byzantine Roman empire of the east. Master of the Orthodox Christian world, he made his empire stretch from the shores of the Black Sea to the crusted ridges of the Balkans, appointing Christian patriarchs with their staff of office, bringing the chief rabbi to the city destined, as all men said, to be the navel of the world.

And he had summoned an Italian painter to his court.

"The portrait, my padishah—it still exists?"

The sultan cocked his chin and stared steadily at Yashim. "I don't know," he said quietly.

There was a silence in the great room. As it lengthened, Yashim felt a shiver pass up his spine and ruffle the hairs on the back of his neck. Millions of people lived out their lives in the shadow of the padishah. From the deserts of Arabia to the desolate borders of the Russian steppe, touched or untouched by his commands, paying the taxes he levied, soldiering in the armies that he raised, dreaming—some of them—of a gilded monarch by the sea. Yashim had seen their paintings of the Bosphorus in Balkan manor houses and Crimean palaces; he had seen old men weep by river and mountain when the old sultan passed away.

He had spent ten minutes in the company of a youth who blushed like a girl, and dabbed his nose, and confessed to something he didn't know. The padishah.

It was the padishah who spoke. "The painting, like the frescoes, disappeared after Mehmet's death. It is said that my pious ancestor had them sold in the bazaar. With that in mind, what Muslim would seek to buy what the sultan himself had pronounced forbidden?"

The word was *harem*. Yashim nodded.

"The portrait has never been seen since," the sultan added. "But Bellini was a Venetian. The best painter in Venice, in his day." His eyelids flickered; he brought the handkerchief to his face, but no sneeze came. "Now we have word that the painting has been seen."

"In Venice, my padishah."

The sultan tapped his fingers on the table and then, abruptly, clambered to his feet. "You speak Italian, of course?"

"Yes, my padishah. I speak Italian."

"I want you to find the painting, Yashim. I want you to buy it for me." Yashim bowed. "The painting is for sale, my padishah?"

The sultan looked surprised. "The Venetians are traders, Yashim. Everything in Venice is for sale."

6

YASHIM took a caïque across the Horn, directing it to drop him farther around the shore, at Tophane. He did not want to see the broken fountain again, or to witness the felling of that magnificent old plane. He made his way uphill, through the narrow alleys of the port; at night, this place was dangerous, but in the afternoon sun it felt almost deserted. A cat slunk low on its belly and disappeared under a broken-down green gate; two dogs lay motionless in a patch of shade.

He found the steps and climbed briskly up the steep slopes of Pera toward the Polish residency.

Most of the European ambassadors had already decamped for the summer. One by one they retreated from the heat of Pera, where the dust sifted invisibly and relentlessly off the unmade streets. They went to villa gardens up the Bosphorus, to conduct their intrigues and negotiations among the bougainvillea and the hyssop. Some of these summer palaces were said to be magnificent—the Russian and the British could be glimpsed, cool and white among the trees, from a caïque gliding down the Bosphorus. The French, the Prussians, the Swedes all had their summer palaces. Even the Sardinian consul took rooms in the Greek fishing village of Ortaköy.

Stanislaw Palewski, Polish Ambassador to the Sublime Porte, remained in town.

It wasn't that Palewski felt the need to remain close to the court to which he was accredited. Far from it: the ordinary burdens of diplomatic life rested lightly on his shoulders. No frowning monarch or jingoistic assembly issued him daunting instructions; no labyrinthine negotiations were ever set afoot by the Polish Chancellery. Poland had no monarch and no assembly. There wasn't, indeed, a Poland at all—except one of the heart, and to that Palewski was bound with every fiber of his body.

Palewski had arrived in Istanbul a quarter of a century before, to represent a country that did not, except in the Ottoman imagination, exist any longer. In 1795, Poland had been invaded and divided by Austria, Prussia, and Russia, putting an end to the ancient commonwealth that had once battled the Ottomans on the Dnieper and at the walls of Vienna.

"You must always try to forget what you have lost," Palewski had once remarked to his friend Yashim. "And I must always remember."

On a whim, because the day was so hot, Yashim went past the gates of the Polish residency and over the Grande Rue to the cluster of Greek coffeehouses that had sprung up by the entrance to an old burial ground. Far away across the Bosphorus, beyond Üsküdar, he could just make out the snowy slopes of Mount Olympos, shimmering in the heat.

Yashim bought a pound of Olympian ice, wrapped in paper.

He knocked several times on the peeling boards of the residency door. Eventually he pushed it open and spent a few minutes wandering alone through the ground floor of the dilapidated building. Out of curiosity he tried the dining room and found it as he had expected, almost impenetrably dark behind the tangle of clematis at the windows; the dining table sagged in the middle, and the stuffed, hard chairs ranged against the walls were green with mildew.

He went through to the back of the house, wondering if Marta, Palewski's Greek maid, was in the kitchen. She was not. Through the open window he spotted a familiar figure half hidden in the tall grass and waded out to meet his friend.

Palewski lay full-length on a magnificent old carpet. He was propped over a book, wearing a broad-brimmed straw hat and a pair of blue cotton trousers. His feet were bare. A glass and jug of what looked like lemonade stood at his elbow.

"I brought you some ice," Yashim said. Palewski jumped. He sat up and pushed his hat to the back of his head.

"Ice? Good of you, Yashim."

Yashim slipped off his shoes and sat down cross-legged on the carpet. Palewski glanced at it. "Marta laid it out here—she says the sun kills the moth."

"But you're in the shade."

"Yes. It was too hot."

A magnificent palace weave of vermilion semicircles on a black background, the design of the carpet echoed the patterns of the caftans worn by the sultans in the glory days of the Empire, when the İznik tile makers were at their best. It must have been more than two hundred years old. The Poles had been at their best then, too, battling the Ottomans on the Dnieper and the Prut.

"I haven't seen this one before," Yashim murmured. He ran his hand across the fine nap and winced.

"Rolled up in the attic. In canvas, too." Palewski stood up. "Fluttering little bastards. Where's that ice?"

He took it to the kitchen, where Yashim heard him banging around. He returned with a glass and the ice shattered in a bowl. Yashim gestured to the book on the carpet.

"Are you thinking of traveling?"

"I drag out the atlas now and then," Palewski said. "My grand tour, suspended."

Yashim nodded. Many rich young Europeans traveled through Italy and Greece when they came of age. Sometimes they came on to Istanbul, confusing the locals with their attempts to order coffee in ancient Greek.

Something moved at the back of Yashim's mind. "When you say—suspended?"

Palewski busied himself with the ice and the jug, murmuring something Yashim could not quite catch. "Half thinking of going away for a while, Yashim."

Yashim blinked. "Up the Bosphorus?" He found it hard to imagine Istanbul without Stanislaw Palewski.

"Farther. I don't know." Palewski pulled a face. "Not that I have a crowd of options. A felon in my dismembered country. Wanted by half the despots in Europe for upholding Poland's dignity in a foreign court." He shook his head. "Paris? Rome? London's safest, I suppose." He groaned. "Boiled beef and gin."

Yashim smiled. "Pera's pretty horrible in summer."

Palewski scratched his ear. "I mean it, Yash," he said gloomily. "The inaugural ball."

Yashim laughed. "You have six weeks to get ready." It was common knowledge that the young sultan would mark his accession by throwing a ball for dignitaries foreign and domestic on their return to the city. "I expect you've still got that glorious coat you wore last time—unless the moths have got it, too?"

"It's not about moth, Yashim." Palewski looked grave. "It's the new sultan."

"I've just met him," Yashim said. "He has a cold."

"Fascinating stuff, Yashim. Maybe I could take a caïque up to the British embassy and cadge an evening in the gardens on the strength of it." The ambassador picked moodily at the grass. "Sultan Mahmut may have been a reformer, but he had a proper sense of his own power. He waited almost twenty years to achieve it, but by the time he was big enough to do what he liked, I was a sort of fixture. He liked the way it broke the Russians' hearts to have me turn up at his functions."

"He liked you," Yashim said.

"That doesn't count in politics. Anyway, he's gone."

"And Abdülmecid?" Yashim watched his friend in silence for a moment. He saw the way his friend was thinking. "He won't drop you."

"I can't agree," Palewski said stiffly. "Mahmut was old and fierce. He was pleased to think that the Ottomans were the only people in Europe who still recognized the Polish Republic. Abdülmecid is young and probably nervous of stepping out of line. The assembled *corps diplomatique* are watching to see if he drinks champagne from the wrong sort of glass."

Yashim frowned. "Are you guessing, or has someone spoken to you about it?"

Palewski dismissed the question with a wave. "Of course not. No one ever will. In case you're wondering, they haven't stopped my stipend yet, either. It doesn't mean a thing. They'll probably go on paying that until I drop down dead. It's the Ottoman way, Yashim. Polite and indirect. You know that."

Yashim had been tracing a pattern in the carpet with his finger. "I could try to speak to someone, if you like."

Palewski blew out his cheeks. "Decent of you, Yashim. Just don't think it would sway the balance."

Yashim drew a long breath. "I could find out if you're invited?"

"It's a bit late, actually. I saw the Sardinian consul yesterday in the street. Grinning like an organ grinder and all ready to move up to his hovel in Karaköy. Had the wretched invitation in his pocket. The Sardinian consul, Yash! Wouldn't surprise me if the sultan asked that French tailor in Pera to come along. It's not an exclusive affair."

Yashim sighed.

"I'm in a difficult position at the palace, too."

He told Palewski about Resid's warning and the sultan's interest in an old painting.

When he had finished he took a sip of lemonade.

"Very weak," Palewski explained grimly, as Yashim choked. "Low-grade stuff, too. I wouldn't use bison grass." He lay on his side, his chin cupped in his hand. "Ask yourself: What if the Bellini does exist?"

Yashim shrugged. "I buy it for the sultan."

Palewski was quiet for a moment. "Do you remember Lefèvre, the Frenchman? He stole old books."

Yashim nodded. How could he forget?*

"I told you then about provenance. About how a book could become valuable if it had a story attached to it. Remember?"

Yashim remembered. Old books, guarded in some monkish scriptorium for generations, could accrue a value far beyond their worth as literature. Sometimes, it seemed, beyond the value of a human life.

"Bellini's portrait of Mehmet could be worth a lot of money, Yash," Palewski said. "A Bellini's just the sort of thing some young milord would want to carry off in triumph to his big house. And a Bellini portrait of Mehmet the Conqueror—so much the better. Exotic. Story attached. Impresses his friends."

Yashim's chin sank onto his breast. He thought of the İznik tiles he had rescued. To him they were priceless, irreplaceable. They were beautiful works of an artist's skill and imagination—but in Istanbul they were treated like old bricks.

He took a sip of Polish lemonade.

"Imagine if some turbaned Ottoman dignitary arrives in Venice with instructions to buy the painting and a sultan's purse at his disposal."

Yashim's nose prickled against the vodka. "I pay too much," he said simply.

"You're a sitting duck, Yashim. You'll pay double for an artwork that many of Abdülmecid's subjects will think is blasphemous. Mahmut left the Ottoman state almost bankrupt: it's an open secret. Resid is right. This, Yashim, is a watery command."

"But if I don't go . . ." Yashim trailed off.

"Well, you're in a fix, Yashim. If you don't go, the sultan may resent it. If you do, Resid will never forgive you."

Yashim snatched up Palewski's atlas and bent his head over the map. Mountains on the atlas were shown as a scattering of tiny peaks, cities as small black dots. The edge of the land was represented by a pretty shading, in blue.

His first commission from the new regime—and already it was com-

* See *The Snake Stone.*

promised! Resid wanted him to stay and forget. The sultan wanted him to go. Resid was right: Palewski said so, but the sultan ruled.

Yashim laid a finger on the map. "You're right. I can't go." He picked out the Latin inscriptions. Adriaticum. Ragusa. Venetia. "But you can. You can go and buy the sultan's Bellini, my old friend."

Palewski opened his mouth and shut it again in astonishment. "Me?" He sat up. "Yashim, you must have taken leave—"

"The grand tour—resumed," Yashim interrupted. "And more important, the sultan's gratitude."

Palewski looked at him uncertainly.

"The Conqueror, restored by the Polish ambassador to the city he won? I think it's worth an invitation to the inaugural ball."

His friend looked up into the branches of the mulberry tree. "Yes, but—the Austrians, Yash. My position. All—this." He waved a hand around the ill-kempt lawn. "What would Marta say?"

Yashim smiled. "Leave her to me. It's summer, and all the ambassadors are away. As for the Austrians, well." He paused. Palewski was scarcely regarded favorably by the Habsburgs. He'd been a thorn in their side ever since he arrived in Istanbul, a refugee from his own estates in southern Poland. The Habsburgs had sequestered his country, and they ruled over Venice, too.

"The answer, my friend, is that you will travel in disguise." And seeing that Palewski was opening his mouth to protest, he added, "And I'll have a drop more lemonade."

7

THE sun rose from the sea in a veil of mist so fine that in twenty minutes it would burn up and be gone.

Commissario Brunelli took the papers between his thumb and forefinger and dropped them into his satchel without a second glance. The aged pilot grunted and gave him a narrow, toothless smile.

"For the friends?"

"For the friends," Brunelli agreed. What the Austrians made of them he had no idea. Nor did he much care. If they combed the passenger lists for foreign spies or political exiles, that was their affair: they could do the work, if it mattered to them so much. His own mind, he felt, was on higher things.

In particular on the sea bass that Luigi, at the docks, had promised him as the customary favor.

The ship creaked slightly in the current. Brunelli shook hands with the captain, a trim and stocky Greek with tight white curls he remembered having seen before, and went to the rail.

Scorlotti was waiting for him in the boat.

"Anything new, Commissario?"

"No, Scorlotti. Nothing new." When would the boy learn? he wondered. This wasn't Chioggia, this was Venice. Venice had seen it all before. "Drop me at the docks, will you?"

Scorlotti yawned and grinned. Then he took up the oars and began to row them across the smooth waters of the lagoon.

By the time Palewski reached the deck, Commissario Brunelli was nothing more than a speck of color laid, so it might have seemed, by the tip of a brush on the loveliest canvas ever painted by the hand of man.

"So this is Venice," Palewski muttered, shading his eyes against the shards of sunlight bouncing off the sea. "How ghastly."

8

STANISLAW Palewski's words were not spoken with any animus against the Queen of Cities. The previous evening he had celebrated his impending arrival with Greek brandy, toasting the islands of the Dalmatian coast as they slid by and revealed their coves and whitewashed villages to him one by one. In the morning the rattling of the ship's anchor chain through the davits, and the ship's bell five minutes later, had woken him from a befuddled dream rather earlier than he was used to. Worse still, the ship's cook no longer offered coffee to the paying passengers: they had arrived.

He ran his hands through his hair and groaned softly, squinting at the view.

Gorgeous it was, with its domes aflame in the morning light and a soft mist dispersing around its pilings and water stairs, yet Venice in 1840 was not quite the Adriatic queen of former times. Once, with her islands and her ports scattered across the eastern Mediterranean, she had considered herself sovereign of a quarter and an eighth of the Mediterranean. Each year her doge, with his ring, renewed his marriage to the sea; each year it cast back treasures on her shore—silks and spices, furs and precious stones, which the Venetian merchants sold shrewdly in the north. But with each passing year, too, her grip had loosened: the Ottomans had gained; the current of trade and wealth had ebbed toward the Atlantic. In a whirlwind of partygoing, the Venetians had pavaned insensibly toward Nemesis. Napoleon had come and had been what he predicted: an Attila to the Venetian Republic.

The Austrians took over what Napoleon could not hold for long, and for thirty years the old port had decayed under the indifference of the Habsburgs, who preferred Trieste.

Palewski found the view consoling, all the same. Venice in the flesh was remarkably like the Canalettos that hung in the British ambassador's residency, only much larger—a full panorama of drabs and browns, blotched here and there by puffs of iridescent pastel; close in, a drunken regiment of masts and spars; far off, the campaniles of the city's thirty-two churches; shimmering blue water beneath his feet and overhead the clear summer sky. He thrust his hands into his pockets and felt the jingle of silver coins there for the first time in years.

Palewski had grumbled at the tailor who fitted him in Istanbul, and at Yashim, too, but in his heart, where every man carries at least an ounce of vanity, he was rather pleased. He had always been elegantly, if a little shabbily, dressed, but now he wore a waisted coat over a deep-fronted waistcoat, stovepipe trousers of the latest cut, and shiny black shoes pointed at the toes. His mustache was neatly, even tightly, trimmed, while his hat—blacker and more lustrous than the one he habitually wore around Istanbul—was also three inches taller. He sensed that he carried the air of a man of the world, one whom the world was unlikely to fool but who looked on it with kindly interest.

Did he look like a citizen of the United States? As Yashim had pointed out, the beauty of being an American was that no one really knew what an American ought to look like.

"Have my bags sent on to the Pensione Inghilterra," he told the purser as a boat drew up alongside.

It was a gondola. To Palewski, used to the graceful open caïques of Istanbul, it suggested something more sinister, with its beaky prow and tight little black cabin in the middle. As the stocky gondolier helped him from the ladder, Palewski doubled up and stepped down into the cabin, removing his hat. It was organized like a barouche. He found a seat and sat down; the bench opposite was of tattered leather and the air smelt musty and damp. When he drew back the curtains and dropped a window, he was surprised to find himself already moving at some speed along the Riva dei Schiavoni.

With a jolt he recognized that the coloring, the little stone windows with pointed arches, even the disjointed roofline, reminded him of Cracow. "Why," he exclaimed aloud, "this isn't a Mediterranean town at all!"

He identified the Doges' Palace, and the two pillars that stood beside it at the water's edge: he had seen them in the Canalettos. The palace seemed to be upside down, all the lightness expressed in an arcade of slender columns was at the bottom, with the bulk of the building pressing down from above. He craned his neck for a glimpse of its reflection in the water, but he couldn't see beyond the legs of his gondolier, and at that moment the great white church of Santa Maria della Salute reared up on his left-hand side, ushering them into the Grand Canal.

The traffic thickened. Black gondolas swept past them in the opposite direction, their curtains drawn, though now and then from their dark interiors Palewski caught sight of a white-gloved hand or a set of mustaches. Slow, deep barges carrying vegetables or dressed stone or sacks were being worked forward by men leaning on long oars. The oarsmen exchanged shouts with one another, especially when their barges were moving empty. A *traghetto* carrying a parcel of nuns shot out from a landing stage. Palewski's gondolier braked with a whoosh and unloosed a rich slice of impenetrable dialect, which seemed to be returned: fists were shaken; the nuns looked away. Palewski smiled. The nuns in their habits reminded him of ladies at home, ladies in Istanbul.

He was aware now of something he had already sensed but not understood: the almost total absence of any sound beyond the shouts of boatmen and the liquid notes of water dropping from oars or hissing at the foaming prow of the boats. But as the gondolier pressed down on his sweep, they swung abruptly into a side canal, and sound and sunlight were blotted out.

Palewski started back, as if the bricks were about to strike his face. Twisting in his seat, he stared upward: they were passing down a slimy passage between tall buildings. The windows overhead were framed in stone, with rusty iron bars; patches of fallen plaster revealed an expanse of narrow brick. Here and there, laundry hung limply on lines stretched across the canal. Palewski wondered how it could ever dry. He pulled his coat across his chest and turned to the little window at his back.

"Brrr. Pensione Inghilterra?"

"*Sì, sì.* Pensione." The gondolier jerked his chin.

"Inghilterra?" A doubt had lodged in Palewski's mind. "Pensione Inghilterra?"

But Palewski's question was destined to go unanswered, for at that moment the gondolier stumbled, staring into the water.

"*Sacramento!*" he growled. "A man!"

9

IT had been a man, certainly. The image was still lingering in Palewski's mind as he sat in his apartment at the Pensione Inghilterra watching the reflected light from the water ripple across the façade of the building opposite. He turned his head. Involuntarily he saw, again, the mat of dark hair and the whole revolving, bulbous mass of the dead man's face sliding beneath the surface. The boatman, prodding with his sweep, had brought up the corpse in a roil of bubbles and guided it toward the nearest quay. Palewski had not stayed to see more.

He took a sip of tea. It was barely warm, and with a shudder of disgust he stood up, crossed the room, and emptied his cup out the window. He heard it patter into the water down below.

He set the cup back on its saucer and rang his bell.

"I am going out," he told the valet.

At Florian he ordered wine and a dish of polenta, which arrived smothered in onions and anchovies and put him in a better mood. He asked for grappa. He'd been hungry, thirsty, and thrown by that horrible unexpected corpse floating in the water. Who knew how the poor fellow had got there? Missed his step in the dark, maybe. One thing you could say about Venice: it would never do to trip in the street.

He leaned back and began to survey the square for the first time. At one end, beyond the enormous tower that reminded him, once again, of Cracow, stood a squat church, like a pig in rut. The arcades that lined the piazza on three sides were pretty fine. The pigeons were returning to their roosts with the dusk; little fires were springing up across the piazza, and the air had begun to fill with the scent of roasted chestnuts. It was after nine.

"*Permesso?*"

The man had his hand on the back of a chair. Palewski raised an eyebrow and shrugged.

The stranger pulled out the chair and sat down. He put his forearms on the table.

"*Parlite Italiano?* Good. My English is poor, Signor Brett."

His frank blue eyes looked Palewski in the face. He was a big man in his early fifties, Palewski judged, with a fine head of black hair. How the devil did he know his name?

"And you are, Signor—?"

"Brunelli." He put out his hand. "Commissario. You are welcome to Venice."

Palewski blinked and shook hands.

"The boy at the Inghilterra said you had come out," Brunelli explained. "And I needed a little air. Perhaps a grappa, too."

He clicked his fingers and the waiter came forward.

"Grappa—*due*. The polenta is good here, Signor Brett."

"Thank you, I've eaten," Palewski replied. He eyed the commissario uncertainly. He had told the valet he was going out, nothing more. "How did you know I'd be here?"

Brunelli shrugged lightly. "On their first night in Venice, everyone comes to Florian. Or Quadri," he added. The waiter laid the glasses on the table. Brunelli took a sip. "Or have you perhaps been to Venice before?"

"It's my first time, Commissario." Some functionary of the police, evidently; for a few moments Palewski had allowed himself to forget that he was in Habsburg territory.

He downed his grappa and called for the bill. "Do excuse me, I'd like to walk a little."

Brunelli rose to his feet with surprising lightness for a large man. "Let me walk a little way with you, signore," he said. "I will show you the pillars of St. Mark."

Palewski bowed stiffly. The evening was warm but his hands were cold, and he could feel the beating of his heart.

"You were in Istanbul?" the commissario remarked casually, as they strolled along the arcade toward St. Mark's.

The ship's manifest, of course, would have given this man his name and his port of embarkation.

"I went to buy a statue," Palewski said. He and Yashim had devised this story together. "For a collector in New York."

"Did you have any luck?"

"Not yet. Ottoman bureaucracy is very slow."

The policeman nodded. "Here it is the same. Vienna is a long way away."

Palewski did not reply. He had recognized, with a shock, the gray-coated Habsburg sentries strutting outside the government buildings at the far end of the piazza. It had been many years since he had seen the uniform: columns of soldiers in greatcoats, marching through snow. Vienna seemed uncomfortably close.

"You deal in artwork, Signor Brett." The commissario sighed. "And in Venice?"

"And in Venice, yes. There is a lot to see."

They turned in front of the basilica and began to walk toward the water.

"A strange thought, Signor Brett, that our Tiepolos and Titians may end up in the land of beavers and savage Indians."

"Would you rather see them in Vienna, Commissario?" Palewski tried, and failed, to keep the bitterness out of his voice.

Brunelli's voice came from behind. "Stop where you are!"

Palewski turned around slowly.

Brunelli was shaking his head. "The pillars," he said. "It is very bad luck to pass between them."

"Between them?" Palewski echoed. "Why?"

Brunelli smiled. "Venice is an old city, Signor Brett. Not like New York."

Palewski looked up at the pillars. They were not matched, one green-gray, the other of red granite. On top of the green pillar stood a small winged lion, the symbol of St. Mark, the patron saint of Venice.

"In former days," Brunelli explained, "this is where we executed our criminals and traitors. Their heads went on a pillar over there, by the entrance to the church, until they began to stink."

They skirted the pillars and came down to the waterfront. "The Republic was finished off when I was three years old," Brunelli added. "Many people—my family among them—had great hopes of Napoleon. In the end, he destroyed some churches and stole some of our treasures."

"Treasures, perhaps, the Venetians had stolen from others."

"Yes," Brunelli said mildly. "Perhaps that is exactly what I mean. We rob, and we are robbed. This is the great game of history, Signor Brett. It is played out over our heads—like a meeting of the gods, painted on a ceiling by Tiepolo." He drew a breath, like a whistle. "It may be different in America, of course."

He blew on his hands, to cool them.

"In the meantime, the people still need justice—and protection." Brunelli turned his head and stared out toward the island of Giudecca, across the darkening water.

"This morning," Palewski said slowly, "I saw a body in the canal."

"Yes. That is what I came to talk to you about."

Palewski had believed himself to be in a northern city, but this Brunelli fenced like a Turk. "I thought you had come to check my bona fides."

Brunelli nodded. "That is why I was sent. It is not the same thing."

"I see. You think I knew the man?"

"Did you?"

"I don't know a soul in Venice. Except now you, Commissario. But the body—was pretty far gone."

"Unfortunately, yes. But you weren't there when I arrived."

Palewski frowned. "It wasn't my affair. Another gondolier offered to take me to the *pensione*."

"That's quite all right," Brunelli assured him. "I wished only to ask. You see, the dead man was an art dealer, like yourself. He had been strangled."

His lugubrious features softened. "Well, well, Signor Brett." He clapped him on the arm. "I hope you enjoy your stay in Venice."

Palewski lingered by the water, watching the lights on the Giudecca and the last of the fishermen returning from the lagoon. Then he turned away and retraced his steps to the *pensione*.

The journey took him longer than he had expected; several times he had to double back when the alleyway he was following ended in a set of worn steps going down into some little canal. He began to wish that he had engaged a gondola at the piazza. He wound through one alley after another, almost blind; such light as there was came from votive candles flickering in their little niches above dark doorways and the occasional oil lamp bracketed to a wall where two alleys joined. Nothing—and everything—looked familiar. He had no idea how far he had wandered from his path when a dim light ahead revealed the entrance to the *pensione*. He fell into it with a flood of relief.

He was already on the stairs when a flunky scuttled forward and presented him with a small envelope addressed to Signor Brett. Surprised, Palewski opened it and pulled out a card with the name Antonio Ruggerio printed on the front. On the back was a short note:

A. Ruggerio presents his compliments and will have the pleasure of calling on Signor Brett tomorrow at ten o'clock.

Palewski grunted. "Ruggerio? Who is this man?"

The flunky spread his hands. "Signor Ruggerio is a friend of visitors to Venice, signore. I am sure you will like him very much."

"Indeed?" Palewski turned and wished the man good night.

"Good night, signore. I hope you enjoy your stay in Venice."

Palewski had heard that phrase before.

"Me, too," he muttered, as he climbed the stairs. "Me, too."

10

VENICE slept, coiled in its lagoon like a cat in a basket. It had once been a lion of the seas, but now its claws were drawn. To its Austrian masters it was merely a curio, a decaying backwater with an illustrious past and a sullen population.

The lagoon had long since rinsed the dawn when Antonio Ruggerio sprang neatly from his rented gondola and entered the water gate of the Pensione Inghilterra. He was small, dark, and ambitiously dressed, with a flower in his buttonhole and a pair of white gloves in his left hand; in the other he carried a sheaf of papers done up in a leather folder.

He reached the stairs without breaking stride. At the door to Palewski's apartment he straightened his jacket and ran a hand through his glossy black hair, then knocked.

"Signor Brett! I welcome you to Venice." He took Palewski's hand with both of his and pumped it enthusiastically. "So I may introduce myself: Antonio Ruggerio. I hope you are comfortable at the Inghilterra?"

Ruggerio's eyes swept the room. He knew it too well to linger on the rococo furnishings or the Axminster carpet picked out with an Oriental motif. What interested him—what he understood, almost as a science—was the scattering of personal possessions the American traveler had added to the familiar scene. A good valise, the polished traveling trunk with curiously florid brass corners, the ivory hairbrush on the dressing table, and a magnificent top hat and cane.

"Comfortable enough," Palewski said cautiously.

"You are here, Signor Brett, at the best time of the year in Venice!" Ruggerio inhaled theatrically: it was a delightful scent, the odor of money. He would not lie if he could help it. For a wealthy visitor, any time was the best time in Venice.

"What are your plans? Where do you want to go? The Salute? San Marco? Ah, to be for the first time in Venice! Signor Brett, do you know what? I, Antonio Ruggerio, envy you! It is true. The Ruggerios (you will have heard our name spoken, as that of an old family, aristocrats of Venice; between gentlemen I need say no more) have taken every pleasure from this city—but that one. Do you know our little Tiepolino? I will introduce you to him. To Tiziano, too—you call him Titian. What a prospect, signore! For a man like yourself, in the full vigor of his energies, to come to Venice for the first time! I am so proud—and so happy for you." He bowed with almost comical speed. "Have you eaten some breakfast?"

"Breakfast? I—"

The little man wagged his finger. "I know, I know. A *pensione* breakfast—a little roll, a watery coffee, *e basta*! Come. I will show you how a man should eat in this city." He made a dive. "Your hat. Your cane. My gondola is down below. We shall go to the Rialto. Like Shakespeare. Come."

Palewski had adopted the character of an American, but he was not a morning person. Slightly dazed by the fellow's torrent of words and enthusiasm, he took his hat and cane and followed downstairs to Ruggerio's boat.

All the way to the Rialto Bridge, seated opposite him on the gondola, Ruggerio radiated good nature and camaraderie, sprinkled with statistics, ancient gossip, and a little sightseeing information. The gondolier, at his bidding, sang several verses of an old song as he rowed them up the Grand Canal.

"He sings of a woman," Ruggerio explained, quite superfluously as it seemed to Palewski, who supposed most songs were about women. "She is the Queen of Cyprus, Caterina—we will see her picture later. By Bellini. Not a beautiful woman, but a great one. And the painting is a gem of the Renaissance."

Palewski had started at the mention of Bellini. He wanted to speak, but his new friend was already gesturing out of the window. "Palazzo Mocenigo. Byron lived here. Ah, that was a man. I knew him."

Palewski raised an eyebrow, and Ruggerio put up a hand. "I am older than you think—but Byron and I, we were both young in those days. We swam together many, many times. Here, in the Grand Canal. My friends say to me—you are crazy, like Byron! Perhaps. What a beautiful man."

He whipped out a silk handkerchief and trumpeted into it, then tucked it back into his sleeve. "Every palazzo tells a tale, Signor Brett. But you must know where to begin. It is my pleasure. We will have a lovely day. And your accommodation, too. We will see to that. How long will you stay with us?"

Palewski was growing used to Ruggerio's sudden changes of tack. "A few weeks. A month."

Ruggerio closed his eyes and his hands swam before him in ecstasy. "A month!" He echoed, emphatically. "In La Serenissima, a month is like a day. But we can see everything," he added hastily. "In a month, you will almost be a Venetian yourself." He laughed. "And here we are—breakfast!"

The gondola glided in between poles sunk in the water. Ruggerio handed Palewski out onto the pontoon, then sprang up after him. He bent a little closer. "Signor Brett, a small tip to the gondolier if you think it would be appropriate—he has sung, and he would appreciate it. No, no, five is too much—I will give him three. Already you see I am able to offer you some service—to protect the innocent traveler, ha ha!"

He pushed his way eagerly into the market throng, Palewski in his wake. Now and then Ruggerio would turn around to check that his new American friend was following as they weaved between the stalls, dodging porters clattering their trolleys across the cobbles, slipping along the arcades until Ruggerio stopped outside a small café and bowed.

"My visitors are always happy here," he assured Palewski. "Even the Duke of Naxos! Small, but very clean. Come."

The café was nothing more than a wooden counter ranged with plates of fried fish, octopus, salami, and olives. There was nowhere to sit, but Ruggerio seized a few plates and bore them off to a high table, snapping his fingers for coffee.

"May I suggest a prosecco, also? *Allora, due vini, maestro!*" He took some bread from a large open basket on the counter and beamed at his guest. "So—wine, good food, a little coffee, and the Rialto in Venice! Is not life good, my friend?"

Palewski had to agree with him. It had been many years since he had drunk wine among strangers, in open view. The sensation was agreeable, if peculiar at first, like the sight of unveiled women prodding the vegetables or drifting down the canal in a gondola. Many Europeans came to Venice because it offered them—in their imagination, at least—a glimpse of the Orient with none of the inconvenience: Byzantine domes and mosaics, strong colors, picturesque poverty, and an air of licentious freedom, comfortably offset by a familiar battery of French-speaking hoteliers, Catholic churches, and Renaissance art. These visitors, unlike the Polish ambassador, were often struck by seeing women who were, in fact, veiled according to a custom that went back to the days of Byzantine influence. But in Palewski's world all women, even Christians, were veiled in the street; to him in Venice it seemed that any man could admire a woman's features. Some of the women were very beautiful, he noticed.

Ruggerio caught his eye and winked. "In Venice we have the most beautiful women in the world. You think the husband is jealous? The father—yes. But after a woman is married—*altra storia!* She takes admirers! Why not? The husband—he, too, plays the game."

When they had eaten, Ruggerio laid his hand on Palewski's arm: "Twenty lire only will be enough. They all know Antonio Ruggerio. No cheating." He shook his head. "It happens."

The Venetian aristocrat's gondola was not to be found at the landing stage. Ruggerio looked annoyed, but his spirits soon recovered. "No matter. We will take another."

"But where?" Palewski asked. "Where are we going?"

The little Venetian amused him, he had to admit. Ruggerio was transparently a fraud, but he was engaging company and he was determined to show him around the city. He was a cicerone: a guide, a paid companion, and Palewski was not without means, with Yashim's commission.

"Where we are going?" Ruggerio looked surprised. "We are going to find you somewhere to live, Signor Brett. Nobody," he added, with emphasis, "nobody lives in a hotel in Venice for a month."

11

Two days later, gazing down upon the Grand Canal from the vestibule window of his apartment, a glass of prosecco in one hand and a telescope in the other, Palewski reflected that life, indeed, was good. He owed his present sense of good fortune to Antonio Ruggerio, which offered little scope for complacency. Ruggerio was, in many ways, an absurd pest; contentment that rested on his infinitely mobile shoulders could scarcely be supposed secure. But there it was: he had spent a day with the able cicerone, reviewing apartments to rent for the month.

There had seemed no end to them, each one larger, darker, more dilapidated, and more expensive than the one before, each one entangled in some way with families of title—the titles, it seemed, growing longer and more sonorous and hollow, until Palewski had prodded his guide in the other direction and stipulated something modest.

And Ruggerio, finally swallowing the blow to pride, and pocket, had brought him to this perfectly serviceable little *casa* on the banks of the Grand Canal, not far from the ruined bulk of the Fondaco dei Turchi: an apartment on the second floor sandwiched between the pleasant Greek landlady and her Venetian husband above, and a renowned but aging opera singer below. The ground floor, lapped by the canal itself, was given over to a quiet and unfashionable café, where watermen sometimes ate their lunch and where Palewski was sure of a dish of rice and a bottle of black wine in the evening.

He wondered what Yashim would make of these risottos, which bore a family resemblance to pilaff, only the rice was thicker. Yashim believed Italians had learned to cook in Istanbul. And certainly the Venetians, who had lived, fought, and traded so much in and around the fringes of the Ottoman world, ate very like the Turks. They had the same particular preferences, Palewski observed, for dozens of little dishes, like mezes, though the locals called them *cicchetti* instead, and they were as finicky as any Ottoman about the provenance of certain fruits and vegetables. In Istanbul, one ate cucumbers from Karaköy, or mussels from Therapia. In Venice, Ruggerio insisted that the bitter leaves called radicchio should come from Treviso, the artichokes from Chioggia, and the fresh beans from a little town called Lamon, on the mainland. Neither the Turks nor the Venetians seemed to value fish.

Ruggerio had given him a whirlwind tour of the city's treasures and marvels simply, as he said, to help Signor Brett familiarize himself with the disposition of the city, its churches, palazzi, and artworks, although Palewski had begun to suspect that the cicerone was disappointed in him and was looking for more valuable *clienti*. Some days Ruggerio arrived late; once, not at all; other times he often seemed distracted.

The idea that Ruggerio might, at last, begin to leave him alone was a relief to Palewski. It contributed to his sense of well-being as he trained his telescope on the landing stage opposite and watched a gondolier handing up a large packet of a woman onto dry land, along with her tiny dog.

He laid the telescope aside with a smile and took a printed card from his pocket.

MR. S. BRETT
DE NEW YORK
connoisseur

For the first time since his arrival in Venice, he felt he was being useful to Yashim.

Ruggerio would deliver the cards to various dealers and collectors he knew, expressing the hope that they would call on Signor Brett to discuss his own collection and theirs. Ruggerio would have preferred to present the American connoisseur to the dealers in person, but Signor Brett had been firm on the point. In a society as small as Venice a man would be judged by the company he kept. Ruggerio, foppish, quaint, and ingratiating, was not the man to present an American dealer to Venetian art circles. Palewski was fishing for a Bellini. Whatever the bait, the hook had to be clean, sharp—and expensive. A man like Ruggerio would merely foul it, like weed.

Quite what the bait would be, Stanislaw Palewski had no idea. It was unlikely that the Bellini was on open sale. Discretion would be required, not least because the Austrians, by all accounts, watched the market jealously.

He stood up, stretched, and went to his bedroom, where he found his battered leather-bound copy of Vasari's *Lives of the Painters.*

He read it again at the open window, listening to the shouts of the gondoliers and the backwash of the boats and skiffs below, locating in his mind's eye Vasari's comments about churches and paintings in the city. He was not a true connoisseur of painting, but by the time he had finished the chapter about the Bellinis, and his bottle, he knew what he needed to know.

He sensed that Mehmet II, the Conqueror of Istanbul, had created a little revolution in Venice.

12

SIGNOR Brett's card, too, created a minor stir in the city.

Gianfranco Barbieri stood for a long time at the great arched window on the piano nobile of his Zattere palazzo, looking out across the canal to Giudecca. He tapped the card against his perfect teeth, wondering who Brett was and whom he worked for. What kind of a man came from New York? A financial man, no doubt: Gianfranco always seemed to be reading about another American banking scandal, another astonishing default. People got burned lending to Americans. But they got rich, too—why else would they go on lending?

He would have to be careful.

He touched his fingertip to the small scar on his lip. The scar was not unattractive, and it gave him a mildly quizzical, amused expression, as though he were smiling at something only he could see.

Gianfranco liked to think of himself as a very careful man.

Across the city, close to the Arsenale, another man was pondering the arrival of Brett's card.

"Popi" Eletro rubbed the ink with a heavy thumb, then ran the lettering beneath a nail that looked hard and yellow. The card itself was unfamiliar: plenty of rag, but not Venetian. Not French, either. He would have said Turkish, but it was probably American, like the man. He grunted and stared up at a Canaletto on the wall. Canaletto in the land of bears and Indians?

There was money in furs.

His eyes slid from the first Canaletto to another three hanging beside it. Big pictures. Worth money, as soon as the glaze dried. What a shame this Brett couldn't buy them all! Four matchless Canalettos. All of them, unfortunately, identical.

Popi levered himself from the swiveling leather chair and reached for his hat.

It was time, he thought, to visit the Croat.

He'd have had his drink by now; he'd be ready to work again. If not, well, sometimes you needed to be cruel to be kind.

Popi walked, scowling, from the Arsenale toward the Ghetto. It was a long, difficult route: as late as 1840, few of the canals had been provided with pavements and the fashion for filling them in had not yet begun. Districts were still preserved as the islands they had always been, clustered around their church, their *campo*, and their well, speaking a dialect that marked them out from other islanders in the city.

Popi did not ponder the irony that a man who made his living from canals should detest them, but it was so. They were sluices of gossip, in his opinion—gondoliers to recall the address you visited, boatmen to note your passing. Beggars and idlers hung about the bridges, and in the dankest, dirtiest dark bends of a canal the inevitable old crone was forever craning her neck from some upstairs room for a better view. You took a gondola only if you wanted to be noticed—visiting a rich American art collector, for instance. Otherwise you used the pavement and walked the long way around.

In the Ghetto he found firmer footing, where the Jews had been crowded up behind their gates. The air was filled with floating goose down, like a gentle snow, for the people here used goose fat where other Venetians used pork, and it reeked of more than the sewage that offended visitors to Venice elsewhere in the city. It stank of old fish and rags, and the sourness of confined spaces. Napoleon had had the gates demolished, but everyone knew that they still existed in the Venetian mind. A few rich Jews had moved away, and a few—a very few—impoverished gentiles had taken rooms in the Ghetto, but otherwise little had changed in forty years.

Popi stumped along, looking neither left nor right. Something in his manner made the women working in their doorways draw in their feet as he approached; the men shrank to the wall as he passed. It was not that Popi looked official: when the Austrians sent patrols through the streets the people just watched them go, sullen and unmoving. It was, perhaps, that he came from the other Venice, a Venice that festered beneath the golden afternoon light and the fine tracery of a Byzantine façade, a Venice unimaginative visitors would never penetrate, no matter how much poverty or wretchedness they passed by, trailing their fingertips in the water until their solicitous gondolier hinted that it would be better, perhaps, to keep their hands folded on their laps. How could they, when even the more engaged, more lively minded visitors to the city allowed themselves to be seduced so readily by the prettiness of its whores and the cheapness of its *appartamenti*?

The people of the Ghetto shrank from Popi as a man of thalers and kreuzers, and of little accounts kept rigorously in black books that had the power to ruin lives.

Popi stopped to stick a cigar in his mouth and lit it with a match, then carried on up the narrow *calle* like a steam tug. After several turns that he executed without stopping, he ducked into a low doorway, crossed a small dark hallway, and found the stairs. He began to climb, slowly, to the top.

The stairs were dark. At each landing, narrow passages radiated into a deeper blackness relieved occasionally by a tiny opening, without glass, which gave onto a narrow well of light. On the lower floors the light was blocked by the accumulated rubbish of many centuries—moldering feathers, desiccated rats, pigeon droppings. Reaching the fifth floor, Popi ignored the stairs and pressed on down a corridor barely wide enough to let him pass. Stooping, he fumbled his way until his outstretched hands encountered another set of stairs, running up and back the way he had come. He took the cigar from his mouth and stood leaning against the wall, waiting for breath. Then he began to climb again.

Pressed into their narrow space, the Jews had built their houses higher than anyone else in the world.

Now, when he leaned against the wall for breath, Popi could feel it flex against his weight; another piece of plaster crumbled and fell to the floor.

At last, holding the stub of cigar at eye level, he perceived a door. He hit it with the heel of his hand, and it swung open, drenching him in sunlight.

Popi blinked, tears starting to his eyes. The cold reek of cabbage and drains that had followed him up through the warren of stairs and passages was swept aside by an overpowering sweet smell of alcohol and decay, wafted out on a raft of summer heat.

He coughed and stepped through the narrow doorway.

The first thing Popi noticed were the flies. They crowded the skylights and crawled across the sloping ceiling, buzzing and falling, swirling in the dust on their wings. With an exclamation of disgust he lunged at the nearest skylight.

The room was in disarray: tangled bedding, empty bottles, lumps of bread were strewn across the floor. The easel that normally stood beneath the window was overturned. Only the box of paints and the jar of brushes were in place. In the middle of the room, naked on a high stool, sat the Croat himself: waxy, immobile, his eyes staring on vacancy. His thin shoulders were flung back. His back was straight.

Popi's first thought was that he must be dead.

He stepped closer. The Croat continued to stare. Only when Popi was close enough to smell the man's skin did he realize that his lips were moving, minutely, horribly, like hairless caterpillars.

Popi took a step back: the Croat, alive, repelled him more than the notion of the Croat dead.

Popi was not unimaginative. He could tell, for instance, that the Croat was somewhere where Popi and the drink and the stench and poverty of his life could not reach him. He sat like a prince upon his throne, issuing soundless orders, perhaps, to the invisible minions who flitted before his glassy stare.

But Popi was unsympathetic.

He snapped his fingers in front of the unseeing eyes.

Nothing happened.

"I'll bring you around," he muttered. He took a drag on his cigar, lowered the glowing tip until it reached the level of the Croat's naked belly, and stubbed it out.

Way below, in the street, some people thought they heard a high-pitched scream, but the gulls were wheeling overhead, too, and they couldn't be sure.

13

YASHIM was reading the latest novel from Paris, a rather improbable account of the life of Ali Pasha of Janina lent to him by his old friend the valide, the new sultan's grandmother. The subject matter had taken him by surprise. Yashim was used to discovering Parisian life. Reading *Ali Pasha*, he felt, was rather like peering through a keyhole, only to see an eye looking at you from the other side.

"I find this Monsieur Dumas *sympathique*," the valide had told him. "His father was a French marquis. His mother came from Santo Domingo."

Yashim nodded. The valide herself was born on another Caribbean island, Martinique. The extraordinary story of her arrival in the harem of the Ottoman sultan, and of her inexorable rise to the position of valide, or queen mother, would have challenged the imagination of Monsieur Dumas himself.*

"The novel is a bagatelle, Yashim," the valide added. "I'm afraid it kept me up all night."

Yashim found the novel riddled with falsifications but also surprisingly energetic. It was certainly unlike anything he had read before. He wanted to discuss it with the valide, but a visit was out of the question. Even though she did not live in the palace of the sultan, his presence was sure to be noted. The sultan expected him to be in Venice, on the track of the Bellini.

Resid was right to hint that the sultan's infatuation with a painting he had never seen would pass as he grew into the responsibilities of office. Yet the deception bothered him. Not merely the disloyalty, if it was such. What mattered more was the complicity he shared with Resid Pasha and the vagueness of Resid's support.

What if, after all, Resid believed he had gone to Venice?

It was also an irksome restriction: he felt in a sort of limbo in his own city. He read, he went to the hammam, he cooked and ate, but in his heart he knew he was simply marking time. Two Thursdays came and went without the customary dinner he was used to preparing for his friend Palewski; the second time he went out to a *locanta* in Pera and found himself ordering an old palace dish, *ekşili köfte*, meatballs in a sauce of egg and lemon. Several times, too, he found himself outside the Polish Residency, and on these occasions he unfailingly went up the crumbling steps and knocked on the door, to see if Marta had any news.

Only his visit to Malakian, in the Grand Bazaar, had eased his sense of idleness. He found the old Armenian cross-legged, as always, outside

*See, however, *The Janissary Tree*.

the tiny cubicle that held his queer and fascinating collection of antiques, impassively watching the crowds that swirled down the covered lane.

"You are well, Malakian efendi?"

"I did not expect to see you, Yashim efendi. I am well, thank you." He patted an empty stool. "I have something for you. You will have coffee?"

When Yashim was sitting down, Malakian clapped his hands and sent a little boy running through the crowds.

Life was returning to the bazaar, Yashim noticed. The sultan's death had cast a pall over the city, like an echo of the days when the death of a sultan stopped time in its tracks and the city waited to learn which of the sultan's sons had won his way to the throne of Osman. But that was long ago, when the sons of sultans were trained to govern and to fight. This time there had been no contest.

The boy returned, a tray in his hands. Malakian took the coffee and handed a cup to Yashim. For a few minutes they talked about business.

"It dried up," Malakian agreed. "Many of the caravans delayed their departure. But the bazaar, too, was empty, so I could neither buy nor sell." He shrugged. "It was good to have a little quiet. But now they are come again."

"The caravans?"

"You understand how it is, efendi. I have only this small shop—I do not have caravans at my command. But the drivers, they will pick up some little thing and bring it to me. Look. Two French pistols." He opened a wooden box and brought out the guns. "From Egypt, I believe."

Yashim turned them over in his hands. "Good quality. But old now."

Malakian sighed. "Some things get better as they grow old. But guns? You are right. We make always newer ways to kill."

He replaced the pistols in their box. "I will sell them to a French-man, so that he can say his father was with Napoleon. For you I found this."

It was a small knife with a four-inch blade and a wooden handle bound with cord.

"A cook's knife," Yashim murmured. "Very comfortable."

Malakian bent forward and pointed to the mottled blade. "Like me, you think it is not interesting. But then I saw this."

Yashim turned the blade and noticed a faint inscription along the flat edge.

"*Ammar made me*," he read slowly, squinting. The Arabic was worn, almost smooth. "What's this?"

Malakian wagged his head. "Damascus steel."

"That's unusual," Yashim admitted.

"Unusual? Here is the soft steel—here, and here—to protect the edge. It rusts, of course. On either side, the soft steel—and between them, the true blade. You see how it shines? Even now bright. Such a plain knife, for cooking. Do you like it?"

Yashim grinned. The best steel in the world. A blade fit for a warrior—in the kitchen. Of course he liked it.

"It must have been made for a sultan's kitchen," he said.

"Of course. I hear you like to cook, so I make it a present. You can give me one asper."

"One asper?"

"We say, Yashim efendi, that you cannot give a knife. But if you pay me a little coin, it is all right."

Yashim dipped into his pocket. Everyone had his superstitions. "Thank you, Malakian efendi. I shall treasure it."

"You should use it," Malakian remarked. "Have it sharpened."

Yashim nodded, touched by the old shopkeeper's generosity. But then Aram Malakian was an extraordinary man. So much slid between his fingers—so much knowledge was stored in that enormous head.

"Do you know anything about an Italian painter, efendi? His name was Bellini. Centuries ago, he came to Istanbul and painted a portrait of the Conqueror."

"Bellini, hmmm." Malakian frowned and tugged at one of his enormous earlobes. "I hear of this name before. Bellini. I remember."

"Four hundred years ago," Yashim added.

Malakian gave a dry smile. "I do not remember this Bellini personally, Yashim efendi. But there is something I recall." He gazed at the ceiling. "Metin Yamaluk."

"The calligrapher?"

Malakian nodded. "And his father and grandfather before him, also, and their fathers, to the time of Sultan Ahmet, I believe, who built the Blue Mosque. The family came from Smyrna."

Yashim could vaguely recall meeting Yamaluk in the Topkapi Palace, where he worked in the copying room. But that was years ago, and the calligrapher had been an old man already.

"Metin Yamaluk is still alive?"

"If God wills. He retired years ago, it is true, but he still works. His hand is more elegant than ever, in fact. I remember he had a book he sometimes liked to look at. He said it gave him refreshment—but he was also ashamed, because it was a pagan book, of pictures, very well drawn. It came from Topkapi, Yashim efendi."

Yashim frowned. "Stolen, you mean?"

Malakian paused and stared at Yashim. "Stolen!" He spat. "This knife. I give to you. You think—stolen? We give it back to—who, efendi? The Sultan of Rum? The Caliph Harun al Rasid? The son of a son of a cook?"

"No, of course, I didn't mean—"

"Yashim efendi." Malakian put his broad hands on his knees and rested his weight there. "When I was a boy, I played chess with my god-father. He was a merchant. He traded to Baku, Astrakhan, and up the Volga. He would tell me about the chess set he had been given by his father. The white pieces carved from camel bone, the black from Indian ebony. It came from, I don't know, maybe Samarkand or old Kiev. He said that every piece contained inside it, like in a little cage, a tiny image of it-self. A king inside a king. A pawn in a pawn. You could see it, and hear it rattle, but there was no way into it."

He sighed and rubbed his ear. "I wanted to see that chess set so much. But when I asked him if he would bring it to the house, he told me he didn't have it anymore. I asked him where it had gone, and he only smiled and shrugged. Sold, or lost, or stolen—which? I wondered, every time I wondered."

"Perhaps," Yashim said carefully, "it was simply—left behind."

The old Armenian cocked his massive head. "Much better, Yashim efendi." He made a slow, sweeping gesture, taking in the pistols in their box, the knife, the shelves at his back. "Left behind," he said in his deep voice.

"Who knows?" Yashim said slowly. "Perhaps one day, Malakian efendi, it will come to you. A caravan driver with a chess set."

"You understand too much, Yashim efendi," Malakian said. He sounded sad. "Metin Yamaluk lives in Üsküdar. He said the drawings were by Bellini."

14

PALEWSKI was right that Antonio Ruggerio had been disappointed by his choice of lodgings, but the cicerone had not abandoned him yet, by any means.

He presented himself early at the American's apartment, anxious that Signor Brett should not give him the slip. He need not have worried.

"Perhaps the signore would prefer if I were to return in—one hour?" he suggested, once he had caught sight of Palewski's bleary face at the door.

"Just come in, Ruggerio. What time is it?"

Palewski excused himself to dress, leaving the Venetian sitting at the window in the vestibule. There was nothing in the room but an empty bottle of prosecco, a glass, a copy of Vasari's *Lives*, and the gentleman's splendid top hat, sitting by the pier glass on a little marble console. Its shiny nap had already encouraged Ruggerio to draw important conclusions about the American collector.

Ruggerio got up and walked stiffly up and down the vestibule, kicking out his legs, hands clasped behind his back. Eventually he came to a stop by the hat and pulled some faces in the mirror, rocking gently on his toes. He put out his tongue. He wagged his head from side to side. He cast a quick furtive glance toward the bedroom door and very gingerly picked up the hat and put it on his own head.

Ah, what a hat! It was a good fit. Ruggerio glanced again at the closed door, then at his own reflection. Even he could tell what a difference the hat made: he looked taller, younger, richer. Yes, it was the sort of hat a man like him needed.

He took off the hat and glanced inside for the maker's name. *Verbier: Constantinople.*

He laid the hat quickly back on the console. He returned to the window, where Palewski found him a few minutes later flicking through Vasari's *Lives*, pondering a handwritten dedication in a language he didn't know. Ruggerio snapped the book shut and laid it aside.

Palewski picked it up and dropped it into his pocket. "Breakfast, Ruggerio. Breakfast and Bellini."

"Bellini? Certainly, maestro!" As he followed Palewski out the door, Ruggerio glanced back into the room with a puzzled frown.

"The Rialto, signore?"

Palewski considered. "I'd rather go somewhere we can sit, my friend. But let's walk for a change. If we can?"

"Of course, of course. Please, follow me. But take care—the stones are uneven."

Palewski was glad to be moving on foot. However disorienting, threading the narrow alleys and *fondamenta* gave him a sense of the city's shape in a way a gondola ride did not. In a gondola he was just a parcel to be delivered, swaying to the rhythm of the oar and exclaiming like so many before him over the beauty of a view or the intricacy of a doorway. On the water he was always lost, *all at sea*, as the English said.

They walked in file, Ruggerio leading the way. Off the canals Venice seemed less dreamlike. In the dark, narrow courts, each with its old stone well, sunburned children sat on the stones picking through baskets of shrimps, or threading beads; a few *nonni* sat on tiny stools in a patch of sunlight, bending over their sewing with weak eyes. Men as brown as gypsies sat outside their workshops, planing, hammering, sewing, making an industrious racket you scarcely heard as you drifted along the canals, too low down to peer into anyone's shop.

Grass sprang through the uneven stones, and there was rubbish everywhere. Once or twice, a mound of dirty rags actually stirred and a hand protruded, begging for alms. Such was the fate of those who had no work, and the sight made Palewski flinch as he groped for coins. He was not used to it. In Istanbul, such abject beggars did not exist; they seemed to be everywhere in Venice.

At turnings, Palewski stopped and glanced around to get his bearings. He noticed that the buildings had a strange way of muffling and amplifying sound, so that the bright childish echo of a *campo* was snuffed out while the sound of a falling hammer followed them relentlessly over bridges and down passageways. Sometimes, as he looked back down the alleyway they had just left, he had a curious sense of being followed; another trick of the winding streets, he thought.

"Signor Brett!" Ruggerio exclaimed, when Palewski paused for the twentieth time. "I think one day you will write a book about Venice!"

Palewski smiled and shook his head. "I have heard that everything that can be said about Venice has been said already."

Ruggerio looked pained. "I would say, signore, that on the contrary we have not said nearly enough. Everything that has been said and written about Venice is only the beginning of the first page of the first chapter of the first volume"—he raised a finger—"of the story of La Serenissima. Every Venetian has his own Venice—and every visitor, too. And so, *da capo*, till the city sinks—or the world ends!"

He made a little flourish of his arm. Palewski almost blushed, ashamed.

"And the Republic?"

Ruggerio touched a finger to his lips. "Let us go to the café," he said.

They emerged shortly onto a *campo* where chairs and tables were set out in the sun.

"Now we can sit and have breakfast," Ruggerio declared. He ordered coffee and rolls, cheese and salami. "But this morning, signore, I think— no grappa!" He chuckled, recalling Palewski's washed-out look at the door.

"As it happens, Ruggerio, I think a grappa would be in perfect order," Palewski lied, a little stiffly.

Ruggerio was not put out. "Aha," he beamed, signaling the waiter. "*Un amaro, caro, per favore.* This is something better, Signor Brett."

"Hmph." Palewski took out his Vasari and laid it on the table.

"*Lives of the Painters*," Ruggerio said, touching the leather with a fore-finger. "This is a very old book."

"Yes. I've had it—" Palewski paused; he had been about to say that he'd had it all his life. "A long time," he concluded.

Ruggerio looked away. "Breakfast will be here in a moment, signore, and you can try the *amaro!*"

"And afterward," Palewski added, "I want to look at all the Bellinis in Venice. Gentile Bellini, that is; I'm not so interested in the brother."

He picked up the Vasari and idly thumbed the pages. The more he wanted to look at the title page, with its inscription in Polish, the more he felt Ruggerio watching him. In the end, he gave up. "Vasari doesn't say where they are." He put the book back in his pocket.

"I can help you," Ruggerio said. "Here's our coffee—and your *amaro*."

The *amaro* came in a small, stemmed glass. Palewski picked it up suspiciously, a brown, treacly liqueur that smelled of—what, exactly? Wormwood. Aniseed. He tilted it to his lips.

"Disgusting," he said, after a moment's pause. Some of the throbbing in his temples—the effect, he supposed, of that dangerously black wine—was eased. "I like it."

They spent the morning searching out the works of Gentile Bellini. Palewski was impressed by his companion's resourcefulness. Although Ruggerio knew very little about Gentile Bellini himself, he was unafraid to ask—beginning at the Correr.

"And Correr left all this for us to look at?" Palewski wondered. He was unfamiliar with the idea of a public gallery. There were none in Istanbul, and in Poland, long ago, one simply left one's card at a nobleman's private house and was invited to look around.

The director of the gallery snuffled with amusement. "One day, Signor Brett, Count Correr's example will be followed around the world. Connoisseurs like him, with the means and the eye to build wonderful collections, will leave them to the public—maybe even in New York."

"Why not!" Palewski responded enthusiastically. "After all, they can't take it with them!"

The director drew back and began to laugh. "Ha ha ha! Signor Brett, you are absolutely right!"

On the director's advice they unearthed three Bellinis by lunchtime; two were in churches and one hung in the Accademia. Palewski inspected them carefully, looking for evidence of the master's style. They lunched at Florian, after which they parted at Palewski's insistence. At the apartment he found a card informing him that Count Barbieri would have the honor of calling on Signor Brett at six o'clock that evening, if the time was convenient.

Palewski spent the afternoon dozing on his bed, but he was at his window before six to await the arrival of Gianfranco Barbieri.

A gondola swept up to the water door in a graceful curve. The gondolier pinned it to the wall with his long oar, the doors of the felze snapped open, and a fair-haired man in an elegant coat stepped out and disappeared below.

As Palewski watched, the gondolier slipped his oar into its crooked rowlock and swept the long boat with insouciance across the channel, narrowly missing a heavy barge and another gondola coming in the opposite direction. For a gondolier, Palewski thought with admiration, a near hit was still a miss.

He went to the door and pulled it open.

15

WHATEVER Palewski had supposed, Antonio Ruggerio was telling the truth when he boasted of belonging to one of the oldest families of the Republic. Ruggerios had been present, if not prominent, at the sack of Constantinople in 1204, when the energies of the Fourth Crusade were unexpectedly diverted to the enrichment of La Serenissima. Members of the clan had left their bones all over the Mediterranean—in Cyprus, in the Aegean islands, even North Africa. But for many centuries the Ruggerios had seldom ventured much farther than the Campo San Barnaba near the banks of the Grand Canal, in whose dreary baroque church they were baptized, married, and dispatched to a pauper's grave.

The Ruggerios belonged to a special class of impoverished nobility, the so-called Barnabotti, who had withdrawn from the Venetian administration at the beginning of the fourteenth century, for reasons of cost. Ever since, these families had survived in and around the *campo* on the charity of the state, which provided them with tiny apartments, and on profit from the *casino*, where gambling had been licensed, enabling the Barnabotti to make a living from high-rolling foreign visitors.

Neither the French, nor the Austrians who came after, had felt the Republic's sense of obligation to the Barnabotti. The stipends were withdrawn; rents were introduced; those Barnabotti who were too proud, too old, or simply too unskilled to take on real work lived on in wretched and degrading poverty.

After an excellent lunch with his new friend, Antonio Ruggerio went quickly on foot to the Rialto market with three lire rescued from the bill. The market was winding down, and there were bargains to be had: spoiled tomatoes, wilted greens, bread that was almost fresh.

As Ruggerio approached, various marketeers reached back for a handful of vegetables and offered them with a shrug and a smile; if Ruggerio made to pay they waved him away. "Later, Barone, another day, maybe." Others studiously ignored him, indicating without rancor—and with the special tact and grace of the Venetian—that they had already parted with their leftovers to another of the Barnabotti, or had nothing to give away.

Only the butchers, by the expensive nature of their trade, invariably expected payment for their sausages, their salami, their pigs' feet and calves' brains. In butchery there was no waste.

Ruggerio came away from the vegetable market with an armful of produce and spent several minutes carefully perusing the butchers' stalls. They heard the lire jingling in his pocket and stood in respectful attendance, helping him make a selection.

"The lights are very good," one of them remarked, pulling a thread of meat through his hand. "And with the grass turning, we give a good price."

Ruggerio rounded off his expedition by buying some cornmeal for polenta.

He carefully packed his purchases into a flimsy wooden crate and carried them home.

"What's happened?" His wife looked anxious. "Did he pay you off?"

"No, *cara*, no." Ruggerio laid the box on the deal table by the open window. "I think he was tired. I will see him again tomorrow."

"Pfui."

"I work hard, Rosetta. I cannot be in his pocket night and day."

"Why not? What does he want with his time that he cannot share it with you—or a woman, perhaps?" She cocked her head. "You know who I mean, Antonio."

Ruggerio spread his hands out. "It's difficult."

"Difficult? What sort of a man is he? *Un Americano*. Don't they have women in America?"

Ruggerio stuck out his lower lip. "I'm not sure that he is *un Americano*."

"What's that supposed to mean?"

Ruggerio began to unpack the box. "I don't know exactly. But certain things—yes, some strange things . . ."

Rosetta moved to help her husband. "Strange things, Antonio?"

Ruggerio stood back and watched his wife put the greens on the table. She counted out five tomatoes. They were split, but fresh.

"A book he has. An old copy of Vasari." He shrugged. "And then— I don't know. His hat."

"His hat?"

Ruggerio sighed and ran his hands through his hair. "I know the rich, Rosetta. How they like to eat, the pictures they like. It is my study, after all," he added proudly. Had the Venetians not swum on the currents of trade for a thousand years, appraising, analyzing, supplying a want here, removing a glut there, matching men to their desires? "I know how they dress, Rosetta."

"And so?"

"The rich buy their hats—and their shoes—in London. Maybe Paris if they are French, or young, or have business in the city. It takes time to make a rich man's hat, *cara*."

"Fine. So where does your friend have his hats made? New York?"

"Constantinople."

"I see."

Rosetta, after all, was a Venetian, too. *Constantinople* was a rich word, full of associations: city of gold, city of lost fortune, the heathen image of Venice itself. Once the Venetians had held it in the palm of their hand. But that was long ago, before the Ruggerios and their kind had found their way to San Barnaba. Istanbul had been the enemy after that, cat playing mouse through the Aegean and the Adriatic: the city of sultans and viziers, of careful pacts and sudden wars.

It was not, in Rosetta's imagination, primarily noted for its hats.

16

GIANFRANCO Barbieri ran his hands through his hair. He was about to knock when the door opened.

"Count Barbieri?" the American said. "Kind of you to come."

The count smiled, showing his fine teeth. "I was delighted to receive your card, Signor Brett. You are settling in Venice comfortably, I hope?"

Brett bowed. "I've seen a dozen good churches, two dozen soldiers—and a body in a canal." He stood back to let his guest enter the apartment.

Barbieri responded with an uncertain smile and advanced to the window, where he gazed out onto the Grand Canal as if it were for the first time.

"Champagne?"

A pop, a clink; wine fizzed and subsided in the wide, shallow bowls of two Murano glasses. To Barbieri it seemed as if the sounds of the canal had grown brighter, its colors and movement more vivid. It had been many months since he tasted real champagne.

Brett handed him a glass, and they toasted each other.

"I am sorry," Barbieri said. "A tragedy—I even knew the man. Not well, you understand, but—" He sighed. "Yes, these things happen, even in Venice. I hope you will not allow such an unpleasantness to spoil your stay."

"Nothing of the kind," Brett assured him.

"I admire your choice of season, Signor Brett. I often think Venice is at her loveliest at this time of year. The warmth. The light. Carnevale? Far too cold." He took a sip of champagne. It was very good. "But you will know that already, perhaps."

"The Carnival? No. I was never in Venice before, I regret to say."

"You are from New York?"

"Based in the city, yes."

"In Venice we are a little crazy about the past. *Com'era, dov'era*—as it was, where it was. A very Venetian saying—and said rather too often, I think. I would like to visit your country one day. A young country. We tend to forget that Venice was once a series of muddy little islands, inhabited by refugees from the mainland." He gestured to the window. "Like you today, Signor Brett, we had to build up all this, little by little."

"I'd be proud if we made New York half as beautiful," Brett said.

"Who knows, Signor Brett? It will be another kind of beauty, I imagine. The beauty of the machine age."

"Founded on commerce."

"Of course." Barbieri smiled. "Trade is a very pure expression of human energy. Modern Venice is listless and poor, and produces no art. Why? Because there's no art without a patron. And one is not enough. It takes a wealthy and energetic commercial city to spawn rich men, who then vie with each other to call out what is beautiful." He touched the scar on his lip with his tongue. "Are there rich men in New York?"

"More every day," Brett said.

"So it was in Venice once. Spices, maybe, were your furs." He laughed. "Forgive me, I have tumbled into my own trap—thinking, like any Venetian, of the past."

"I think about it, too," Brett said.

"Of course." Barbieri nodded his head seriously. "One could draw the comparisons too close, and yet—" He put up his hands, as if he were grasping a balloon. "I do not think Venice would have become what it became without men like us."

"Like us?"

He nodded. "We mined, in our time, the treasures that others had stored up. A lion from Patras, for the Arsenale. A column from Acre—to the Piazetta! Even the body of St. Mark—we took it from Alexandria. Go to the church of St. Mark's, and what will you find? A gazetteer. A wild, encrusted guidebook to the cities of the ancient world. Precious marbles, enigmatic statues—and all embedded in a building that echoes the tossing of the waves. We hauled back the treasures of the East, and with them, slowly and cautiously, we forged our style."

He gestured to the window.

"But we took it, mostly, from Istanbul. Constantinople, as it was. We sacked and scoured a city that had never been won by force of arms for eight hundred years."

"You, at least, preserved what was carried off," Brett said. "Lysippos's bronze horses, for example."

"And the bones of saints, and the reliquaries, and the gold. We took glass made in Antioch, and icons painted by the companions of Christ. Before we had been magpies, Signor Brett, snatching whatever was available, and beautiful, and bright. In 1204 we took a whole reference library."

Brett nodded.

Barbieri smiled. "You, Signor Brett, are the Venetian now. And Venice, of course, is Istanbul." He paused. "Tell me, how can I help you?"

Brett poured some more champagne.

"You're a cynic at heart, Count Barbieri."

"Not at all. Perhaps the Barbieri have at last produced an optimist."

"A realist?"

Barbieri smiled. "It is the same thing."

17

HE ordered the deaths without emotion. He had not known that they would die. Even when the killer arrived, unable to speak, handing him written instructions, he had pretended to himself that it would be something else.

But of course when Boschini was found in the canal, dead, he could no longer pretend.

He could adapt.

That's how it had to be in this city. You adapt, or you die.

And the man was good at that. It's what he did, the way he lived.

So he told himself that the people who died deserved to die.

18

PALEWSKI twisted the wire, and the cork popped out into his hand.

"Brillat-Savarin," Count Barbieri said.

Palewski knew exactly what the count meant.

Brillat-Savarin, the French gastronome, had established a sensational fact, which flew in the face of all recognized wisdom.

After the battle of Waterloo, British regiments stationed around Champagne had plundered the wineries. Bottles were popped, quaffed, and tossed into the hedges; old vintages vanished indiscriminately with the latest crop. When order was restored, the champagne houses were left with shattered cellars.

"The champagne makers thought the British had ruined them," Palewski began. "Until every club in London—"

"Ordered another twelve dozen cases!" Barbieri beamed. "The champagne houses made their fortune."

"You truly are an optimist, Count Barbieri."

"A realist, Signor Brett."

Palewski clasped his hands under his chin.

"I am looking for a Bellini," he said.

Gianfranco Barbieri came from a long line of Venetian aristocrats who had been trained, like aristocrats everywhere, not to reveal his feelings easily. He opened his eyes wide and gave a whistle.

"Bellini! No. Bassano, yes. Longhi, Ricci. Guardi—it would not be too much of a problem. But Bellini? That would be a miracle." He blew on his fingertips and laughed. "You would have to steal it," he added.

"It is what America wants," Palewski explained. "Something utterly first class. Better one work by a master like Bellini than a whole gallery of lesser paintings."

"No, no. You must begin slowly. Like us."

Palewski knelt on the window seat and contemplated the Grand Canal.

"Count Barbieri," he began, "I wonder—if, by some stroke of fortune, someone in Venice was in a position to offer a Bellini on the market—it's a hypothetical suggestion—you would know about it, I suppose?"

The count shrugged. "If it were to be offered through the usual channels, then yes, I would know of it. But for such a painting—well. This is Venice, Signor Brett. Not all traffic passes down the Grand Canal."

"I understand," the American said.

Barbieri set down his glass. "I am expected at the opera, Signor Brett. There's no reason to be disappointed. If a Bellini should suddenly appear . . . In the meantime, I can show you at least three works that would delight you. They would cause a stir if they were exhibited in London or Paris. A fourth, I think, would interest you also."

They shook hands at the door. "Your neighbor is an old friend of mine. Carla d'Aspi d'Istria. She's having a little gathering tomorrow night. Do drop her your card, I'm sure she'd be delighted to meet you."

Later, Signor Brett did take a few steps along the alley to a large green door, where he delivered his card to his neighbor.

On his way back he looked into the café. He was hungry; something smelled good. He ordered wine and a dish of rice. To his astonishment it arrived looking black as if it had been burned.

"*Risotto al nero de seppia*," the girl explained. Palewski ate it all; it was delicious. But it was very black, and he could not quite escape the impression that he had been offered death on a plate.

19

MARTA served Yashim tea in the ambassador's drawing room. She had kept the windows closed, she explained, because of the dust. The room was warm, and two flies batted sleepily against the windowpanes.

Yashim dropped into his usual chair by the empty grate and looked around. He was accustomed to seeing a jumble of Palewski's books and papers spread out in haphazard order over the tables, armchairs, and even across the floor. Now Palewski's pince-nez reading glasses sat primly on an open book on the desk.

"I wonder how he is getting on, in the *Dar al-Hab*," Yashim said, when he had thanked her for the tea.

Marta pursed her lips and nodded. "The lord has sent me a note," she said.

"A note?" Yashim turned in the chair.

A curious, almost wary, expression passed across Marta's serious face. She began to dust the window ledges, humming to herself.

"He is in Venice, efendi. It must be very beautiful."

'So I understand." He paused. He noticed Marta's hand slip surreptitiously to her breast. "Is that what he writes about, Marta, in his note?" She caught his eye, then looked away. "The writing is very small, efendi."

Yashim nodded. "Yes, of course. I'm quite used to his small writing. What if I try to read what it says?"

He could almost read the conflict in Marta's mind. At last she nodded and fished the note out of her jacket.

It was written in Palewski's best classical Greek script and illustrated with little ink drawings: Palewski sitting in his window seat with a bottle of wine, a cheerfully waving gondolier, Palewski with one foot on the quay and the other improbably far apart on a gondola, and a man swimming with a top hat. It was an affectionate and amusing letter, and ended with an exhortation to Marta to look after Yashim. Yashim read it aloud, laughing at Palewski's jokes; even Marta allowed herself a smile.

It made no mention of the Bellini and gave no indication of when the ambassador would return. But it ended with the suggestion that Marta might be lonely in the empty house.

Marta took the letter back and scanned it, as if committing its meaning to memory. Then she tucked it back into her jacket.

"Yashim efendi," she said. "Do you think the lord would be unhappy if I went home until he writes to say he is coming back? I could still come in, every day or two, but I am afraid that without him, there is—there is not much for me to do."

"I'm sure your mother and father would like to see you."

Marta nodded and looked pleased. Her family lived up the Bosphorus, in the Greek village of Karaköy. Yashim had met them, and her brothers. She had six, and they were devoted to her.

"Thank you, efendi. I will go this afternoon."

Yashim walked slowly back to the Golden Horn, taking the steep and crooked steps that led from the Galata Tower. Halfway down he became aware of an unfamiliar murmuring from the shoreline below.

From the lower steps he gazed out over a crowd gathered around the gigantic plane tree. Its branches cast a deep pool of shade over the bank of the Golden Horn, where the caïque rowers liked to sit on a sweltering day, waiting for fares. The lower branches of the tree were festooned with rags. Each rag marked an event, or a wish—the birth of a child, perhaps, a successful journey, or a convalescence—a habit the Greeks had doubtless picked up from the Turks, and which satisfied everyone but the fiercest mullahs.

Yashim heard the distinct rasp of a saw; he realized that there were men in the tree. There was a sharp crack, and one of the branches subsided to the ground; the crowd gave a low groan. He scanned the faces turned toward the plane: Greeks, Turks, Armenians, all workingmen, watching the slow execution with sullen despair; some had tears running down their cheeks.

Two swarthy men in red shirts started to attack the fallen branch with axes, stripping away the smaller growth: Yashim recognized them as gypsies from the Belgrade woods. They worked swiftly, ignoring the crowd around them. Out of the corner of his eye, Yashim caught a sparkle of sunlight on metal: a detachment of mounted troops was drawn up beyond the tree. Perhaps the authorities had expected trouble.

He looked more carefully at the crowd. Most of them, he guessed, were watermen for whom the felling of the tree was a harbinger of bad times to come. What would become of them, when people could walk dry-foot between Pera and old Istanbul? But the tree was an old friend, too, which had sheltered them from the heat and the rain, accepted their donations, brought them luck, sinking its roots deeper and deeper with the passing decades into the rich black ooze. No one had turned up to witness the destruction of the fountain: that, in the end, was only a work of man. But the plane was a living gift from God.

A second branch, thirty feet long or more, fell with a crack and a snapping of twigs, and the crowd groaned again. For a moment it seemed as though it would surge forward: Yashim saw fists raised and heard a shout. Someone stepped forward and spoke to the woodmen, still hacking at the first branch. They listened patiently, staring down at the tangle of twigs and branches at their feet; one of them made a gesture and both men resumed their work. The man who had interrupted them turned back and pushed his way out of the crowd.

Yashim watched him: a Greek waterman, who stumped away to his caïque drawn up on the muddy shoreline and stood there, looking up at the sky.

Yashim followed him down the steps.

"Will you take me across to Fener, my friend?"

The Greek hitched his waistband and spat. "I will take you to Fener, or beyond."

As they pulled away, Yashim turned his head. Two more branches had fallen, and the tree looked misshapen. He could hear the rasp of the saw and the *toc-toc* of the woodman's axe. A team of horses was dragging away the first bare branches.

The rower pulled on his oars, muttering to himself.

A hundred yards out, Yashim noticed a crimson four-oared caïque cutting up the Golden Horn at an angle that would soon bring them close together. A young man sat in the cushions, and Yashim recognized Resid Pasha. Normally he would have directed his rower to avoid the imperial craft, but this time was different: it would be better if Resid did see him. He wondered if the vizier would salute him.

Sure enough, as the two caïques got within hailing distance, Resid Pasha leaned forward and signaled to his boatmen. The caïques drew level, and the boatmen rested on their oars.

Yashim touched his fingertips respectfully to his forehead and his chest, while Resid's hand fluttered briefly to his scarlet fez.

"How glad I am, Yashim efendi, to see you in our pleasant city!" The young man inclined his head and winked. "Summer is such a *healthy* season to be here, I think."

"I followed the counsel of someone experienced, Resid Pasha," Yashim responded politely.

The young man smiled pleasantly. "Very well, Yashim. It will suit you, in the long run. Indeed," he added, clearly enjoying the little joke, "I have heard that certain other cities are positively dangerous to the health at this time of year."

"None, I would hope, that are under the mantle of God's protection, both in this world and the next," Yashim replied. He was fairly sure that neither rower could understand a conversation spoken in the pompous language of the Ottoman court.

"No, no, certainly not. Here all is serene. But one hears a great deal about death in, say, Venice."

"In Venice?" Yashim echoed.

"Well, well, it shall not spread. Inshallah."

"Inshallah," Yashim returned automatically. A covey of shearwaters skimmed past, almost touching the unruffled surface of the Horn.

"Soon, I hope, the time will be favorable for me to visit the esteemed pasha once again?" He wanted to know how long Resid planned to keep him under wraps. He wanted to visit the valide.

The young pasha nodded. "I will send for you, Yashim. Two weeks from now, I imagine, would be auspicious for us both. I shall be very pleased to see you."

He waved a hand at the boatmen, who dipped their oars. "Seeing you, my friend, has given me great pleasure." He gave a nod, and the caïque pulled away.

Yashim watched them go. Two more weeks! He gave a signal to his boatman. To his surprise the man was looking at him with something like anger.

"You should have told him about us, efendi," he said bitterly. He glanced over Yashim's shoulder. "You should at least have asked him to save the tree."

"Do you think it would have made a difference?"

The boatman looked at Yashim in his plain brown cloak, then up the Horn at the crimson caïque.

"Nothing surprises Spyro anymore," he said.

20

COMMISSARIO Brunelli left his house in Dorsoduro early and walked to the *traghetto*, where he stopped for a *caffè corretto*. On days like these, when his son was more than usually difficult and rebellious over breakfast, the café between home and the Procuratie was his single guilty pleasure. That morning he had been presented with a scowling boy, muttering darkly under his breath, all thanks to a spot of unpleasantness at La Fenice the night before.

He sighed and leaned his elbows on the counter. La Fenice was the only public place in the city where the barrier between Austrians and Venetians was regularly breached. Austrians occupied the boxes and Venetians pointedly arranged themselves in the stalls, but at least for a few hours the two sides shared the same space and applauded the same artists. Trouble, when it began, generally occurred afterward as the opera lovers streamed out of the tiny theater onto the constricted quay.

Last night's affair, if Paolo was to be believed, had involved an Austrian officer commandeering a gondola reserved by a Venetian family. An altercation had arisen, in which the gondoliers themselves had joined, before the officer, according to Paolo's story, had been driven off with his lady friend, to the universal hissing of the Venetian crowd. No doubt there was another side to the story, as Brunelli had attempted to explain to his son. Even Austrian officers could make a mistake.

He stirred two sugars into his little cup. Paolo pretended to see all Austrians as pigheaded triumphalists, riding roughshod over the sentiments of the people. At the same time he imbued them with complete omniscience, as if any slight must be carefully and brilliantly contrived.

"The boy is not rational!" he had appealed to his wife, after Paolo had heard him out in glowering silence across the table.

His wife had ruffled his hair. "He is a boy," she had remarked.

"Well, I'm off," Brunelli had said, scraping back his chair. "I have some oppression to carry out."

To make matters worse, Finkel would be in a bad mood today.

Brunelli took as long over his coffee as he dared, then crammed his hat onto his head and went out to find a gondola.

Twenty minutes later he entered the Procuratie beneath the gilded double eagle of his ultimate employer, the Emperor Francis II. Under the eagle, as he reminded himself, lay a lion of St. Mark, patron saint of the city of Venice, carved in stone.

Stadtmeister Gustav Finkel arrived fifteen minutes later than Brunelli. He was a short man with a big paunch, a red face, and white mutton-chop whiskers. He marched down the corridor to his office and shut the door heavily behind him. Half an hour later, as usual, he put the last of his papers aside and called for the commissarios' reports.

Later in the day, an hour at most before lunch, he might call someone in for a review. He liked to keep these sessions short.

"So, Brunelli, it looks like your man was killed by a common thug. A robbery gone wrong. Is that also your conclusion?"

Brunelli considered this surprising assessment. "A common thug, Stadtmeister?"

Finkel leaned across his desk with a pained look on his face. "Let us not delude ourselves, Commissario," he began, using the phrase that had become a standing joke at the Procuratie. "Venice may not be a city associated with violence, but there is a low and persistent level of insolence, insubordination, whatever, that left unchecked can all too easily lead in this sort of direction. I'm afraid that people are very like children," he added.

Brunelli nodded. The stadtmeister had just two years to go before he retired to the muddy Mitteleuropaisch spa town in which he had chosen to spend his declining years. If the art dealer's murder could be linked vaguely to the affront to an officer outside La Fenice, and various similar incidents, then his final report—which would never, in all probability, be read—could be filed and forgotten.

"Like children," the stadtmeister repeated. "And let us not delude ourselves, these things are more likely to happen late at night, are they not? Well?"

"You mean in the dark? I suppose that's true, Stadtmeister."

"Yes, of course. Take last night—an ugly scene outside the opera. I shall have to report it, I'm afraid. If I had my way, I would get everyone into their own homes by ten o'clock. Then we'd see little more of this tiresome behavior."

Even murder, Brunelli reflected, could be swallowed if it was ground down small.

"You are going to recommend a curfew, Stadtmeister?"

"We shall see," the Austrian returned cautiously. "In the meantime, is there anyone you actively suspect of killing your man?"

"Not yet."

"Hmmph. You should check the port register. See if any boats have sailed in the past day or so. It could so easily have been a sailor, you know."

Brunelli said nothing. The port, like the low-level rebelliousness of the people, was one of Finkel's treasured explanations for almost anything untoward—blithely disregarding the fact that Venice, these days, scarcely was a port at all. Austrian harbor dues and import duties, along with the neglect of the channels, had seen to that.

"Will that be all, Stadtmeister?"

The Austrian glanced involuntarily at the clock. "That will be all for now, thank you, Commissario," he said. He opened a big ledger on his desk and bent his head over it, gripping his whiskers in either hand.

Brunelli bowed and retreated. The ledger did not fool him much. In five minutes Stadtmeister Finkel would be going down the corridor to his gondola, and lunch.

21

YASHIM took the knife from the table and hefted it in the palm of his hand. Years of sharpening had taken the blade down a fraction of an inch. He had asked the sharpener to take out the slight bell where the curve met the straight, and the knife weighed equably between his fingers. The grip, he supposed, was new.

He had known what he wanted to do the moment he saw the artichokes in George's stall. The appearance of the first tiny artichokes always made up, he felt, for the disappearance of asparagus.

"Is summer!" George waved a bunch of the greeny-purple artichokes under his nose. "Not more to wait, Yashim efendi. You wants?"

Yashim, who felt he'd been waiting weeks already if not for summer then at least for Palewski to come home, seized a dozen. He bought broad beans, fresh onions, lemons, and a fistful of dill and parsley.

At home, he halved a lemon and squeezed the juice of both halves into a bowl of water. He set an onion on the board and chopped down on its spiraled top, wondering how many hands had held this knife, and how many times it had been asked to perform the same simple function in Damascus, or Cairo.

Smiling, almost dancing around the blade, he sliced the onion in half. He sliced each half lengthways and sideways, watching his fingers while he admired the fineness of the blade.

He set a pan on the coals, slopped in a gurgle of oil, and dropped in the finely chopped onion. He reached into a crock for two handfuls of rice. He cut the herbs small and scraped them into the rice with the blade.

He threw in a pinch of sugar and a cup of water. The water hissed; he stirred the pan with a wooden spoon. The water boiled. He clapped on a lid and slid the pan to one side.

He began to trim the artichokes.

Summer was good. The knife was even better.

He smiled as he slid the blade smoothly across the tough tips of the leaves; inside was the choke, which he lifted with a spoon. One by one he dropped the artichokes into the lemony water.

He thought of Malakian, waiting for that chess set to appear one day. At least he could make him supper in exchange for the knife.

The rice still had bite, and he took it off the heat. As it cooled he ran his thumb down the soft fur inside the bean pods, trying to remember his first meeting with the old calligrapher.

Metin Yamaluk had been working on a beautiful Koran. It was probably the old sultan's gift to the Victory Mosque, built as a thanksgiving for his deliverance from the Janissaries sixteen years ago. Like all Ottomans, Yashim had a respect that bordered on reverence for the bookmaker's art, but it was dying all the same. For many years, the ulema and the scribes together had successfully resisted printing. First the Greeks and then the Jews had set up presses, and now the sultan himself had ordered certain scientific works to be printed in Arabic. One day, Yashim supposed, they would print the Koran, too.

He sighed and dipped a finger into the rice. He took an artichoke out of the water, shook it dry, and stuffed it, scooping up the rice in his fingers and pressing it in. As each one was finished with a little mound of rice, he put it upright in an earthenware crock.

When the crock was full he sprinkled the artichokes with the beans and a few chopped carrots. He drizzled them with oil, around and around, then threw in a splash of water and the rest of the dill and parsley, roughly chopped. Over the top he squeezed another lemon.

He covered the pan with a smaller plate, to weight the artichokes down, and settled the earthenware onto the coals. He set the rice crock on top of the plate. It would be done in an hour or less. He and Malakian would eat it later, cold.

Perhaps he would go to Üsküdar later, after all. Take a caïque, enjoy the cool breezes on the Bosphorus, maybe stop for tea in one of the cafés that lined the waterfront. He liked to go there: it was a little Asian village, really, scarcely a town, in spite of its magnificent mosques. And Yamaluk, and his treasures—why not?

Perhaps, somehow, the Bellini book would help.

22

IF Istanbul was a city of dogs, then Venice—from the lofty symbol of St. Mark to the lowest denizen of boatyard and alleyway—was a city of cats. The winged lion stood only wherever the Austrian authorities had found it inexpedient to remove it, but the ordinary cats of the city still prowled by night through the *campi*, the gardens, and the ruins of Venice, in search of food.

By long tradition, the pigeons on St. Mark's Square, like the impoverished nobility of San Barnaba, were fed by the state. The cats fended for themselves. Mostly they preyed on the rats who had long since colonized the city, breeding easily in the damp, crumbling foundations of Venetian houses, beneath rotting vegetation in the little landlocked gardens of the well-to-do, and in empty attics.

A she-cat, when her litter is due, looks for a dry and quiet place where she can raise her kittens undisturbed for the first few weeks. An empty building makes an ideal shelter even if, after years of abandonment and decay, it is not perfectly secure. The Fondaco dei Turchi was such a building. Grand, forlorn, shuttered, and rotting, it fronted the Grand Canal not a hundred yards from Palewski's own snug billet, a perpetual reminder to the Venetians of the decay of trade and the passing of the heyday of their commercial power. The Turks, who once used it as their caravanserai, filling it with muslins and silks, gems and precious metals, had found no further use for it once the Republic was dead; rumor had it that the fondaco—which rivaled the fondaco of the Germans, not far off—had been sold to a Venetian speculator.

The cat was not interested in the rumor, nor did she appreciate the Byzantine architecture of the old palace, built in the twelfth century in the fashionable Eastern style. What interested her, as she prowled the dark stairs and investigated the empty rooms, were ratholes and rubbish heaps, scraps of wood, paper, and old fabric that cluttered the corners, areas of greenish damp and fallen plaster, and above all the distance between her nest and another, composed of a candle end, a cloak, a pitcher, and a plate on which the cat found some scraps of bread.

She wolfed them hungrily, and fled.

23

POPI Eletro stood in his studio with his back to the light, gripping his lapels with his stubby fingers, his head cocked to one side.

It was amazing, he thought, what human beings could endure.

He bent closer to the canvas.

Good. Very, very good. Even without the varnish—a triumph.

His expression didn't change. "The other one," he said gruffly.

The Croat tenderly lifted the canvas from the easel and set it down against the wall. He picked up another and removed its blue paper wrapper. Popi saw him hesitate for a moment before he set it on the easel.

Popi gave a grim little smile and started to look for the flaw. It was only a matter of scrutiny. Ever since he had found the Croat silent and imbecile in a little church on the Dalmatian coast, he had perfectly understood the Croat's cravings.

Soon after he had learned to recognize his pathetic evasions, too.

It had been five years since Popi had learned that a sojourn on the Istrian islands would be good for his health. The diagnosis was not made by a doctor, but so it had proved. One day, crazed with boredom, he had walked the long mile to the hilltop church and found the Croat drawing pictures with a stick of charcoal on the marble steps.

He had been astonished. Popi Eletro had not, until that moment, given much consideration to art, but it was a Venetian consideration. He watched shapes and figures flow from the man's hand like water. So when the Croat proudly led him to the parish priest, and the priest showed him what the Croat could draw and paint on paper, Popi had discovered an interest in the full commercial sense of the term.

Art, Popi reasoned, could make him money.

"It is a gift from God," the priest would say. "The only one he has—but a gift to make him happy!"

Now Popi bent close to the picture. A perfect Canaletto—with a flaw.

In the end it had been so easy. One night he led the Croat to a bar in town and got him drunk, and by morning they were miles from the wretched little church and its pious priest. The Croat was dubious but also excited: Popi gave him paper and pencils, and he sketched his way easily to Venice.

Popi took the room in the Ghetto. They had lived there together for six months.

Popi had learned then what made the Croat tick. His simple pleasures.

And the seagulls cried in just the same way.

24

PALEWSKI had scarcely finished his breakfast when the maid introduced a liveried servant, asking if he would care to drink coffee with the
Contessa d'Aspi d'Istria.

"What, now?"

The footman bowed. "If it is convenient, signore. The Palazzo d'Aspi
is just next door."

The Ca' d'Aspi had been built by the contessa's sixteenth-century fore-
bear, the hero of a naval engagement with the Ottoman fleet who had
become very rich importing mastic from the island of Chios. It was a
medium-sized palazzo, with five exuberant Gothic windows on each floor
and a liberal sprinkling of colored marble embedded, like nuts in nougat,
in the façade. It contained a great deal of martial trompe l'oeil decoration,
a ceiling by a pupil of Tiepolo and, beyond the grand piano nobile apartments where the contessa entertained, barely a stick of furniture.

The contessa had inherited, along with the palazzo, almost a thousand acres of farmland on the mainland and a Palladian villa near Padua,
but the land had not recovered from successive invasions of French and
Austrian troops, who slaughtered the livestock and allowed the complex
system of dikes and sluices to collapse. The villa lacked a roof.

The footman led Palewski up the stairs into a small vestibule decorated with frescoes of cupids pouring cornucopias of fruit into the laps of
languid women.

"I shall inform the contessa of your arrival, Signor Brett."

He was forestalled by the arrival of the contessa herself, flinging back
the door.

Palewski's first impression was of a Tiepolo sprung to life, Beauty herself, perhaps, descending from her cloud. She was wearing a brown riding skirt, a well-fitted white blouse, and a man's jacket. Her feet were bare and her hand was on her hip. In her hand she held a foil. She was breathing hard.

"Signor Brett?" She saluted him with the foil and smiled. "Carla d'Aspi d'Istria. How kind of you to come."

Palewski stammered a greeting.

The contessa was tall and slim shouldered, even in a man's jacket; her waist was slender. She had the soft complexion of a much younger woman, beneath a heap of long blond curls for which, one summer after another, she had sat on the roof with her hair drenched in lemon juice and a brim to keep the sun off her skin. This morning she wore her hair tied back with a black ribbon, but some stray curls had escaped, and one was plastered damply to her forehead. She looked flushed, and her blue eyes sparkled beneath dark lids. Although her fair hair and blue eyes belonged to the classic canon of Venetian beauty, she had the straight, well-defined nose, and the full upper lip, of a Greek, reminding Palewski of certain lovely women produced by the Phanariots of Istanbul, the old Greek aristocracy. Only her mouth was perhaps too wide: it suggested—well, Palewski wasn't sure what it suggested. And when she smiled, he thought, it was perfect.

She was smiling now. "Come through, signore. As you see, I was practicing my art. I fence—does it surprise you?"

'I think everything about you surprises me, madame."

She laughed. "How so?"

Palewski followed her into the salon. It was a huge, high-ceilinged room with four long windows looking onto the canal and a floor of shimmering colored marble.

"I expected the contessa to be an old lady with a lorgnette and lots of tiny spoons," Palewski said.

Carla shook her head. "Not the Aspi style at all." She flicked the point of her foil and held it to his chest. "We die young."

Palewski took the foil by the button on its tip. "Not fighting, I hope."

She shrugged and flipped the foil out of his fingers.

She pointed to the far wall, where a display of weapons was ranged above a large canopied fireplace: glinting scimitars cocked like eyebrows, two splayed fans constructed of long old-fashioned muskets, and a triumphal tableau of pikes and spears and small bossed shields. A stout gilded pole rose from the almost baroque array of weaponry, topped by a curious arrangement of three brass balls, one above the other in order of size.

"A Janissary standard!" Palewski exclaimed in surprise.

She looked at him curiously. "We took those in the Peloponnese. An ancestor of mine, who fought with Morosini."

Palewski nodded absently. Long ago, as a boy, he had spent hours playing with just such weapons in the big house in Cracow: martial souvenirs seized from the Turks at Vienna in 1683.

"Now you have surprised me," she said. "I didn't think you would be an expert in Ottoman weaponry, Signor Brett."

Palewski gave a gesture of demurral. "I've been in Istanbul, that's all," he replied.

"I was born there," Carla said.

"Touché, madame," Palewski said.

Carla cocked her head to one side, regarding him critically. "Do you fence, signore?"

Palewski smiled. "A long time ago."

"Very good," she said. She indicated a trolley that held a collection of foils, masks, and plastrons.

"No, no, madame." Palewski laughed. "I haven't fought for thirty years. You'd overpower me."

"You don't really think that, Signor Brett."

Palewski blinked: it was another point to the contessa. He didn't think she would overpower him, but he was less sure now.

"Best of five points, signore. A friendly bout."

"I—I was never much on foil, madame."

"Indulge me, Signor Brett. A practice round. Five points. Then we can have coffee."

Palewski took off his coat and slung it over the trolley. He put on the half plastron, buckled it at the side, and selected a foil.

You are a fool, he told himself. An old fool.

He had the blade in the air before he noticed it had no button on the tip.

The contessa slipped a mask over her head.

Palewski chose another blade, checked the button, and felt its weight. He put on his own mask.

Carla backed from him, left hand up, foil in sixte, her bare right foot pointing forward. She glanced down and tamped her left heel on the marble floor.

She stood motionless, awaiting her opponent.

Palewski went to meet her, and as soon as their foils touched he took his stand.

He acknowledged immediately that he was not in condition. He lacked the suppleness of the younger woman, who was turned at the waist to present him the narrowest target. It had the effect of emphasizing her figure, and Palewski frowned.

He put up his left hand.

In the wrist, he thought: all in the wrist.

"In guardia," Carla murmured.

They crossed swords. Palewski made a feint to quarte, Carla parried in sixte, he returned and she counterdisengaged, following the movement with a swift step forward and a simple thrust in quarte.

She stepped back. *"In guardia."*

Palewski compressed his lips. The attack had been a mistake. This time he allowed her to develop it, trusting to his parries and solidifying his defense while he tried to get used to the feel of the sword.

It had been a long time, as he had said.

This time it took her four attempts to touch.

Better. *"In guardia."*

The action was all in the wrist, but Carla moved lightly, too, gaining and breaking ground with speed and confidence. Twice Palewski was able to parry a feint to sixte.

He took her lunge to quarte on the hilt and pushed hard: her arm flew up and she sprang away. Palewski heard her laugh.

"So, a hussar!"

Palewski ground his teeth and said nothing.

She opened in octave, made a feint to sixte—her favorite—and then followed it up with a low attack in septime, which Palewski managed—only just—to parry, returning to octave before she parried in octave and took the point of his foil wide.

She made a flèche and won the point.

The bout was hers.

Palewski, with nothing to lose, found himself relaxed. He'd lost, what of it?

"*In guardia.*"

She opened her attack with the feint to sixte, but this time Palewski was ready for her. He parried with an indirect riposte that went home and struck her chest.

"Touché, madame," he muttered.

Carla arched her body and eased her hands along her outstretched leg, to the floor.

Palewski put up his foil.

"*In guardia.*"

Carla's foil flipped into guard: she stamped and stepped forward with a feint to octave.

Palewski had anticipated the feint—and she had guessed he would. Now she took him by surprise by executing a beat to his blade. With a delicate disengage she placed the point of her foil neatly into the center of Palewski's chest.

She held the blade there, curved, for a fraction longer.

Then she pulled off her mask, undid the ribbon, and tossed her hair over her shoulders. "Fencing—it's like conversation, don't you agree?"

Her blue eyes were full of mischief.

"What did you learn about me, Signor Brett?"

Palewski took a deep breath and nodded. "You didn't give much away, madame—neither points nor traits."

"There must be something. Or am I too cold?"

"Cold? I think you're controlled. Very sure of yourself. A little dangerous maybe—to yourself and others."

He was looking at the pattern of pink, green, and gray marble laid out on the floor.

"To myself? I'm not sure I understand."

Palewski looked thoughtful. Most people, he reflected, shy from pain, but he could hardly tell the contessa what he had sensed about her, even if it were true.

"Perhaps if I knew why the d'Aspis die young, madame?"

"Ha!" She considered him in silence for a moment. "As for you, Signor Brett, New York is not where you learned to fence. Or would it be better to say, where you learned to wield a sword?" She paused, long enough to gauge his reaction. "I practice for an hour every day—and you won a point off me. But just now you wanted to fight saber, I'm sure of it."

Palewski gave a shrug. "I've picked up some bad habits. It was a long time ago."

She ran a fingertip along the line of her cheek. "An American sabreur," she said thoughtfully. "The War of 1812, perhaps? Cavalry action along the Canadian border." The irony was inescapable.

Palewski looked down at the floor. "This pattern—you use it, don't you? To fence."

He felt her watching him. After a moment she said, "You're very perceptive, Signor Brett. Yes, I use it: it helps me to concentrate. To keep control, as you put it."

He nodded. The pattern made an endless knot, woven from four triangles in a square.

"Is it Venetian?"

"You don't recognize it?"

Palewski shook his head. "It's very beautiful."

"Yes." She rang a bell, for coffee. "And also a grappa, Antonio, for Signor Brett."

She smiled. "I always imagine that hussars drink grappa—but there, Signor Brett, I'm making you cross." She half lowered her eyelids. "Forgive me."

"The hussars—are boors," he explained. "I hope you don't find me too boorish."

She gave a peal of laughter and covered her mouth with her hand. "I was being—complimentary. Don't the hussars say that they always make the people run—the men away, and the women into their arms?"

Palewski gave a weak smile. "Whatever they say, madame, it was true only of the lancers."

She gave him an almost tender look. "The lancers."

"You were telling me about the pattern on the floor," he said uncomfortably.

"The Sand-Reckoner's diagram," Carla said. "It has other names— this one, from Archimedes' effort to calculate the size of the universe." She smiled. "Now you know—and here's your coffee."

Palewski took the grappa, downed it, and replaced the glass on the tray. He drank the coffee standing, as she did. There was barely a stick of furniture in the salon.

"Barbieri told me you were hunting in Venice for something rare."

I found you, Palewski thought. Aloud he said, "Yes. I mentioned Bellini, and he laughed at me, just about. Said we'd have to steal it."

"Steal it? A respectable man like Count Barbieri?"

"It sounded like a joke."

She gave a wan smile. "I didn't know the count was capable of a joke where money was involved. But Bellini? I admire your ambition, signore— but I doubt you will succeed."

"Perhaps not. It was just a rumor. I was acting on impulse."

"Yes, Signor Brett. That I can believe."

"You divined as much from my fencing, madame."

"Perhaps before. It was the way you accepted my challenge. After all, you came here expecting to have coffee with an old lady," she added with a laugh. "I'm glad you gave me a bout. It was—gallant of you. I hope you will come back. I practice every morning, at this time."

Palewski bowed.

"But come tonight, as well," she said, holding out her hand. Palewski brought it to his lips. "Seven o'clock. And Count Barbieri will be here. You never know, signore, he may have stolen you a Bellini already."

25

THE Croat was getting worse: his moods, his withdrawals, were becoming more frequent. Even his products were less reliable. In a year or two, Popi considered, he might be useless to him.

He saw it finally: the shadowy figure of a man in a top hat standing at a window overlooking the Grand Canal.

Drawn obviously from life—what of it the Croat ever saw. Nobody had worn top hats in Canaletto's day.

Popi brought his index finger up slowly so the Croat could see and pointed at the offending image.

"Change the hat," he said. He did not think that after all this time he would need to say, or do, any more.

The Croat did not even glance at the picture. He simply stared at Popi with an expression of sullen disappointment.

"Change the hat," Popi said slowly. "Then we varnish the pictures. And then, my friend, two bottles." He held up two fingers.

The Croat looked at the fingers, then for the first time at the picture. It was agreed.

Popi's jaw worked. Two bottles—if he kept his side of the bargain the Croat would be incapacitated for a week. But at least Popi would have something to sell the American. He couldn't afford to wait.

"Take this one through to the studio," Popi said.

The Croat lifted the painting down and carried it into the back room, where Popi kept his paints and varnishes.

Popi sat down at his desk and began to compose a letter to S. Brett, connoisseur. A meeting really ought to be arranged, perhaps—if Signor Brett thought it convenient—sometime next week.

Next week, when the varnish would have hardened on his Canalettos.

26

PALEWSKI went home to change his shirt and spent a few minutes in front of the mirror with his elbows out and his hands by his chest, flexing his torso from side to side.

"Psha!" he exclaimed aloud. "You're an idiot, Mr. Brett!"

There was a note on the table below the mirror. It was from Ruggerio, regretting that he was unable to accompany Signor Brett that day. He suggested various places he might like to visit on his own—none of them, Palewski noted with amusement, likely to involve much outlay of cash—and the possibility that they might visit the Murano glassworks together the following day.

"The Murano glassworks! Twenty percent commission and a decent lunch!"

But why should he be led everywhere by Ruggerio? Why shouldn't he go on his own? A leisurely ride across the lagoon was no less than he deserved after his energetic bout with the Contessa d'Aspi d'Istria.

But as the gondola moved out onto the calm blue waters of the lagoon and Palewski turned his head for a better view of the city, he remembered something about an Armenian monastery and changed his mind. The gondolier looked doubtful. Murano had been decided on, and he was looking forward to visiting a café on the island while his padrone toured the manufactories. When Palewski, mistaking the source of his indecision, promised to pay him ten lire more, he agreed to forgo the pleasures of Murano society and take his fare to San Lazzaro.

The truth was that Palewski, without quite realizing it, was suffering from homesickness. Many an evening he had spent with his friend Yashim, drinking bison-grass vodka and lamenting his lost homeland, ripped apart by the greed and brutality of its enemies. Yet Palewski's desire for Poland, while genuine and deep, had an air of daydream about it. It was not visceral, as his feeling for Istanbul was turning out to be.

In another city—Paris, say, or even New York—the feeling might have been allayed by the excitement of novelty, but in Venice he was constantly running up against reminders of the city he called home. Venice, in the European mind, was a city half Oriental already, and certainly it made Palewski feel giddy, as though he were looking at a familiar scene down the wrong end of a telescope. Pacing the narrow alleys in Ruggerio's wake, he would be struck by some grace note of Istanbul—in the effort of a cat, for instance, to catch a bat at dusk, or by a porphyry column no doubt looted from the same classical ruin that Constantine had looted for his city centuries before. Sometimes it occurred to him in the shape and dimness of a doorway, or it might be the sound of the Orthodox monks chanting in San Giorgio dei Greci. It was even a puzzle to decide whether Venice or Istanbul had more shoeshine boys, all ragged, all alike, squatting on the pavement behind their little wooden boxes.

In the Campo dei Mori he had seen a relief of a camel led by a man in a turban and almost burst into tears, without knowing why, and he had stared forlornly at the busted shell of the Fondaco dei Turchi, on the Grand Canal, for almost an hour, savoring its decline and its crumbling Byzantine fenestration. With its blocked-up arcades and bricked-in windows, the old palazzo of the Ottoman merchants looked like the survivor of some drawn-out siege.

To make matters worse, he inhabited the identity of a stranger, and an American to boot. He missed his embassy. Half overgrown with creepers, and in want of a new roof, it was still a comfortable sort of place for a man who enjoyed his own company and that of his books. He had now read Vasari three times and was beginning to feel a kind of mental restriction from prolonged acquaintance with the author, as if he had eaten nothing but potatoes for a week. He missed his friends. Here in Venice he was hounded in the most polite and remorseless way by waiters and gondoliers and landladies demanding—well, money, certainly, but he had enough of that. What exhausted him were their demands for a decision. At home he had only to think of tea, or a brandy after dinner, and it was there, in his hand.

Marta would fetch it for him, before he had even asked for it sometimes. He took off his top hat and let the breeze ruffle his hair.

Venice from the lagoon was too flat to look like Istanbul, though the shoulder of Santa Maria della Salute, its great white dome, recalled the domes of Istanbul, and the rooftops looked crowded and orange like the roofs of the houses that crowded the shores of the Golden Horn.

He shaded his eyes and gazed ahead to a spire and a low red wall topped with greenery rising almost miraculously from the lagoon. The gondola advanced with a thudding swiftness while Palewski gazed almost blindly on the rosy apparition, lost in thought.

An hour later he wondered why he had come at all. The brightness of the lagoon had given him a headache. Now he strained his eyes to see the treasures that the gentle Armenian priest was lovingly laying out for his inspection in the dim scriptorium. At first, the thousands of ancient volumes in their shelves had heartened him, but, after all, they were all written in Armenian, except for a rather beautiful Koran. It was a gift to the monastery from the Aspi family, he noticed, its pages decorated with tendrils and lilies, and on the frontispiece a rendition of the pattern on the contessa's floor. Palewski saw his hands were trembling.

He asked for a glass of water, which momentarily broke the flow of the priest's gentle speech. He went out into the monastery garden to drink it and sat for a few moments beneath a tree in the shade.

"Come, signore," the priest said softly. "I will take you to Father Aristo, who is doing a wonderful work. Our first Armenian-English dictionary. The great poet Lord Byron asked that this should be done. Peace to his memory. He studied here, for almost a year."

"I'm afraid I'm not feeling very well," Palewski said. Then, not to sound rude, he added, "Byron studied here?"

"Every week, efendi. He wanted to learn Armenian, for the good of his mind." He paused, smiled. "I am afraid he was not a very diligent student."

Palewski stood up. He felt light-headed. "Can you tell me where to find my gondolier?"

The priest nodded, disappointed. "I will take you to him, if you prefer."

"Thank you." Palewski reached into his pocket and brought out some banknotes. "You have been very kind."

They went through a gate to the landing stage. In the gondola Palewski relaxed and closed his eyes. He unbuttoned his coat to feel the breeze and lay back against the cushions. The next time he opened his eyes he found himself in the Grand Canal again: he must have slept. His hands were cold.

Back in the apartment he paused only to pick up a card from beneath the mirror in the vestibule and to remove his shoes before he tumbled headlong onto his bed. He read the card at an angle: it was from the Contessa d'Aspi d'Istria, repeating her invitation to a reception that evening. After a few minutes he reached out and flicked up the counterpane, and in a moment he was asleep.

27

ON the piano nobile of the Ca' d'Aspi crystal goblets sparkled in the light of hundreds of candles set into candelabra of old glass, all reflected in the mottled mirrors that lined the walls. Down the center of the great room heavily embroidered linen hung in folds from the table, as though carved from pure stone. The curtains were not drawn. As the evening wore on, the glass of the tall windows, too, came to reflect the brightness of the room; from outside, on the Grand Canal, it looked as though the whole palazzo was aflame.

Stadtmeister Finkel, passing in a gondola on his way back to his fat blond wife, saw the lights and sighed. One thing was for sure: neither the stadtmeister, nor his superior, nor any member of the Austrian administration would ever attend a Venetian party, thrown by a Venetian. Only the year before, at Carnivale, the stadtmeister had inaugurated a ball at the Procuratie that not a single native had deigned to attend. The elegant officers had stood in their white gloves and immaculate uniforms like mustachioed wallflowers while the band played mazurkas and the candles burned low in their sockets.

Very faintly now he heard the strains of a quartet floating through an open window.

"*Der Teufel!*" he grunted, turning his thick neck to address the gondolier. "What are we dawdling for?"

Having given the band the signal to play, the contessa threw back a window and stood there for a moment, looking out.

She turned from the window with a radiant welcome for the man who had just entered the room.

"Dottore—I'm so glad it is you. If I am lucky I will have you to myself for a few minutes, at least. Somehow at these occasions one never manages to talk to the people one wants to talk to. Come, sit at the window here with me. In Venice," she added, with a sudden change of tone, "we need never tire of the view."

The professor, a small, barrel-chested man with a beautiful head of wavy gray hair, lifted a glass from a liveried attendant. He spoke in low tones to the contessa, who now and then wrung her hands. "Idiots!" she murmured. "It is barbarism!"

The professor spread his hands ruefully. "What to do? The Austrians have never been refused. In Prague, in Cracow, they can take what they want. Destroy what they like. And the emperor will act like a new Napoleon. I do not think he was happy when the horses of St. Mark returned from Paris."

The contessa clenched her fists. "We shall see the Bandieras this evening, Dottore. Attilio and his brother are not afraid to act. But money, yes." She wrung her hands.

The room was filling up. Out of the corner of her eye the contessa noticed a man standing uncertainly in the doorway. He was tall, pale, and good-looking; his clothes were immaculate. The contessa swiveled and held out her hands with a charming smile.

"Signor Brett! But how wonderful you could come. You see, Tommaseo, we are neighbors now! But yes—Signor Brett has come all the way from America to share my view. Is it not so?" She laughed, and light played in her eyes.

Palewski smiled. "Had I known I might share a view with you, madame, I would have left America sooner," he said.

"*Basta*, signore." The contessa raised a hand, but she looked pleased.

The contessa touched his arm. "Let me introduce you to Tommaseo Zen—he is a recluse, but for this evening we have dragged him out. He lives on Burano."

She snapped her fingers, and a glass of prosecco appeared in front of Palewski. Before he knew it, he was talking to a quiet young man about the flora and fauna of the lagoon, and his glass was empty. A footman materialized with a bottle.

"There is a type of clam, also," the young man was saying, "that is unique to the lagoon. It exists only here and, so I understand, at the mouth of the Canton River, in China."

"Perhaps Marco Polo—" Palewski began, then stopped. A wave of exhaustion swept over him. He fought for a moment to stay on his feet and pressed the cold glass against his cheek.

"Signor Brett, I believe you have already met Count Barbieri?"

Palewski turned. The room was spinning. He murmured a greeting and shook hands.

"Signor Brett was telling me such interesting things about his country," Barbieri said.

The contessa smiled. "Tell me, *amico*! Tell us—what is it about America you love?"

Palewski focused on her lips.

"Many things," he said cautiously. "A wonderful country."

He was aware that a hush had fallen on the company.

"It is a very big country," he began. What had he said yesterday? "We are a people of independent education. Who know how to eat well." He saw someone raise a finger and wag it at the crowd. "Just like here, in Venice!"

It was his finger. He snapped it shut and put his fist behind his back.

"We have great cities, too, like Venice," he added, remembering. "New Orleans is like Venice. Boston is like Venice. New York is like Venice." That surely wasn't true, he thought. He rocked on his toes and peered around at the assembled guests, hanging on his every word.

"Like Venice—but no canals."

"And art?"

"Quite. Instead of canals, the American people have a desire for art."

The contessa looked surprised. She took his arm and steered him to one side. "I'm afraid we are plaguing you with our foolish questions. Forgive me."

"No, no—it's just . . ." Palewski felt her squeeze his arm. "A touch of sun, Contessa. Day on the lagoon." He shook his head. "I think I rather need a rest."

"But no, Signor Brett, we must apologize. I will send Antonio to see you home. When you feel better, please come to visit me again."

Palewski inclined his head. "That would be delightful," he murmured. Right now, he wanted only to lie down.

Outside on the stairs he felt a little calmer. Antonio, the footman, held his coat over his arm and walked him back downstairs and out into the street. At the door of his building Palewski fumbled for his key, and found some change.

"No, signore. *Grazie a voi*," Antonio said with a rich smile, backing away.

The ambassador tottered into the hall and leaned heavily for a moment against the wall, rubbing his forehead, before taking the stairs slowly, keeling like a drunken man. He should have stayed in bed, of course—but then he would not have met the contessa again. What a charming person! And he had been complaining that everyone in Venice wanted something from him!

He turned the key in the lock of his apartment, but the door was fast; he turned it again, and it swung open.

He kicked off his shoes and made his way groggily across the room, shedding clothes as he went.

Stanislaw Palewski, Polish ambassador to the Sublime Porte, alias S. Brett, connoisseur, flung back the covers and collapsed into his bed, stark naked.

Just like the woman he discovered there.

"Ah! *Mio caro*," she said, putting out her dimpled arms. "I thought I would have to wait too, too long."

It seemed to Palewski that the introductions had been peremptory, at best.

He gave a groan, and before his head hit the pillow he was fast asleep.

28

SCARCELY one hundred yards from where a baffled courtesan was sitting up in Palewski's bed, arms folded and a frown on her pretty face, Count Barbieri was taking leave of the contessa.

"I regret, Carla, that I have some matters to arrange."

"Some matters? How mysterious you are, Barbieri."

He did not miss the absence of a smile. He was about to reply but thought better of it; instead, he kissed her hand. "I wish you fortune," he said, glancing at the tables that the footmen had already set up.

"We will see you next time, then," she replied, turning from him.

Downstairs, he made for the water gate, where his gondola was waiting; the jetty creaked and for a moment he paused, looking up at the stars. Brushing the slender mooring pole with one hand, he stepped lightly into the fragile craft and sat down, leaning back against the cushions. He'd been right to leave while the night was still beautiful, before he lost money.

Barbieri raised his head and contemplated the stars. He felt the gentle dip of the boat as the gondolier took his place on the deck behind him.

Upstairs, the contessa was leading her guests to the gaming tables.

The gondola moved forward from its mooring with a soft sigh. The light from the contessa's windows purled on the inky surface of the canal; overhead, the stars hung brightly in a moonless sky. In no other city in the world, the count was thinking, could one so well appreciate the heavens.

It was a suitable reflection for a man who was about to die.

For rowing a gondola is not easy, and the count's throat presented an unblemished target.

The killer let the oar slide soundlessly into the water and unsheathed his knife.

29

ISTANBUL, where Palewski had lived for so many years, was widely considered to be a healthful city: a wind that blew from the Dardanelles, even in summer, agitated and purified the air, while the swift current of the Bosphorus, running down from the Black Sea, acted as perpetual sluice.

Perhaps that was why, in 1204, the aged and blind Doge Enrico Dandolo had proposed moving the entire enterprise of Venice, lock, stock, and barrel, to the shores of the Golden Horn. He had just conquered Constantinople with Crusader help, and the chance would not come again. His proposal was rejected.

Venice, according to the wisdom of the day, was a sickly place. Miasmas, which carried the risk of disease, rose from sluggish canals choked, as they usually were, with rotting garbage and raw excrement. The passage of a gondola stirred the depths of these little open sewers and occasionally raised a stench; everyone knew that bad smells, if inhaled, were dangerous.

It was also a plague city, or had been, when it traded with the Eastern ports. In those days, Venice had been famous for San Lazzaro, the island on which new arrivals could be confined for forty days—*la quarantena*. Now, with the decline of trade, and in the face of official indifference, quarantine laws had been suspended. So few ships bothered to pay the Austrian harbor dues to enter the lagoon in the uncertain hope of trading with an impoverished population that the stern regulations of a vigorous Republic had been allowed to lapse. It remained a city of rats—those soft plops that Palewski sometimes heard beneath his windows at night were proof of that. But plague—the bubonic plague of medieval Europe—had not, in fact, broken out in Venice for many years. Only cholera remained a recurrent problem.

Cholera! When Palewski woke the next morning to a bright blue sky and stomach cramps, he groaned, and sweated, and half supposed that he was going to die, a friendless stranger in a strange city. He would pass from the record unremembered, laid beneath a stone—if anyone gave him one—inscribed with a fictitious name. If he lived, he thought, he might at least have been able to scrape together an acquaintance with the contessa, even, perhaps, to become a friend. But she would cut him when he died, for sure.

Such thoughts—the heat, his tangled sheets, the shouts of healthy men passing on the canal outside—served to oppress his spirits. He was unaccountably plagued by a dim and dreamlike memory of finding a strange woman in his bed, too, which worried him. Was he losing his reason, as well?

His hand fluttered to his head.

Then the door opened and that very woman seemed to come in, neatly dressed, carrying a steaming bowl of chicken soup.

"*Ecco!*" she said. Behold!

Palewski scrambled up beneath his covers, revived by the smell of the broth. The woman who brought it in was plump and dark; she had little hands and a face as sweet as a Madonna's, with liquid brown eyes, a pert nose, and a dimple in the middle of her chin. She drew up a chair to the bed and sat down.

He looked at her. She dipped the spoon into the soup. He made a weak effort to reach for the spoon, but she swept it back and tut-tutted so that he lay back against the pillows and let her bring the spoon to his lips.

If the smell of soup had revived him, the soup itself perfected the cure.

A touch of sun! A headache, perhaps a chill: nothing more. Of course—that ridiculous expedition to the Armenians, across the lagoon in the heat of the day! No wonder he had been out of sorts. And then fizzy wine on an empty stomach. He'd woken up hungry, that was all.

And now this wonderful girl had cured him. He turned his head.

"I don't know your name?"

"Maria," she replied with a smile.

Palewski reached out and put his hand on her knee. "Maria," he croaked. "What a lovely name! And do you know, Maria? I feel much, much better now."

30

"WHAT would I tell you?" She stood by the window, where only the night before she had sat with the dottore, speaking of stone lions. "To me, Commissario, this is my house. These are my friends."

Brunelli felt the heat flush in his cheeks.

"I might point out that one of your friends has been killed," he growled.

His eye fell on a monstrous display of barbaric weaponry above the fireplace. Pikes, cutlasses, sabers—all of it, no doubt, stripped from the corpses of fallen Turks on some godforsaken battlefield far away. It was unlikely, he thought, that whichever scion of the house of Aspi had fought that day had killed them personally. That would have been a job for the ordinary men, the common soldiers, the Venetians who fought and who went down unrecorded.

"What you think of me, or the work I do, is of no consequence," he added. "I hear the same from my son."

The contessa flung him a glance of contempt. "Even your son."

"My son is young. He does not, I think, understand what death means. He does not understand about justice."

The contessa said nothing, merely wrapped her arms tighter about her body and stared through the window.

"Justice," he repeated heavily. Brunelli could guess what she was thinking. They were all the same, weren't they, these aristocrats? Supposing that the law was for little people, people like himself. Still dreaming of the days when they controlled the Republic—except that they gave it up, too, at the first shot. "I believe the count himself would have wanted that much."

The contessa put the heel of her hand to her mouth. Brunelli saw her shoulders heave. After a while she wiped her eyes with her fingers. "The gondolier, Commissario?"

"Mostly bruised. Remembers nothing," Brunelli said brusquely. "Were your doors locked?"

There was a pause. Eventually the contessa said, "It was not necessary. Antonio was downstairs to receive my guests."

"And to bring them upstairs?"

"Yes."

Anyone, the commissario thought, could have come in the street door and walked through to the jetty, while the footman showed the guests upstairs.

"The count—he was the first to leave?"

"He went early. He said he had something to do."

"Do you know what?"

"No. I—I accused him of being mysterious." The contessa's voice was flat.

"What time do you think he left?"

"The time? What does it matter, Commissario? Nine, ten o'clock. We were about to play cards." She tilted her chin. "Why don't you say half past nine? Make it precise. Your superiors will like that."

Brunelli ignored her. "You expected the count to play?"

"Of course."

Brunelli paused. "The stakes—were they high or low?" Venice had invented the casino: it went without saying that nobody played for matchsticks.

"You would probably call them high. A thousand lire, something like that."

Brunelli nodded. He had expected higher. "Which Count Barbieri could afford?"

She gave a brittle laugh. "He didn't run from the tables, Commissario."

There was a knock on the door. *"Avanti!"*

Scorlotti, Brunelli's assistant, entered the room hesitantly. He saw the contessa and bowed.

"Something to report, Commissario."

Brunelli took Scorlotti aside and they spoke together in low voices.

"That's all, Scorlotti. Thank you." When the policeman had gone, he turned again to the contessa.

"I think that's everything for the moment."

"For the moment?"

"Unless there's anything else you wish to tell me now. About Barbieri, perhaps." He paused. "Or anything—I don't know, unusual about last night?"

Something, he thought, changed momentarily in the contessa's expression.

He waited, patient as a cat at a mousehole.

"I—I can't think of anything," she admitted.

He sensed her reluctance. "It might be anything—even trivial. A remark? A guest who didn't show up as usual?"

"No. Not quite that," she said slowly. She put up a hand and began to twine one of her curls around her finger. "An American. He wasn't feeling very well, I think."

"He lost at cards?"

"No, no. He left long before—" Her eyes widened. "He left before the count."

Brunelli was silent for a while. "And the American's name, Contessa?"

But he knew the answer to his question already.

31

YASHIM pushed the door onto a tiny cobbled courtyard. There were pots of rosemary and sage against the whitewashed walls, and a lemon tree grew in the corner, throwing shade over a table and a wooden bench. Beyond the tree was a long wooden screen with slender glazing bars painted blue, which reminded Yashim of a teahouse he had visited once, in Tashkent.

A cage hung from the tree, and in it was a little bird.

Yashim leaned his back to the door and smiled to himself. Through the glass he could see the calligrapher's pens and brushes standing in pots on the windowsill.

He crossed the yard and knocked tentatively on the half-glazed door. Nobody came, so he leaned his arms against the glass and peered inside. Books lined the walls. There was a low carpeted divan scattered with cushions and in front of it a long table with a big oil lamp at one end. There was a block of paper on the table, with some pens and a bottle of ink. By the ink was a little wooden box. There was a door at the back of the room that was closed. It was blue, like the screen.

It looked like a working room—a tranquil studio. There was no sign of anyone working. Yashim tried the door, but it was locked.

He took a few steps back and saw the bench against the wall. He sat down.

Then the street door opened.

32

SHE had let her scarf drop before she caught sight of Yashim. Now she snatched it and pulled it across her face, but not before Yashim had seen the same high cheekbones and the big mouth he remembered from fifteen years before; her eyes were her mother's, he supposed.

He stood up.

"Forgive me, hanum. I am Yashim *lala*—I met Yamaluk efendi at the Topkapi Palace, many years ago."

She hesitated with the scarf. *Lala* was the honorific Yashim often used: guardian, uncle, it was given to a certain class of men who were not exactly men. And Meliha hanum was herself no dimpled maiden. Stouter and shorter than her father, she was a mother and a grandmother, too. But she knew the ways of the palace.

She let the scarf drop.

"You gave me a fright, Yashim *lala*, sitting there," she said. "I thought you were my father."

"I am sorry, hanum, I did not mean to intrude. When no one answered the door, I looked inside. I am afraid I was overcome by the beauty of this place."

"It is—very tranquil." She sounded uneasy.

"I had hoped to speak to your esteemed father," Yashim said hurriedly. He felt awkward. "Please. I can come another time."

Meliha hanum closed the street door and took a few steps into the courtyard. "I have not seen you before, Yashim efendi. Are you a friend of his?"

"We have met, hanum. I come as a friend."

"Yamaluk efendi passed away a month ago."

"My condolences, hanum. I am sorry to hear it."

A silence gathered between them.

"The peace of God be with him. I did not mean to intrude upon your grief." He moved past her, toward the door.

"It is no intrusion. He was an old man," she said. "I—I could show you the room he worked in."

There was a pride in her voice. Yashim turned.

"I would be honored," he said simply.

"My name is Meliha," she said. "My mother died giving birth to Matun, my little brother. He died when he was eight years old. I was fourteen."

As she turned to unlock the door, Yashim began to understand. Yamaluk had been her father and her mother. Yet she would have had to look after him, too.

"This is the knife for the brushes. This *dawat*—the inkpot—is of Persian lacquer. We kept the best paper here, away from the sunlight." So she guided him around the room, pointing out the articles of her father's craft, touching them with her strong fingers.

A calligrapher's fingers: she had her father's hands.

"I'm told your father did some of his best work after he retired from Topkapi," Yashim remarked. "As if he had rediscovered his energy."

"It's not for me to say," she said quickly. "He liked it here."

"Did you grind his pigments for him, Meliha hanum?"

She didn't reply. Yashim bent over the paper on the table and was struck immediately by the fluid strength of line, the beautiful and painstaking coloring of the margins. He recognized the sura; it was from the Koran.

He took a breath. The ink, he thought, was still fresh.

"Is it forbidden," he asked slowly, "for a woman to transcribe the word of God, when she does it as well as any man?"

Their eyes met.

"It is not forbidden," she said. "But I did it for him."

Yashim dropped his gaze. Yamaluk had trained his daughter; she had equaled him. Now Yamaluk was dead and this might be her last Koran.

He looked around in silence. Yamaluk—or his daughter—worked in patterns, too, transcribing beautifully colored geometric designs. Yashim knew that they represented the mysteries of Creation and were attempts to reveal an underlying form. The İznik tiles he had rescued drew on the same tradition.

He stopped in front of an iridescent pattern of twelve flowers blooming at the edges of a circle.

"The Tree of Life," Meliha said, smiling.

"And this one?"

"It's an astronomical pattern. An old one. It doesn't have a name."

"And this? I've seen this one before."

"Yes—it's Greek. We call it the Sand-Reckoner's diagram, from Archimedes."

Yashim nodded. He knew something about the mathematician who was wantonly killed by a Roman soldier in Syracuse eight centuries before the birth of the Prophet, peace be on him. He did not know that the diagram belonged to him.

"It looks familiar, all the same."

Meliha followed the pattern with her eyes. "The Greeks—I mean the later Greeks, in Byzantine times—liked the diagram, so perhaps you have seen it somewhere in the city."

There was no need to ask which city. To the Byzantines, as to the Ottomans, there was only one city. One Istanbul.

"Think of it as a diagram of possibilities. Explored and unexplored."

Yashim studied the figure. "But couldn't that be infinite?"

"Possibilities aren't infinite. Only impossibilities. The realm of the possible has limits. The grains in a handful of sand could be counted. It's within the bounds of the possible."

Yashim nodded. They stepped out into the courtyard.

"Your father lived alone?"

Meliha smiled. "He was never alone while he had his books. And we live so close. He was always welcome in our house."

"He had a lovely garden," Yashim said.

"He loved the lemon tree. He would sit there for hours in the evening, efendi," she said. She gave a little shiver. "That was why you gave me a fright, sitting there. It was just—where I found him."

"I'm sorry, hanum. But it is a place of sublime peace."

Meliha bit her thumb and looked away. "I—I suppose so."

"A place he loved, his family close by, his books." Yashim sought to reassure her. "It's a gentle way for an old man to go."

"I don't know, efendi. I wish I thought so. He looked—he looked so awful. His eyes open. So afraid." She put her fist to her mouth.

Yashim looked her in the eye. "I'm sorry," he said. There was nothing else to say, nothing that could be said. The knowledge of death was an unspoken bond between them all. "What was he working on?"

"He didn't work much. He had his address to write—he worked on that."

"Address?"

"He wrote an address to celebrate the accession of the young sultan. It was so beautiful. In kufic."

Yashim knew the style: the Arabic letters pointed and sharp. "A warrior's script?"

She smiled. "My father said it would suggest the responsibilities of rulership. The sultan is no longer a child: he understood."

"The sultan acknowledged the address?"

"My father presented it to him in person," she said proudly.

Yashim nodded, glad for her and for the old man, glad that the new sultan had had the grace to receive him, too.

There was one last thing. "I was told that your father had a wonderful book of drawings. By a Venetian."

Meliha looked at him sharply. "Told? By whom?"

"Aram Malakian. His friend, and mine."

"Malakian," she echoed. Then her tone hardened. "And did Malakian also tell you about the diagram?"

Yashim blinked. "Forgive me, hanum. The diagram?"

She stared at him intently.

"The Sand-Reckoner's diagram." She gestured to the calligrapher's room. "Which we just discussed."

Yashim returned her gaze. "I'm sorry. I don't understand."

Meliha sighed and let her shoulders fall. "No, Yashim efendi. I should apologize. And Malakian is a good man." She bit her cheek. "My father's death is still too fresh for me. The diagram was in the album, which he loved. The Bellini album." She hesitated. "I wondered if he had taken it to show the sultan."

"Did he?"

She shrugged helplessly. "I don't know. I didn't notice it had disappeared until after my father's death." She frowned and added, "But I wouldn't think so. It came from the palace years ago, into our family. I think if he had taken it to show the sultan . . ." She trailed off.

"Yes—the sultan might have thanked him for the thoughtful gift." Yashim frowned. "But you can't find it?"

She smiled brightly. "It will appear, inshallah."

"Inshallah." Yashim bowed. "I am grateful to you, hanum. I am sorry I could not meet your father, but it has been an honor to meet his daughter."

On his way down to the shore he passed a little mosque and stepped inside.

When he knelt on the carpet, and looked up, he saw that inside the dome was written *There Is No God but God* in black against the white plaster. He bowed his head and murmured a prayer for the dead.

When he lifted his head again he noticed the imam sitting by the screen, reading a Koran.

The imam nodded at him.

"The inscription—it's by Yamaluk efendi?"

"Indeed so, efendi. A light gone from our world."

"I have met his honorable daughter, imam. She said that he died—strangely."

The imam pursed his lips. "Yamaluk efendi did not fear death."

"But?"

"But the fear of God was in his face when he died." He placed his finger in the book. "I am sorry for his daughter. Her father must have died after she left him one evening. In the morning he was already cold. He had apoplexy, I suppose. Well, it was quick. God is merciful, efendi."

"God is indeed merciful, imam," Yashim replied uneasily.

33

PALEWSKI heard the knock on his door and clambered out of bed. It would be Ruggerio, he supposed, as he drew on his dressing gown. Ruggerio pressing the rich American to take him to lunch again.

It took Palewski a moment to place the heavyset man with the crumpled face in his memory.

"Come in, Commissario," he said, suppressing a guilty start by wrenching the door wide. A wave of yesterday's unhappiness washed over him: he felt like a hunted and friendless fugitive.

The commissario walked over to the window and stared out at the Grand Canal.

It struck Palewski that Barbieri, too, had been unable to take his eyes off the canal. One might have thought that the novelty would wear off.

"Can I help you, Commissario?"

Brunelli grunted. "For a man who has been in Venice only a few short days you seem to be making quite an impression, Signor Brett." He turned. "I'm not sure it's altogether the impression you wanted."

Palewski frowned and said nothing.

"The other night," Brunelli continued, "you thought I had come to establish your bona fides. I told you that was why I had been sent but not why I had come. Do you remember?"

"You had a body in the canal. I had seen it pulled out. Wasn't much help, I'm afraid."

"It's not a problem, Signor Brett. Except that now, you see, I have another one."

"Another one," Palewski echoed, baffled. It was the commissario's job, he supposed, to deal with bodies in canals. Why should he come to him?

"This second man, I think, you had already met. Count Barbieri."

Palewski's hand flew to his mouth. "Good God—what is the time? I completely forgot—I'm supposed to be seeing him at eleven."

Brunelli looked into his eyes and slowly shook his head. "Not Barbieri, signore. And, I should add, it is already almost noon."

If Brett was a liar, he thought, he was very good.

A simpler man—the stadtmeister, for example—might have drawn the obvious conclusion that Signor Brett was not to be trusted. "Let us not delude ourselves," the stadtmeister might say, "mud sticks for good reason."

But Brunelli, unlike his boss, was not a simple man. He had spent too many years considering his own motivation to assume that he always understood what motivated other people. He was a Venetian patriot, born and raised on these tightly packed islands, and he believed that Venice in all her grandeur and decay, in all her moods, in both her sweetness and her wickedness, offered him a solid and sufficient stage. Torcello, say, or Burano, or the farther reaches of the lagoon, were in the wings; the mainland was scarcely in the same theater.

He was a Venetian patriot who had taken a vow of allegiance to the Habsburg emperor. The paradox infuriated his son, as he had admitted to the contessa: but Paolo was still simple, because he was young and had not faced choices. Paolo had not taken decisions.

Brunelli took one now.

"Count Barbieri was killed last night, as he left the contessa's party," he said. "He was attacked on his gondola, and his head was cut off with a knife."

Palewski sat down on a chair against the wall. "How perfectly horrible."

"Barbieri's head was discovered this morning by a sacristan in the church of San Paolo, not far from here. The sacristan found it on the altar, on a communion plate."

Palewski stared at the commissario. "On a plate? Like John the Baptist?"

Brunelli grunted. "Yes. I had not thought of it that way."

"But what could it mean?"

"I have absolutely no idea."

Brunelli took the window seat and he and Palewski leaned forward on their elbows, looking at one another. After a pause they both spoke together:

"You think I—?"

"I don't think you—"

Palewski was the first to recover. "I didn't kill Count Barbieri, Commissario. On the contrary, I was hoping to do some business with him."

"I am thinking of my report," Brunelli said candidly. "You saw Barbieri at the contessa's party, then you left, early. Some people—a magistrate, for example—might wonder where you went."

"I came back here. I felt ill—a touch of sun, I think."

"Hmmm." The commissario looked troubled. "I don't suppose that anyone saw you later?"

"Later? No." Palewski hesitated. He had a code, and he sensed he should stick to it even when he was in trouble.

Especially, perhaps, when he was in trouble. What good was the code otherwise?

"I'm afraid I can't prove that I was here," he said stiffly.

Brunelli sighed. "It's a shame, Signor Brett."

Their eyes met. The door to the bedroom opened and a young woman stepped out. She fastened a pin in her hair.

"But I know, Commissario, that this gentleman was here." She smiled sweetly. "I was with him the whole night."

34

STANISLAW Palewski closed the door on the amiable commissario and turned back to his other uninvited guest. She looked very pretty with the light in her hair.

"I am in your debt, Maria," he said. "I'm afraid this sounds like a terrible business."

Maria nodded with a smile. The first rule, she had been told, was to keep her gentleman in good spirits. Until the policeman came she had been doing rather well, she thought.

"We could take a little walk," she suggested.

They walked south, arm in arm toward the Zattere. The canals were broader in these parts; the pavements were more even. Here and there rampant roses spilled out overhead from walled gardens. Beggars sat in doorways in the sun, mumbling for alms. Through open windows came the sounds of people eating, the bright clank of crockery and knives, somebody somewhere playing a flute.

Palewski had spent almost half his life in Istanbul, and now the pressure of a woman's arm on his, the rhythm of her smaller steps—first awkward and then agreeable—the musical sound of her prattle (it was, when one stopped to listen, scarcely more), drew him unexpectedly back to another country, long ago.

He felt her hand on the small of his back.

"Are you all right, *mio caro?*"

Palewski squeezed his eyes at the bridge of his nose. In a blinding moment he had seen another woman in his mind's eye and felt the pressure of her arm on his.

"Forgive me, Maria."

"Come. We're there," Maria said. They turned the corner and there was the Zattere, with the long, low silhouette of the Giudecca across the water, the church of San Giorgio, and the barges' brown sails hanging in the summer air.

"Tell me, Maria," Palewski said. "Where are you from?"

She squeezed his arm. "From Venice, silly."

"But last night—how did you come?"

Maria nodded. "It was la Signora Ruggerio. She said I should."

Palewski laughed weakly. Ruggerio, of course.

"I'm glad you did," he said.

Maria squeezed his arm. "Can we have an ice cream?" she said brightly.

35

LIKE many Venetians, Brunelli believed that Venetians ate better than anyone else in the world. And like many Venetians, too, he believed that he ate better than anyone in Venice, thanks to his wife.

That morning, before he knew anything of the unfortunate Count Barbieri, his wife had announced her intention of cooking *seppia con nero* for lunch. She knew that Brunelli was unhappy about their son. *Seppia con nero* was a favorite with them both and she hoped that their differences would untangle across a bowl of steaming squid.

"You're late, Papa," Paolo said when Brunelli arrived.

Carla glanced at her husband. He smiled.

"If I am late, Paolo, it is because I have been working. Not lounging about in the piazza, talking and smoking cheroots."

"But Papa, your work is all talk, too. It's the same as mine."

"Hmmph." Brunelli sat down at the table and closed his eyes. "I smell it. I smell *seppia con nero*." He sighed.

36

In the days of the Republic, affairs of state were debated by members of the Senate, drawn from the noble families eligible for service. No other Venetians had any influence over the Republic's policy.

Real authority was vested in a Council of Ten, elected from members of the Great Council. The ten governed in the name of the doge.

And behind the Ten, pulling the levers of absolute power, without appeal, stood a Council of Three.

All this, a system of absolute rule by a secret cabal, was swept away by the Napoleonic intervention. In 1797 a departing honor guard of Croat infantry had fired a farewell salute; the senators, in panic, instantly voted themselves out of existence and fled the chamber.

But a relic of the old government still survived.

While the contessa's friend lamented the loss of the old stone lions of St. Mark, there was one, at least, whose future seemed assured, even under the Habsburgs. At the back of the Doges' Palace, in a narrow alley with blank windowless sides, a stone head of a lion was fixed to the wall, its eyes staring, its mouth agape.

And into this mouth, the *bocca di leone*, ordinary citizens had always been encouraged to post information that would be of use to the Council of Three. The information, anonymously supplied, would be investigated and, if it proved interesting, could be used immediately—or simply filed away in dossiers that the Venetian state kept on all its more prominent citizens. A whiff of treachery, a sharp commercial practice, a breach of contract, a marital infidelity—hidden knowledge was the tool by which the Venetians governed their state. Knowledge of the world at large had made them rich; knowledge of themselves, they hoped, would keep them safe.

It was not, after all, a very progressive republic, which is why it broke apart when Napoleon touched it, like a bubble of Murano glass.

Far from stopping the mouth of the terrible lion in the name of Liberty, the French had actually widened it: the anonymous denunciation became a tool of the revolutionary government in Paris, too.

And the Austrians, who were never the most zealous reformers, and preferred to leave things much as they had found them, soon took to regularly inspecting the *bocca di leone* themselves.

Naturally they didn't turn up much. The people of Venice were generally reluctant to provide their foreign rulers with information.

But old habits die hard.

Venice was the first city in Europe to have street lighting, but the alley at the back of the Doges' Palace was almost dark when a shadow slipped past the *bocca di leone* toward ten o'clock at night.

The shadow seemed to glide along the alley without a pause, but the lion was fed with a lozenge of paper, very small and tightly rolled.

37

PALEWSKI watched as Maria licked a trace of ice cream from her upper lip.

A slow procession of barges with rust-colored sails was making its way along the Giudecca. Foreign, seagoing ships were rare; Palewski thought of the great three-masted schooners and the frigates that often crowded the Bosphorus at home. Here, the shipping was strictly local: flatboats from the lagoon, island ferries rowed by four men with long sweeps, a huge, covered *burchiello*, or passenger barge, and a shoal of smaller craft—wherries, skiffs, and the occasional gondola—dotted the smooth blue water, sparkling breezily in the late afternoon light.

On the Zattere, the *passeggiata* had already begun. Couples strolled along arm in arm, their children zigzagging around them through the crowd; old men tapped their canes over the cobblestones, stopping now and then to admire the view or to hail a friend; knots of young men, with toppers tilted at rakish angles, lounged on the bridges; the ubiquitous gray uniforms of Austrian officers; a matron sailing by with two young women in tow, casting furtive glances at the loafers.

Palewski shifted his glance from Maria's lips and observed a ragged girl with a tray of matches working her way through the tables. He felt in his pocket for a small coin.

Then he froze.

"Maria!" he whispered urgently. "Kiss me!"

Maria turned her head and smiled coquettishly. "Not here, silly."

Palewski bent his head. It had been the most fleeting glimpse—he could not be sure. Compston in Venice? But why ever not? The young Byronist—it was exactly where one would expect to find him, with the British embassy in Istanbul in summer recess. At least—if it were Compston—he'd not been spotted. He hadn't even met his eye.

Yet Palewski's glance, however light, must have somehow left an impress, for seconds later a meaty hand descended on Palewski's shoulder.

"I say, Excellency! This is too fantastic!"

Looking up with a grim smile, Palewski saw a shock of yellow hair crammed under a top hat, and beneath it the open, ruddy face of the third secretary to Her Britannic Majesty's Ambassador to the Sublime Porte.

"Compston," he snapped, in low tones. "I am not here. You didn't see me."

The young man blinked.

And then, to Palewski's horror, there were three of them.

"Found a friend, George?" Another Englishman, also fair, slightly older than Compston: Ben Fizerly. Fizerly registered Maria's appearance and goggled. "Er, friends, I should say—why, it's Palewski!"

They shook hands.

The third member of the group was not an Englishman. He was tall and very good-looking, with sallow skin and the faint line of a mustache across his upper lip. His eyes, like his hair, were black.

"This is Count Palewski, Tibor," Compston said. "Count, Tibor Karolyi. He's with the Imperial embassy in Istanbul. Um."

Tibor's heels clicked together, and he bowed rapidly. Compston looked embarrassed. An inkling of the situation had finally penetrated his mind.

Palewski, for his part, was thinking fast. Curse his damned fond memories, he should never have walked down the Zattere at this hour! And curse his bad luck, too. Compston on his own he could have managed; even Fizerly too. But Karolyi? Karolyi was a Hungarian. He might sympathize—but he might not. The fact that he was at the embassy, working for the Habsburg monarchy, linked him straight to the people Palewski most wanted to avoid.

"Won't you join us, my dear fellows? Maria will be delighted to meet someone of her own age." He gestured to the chairs, playing for time. "On his lordship's trail, Compston?"

Compston blushed. "Venice, you know. La Serenissima and all that," he murmured, "and, well, ahem." He glanced over at Maria, who was sitting with her hands folded neatly in her lap. She had finished her ice cream.

Compston's blush deepened.

"I know a man in Venice who claims he swam with Byron," Palewski said. "Perhaps you'd like to meet him?"

Before Compston could reply, Fizerly leaned forward. "To be honest, sir, I've had about as much Byron as a man can take. Tibor too, I'm sure. Anyway, we're leaving tomorrow, nine o'clock."

"For Istanbul?"

"That's right."

"What a pity. Your last evening in Venice." Palewski cocked his head. "But this is an occasion, gentlemen! Perhaps—if you're not engaged—you will allow me to entertain you all? I have an apartment on the Grand Canal and some very good champagne."

"I say, sir! But really, we can't intrude—"

"No intrusion, Compston. It would be my pleasure. Waiter, hi! Grappa, if you please. Now, gentlemen, I propose a toast." He paused, holding up one finger like a bandmaster, while the waiter set the bottle and five small glasses on the table. "For you, my dear, and for you fellows . . . and so: Stambouliots together!"

They drank. Palewski refilled the glasses and gave them La Serenissima, then Byron's swim, and finally a toast to the evening that lay ahead, before the bottle was empty.

"To the gondolas, my friends!"

They walked to the landing stage, the young Englishmen flushed and animated; even Karolyi's eyes were bright, as he cast them at Palewski's escort.

"Maria," Palewski said, when the two of them were settled in the leading boat. Venice, he realized, had one advantage over Istanbul, at least. "Maria, I will drop you at the Rialto."

She gave a disappointed pout.

"But I want you to come along in an hour or so."

"I see."

"With a couple of your friends."

"My friends?" She looked at him and raised an eyebrow.

"Maria, my dear. I am asking you to arrange a simple, traditional Venetian orgy."

38

POP! Pop! Corks flew. The boys were in ecstasies.

"I say, Palewski!" Compston's eyes shone. "I say!"

"To Venice," Palewski proposed.

They drank again. Palewski filled their glasses.

"And what is Venice, gentlemen? The city of pleasure. Masques, balls, the Arabian nights reborn—a place of love and squalor, of high art—and low desire."

The young men tittered.

"I daresay you've been to the Doges' Palace? To the Scuola di San Giorgio degli Schiavoni? And the Accademia? Of course, of course. To art, gentlemen! To the glory of Bellini, and Tiepolo, and Titian!"

"To art!" they chorused enthusiastically.

"Tell the truth," said Compston, "I've seen about as much art as I could want."

Fizerly nodded. "Writing it all up for the ladies at home, too. Bit grueling, Palewski."

"Karolyi?"

But Count Karolyi, too, seemed to have flagged beneath the deluge of Venetian art. "It is all very old," he said. "Nothing new."

Palewski nodded. "You are right. It's all old. Wonderful but frozen. To frozen Venice!"

They drank.

"'S'all very well for you, Palewski," Compston declared with a wink.

"I think you are right, Mr. Compston," Karolyi said. "Count Palewski's Venice does not appear to be all frozen." He gave his host a thin-lipped smile.

"To which end, gentlemen, I have arranged for you to meet some charming young friends of mine," Palewski continued smoothly. "I believe I hear them now on the stairs."

He went to the door and pulled it open.

"Here they are. Please consider my home as your own."

He stepped out onto the landing. Maria tapped him with her fan and smiled.

The three young men stood, unsteadily, as Maria and her friends entered the room, laughing.

"Avanti, sorelle!"

39

IT was shortly before eight o'clock that Palewski returned to his apartment from the hotel where he had spent the night.

He found three puffy-faced young men already struggling into their underwear.

"Got to get back to the consul," Compston croaked, shading his eyes. "To get our things." He fished up a pocket watch and stared at it, a look of horror spreading across his flushed features. "Oh my God! Fizerly! We've only got half an hour left!"

"All taken care of," Palewski said crisply. "I had everything sent to the ship."

Compston's eyes filled with tears. "Palewski, old man. I—I don't know what to say. You're the most capital fellow I ever met."

40

THE stadtmeister shuddered. A head on a plate? A drifting gondola with a severed trunk inside? It was outlandish, warped—like everything in this dreadful town, wreathed in mist, drifting on its horrible flat lagoon. Ach, for the mountains, where the water was clear and you tramped the forests with proper rock under your feet! And where a former stadtmeister in the service of the emperor was a figure of respect and awe.

He frowned and pulled back his shoulders slightly.

"I have not lived among these Latins for so many years, Herr Vosper, without gaining some useful insights into the Venetian mind."

Vosper drew his heels together and gave a short nod that might have been a bow.

"It is, I think I may say without fear of contradiction, a degenerate mind. Here and there one finds representatives of the old type, but they are unfortunately rare." He placed his fingertips together and contemplated the ceiling.

"In the aim of understanding the representative characteristics of a people, what are the preliminary indices that must be established, Herr Vosper?"

"I beg your pardon, Stadtmeister," Vosper replied, shuffling his feet. "I am afraid I don't understand the question."

The stadtmeister sighed. "What is the most important influence?"

"Climate, sir."

"Because people from the north are tall and fair, like birch trees, yes.

They work hard, in teams. Ice demands unremitting teamwork. People from the south are dark and short. They are more indolent, also."

"Yes, sir."

"We can observe this phenomenon operating both on the large and the small scale, Herr Vosper. The Nordic type and the Mediterranean type. On a smaller scale, it is true to a lesser degree that the southern Italian peninsula is chiefly associated with indolence and dishonesty, while the northerly regions—of which Venice is a member—are more hardworking and upright. Do you follow?"

Vosper nodded. He could have given the speech himself.

"But we must allow for the interplay between large and small scale, as between the movement of men and history. We must—and do—allow for this!"

He leaned forward. His face was growing red.

"This is what the anticlimatic idiots will not try to understand! Science is a subtle system, Herr Vosper. Subtle but irrefutable, when the evidence is allowed." He balled his fists and pressed them together over his leather-topped desk. "Interplay is a crucial element in the system. How else can men change?"

He paused to consider his own rhetorical question.

"For as long as Venetians represented the northern type within their own, smaller world, they were unmatched for acumen and fair dealing. But for several centuries they have been drawn farther into the orbit of the great northern landmass that is Europe. They have become, in this sense, southerners. Am I correct?"

"Quite correct, Stadtmeister."

"So one observes the corruption of the Venetian mind as a matter of course. We cannot entirely blame them for this, although I believe that the Venetians must also have married too many southerners for their own good. Observe, Vosper, how the traits degenerate. What was once commercial acumen has become mere slyness. The bold trading initiative of the medieval Republic—has it disappeared? Not exactly. It has merely degenerated, on the one hand into a capacity for petty jealousy, on the other into an addiction to bright and pretty things. We see the Venetians of today like children, Herr Vosper. They appreciate pageantry and glitter and pretty women. Hrrmph. Once the Venetians were famous for their forethought, but now? Let us not delude ourselves, Herr Vosper. They think of the next hour, at most the next day!"

"Quite so, Stadtmeister. And you once mentioned that someone was the representative of the old type, I forget his name, Farinelli?"

"Falier. A doge."

"But the new Venetian was Casanova."

"I may have said so, Herr Vosper, yes," the stadtmeister said testily. Could it be possible that Vosper was laughing at him? Casanova was the only Venetian literature he had read, many years before, in a translation eagerly passed around the officers' mess.

But Vosper's empty blue eyes revealed nothing. He was a good man, Finkel thought, good Alpine stock. German-speaking, too. A degree of altitude of course tempered the general climatic theory.

"You mark my words, Herr Vosper," he said, jabbing a finger across the desk. "This will be a crime of passion. *Cherchez la femme*," he added and then, seeing a look of incomprehension on his subordinate's face: "Look for the woman. After that, we can uncover the dead man's rival, and all will be plain." He sat upright and sucked in his stomach. "As I say, it is necessary to understand the Venetian mind. As it now is."

Vosper looked uncertain. "Isn't this Signor Brunelli's department, Stadtmeister?"

"Herr Vosper, let us understand each other. You work for me. Through me, for the Kaiser." He paused, to relish the happy juxtaposition. "We do not question our orders."

"Of course not, Stadtmeister."

"Very good."

When Vosper had gone, Stadtmeister Finkel let himself relax in his chair. He had nothing against Brunelli. A good officer, no doubt, and less prone than others of his class and nation to let the soft haze of the lagoon penetrate his mind; but there it was. Vosper was, like him, an outsider— and Brunelli? *Na und*, a man was the product of his climate.

He took up a scrap of paper from his desk and squinted at it, puzzled.

The writing was very small and it was written in a language that Gustav Finkel, Stadtmeister von Venedig, rather imperfectly understood.

It contained, as far as he could judge, nothing new, nothing he was entitled to do anything about.

Someone was afraid and wanted help.

He tore the paper into little pieces and tipped them into the wastepaper basket.

41

SHE looked at him curiously. "You're in trouble, aren't you?" she said.

"Trouble? I'm all right, Maria, thanks to you."

"That's what I mean, silly. You'd have let yourself be copped for that murder if I hadn't spoken up. What did you mean by that? I was here all night. And now," she added, "it's a different story."

Palewski had blushed, insofar as he was capable of blushing. "Not your affair, Maria. I didn't want the commissario to get you into trouble." He paused, and the girl shot him a droll look as if to say: you couldn't get me into trouble. "What do you mean, a different story?"

"Well, I'd wondered. I thought, perhaps, you were saving your reputation, Signor Brett. But from what I gathered last night, Signor Brett hasn't got a reputation to lose."

Palewski unfolded himself and rose from his chair. "I see."

"I don't speak English, so I couldn't understand what the boys were saying exactly. But Tibor—he was my choice, quite good-looking he was—said a few things in French, and I understand that a fair bit."

Palewski felt weary. "And what, Maria, did you understand?"

Maria pressed her lips together, humorously. "I don't know who

Signor Brett is, but you're a Polish count. You're the Polish ambassador in Istanbul. Go on, I know it's true."

Palewski stood a long time at the window, looking out.

"I don't know how it looks to you," he said at last. "A long time ago, before you were even born, there was a country wrapped around a river. The Vistula. It had, what? Cities, towns, villages, little farms. Hills and mountains, too, but mostly plains, and marshes, and big, deep forests where you'd be afraid to go at night, Maria. There could be wolves in there. But foresters, too, and men burning charcoal all night long. And when it snowed, there were people all wrapped up in fur, whizzing along in the dark on sleighs, laughing and telling stories. And they spoke the language I learned to speak, the people in the towns, and the foresters, and the people rushing through the dark, too."

Maria shivered deliciously.

"It wasn't quite like Venice, Maria, when they came and took it all away. Venice is one city, and you can't change that. You can go from the Arsenale to the Dorsoduro with the same joke, and everyone will laugh except the Austrians. But the Austrians took a part of my country, and the Prussians took another, and the Russians took the most because they are big and fierce like bears in the wood. Venice can disappear only if it sinks into the lagoon. But Poland will vanish if people forget. It needs anyone it can get. Even me, maybe, being its ambassador in Istanbul."

He rubbed his chin.

"The fact is, Maria, I came here only to do a favor for a friend. If you turn me in to the authorities, I'd be sorry. Not for me—that's all right. For the people I think of in the woods, and in the towns, and in the sleighs at night."

He turned, and to his surprise he saw tears on her cheeks.

"*Mio caro*," she said sadly, rising to slide her arms around his chest. "With you, it is like an evening at La Fenice." She pressed her cheek against his shoulder. "I will never betray you!"

Thank God for opera, Palewski thought, patting the girl on her pretty bare shoulder.

42

THE contessa, according to Antonio the footman, was indisposed. Palewski had expected as much. Barbieri's death—well, his murder—would have upset her.

Palewski took lunch at an outdoor table in one of the little restaurants off the Rialto, from where he could look across the Grand Canal to the row of palazzi that lined the opposite bank.

On the whole, he felt, it was a pretty but unsatisfactory view, in which the eye was invited to glide, like a gondola, along a single plane, a view that lacked depth. Even the water served only to reflect the wall of pretty color overhead.

He was used to the dynamic jumble of the Istanbul streets, where covered balconies jutted out over the street and whole buildings were jettied forward on the upper floors; sometimes, whole rows of masonry were made to fold in and out like a concertina. In Venice, builders gave their attention to the windows, carving them into extraordinary shapes, and to the surfacing of the walls, but indentation was a mere suggestion, a sort of trick of the light.

Venice was theater in so many ways: even its buildings looked like painted flats.

He sipped his prosecco and tried, for the twentieth time, to make sense of his position. He had made no progress whatever on the Bellini hunt. If the sultan's information was correct, and the painting really had reappeared in Venice, it was a very slow sale. Barbieri had seemed to hint at the possibility of theft, but he never mentioned the portrait of Mehmet II.

If Barbieri knew of anyone trying to sell the portrait, he would presumably have offered to negotiate—on commission—for Palewski to buy it. But he hadn't offered; therefore, he knew nothing about it. And now, bizarrely, he was dead—just like the art dealer whose corpse Palewski had seen floating in the canal on the morning of his arrival.

It was a coincidence that two art dealers should die, in curious circumstances, within a week of each other.

At the back of his mind lay one uncomfortable thought: Was it possible that the coincidence extended to his own arrival in Venice?

The waiter delivered a plate of *frutti di mare*: oysters, clams, prawns, and a half lobster. Palewski downed the oysters hurriedly, relishing the tang of the sea and hoping they would help clear his mind.

He would have liked to speak to someone, thrash it out. He thought of Yashim, drumming his heels in Istanbul: how he wished Yashim were here now with him! It had all seemed pretty simple when they said goodbye. The Brett plan—the printed cards, the expeditions to tailors and hatters and bootmakers on La Grande Rue de Pera. Outwitting the Habsburg bureaucracy had seemed like the easiest, most satisfactory thing in the world. A few weeks in Venice; a few introductions; a deal, or not, as it might turn out—and *basta!* as the Italians say: home again.

Instead of which he'd had murders, the police, Compston and his friends, a bout of fever . . .

And, he thought, something else, too: a sense of being not quite in command of his own destiny. Like an actor in a play, speaking lines that were not, really, his own.

He grabbed the lobster and stabbed it with a fork to pull away the succulent white tail.

He had known nothing about the fellow in the canal: the man was already dead when he arrived.

He squeezed a wedge of lemon over the cold lobster.

As for Barbieri, they had met once, twice, allowing for the brief encounter at the contessa's palazzo. If someone, for whatever reason, had tried to prevent Palewski from learning about the Bellini—well, that made no sense. Barbieri truly knew nothing, and who would want to keep him from making an offer on the painting? A painting that, he was increasingly certain, did not exist.

Which brought him back to his own position in the city. The boys from the Istanbul embassies were safe on the high seas. It would be a week, at least, before any of them could report to the Austrians in Istanbul, and another week before the information would reach the Austrian authorities in Venice. Maria and her courtesans he would simply have to trust. As for that commissario, Brunelli, it was hard to judge if—and of what quite—he was suspicious.

Two more weeks: he owed Yashim that much, at any rate. After that, it would be dangerous to remain in Venice. And if, by then, he had failed to turn up anything on Bellini, it might be said that the picture was not available or did not exist.

A man Palewski had never seen before dropped suddenly into a chair beside him.

"Signor Brett," the stranger said. "I understand you are looking for a Bellini."

Palewski started. "As a matter of fact, I am," he said.

"In which case, signore, I may be able to help."

43

"It is not any painting you seek, signore?"

"No," Palewski admitted. "Not any painting."

The man smiled. "But I wondered about that." He fished into his breast pocket and withdrew a card. He glanced at it.

"*Connoisseur:* it means much."

Palewski watched him. The card, he recognized, was his own.

"But also—nothing." The man snapped the card down on the table.

Palewski's expression did not change. He looked at the man: he was quite fat, with smooth jowls and small, wet lips. His eyes were large and black. His head was shaved clean.

"You have the advantage of me, Signor—?"

The heavyset man looked at him for a long time before he answered. "If you like, Alfredo. It's not important, Signor Brett."

There had been the slightest pause, as if he had glanced again at the card to check.

"Bellini went to Istanbul in 1479," Palewski said. "He painted a portrait of Mehmet the Conqueror, which later disappeared."

Alfredo sighed. "I am a very little man, Signor Brett. Please, I would like you to understand. I cannot sell you a painting. I have children. I have a wife. My parents live with us, and my father has gone blind." He nodded, as if to acknowledge sympathy.

Palewski said nothing.

"I work for another, a very great man, Signor Brett. Many people in this city will show works by inferior artists. You can buy a Canaletto very cheap here."

"I'm not interested in a cheap Canaletto," Palewski said.

Alfredo clasped his hands. "Of course not. Otherwise, Signor Brett, we would not be talking. Let me tell you something about Venice. It looks poor, doesn't it? Sad, and patched up, and gray, even on a beautiful day like this. A city without an income. But do not misjudge it. Venice is also a city of extraordinary wealth—as our friends from Vienna know all too well."

He put his finger on the table and held it there.

"We are surrounded, Signor Brett, with considerable treasures. You know the Correr?"

"Yes."

"What did you like there?"

The question surprised Palewski. "I liked the Carpaccio," he said, after thinking. "*The Courtesans*."

The man smiled. "I like it too, Signor Brett. I agree with your choice. Correr was a rich man, a man of taste and connections. Would it surprise you to know that he considered that painting a poor specimen of the master's art? Relatively speaking, of course. Correr, you see, knew better—he had seen things that he could never put his finger on again.

"We know that for a thousand years, Venice has been plundering the world. With her wealth, she was able to produce her own masters, too. This city was never captured, never plundered. Three hundred families held the reins of power—and access to wealth—in all those years. Oh yes, the Corsican took things that belonged here—the bronze horses from St. Mark's, the Veroneses and the Titians from the churches. Big, grand thefts—for what? To symbolize his mastery of the Veneto. A pagan triumph, nothing more. There was no stripping of the palazzi. Perhaps, had he been given more time—who knows? The Austrians—they try, here and there, to take artworks from the city. But the world is watching them. In the meantime, the old nobility have become clever."

"Clever?"

"These sad old buildings"—Alfredo gestured vaguely toward the canal—"appear to be shuttered up, stripped out, half abandoned. A city in decay—of course." He leaned forward. "But if you could see what really lies inside those walls, not even on display, but in an attic somewhere, under a Persian rug, or locked up in a shabby trunk—well, I need hardly say that you, Signor Brett, would go half mad with joy—and with desire."

Palewski thought of the contessa's palazzo. It had seemed bare, but perhaps it was just a façade, a cautious reaction to the dangers presented by foreign occupation. There were villages in Thrace and Macedonia, he recalled, that scarcely looked like villages at all: mere rubbish heaps. They were inhabited, he was reliably informed, by people who did all they could to disguise their wealth, the better to evade the state's taxes.

"There are treasures in Venice that even their owners do not know exist," he said, in a low tone of wonder. "But sometimes, Signor Brett, these treasures come to light."

"Your patron knows about these hidden things?"

Alfredo shrugged, as if the matter were beyond dispute. "I would say more. A palazzo, dear signor, is not a shop. The old nobility of Venice are not shopkeepers, who ticket their goods for sale. And they have discretion. You must understand that these treasures belong in some sense to the patrimony of Venice, even if she is fallen today. They belong to old families. They constitute a history of a house, and the people who have lived there." He paused, frowned, looked for the proper explanation. "Aha—it is like these pieces can be compared to a beautiful daughter. Her marriage, when she leaves the house, is not left to chance. It is a matter for full and delicate consideration."

Palewski nodded. He wondered whether Signor Brett, of New York, for all his wealth, was quite the kind of catch a patrician Venetian would consider for his daughter—even if she were made of canvas and oil.

Alfredo seemed to have read his thoughts. "My patron understands these delicate matters," he said. "I think, before I was sent to you, that your case was hopeless. In Venice you can buy—what? Anything—a friend, a woman, a nice house." He glanced at Palewski as he spoke, and Palewski flushed slightly. "But a work of art? This is different."

He cocked his head. "Let me be frank. My patron, he is not unhappy to see you in Venice. You are something new, signore. For many years, we arrange matters between our clients—his clients, I mean—and his Venetian friends. These are very important works, and the prices are, well—who can pay? The French? Hmm. Some. Some Russians. Some others, Swedes, princes, yes. But the English—these are the best. The famous Byron, pah! But Byron's friends, lords, like him, with palazzi of their own. For many years we have dealt with these men. Only these, I would say."

"And now you'd appreciate a little competition."

Alfredo smiled. "You understand me very well, signore."

Palewski signaled to the waiter. "Two brandies," he said. To Alfredo he said, "You know nothing about me."

Alfredo laughed, to Palewski's surprise. He waited while the waiter set the brandies down in two huge balloons.

"You exaggerate, Signor Brett. I think you might be surprised how much we know about you."

He slipped his hand beneath the bowl of his glass and swirled it violently so that the caramel liquid left an oily sheen on the inside, then he raised it to his nose and inhaled deeply.

"But in fact it doesn't altogether matter. Yours is a big country, Signor Brett, as I think you have already remarked."

Palewski looked up, and their eyes met.

"I'm glad we've had a chance to talk," Alfredo said. He inclined his glass toward Palewski. "To Bellini," he said quietly. Then, without waiting for a response, he drank the liquor and got up.

"We haven't really discussed Bellini, Signor Alfredo," Palewski said.

"I was always talking about Bellini, Signor Brett."

He turned to go, then stopped and looked around. "We'll meet again. The bill is taken care of," he added, with a flicker of a smile.

With that he was gone, through an arch of the arcade in two quick strides.

"Exit right," Palewski murmured to himself. "*Signor Brett onstage, drinking brandy.*"

He looked down and recognized the list he'd been writing, balancing the options.

He tore the list into little pieces. That done, he got up and went to the edge of the canal, where he let the pieces drop from his fingers into the water.

"*Curtain.*"

It was not what he had expected. It made him uneasy.

Afraid.

He would miss the rendezvous, he thought.

44

"SIGNOR Brett."

Palewski glanced around and recognized Alfredo. They walked in step, neither man saying anything, until Alfredo gestured to a pontoon.

He walked to the rail and leaned on it, looking out toward Giudecca, and then half turned toward Palewski and smiled.

"What do you know about the Bellinis, Signor Brett? As a family, I mean?"

"The Bellinis? Father, Jacopo. Good painter, highly regarded in his day. Two sons—Gentile and Giovanni. Vasari says they were very loving. Giovanni was working on the frescoes in the Doges' Palace when Mehmet's invitation to the best Venetian painter arrived, and Vasari suggests that the Senate didn't feel they could spare him. So Gentile was sent."

"Oh, I think Gentile was good enough for the job, Signor Brett. We should allow him that. When Bellini left, Mehmet gave him a title."

"He didn't use the title."

"Of course not. Mehmet also gave him a gold belt, weighted with coins. It was kept by the Bellini family for many years."

Palewski leaned on the rail. "Well?"

"Signor Brett." Alfredo seemed amused. "My patron has spoken at some length to the very owner of the painting you seek."

"The portrait of Mehmet the Conqueror? By Gentile Bellini?"

"My patron saw it several months ago. And again this morning. Before that—well, it has to do with those gold coins, Signor Brett, and also Tiziano, your Titian. He was a pupil of Bellini."

"Of Giovanni, surely?" Palewski had not spent those hours reading and rereading Vasari for nothing.

"Of Giovanni, yes, but they were a close family, Signor Brett. And I think, more importantly, we should remember how close the Venetians and the Ottomans were. When Venice sent a bailo to Istanbul, it sent the best, and there were many other merchants, too."

"Someone bought the portrait and brought it back?"

"Someone who would have known the quality of the work."

"Who?"

Alfredo smiled and spread his hands. "A little too direct, signore. I cannot tell you the name now—but of course, in due time . . ."

"And what is the deal?"

"Sixteen thousand kreuzers. Just under six thousand sterling, if you prefer."

Palewski turned to the rail. Six thousand pounds! Enough, he supposed, to keep a palazzo for a lifetime, with a gondolier in perpetual attendance! Less than the sultan spent in a month on candles, too, no doubt.

"I do not wish to influence you," Alfredo remarked. "Believe me, I understand it is a lot of money. But my patron has sold many paintings for very much more. Bellini is not in fashion, to be honest. Tiepolo, Titian, Veronese—very well. We sold a Titian last year to an Englishman for fifteen thousand."

Palewski gave an imperceptible nod. He had done some homework: Alfredo was right.

"Fashions change," the dealer observed. "Canaletto—once, two thousand, three thousand. Now you can buy him for eight hundred. There is always another, if you miss one." He shrugged. "But a Bellini—that, Signor Brett, you can buy only once. If you permit me, I shall leave you with your thoughts. You can find me in Costa's little bar—it's close to the end, down a few steps. The evening is getting chilly."

They shook hands. "Thank you, Alfredo. Give me five minutes."

Italians, he smiled to himself: always afraid of the cold. Then he remembered something he had not thought of for many years—a companion he'd loved, a man who joked and was generous and knew how to fight. But when Ranieri had lost his horse on the long retreat, he died before Palewski found him blue and stiff in the Russian snow.

He blew out his cheeks and leaned against the rail. The sunlight was gradually dragging itself from the Giudecca, dropping the spires and the old faded housefronts slowly into the shade. A grayer tide was moving in from the east as the still waters lost their sparkle: the gray ordinary light of all cities in the early dusk, when they lost their beauty and had not gained the shimmering jeweled presence of the night.

He hunched his body against the rail, thinking of another age, when the sun over Italy had set on promises and hope: the promises of a tyrant and the hope of simple men. He had never expected to come back, had he? The gesticulations, and the imprecations soon forgotten, the musical staccato of the language, and beneath his hands the heartbreaking dent of a woman's back as they walked together in the evening light.

Now he was back, and soon he would be gone.

He touched the scarf closer to his neck, wondering if the Italians were right and if there was a coldness about the dusk.

Six thousand sterling. Yashim would be pleased.

And a man in a wineshop, ready to talk terms.

Stanislaw Palewski patted the rail and turned back to the Zattere, and made his way along it toward a darkening sky.

45

SIGNOR Ruggerio, stepping out of his house in San Barnaba to buy a small cheroot from the corner shop, was surprised to find himself accompanied by two men he vaguely remembered who held his arms and suggested a drink together, somewhere outside the *campo*.

Somewhere, in fact, beyond a certain little network of alleyways, a distinct island of mud and pilings and pavements faced about with small canals, which constituted the parish of San Barnaba.

They took him over a bridge.

They gave him a glass of wine.

"He's money," Ruggerio said, prudently swallowing his jealousy along with his *rosso*—for nobody likes to lose a client. "That's for sure. The question is, where's it from?"

The men, it seemed, liked the way he talked.

"That's for you, Barone," one of them said outside the bar, tucking a cheroot wrapped in a note into his breast pocket. "I expect you can find your own way home?"

"You know how it is, gentlemen," Ruggerio replied nervously. "At my age, you begin to forget everything."

One of the men reached out and tweaked Ruggerio's cheek. "I'm delighted to hear it, Barone," he said. "Sleep well."

46

PALEWSKI walked slowly back to his apartment. It had occurred to him, ironically, and with curiosity, what might be done with six thousand pounds.

Now and then he heard footsteps approaching; a dark figure would loom out of the narrow passage, his shadow lengthening with every step, and he would pass with a muffled greeting. Sometimes he heard footsteps behind him. He walked slowly, savoring the money, and let them pass.

Six thousand would buy him a regiment, or a library, or an assassin. He wondered about that. He wondered, too, what it would be like to own a newspaper, perhaps in France, editions in Polish and French, articles about poetry and music, and above all the truth about Poland and the Poles. Mickiewicz was a good poet. Herzen—he'd contribute on the Russian side. Yes, six thousand pounds would go a long way in the diaspora, into garrets and drawing rooms.

And then again, not far enough. Better, perhaps, to go to New York, like Signor Brett, selling Canalettos to the newly rich? He smiled broadly and turned left. Australia! A new life. A new life certainly, but even in his dreams he was unclear what a life in Australia might entail.

Six thousand: two dropped on opium from Bengal, two on a cutter. Sold to China. Palewski Taipan, the richest man in Amoy! He gave a short laugh.

Footsteps again rang out on the cobbles behind him.

He stopped to look about and failed to recognize the alley. There were no lights beyond. He realized he'd taken a wrong turning; to make sure he went to the end of the alley and found himself looking through an archway at a set of slimy steps and a canal.

He swiveled around and began to retrace his steps, hearing their uneven echo in the dark ahead.

47

MARIA was sitting quietly in a chair when she saw the door handle turn.

The first man had a scar that ran from his eye to his mouth; he was thin and Maria guessed him to be about forty, forty-five. The other man was younger, bigger, and puffy eyed. He looked like a drinker.

Neither of them looked like friends of Signor Brett.

"Waiting for someone?" The man with the scar stood in the doorway, stropping his hand with his gloves. He looked annoyed.

"I'm waiting for Signor Brett," Maria snapped. "Who else? Hey, you can't come in here," she added, as the big man walked past her and glanced out the window.

The man with the scar ignored her. He closed the door behind him.

Maria felt afraid.

"Who are you? What are you doing here?"

The scar-faced man walked up to her and looked into her face. "Tell us about your boyfriend, my dear," he said.

Maria stuck out her lip. "There's nothing to tell. He's American."

"American? Oh-oh. It's not what I hear, pretty one. Like, where he buys his hats."

"His hats?"

"You heard what I said. Istanbul. Constantinople. You have heard of Constantinople? I do hope so. I do hope you're not stupid."

"I don't know what you're talking about," Maria said.

The scar-faced man stood looking into her face. His eyes were expressionless.

Without warning he drew back his hand and slapped her hard across the cheek.

Maria gave a cry and staggered sideways.

"I don't like lying women," he said. "I don't like whores."

"I'm not—"

He slapped her again.

Maria looked up: the candlelights were huge and blurred. She felt dizzy. "This is his room," she said thickly. She could taste blood in her mouth. "Get out of here." She sounded drunk; her head was pounding. "Get out."

There was a faint whistle; the scar-faced man pointed a finger at Maria, who was kneeling on the floor.

Maria tried to move but the other, silent man took her arms and dragged them roughly up behind her back.

"Another sound out of you, and you can kiss your lover goodbye." Scar-face went to the mantelpiece and pinched out the candle.

The silent man shoved her ahead of him, through the doorway. At the door scar-face looked at Maria and said, "Where's your bonnet?"

She shook her head. He went inside and reappeared with it, crushed up in his hand.

"Now we're going to make you look all pretty." He dropped the bonnet over her head and tied it around her chin. "We're going to walk downstairs and out the door and if you make one move, one sound, I'm going to stick this blade between your ribs. One shove, and I twist it around, *carissima*."

She was aware of going downstairs. One arm was behind her back and the pain as they jolted down the steps made her want to cry out. She wanted to sob, but her lungs felt paralyzed. She pressed her lips together and they passed out into the night.

Another man joined them at the corner.

"A little information," scar-face said. "But right now she doesn't speak our language too well. I think I can change that."

The newcomer grunted. "Place clean? The man says it's got to be clean."

"Just this one piece of dirt," scar-face said. "But we've taken it out."

The man undid his bandanna. Scar-face used it to blindfold Maria, removing and replacing her bonnet.

"Let's go. And you, *cara*—remember what I said. Keep your head down."

They walked, or stumbled on, for a few minutes: Maria lost all sense of direction. Once the man holding her pulled her back so roughly she almost fell, her leg crumpling under her; she felt the heel snap off her shoe. The man pulled her upright by the hair at the back of her neck. She supposed that they were avoiding passersby, but she couldn't call out. Eventually they crossed some rough ground, and she could hear something scraping; then the stench of mold, as if they were in a cellar, and the air was damp and fetid.

Her hands were tied behind her back and she was shoved violently forward. A sharp edge caught her on the shin and she tripped, turning her head to avoid smashing her face onto the stone floor.

A door slammed.

Maria was alone.

Slowly she began to scrape her way across the floor. She found a wall and huddled up against it, her knees drawn up to her chin. The cold seeped through her thin muslin dress in a moment, and she began to shiver uncontrollably.

48

PALEWSKI skirted carefully around the dark bundle of rags crammed up against the step and wall of the last bridge, and looked ahead to see if the restaurant was still open.

By the faint street light he saw a couple, with another man beside them, walking up the narrow *calle*. The man looked drunk.

Inside the restaurant he took off his coat and ordered a bottle of wine. The place was almost empty, and he asked the waiter for something easy, something quick. He didn't want to keep them up.

The waiter smiled. "We await your pleasure, Signor Brett. What you want to eat, you may eat. Please."

He ordered a dish of calves' liver.

"A few minutes, signore. Your wine."

Palewski ate hurriedly, his thoughts returning to the letters of credit that Yashim had provided. As soon as he finished, he placed some coins on the table and returned to his apartment, where he lit a candle and rummaged in his portmanteau for five thick and heavily folded sheets of paper, of the finest legal grade.

The money, he noticed, to be drawn in Trieste rather than Venice, on two separate banks.

He raised an ironical eyebrow at that. Venice, where the very business of credit had been invented, could no longer furnish a traveler with funds. Alfredo was right: it was a city with capital, of a sort, and no income.

Selling off its heritage, bit by bit.

He undressed, climbed into bed, and reached for the Vasari he'd left on the table with his afternoon nap. His fingers closed on thin air, and he looked around, surprised. It was as if the book had jumped from his grasp to lie a few inches farther off.

The mattress creaked as he leaned across.

Vasari! Again!

He changed his mind, blew out the candle, and in a few minutes he was asleep.

49

SWARMS of beggars were retreating from their pitches as night fell.

Some were carried away by charitable friends, but the famous legless beggar of San Marco, using nothing more than his fingertips, wheeled himself up a side alley where he was released from the wheeled board by a faithful servant and slowly and painfully stood up, cracking his joints.

A furious German soldier, reddened by false piety and wine, stumped off on a wooden leg to one of the more forlorn wineshops of the city. A wraithlike woman, preternaturally skinny, and clutching to her breast a tiny, malnourished baby in a shift, stuffed the baby headfirst into a bag. It was only made of wax and wood, and she scuttled away to prepare dinner for her husband and five children.

All over Venice, under cover of darkness, tiny miracles were being performed. All over the city people found tongues, limbs, parents, and appetites. The halt walked; the weak took up their beds; the idiots and the insane, with looks of innocent cunning, counted their takings and found their way to a mug of wine or a dish of polenta.

On Palewski's bridge, the bundle of rags stirred, too. What emerged from its nest was, at least, a man; he had sores on his shaved skull and a dirty yellow beard. He pissed into the canal, then made his way painfully up the alley, clutching a few kreuzers in a grimy hand.

Nobody passed him. Across the next bridge, he spotted something pretty on the ground and stooped to pick it up.

It was a little pointed object made of hard red leather and for a few moments he held it to his eye as if assessing its value. But even in Venice, among the poorest of the poor, a heel is worth nothing without its shoe; the beggar spat and passed on.

Later, having eaten half a slab of polenta, with the other half tucked away, he returned to his bridge.

He snuggled deep into his bed of rags and pondered, dreamily, the comings and goings on the street.

50

IT was not until the evening that Alfredo called on Signor Brett.

"The viewing is arranged," he said.

"Very well," Palewski replied. "Tomorrow then. Eleven o'clock?"

Alfredo nodded slowly. "Signor Brett, one thing I must explain," he said, with a wince. "It is very Venetian, I'm sorry about it. The owner would like us to look at the portrait tonight, if possible. If you want some time to dress, it is no problem. I can wait. Afterward, we can take a gondola."

Palewski sucked his teeth. "To be frank, Alfredo, I'd like to see the painting by daylight. At eight it will be almost dark."

"Of course, signore, I understand." Alfredo had his hat in his hand, and he began to turn it by the brim. "I think it will still be a very good opportunity to see the painting tonight. I would say, you can spend more time with it—alone, also, if you would like. It would be no problem. If you prefer for now, signore, I can wait for you downstairs."

He got to his feet and gave a little bow.

Palewski blinked a couple of times and said, "Is something wrong?"

"No, signore," Alfredo said emphatically. He spread out his hands. "I shall wait for you outside?"

"Give me five minutes," Palewski said thoughtfully. When Alfredo had gone he adjusted his stock carefully in the mirror.

Damn, but he was so close!

He'd all but scripted the sultan's speech. Now he murmured his own modest reply to the reflection in the glass. *No credit for discovery . . . blah blah . . . painting of venerable ancestor . . . not from me . . . proud nation . . . day of deliverance . . . blah blah . . . your house among the greatest, and oldest, of friends . . . et cetera, et cetera . . .*

Yashim had been right, as usual—tracking down the Bellini was the coup of the year. Abdülmecid would eat from his hand.

He sighed and pulled on his overcoat.

51

SOMETIMES Maria would wake up wondering where she was and, as the truth returned, try to fend it off for a few more moments, but her swollen lip and the cord around her wrists that chafed and bit into her skin made it impossible to resist the dread reality.

More than anything, perhaps, she hated to be alone.

She got gingerly to her feet. Her leg ached where she had cracked it on something. With her back to the wall she worked her way around her cell, groping with fingers stiff with cold across the smooth walls, searching for anything she could use. She found the door, and kicked on it and shouted until her feet were bruised. It was a thick, heavy wooden door but it had a handle, too, and after many attempts she succeeded in using the handle to inch the blindfold off her face.

The darkness remained absolute.

Something that felt like a low stone table stood in the middle of the room. For a while she worked at trying to rasp the cord against the edge of the table, but it was her wrists that suffered. Eventually she gave it up and shuffled back to her original position against the wall, knees drawn up to her face, whimpering with cold, and pain, and the terrible fear of knowing nothing and expecting anything.

She would not tell them anything about Signor Brett, come what may.

But by the time they came, she could scarcely remember her own name.

She had lost track of time; she felt no pain. She moved her thick tongue in her mouth and very quietly sounded out the only word she knew: *acqua!*

52

ALFREDO was waiting at the foot of the stairs.

"I'm here, as you see," Palewski said drily. "But explain to me, clearly and simply, why tonight?"

Alfredo took his arm. "Come," he said. "I will tell you as we go."

A gondola was waiting on the water stairs. Both men climbed in, and the gondolier pushed off.

"You see, Signor Brett, it is something you must understand about the people we deal with—the old nobility of Venice. In former times, when Venice was a great power, these people were very careful to do what was good for the state. Only the youngest son was allowed to marry, for a start. His brothers, they fought in wars or put their energies into trade. So the inheritance was undivided, to the advantage of the state."

"I've read about that."

"Of course, signore. But today, in these times, it is a little different."

"So?"

"So maybe the older brother, he decides to have a share. He says—I have no wars, no trade, and the Republic is finished. Please, brother, share with me!"

Palewski nodded. "I understand. The youngest son, in practice, took the lot—but legally, he wasn't entitled to it. Very shrewd."

Alfredo gave a relieved smile and patted Palewski's hand. "There— I am very glad you understand, Signor Brett. I like you. I think America is a good country. We have no problems together."

Palewski was vaguely aware that Alfredo hadn't really answered his question, but the air of bonhomie was hard to break. Alfredo looked happy and relieved.

"The owner has arranged a special viewing," Alfredo was saying. "But I should say, he asks us to be very discreet. The palazzo is in very many hands." He shook his head sorrowfully. "In former times, just the family—but today, when things are hard for these people, they must divide and divide. But you understand how it is for them," he added, with an encouraging smile.

"We don't want to disturb the neighbors, you mean?"

"If you like, signore. Because of—the friends."

Gli amici: the epithet was universal, and wholly ironic.

"I imagine that the friends do not approve of our undertaking?"

Alfredo gave his wince again in half agreement. "You never quite know with friends," he said.

Palewski chuckled. If this thing came off, it wouldn't be just Poland exalted. It would be the Austrians discomfited, too. He found himself half looking forward to the sultan's ball, just for a sight of the imperial ambassador swelling up in impotent fury, like a nervous frog.

Lamps on the canal were being lit by barefoot men with long tapers, and a few windows shone feebly overhead. By day, when large swathes of the buildings were shuttered up, perhaps half abandoned, the canal had a forlorn and forgotten look, like a silted creek. By night, in spite of the lamps, it was almost sepulchral, and the shutters showed like dark caves in some ancient cliffside necropolis.

"*En avant, légionnaires,*" Palewski muttered, and at the same moment the gondolier made a pass with the oar and brought the elegant dark prow swooping around in a tight quarter turn that made the water hiss against the frail hull. With another twist of the oar the gondola shot forward into a cavernous boathouse.

Palewski had seen these canalside openings, and heard about them, before, but he had never actually been into one, with the gondola sweeping beneath the low arch, the gondolier bowing, and shadows racing in the sudden gloom. It was more like the entrance to a prison than a palace, Palewski thought, as the gondolier unhitched his lamp and raised it overhead. Above, he saw only the curve of the damp stone vault. To one side of the ancient water gate was a narrow pavement, which led to a wooden door banded in iron. The pavement was slimy with algae, and the base of the door, also tinged with green, was ragged and in need of repair.

Alfredo was the first out, onto the ledge. He put out a hand.

"Be careful, Signor Brett. The floor is wet and we don't want you to fall in."

Palewski accepted the hand and stepped up onto the pavement. In spite of the warning he almost skidded: only Alfredo's surprisingly strong arm prevented him from falling backward.

"Thank you, my friend." He smiled.

"The palazzo is divided, as I said." Alfredo's voice was little more than a whisper. "I do not think anyone uses this entrance so much."

"So how do we get in?" Palewski, too, was whispering. It's like a bloody dungeon, he thought: the Rescue of Mehmet the Conqueror!

Even as he spoke he saw a flickering light growing beneath the ratholes of the moldy door, and in a moment someone was drawing back bolts and the ancient hinges were creaking on their rusty pins.

"This is Mario," Alfredo whispered. "He works for my patron also. We can go quietly, I think."

They stepped through the door and into a narrow passageway faced with well-dressed stone. Mario nodded at Palewski. He was a sturdy man with very short-cropped hair and wide, Slavic cheekbones, and he held a candelabra with three candles that guttered in the draft.

"Signor Brett very kindly agreed to come tonight," Alfredo explained. "So, we are expected?"

Later, it was this curiously stilted introduction that Palewski would remember, the moment when he should have wondered who, exactly, was in charge.

Mario now leaned forward and spoke to Alfredo, but either he spoke in a thick dialect or he had something wrong with his speech, because Palewski could not understand him.

"I see. But he has left us to go in?"

Mario nodded.

"It is nothing." Alfredo turned to Palewski and put a hand lightly on his arm. "The owner wanted to be here to meet you, but in fact he has been called away. We can go on. You see how he trusts us," he added.

At the end of the passage, at the foot of the broad marble stairs, Mario produced a key and inserted it into the lock of a side door, which presently swung open.

They entered, Mario leading the procession with his candles, rather like a chaplain with his acolytes, Palewski reckoned, or a tomb robber.

It was an enormous, low-ceilinged room, bare of furnishings. Two long windows, shuttered on the outside, gave onto what Palewski presumed would be the alley at the front. He supposed that another door at the back of the room opened into a storeroom on the canal side of the building.

And at the far end of the room, lit by Mario with his candelabra, stood a table draped in green velvet. Against the folds, like an egg in its nest, lay a small painting.

"Signor Brett." Alfredo's face was serious. "*The Conqueror*, by Gentile Bellini." He made a motion with his hand. "Please."

Palewski stepped slowly, almost reverently, across the room toward the little painting, his hands involuntarily clasped behind his back.

And there it was. It was unframed—no one would expect to buy a painting without having it first removed from its frame. It was very dark, and the glaze was crackled with age. Even in the uncertain light of Mario's candelabra, the form and composition were unmistakable.

Stanislaw Palewski, who knew what a sultan looked like, found himself looking at one now.

Coolly returning his gaze, instantly bridging the gap between the fifteenth century and the nineteenth, was Mehmet the Conqueror himself, the young genius upon whose shoulders centuries of Ottoman dominion, and Ottoman civilization, had been built.

Then there was a commotion at the farther door, and Palewski's gaze was arrested, instead, by the figure of a man without a coat who burst through, glaring, with a long-nosed pistol in his hand.

Everybody froze.

The man raked the pistol around the room, taking them in. He was a tall, well-built young man with a shock of yellow hair and sideburns, but his face was suffused with blood and from the way he moved Palewski could tell that he'd been drinking. For a few seconds his mouth worked in silent fury, and then his eye fell on the Bellini.

"I knew it! By the Mother of God! What's this—you pack of thieves, creeping into my house like snakes? Where is my brother?"

He made a rush at the table and with his free hand he snatched up a corner of the velvet and tossed it furiously over the painting. Mario backed away, lowering the candelabra, and the stranger's shadow leaped to the ceiling.

"Mother of God! He would sell it—of course, under my nose, beneath my own feet!" Spittle flew from his lips. "That bastard! I could kill him now."

"Signore—" Palewski began.

"You? What are you—a thief?" He wheeled and went down on one leg in a half crouch, pointing the pistol with both hands at Palewski's face. "You signore me, do you!" He was snarling now. "You signore me? In my house, in front of my Bellini? Yes, I'll give you signore!"

There was a click as he drew the safety catch.

"You think I'm crazy, hah? The crazy little brother? Crazy, *pazzo indemoniato*, when my brother steals from me and hasn't the nerve to tell me to my face? Maybe, yes—maybe I am a little bit crazy." He drew himself upright and cocked his head first to one side, then the other, like a marionette. His eyes were wild. "Does it frighten you, signore? Are you afraid now, you and your thieves, to meet a man who is half crazy because his brother wants to steal from him? Are you afraid, hah?"

Palewski stood perfectly still, his face an expressionless mask. "Put the gun down," he said quietly. Out of the corner of his eye he saw Mario inching forward.

"Put the gun down," the drunken brother mimicked in a nasty, childish voice. *"Run away and play! We've only come to steal your wealth!* So—fuck you for the bastard of a leper!"

Mario sprang. The last thing Palewski saw before the candles spun away and went out, plunging the room into darkness, was the crazy brother swinging around with his pistol in the air.

The two men went down with a crash; Palewski dropped to a crouch, arms in front of his face. There was nothing he could do. The man still held a loaded pistol and the smaller a target he could make of himself, the better. He could hear them grunting and scuffling on the flagstones, and then someone cannoned into him and sent him sprawling backward.

A furious grunt, a crack as if someone had struck his head on the stone, and then a thunderclap as the pistol fired and a man screamed.

"Mario!" It was Alfredo, calling out from the doorway.

The scream descended to a bubbling groan. Palewski heard someone drag himself across the flags, panting.

"Here." It was Mario's voice.

A groan from the dark.

Palewski's hair stood on end. "Lights, quick!" he commanded.

"Don't be a fool!" Alfredo's voice spat out in the dark. "Let's go, now!"

"And leave this man?" Palewski asked.

Alfredo must have found him by his voice, because a hand fell on his arm and a voice hissed, "Don't be stupid. If he dies, he dies. But if he lives—he'll say that you shot him."

"Why me?"

"He was drunk. You're the one he'll remember. Come on." He pulled Palewski toward the door: he was surprisingly strong. "The police will come—a shot, like that! Mario, get the door."

The door swung open and its faint outline appeared in the darkness. Alfredo rushed Palewski toward it, and they passed through into the hall.

"We can't leave by the street—it's too dangerous," Alfredo said.

Palewski allowed himself to be led along the corridor, but when they had wrenched open the moldy door at the end, Mario swore.

"*Madre!* The gondola—it's gone!"

53

"MARIO—check the front door!"

The man reappeared in half a minute. Palewski heard his boots ringing on the stone floor of the passageway.

He whispered something urgently to Alfredo, who gripped Palewski's arm.

It was as if no one could quite bring himself to contemplate the obvious. They stood together on the slippery ledge, and Palewski could hear them all breathing hard.

He started to remove his shoes. He took off his jacket, then his trousers, tied the laces of his boots together and slung them around his neck. He held his clothes in a bundle and sat down on the cold stone, his feet in the water.

"Come on," he urged—and then he was in the water, gasping with shock, thrashing out toward the low mouth of the water gate.

54

THEY gave her water, though not before they had amused themselves by trickling it anywhere but on her lips.

When the strong man saw her bend her head, trying to lick the water from the muslin of her own dress, he laughed excitedly.

The scar-faced man looked at him with disgust. Perhaps that was what made him decide to reach around and cut the cord that bound Maria's wrists.

"She's not going anywhere," he said.

Even with her arms free, Maria had to have the jug held to her mouth: her hands were swollen and the muscles in her arms could not obey her.

"Changed your mind yet?" The scar-faced man held her by the chin. Maria closed her eyes, waiting for the sting.

Instead, he pushed her away. "We'll see you again, pretty one. Don't you worry. We'll be back."

They left her in the darkness. She heard the bolts ram home through the thick door, and she folded her fingers over the raw skin on her wrists and wept.

55

WHENEVER Palewski closed his eyes he was plunged back into darkness. The sound of that bestial cry would lift him from the pillows, grinding his teeth. He had seen and heard men die. Sometimes they died silently like Ranieri in the snow. Sometimes they raved. But too often he had heard that cry of an animal in fright or pain.

What am I? he asked himself once. He did not think he was a coward. But he had saved himself, certainly. Saved himself for what? For Poland? He sneered at the thought. Was it true that everything he did was purely for the motherland? Then why bother with Bellini and a sultan's ball at all? Why not take the money and set it to work? Perhaps that was what a braver man would do.

Hours passed, drifting between sleep and wakefulness. He saw the dawn gather at his window; he had forgotten to close the shutters. For some the dawn brings hope, but for Palewski it was as if the sun were spying through the glass on a man who was no longer young, half sick with brandy and sour dreams, primping and petting on tyrants and courtesans.

A man who let another die alone.

A man too frightened to strike a match in the darkness.

Then the sun slipped from his window again and he lay immobile on the pillows, seeing the window through a tangle of black lashes, until he finally noticed Yashim near the foot of his bed.

"I've failed," he murmured, feeling no surprise. Yashim only smiled.

Palewski felt no desire to open his eyes. In his dream he was running across snow, like a hare on the thin crust, and the surface of the snow was pockmarked by the little holes into which his friends had sunk, one by one. He ran hither and thither across the snow, whining and wringing his hands, knowing that if he tried to crack through the crust to save them then he, too, would slide through it like a hot coal.

And when he opened his eyes with a jerk the room was as empty as it had always been, and someone was knocking on the door and calling out, "Signor Brett! Signor Brett! Are you at home?"

56

PALEWSKI let Ruggerio prattle on. It was battle enough simply to lift his hand and take the morsel of bread from his plate and put it to his lips.

The sun was already warm on his back, but he felt a shudder pass across his shoulder blades. He rested his hand on the cloth and then put it out again, to take a thin fluted glass of the *amaro*.

He tilted the glass and the liquor ran into his mouth and he made an effort with his tongue and it went down.

"I thought I'd lost you." The cicerone was beaming across the table.

"Lost me?" Palewski leaned forward and examined the Venetian as if for the first time.

Ruggerio looked disconcerted. "I mean only to say, signore, we have not seen each other for a few days. But if you are busy, then Ruggerio is happy!" He winked, grinning again. "Maybe la signorina Maria opens up—a little Venice, also? With her, signore, you see many attractive sights, no?"

Palewski stared at him, expressionless.

"A little Venice, signore, between a woman's thighs!"

"I haven't seen the girl for two days," Palewski said coldly.

The grin faltered and congealed on Ruggerio's face. "Are you sure?"

"Two nights," Palewski admitted. "She's a damn nice girl."

Ruggerio looked uneasy. "I think so, too. Very clean," he murmured. He was silent for a while.

Palewski reached for the coffee.

"I'll be leaving in a day or so, Ruggerio."

"But Signor Brett!" Ruggerio's face fell. "I think your matters are not yet arranged—you must give us time." His eyes widened. "Is it—is it because of Count Barbieri?"

"It's a business matter." Palewski dabbed a napkin to his lips. "The rent is paid on the apartment. I owe you for your time, of course—and Maria's, too."

Ruggerio drew himself up. "You are too kind, signore. Of course, I will be grateful for any gift you choose to bestow. I can take care of the girl, also—she was not with you last night? I am sorry for that." He pursed his lips. "But I am afraid it is not quite so simple. My honor, also, is at stake."

"Your honor, Ruggerio?"

Ruggerio leaned his head to one side. "Signor Brett, I am surprised you do not appreciate my difficulty." He sounded severe, cross almost. "I deliver your cards to the most prestigious dealers in Venetian art in the city. The card says—what? That you are from New York. That you collect art." He looked upset and waved his hands. "Forgive me, Signor Brett, but such a card you can buy for a few lire at the printers. If you see *cunt* written on a wall, do you stand to it?"

Palewski smiled in spite of himself. "Of course not."

"Of course not. That's very good, signore." Ruggerio seemed to be working himself up into a passion. "It is the same with this card. You think the dealers become stiff because you have a card with a name written on it? No, of course not. Yet Count Barbieri—he died, but he came to see you. At the Correr, the director made time for you. Signor Eletro—he, too, starts to think about this Signor Brett. They must think—and it is I, Antonio Ruggerio, who brought them something to think about!"

He grabbed out and his hand collided with Palewski's glass. He snatched it up and drained it.

"In a month, I tell them, you must flush out the greatest of your pictures. I tell them, Signor Brett is a friend to Ruggerio, a good man, with a keen eye and some money to spend. I admit I said that—or why would they come? For a card? Pah!"

"You have been more than kind, Signor Ruggerio—"

"Barone."

"Barone Ruggerio. I apologize. I am at fault, and I acknowledge it freely."

But I am always at fault, he thought. He shook his head, to block out that cry in the dark.

"I have put you in a position of some delicacy, I understand," he continued. "But what must be, must be. How can I make it acceptable to your honor?"

How, he wondered, how does a man regain his honor?

Ruggerio's anger seemed to collapse.

"Once," he began, "I told you that the story of Venice is never written. It can never end, because no one writes the same story twice. You tell me you must go away." He reached out for his coffee. "You will be back. You must come back."

Palewski remained still. Was that it, then? No one could write the same story twice?

"And Maria? I'd like to leave her something—it's a pity she could not come herself."

"Have no fear, Signor Brett. Upon my honor as a Ruggerio, I will see that she gets whatever you choose to give her."

Palewski grunted. "Where the devil is she, Ruggerio?"

"Ha ha! But you know how it is, Signor Brett, with women. And where would we be without them!"

"I must take a ship in Trieste," Palewski said brusquely. "Perhaps you can find out for me the sailings in the next few days?"

"I want only to help," Ruggerio said.

"Meet me at Florian, then, at twelve," Palewski said, praying that he could be there, too.

They shook hands and Ruggerio departed, bowing and scraping.

"Shame about the girl, though," Palewski murmured to himself later, as he stood with his hands in his pockets and watched the barges and gondolas slip past beneath his window.

57

MARIA awoke to the dark. It was almost her element, as if she had lived for so long without light that darkness could no longer shock her. It could no longer make her weep.

She moved her arms, flexed her fingers. Her wrists began to burn: perhaps that was a sign that they were healing, too.

For a while she sensed nothing more than the strange scatterings of color that formed and reformed in the darkness, like evanescent patterns in oily water. But then, very distinctly, she heard the scrape of bolts being drawn back and then the creaking of the door.

Her heart went to her mouth, and then—nothing happened.

She was aware of a new smell. She sat up in the dark and felt someone or something feel her feet.

It was a hand, a human hand—and then another hand came around to meet hers and in it was something that smelled sweeter than she could have possibly imagined.

She took the bread and crammed it into her mouth.

They might take it back, at any time. It might be a trick, like the water they had poured across her breasts.

But why, she wondered, was there no light?

And then, slowly and wonderingly, she became aware of the smell of roses.

"*Grazie,*" she whispered. "*Per il pane—grazie, caro.*"

"It's nothing. Can you walk?"

"Yes."

"Let's get you home."

58

PALEWSKI took a gondola at the landing stage and instructed the gondolier to row him down the Grand Canal.

The palazzo with the water gate was one of the largest on the canal. Most of its shutters were closed.

Palewski paid off the gondola at a nearby stage. In his mind's eye he had imagined a blind alley, with windows overlooking it on the ground floor, but the entrance turned out to be a gate that opened to his touch. Inside was a courtyard with a wellhead in the middle and to his left a stone staircase rising to the first floor.

Some small children were playing, watched by an old lady engulfed in black silk who sat on a bench in the sun.

"Good morning," Palewski said politely, raising his hat.

"Good morning to you, signore. Are you lost?"

"Perhaps I am."

"Ah," she smiled. "This is the Palazzo d'Istria, signore."

"I've heard the name."

"Heard it? Excuse me—Bepi, is that kind? It doesn't matter—a boy should never strike a girl. Come here, cara. Come to Nonna. That's right. That's better."

The little girl settled into the old lady's lap. "A century ago, the Istria family were very gay, signore. You would have known the name then, for sure."

"I have met a contessa, Contessa d'Aspi d'Istria. A very charming lady."

"Ah yes. It is a sad story."

"I can stand a sad story," he said. "If I may?"

"Please." She patted the bench and he sat down beside her. The little girl peeped up at him through a tangle of black hair and her grandmother started to pull her fingers through it. "Lucia d'Istria was a great beauty, signore. She married Count d'Aspi. A very good match—two old families." She leaned sideways to confide: "The Aspis had the money, but the Istrias had the beauty, like Carla."

"Yes, I see."

"This was in the days of the Republic, of course. Three hundred guests, and the women—so beautiful, in those days. I was there, and beautiful, too, why not? I was quite young. Married, of course . . . You should have seen it, signore, the color—even the men! Men did not always wear black, as they do today.

"They lived here in the early days. There was a son—Luciano—and also the daughter you have met." She shook her head. "We could believe that they would be happy forever." She batted her fingertips against the ground, as though she were shooing mice. "Now, off you go, little one. Bepi will be nice now—won't you, Bepi? And you, signore—do you have children?"

"No," Palewski said.

She patted his hand. "That's not unusual in Venice now. As I was saying—the Republic fell, and in the war the Aspis lost a lot of good land, on the mainland. Luciano was killed fighting the Austrians, poor boy. Lucia—I think she only lived for her son. A shame for the girl, that was, too." She heaved a sigh. "Count d'Aspi used to sit on this bench, with his chin on the top of his cane. He said he had lived too long. It had all turned to nothing, you see."

"And the daughter? The contessa?"

"She is the last. Last of the Aspis, last of the Istrias. But she'll never marry."

"Why not?"

"That's right, Bepi. Good boy." She seemed not to have heard him. Palewski stood up, watching the children.

"Are there many families living here now?"

"In the palazzo? Few enough. My son, the doctor, took the piano nobile when he married. I'm afraid it's an extravagance. I have an apartment above and of course it's very convenient for them. The Gramantes upstairs. They're trade but quite respectable."

"And your family, *signora mia*. They are all well?"

No gunshot wounds?

He saw her reach out surreptitiously to touch the bench. "Since you ask, yes. Thank God for children, signore."

Palewski bowed. "Thank you for talking to me. I shall resume my walk."

How peculiar, he thought, as he wound his way toward the piazza. It evidently wasn't the doctor who got shot, nor his brother, for that matter. But nobody else lived in the palazzo.

I wonder how this will end, he asked himself.

He caught sight of Ruggerio, sitting at a table, and was about to join him when he noticed a man standing back in the shadows of the arcade, signaling to him.

"Are you crazy, Signor Brett? The piazza, today?"

"I'm in the hands of Fate, Alfredo."

"You might be in the hands of the police, signore, unless we move quickly."

Palewski raised an eyebrow.

"The brother—he's not as crazy as he seemed," Alfredo went on. "He took a bullet in the shoulder and I think it sobered him up. In fact, we owe everything to him, as it turns out. He tells the police that it was an accident, no one else involved."

"And they believe that?"

Alfredo shrugged. "For the moment yes, why not? Come, let's walk. The band is about to play."

The arcade was growing more crowded by the minute: patriotic Venetians were sweeping from the piazza to avoid the appearance of enjoying the Austrian band.

They crossed beneath the Procuratie.

"Why did he want to mislead the police?"

"The Venetians have no love for them, signore. And a family like this—they try to solve their own problems."

"What are they called, this family?"

"Please, Signor Brett, I am not at liberty to say."

"After all we've been through, I'd have thought . . ." He trailed off. "I was at the palazzo this morning. There's no old family there."

"This morning? Why? Whom did you speak to?"

"An old lady. She told me the whole story of the place. She didn't say a word about last night."

Alfredo blew out his lips. "The owner of the painting wants to be discreet. If he invited us to his own palazzo, you would soon know his name."

"But you were saying to me—"

"Signor Brett, if a client wishes to be discreet, I am discreet also. You cannot expect less."

"Then—why was the brother there, too?"

Alfredo stopped and turned to face Palewski. "Signore. I will answer these questions, which have very simple answers. And then we must go on; there is not much time. Maybe in America, a man may also have a mistress? Good. So in Venice, it is normal. He cannot bring that woman to his house so he takes a little *casino*—a room in another's house—where they can go for their enjoyment. It is very discreet. No one will talk about it, not even an old lady. But maybe she knows nothing about it herself."

"But the shot?"

"You are not a Venetian, Signor Brett: you ask too many questions. What happens between a man and his mistress is of no consequence to anyone. A shot? Broken china? The crack of a whip? Do you understand what I am saying?"

He turned and walked on. "Enough. What is important for us is the brother. He does not know who you are, although he could probably recognize us both. So it is important that he should not see us, for obvious reasons. I would not particularly suggest eating at Florian, signore."

"But he's made no charge, you said?"

"It remains a possibility. A threat, if you like."

"The whole thing's a mess," Palewski said moodily.

"No. What happened last night looks unfortunate, to say the least, but also in a way I think it has been of benefit. A letting of blood, to relieve pressure, no? There is still a good chance, for you. The brother has spoken to our client. He will not object to the sale, but he wants his share."

"His share," Palewski muttered. "Last night he acted as if he couldn't live without Bellini."

"There is compensation for everything."

"Compensation?"

"It means, unfortunately, that the price has risen."

"Oh," Palewski said. "I'm to pay him his share, is that it?"

"Not completely. My patron has discussed this with them both and persuaded them to be moderate. Now the client has agreed to lower his price, for the sake of peace. Seven thousand, this is their last price. But you have seen the picture. You know what it is worth."

"I've seen a man shot over it, yes."

Alfredo gave a rare, dry smile. "As authentication, signore, it's pretty conclusive. Do you agree?"

"Very well."

"I have taken some measures to help you, signore. There is a sailing to Trieste this evening. Tomorrow, at twelve, having visited your bankers, you can return. You will be here for a second sailing tomorrow evening—to Corfu. From Corfu you can choose any destination you like—but not, I think, Venice or Trieste."

"Why doesn't someone simply accompany me to Trieste, with the painting? Then I can leave directly, from a major port."

"A very good question, Signor Brett. The brothers do not trust each other farther than they can spit. The only solution is for them both to receive the money together when the painting changes hands—and then, signore, to see that you have actually left the city."

"They want me waving from the poop, with the Bellini in my other hand?"

"Please, Signor Brett. No jokes. Return to your apartment. I will call for you at five and see you to the Trieste boat."

"Do something for me, would you? There's a cicerone, Ruggerio, sitting now at Florian. Small fellow, spectacles, sixty-odd. He expects a good lunch—will you give him this, with my compliments, and ask him to look in this afternoon?"

"Ruggerio. Spectacles? Very well, signore."

He took the banknote, and they shook hands. *"Arrivederci!"*

59

"HA! Maria Contarini! *La duchessa* herself! A very fine time to be coming home, to be sure—and your father out worrying himself into the grave, with not a soul to help your mother look after your poor brothers and sisters!"

"Mama, I—"

"Look at the state of you!" Signora Contarini hissed. She grabbed the girl's arm and hustled her into the tumbledown shack, banging the door. A dozen pairs of eyes had seen her daughter come home.

"That beautiful dress—it's a rag! *Madonna*—if I didn't have more work than the good Lord sends hours I'd be dead of worry, Maria Contarini! Where are your shoes? What happened to your dress?"

She glanced at Maria's swollen face, and her hand went to her mouth. "My God, my God, what has he done to you?"

Her powerful arms swept the girl to her bosom.

"Maria, *ragazza mia!*" She flung her daughter back, at arm's length, to see her better. "*Ti prego!*" Her voice dropped an octave. "If I find the man who has done this to you I will tear him apart with my bare hands—I, who bore you, my little one!"

She hugged Maria again, then thrust her away to inspect her ruined clothes, her pale, bruised face, and the welts on her wrists.

Finally *la signora* enveloped Maria in a damp embrace.

"I am going to buy meat," she declared grandly, stroking Maria's black hair.

"Mamma, please. The man outside—"

"The scarecrow. Did he do this to you?"

"No, mamma. He got me out. Please!"

Maria went to the door.

"What are you all staring at?" she shouted. The courtyard was full of folded arms. Above those arms, dozens of curious eyes.

But the man who had brought her back was nowhere to be seen.

"Did you see him? Did you see him go?"

A woman spat. "He left," she said grimly. "You do look a sight."

Maria cast a wild look around the courtyard and went back in, slamming the door.

Finally, standing in the smoke-stained den that served them for a kitchen, her chin wobbled and she burst into tears.

"Mia poverina," her mother cooed, putting on her bonnet and gathering the girl into her arms all at once. "Don't mind them. You just sit right here, and your brother will look after you. Aurelio!"

The shambling figure of a young man broke from the shadows around the fireplace.

Signora Contarini nodded and sailed out with her nose in the air.

Like most Venetians, the signora did not hold with eating much fish, which could be bought in profusion, very cheap; her family ate it only when the church made it an obligation. In general she fed them a diet of onion, garlic, green leaves, and polenta; a few mushrooms, in season, a little risotto, and the occasional slice of pancetta might also make an appearance in her kitchen.

To buy meat she walked as far as the Rialto and spent a long time studying the different cuts, weighing up the relative advantages of beef—which made the best stock—or horsemeat, which was particularly suitable for a delicate patient. The butchers treated her with grave gallantry and patience, for although she was a rare customer it was women of the signora's sort, who bought seldom but with determination, who kept them in business.

In the end the argument for stock won out. Maria, she reasoned, was weak and wounded, but she was not actually ill. The signora selected a fat shin and took it home in her basket, wrapped in a few pages of the Venetian *Gazzettino*.

60

PALEWSKI was astonished how fast his mood had changed.

Alfredo's revelations had bucked him up immensely. He could hardly be accused of cowardice now. The wretched brother was not, after all, dead: far from it! He appeared to be up and about, and scheming like some old Byzantine exarch.

The simile struck Palewski as particularly apt. What was Venice, after all, but some sprig of Byzantium that had somehow taken root and forced its way intact into the nineteenth century like brambles in a church roof? Armenian priests, mosaics, scheming aristocrats—why, even the Fondaco dei Turchi was a Byzantine palazzo.

He smiled grimly. What was a bullet here or there, now that the brother had won his share? And so the deal was back on track—for a thousand more, it was true, but still a very decent buy.

The ambassador would, after all, go to the ball.

61

SERGEANT Vosper was a slow and methodical man, for whom orders were orders. Other than questioning the procedural validity of taking over another man's case, he did not doubt his chief. Finkel had analyzed the murderer's motives. Vosper's job was to furnish the supporting evidence.

The contessa, of course, would be able to name the guilty lover easily, but Vosper was not a policeman for nothing. He was sly enough to know that she would refuse to give away the name—even if she suspected him. She was probably flattered by the passions she had aroused. Questioning her was, therefore, a waste of time.

The truth was, Vosper was slightly scared by the prospect of interviewing the Contessa d'Aspi d'Istria, with her titles and protocols, and the opportunities for making a fool of himself. But Vosper's own aunt had been in service, many years ago, and he knew how to talk to servants. He knew, too, that servants kept their eyes open; they were a mine of information.

"So, Andrea?" he said pleasantly to the contessa's footman, as he slipped into a chair in the little café on the Campo Santa Maria Mater Domini.

"It's Antonio. Who are you?"

"Police. Don't worry, I'm not here to put a finger on you. I just want to have a little chat."

"It's Barbieri, is it? I know nothing about it."

"I see. And what makes you so sure it is about Barbieri?"

Antonio looked at the policeman and frowned. "What else would it be?"

Vosper considered the question. He couldn't think of an answer, so he said, "The contessa, your mistress. She's an attractive woman."

Antonio didn't respond.

"Unmarried, curiously." For Vosper, an unmarried woman was a rare and rather unappealing idea. "But she has men in her life, I'm thinking. Admirers."

Antonio looked blank. "It's not for me to say."

"You can confide in me, Antonio, because I am a policeman." Vosper took out a toothpick and put it into his mouth; he saw no point in beating about the bush. "I wonder, has anyone new come calling on her recently? A new friend, perhaps?"

Antonio smiled to himself. He didn't have much time for the friends, or their policemen. "You mean, the American?"

"The American," Vosper returned, noncommittally. "Tell me about him."

Antonio obliged. There was very little to tell, but he was reasonably sure that a fellow as stupid as Vosper could waste a lot of time pondering Signor Brett's involvement in the case. He hoped Signor Brett would not be much inconvenienced: he had seemed like a decent man.

"He took the neighboring apartment? Interesting." How better to manage an affair?

He found the details of Brett's last—albeit first—public visit to the palazzo interesting, too.

"He felt sick, you say?" Sick with jealousy, no doubt. Brett had seen his rival in the room. He left early and then, having carefully brought Antonio to the door of his apartment to establish an alibi, he waited until the coast was clear and doubled back.

An open-and-shut case, just like the chief said.

"Thank you, Andrea, you've been most helpful."

"My pleasure," Antonio said.

Only one thing troubled Vosper as he made his way back to the Procuratie.

He was not, he would have admitted, the brightest candle in the chandelier. So why hadn't Brunelli pounced already?

62

BRUNELLI returned to the Procuratie after a quick lunch, to find an anxious Scorlotti waiting for him in the office.

"Trouble, Scorlotti?"

"Vosper's taken over the Barbieri case, Commissario. The chief told him it was a crime of passion."

Brunelli sat down heavily at his desk and rubbed his eyes. He felt terribly tired.

"Thank you, Scorlotti."

"Aren't you—I mean, don't you want to see the chief?"

Brunelli looked up. "Frankly, Scorlotti, no. He won't be back from lunch for another hour or two, anyway."

"Not today, sir. He's in his office. Vosper thinks he's found the murderer."

"Well, that was quick. At least he ruled out suicide."

Scorlotti grinned.

"So." Brunelli clasped his hands in front of him and swiveled on his chair. "Who did it?"

"The American, apparently. Brett."

"Ah, yes." Brunelli nodded slowly. "Has he asked to see my notes on the case?"

"Not necessary, the chief says."

"No. No, of course not." He stood up. "If anyone asks for me—I don't suppose they will, Scorlotti, but you never know—tell them I've gone for a walk."

"*Bene*, Commissario." Scorlotti hesitated. "It's a mess, isn't it, sir?"

"For Signor Brett, Scorlotti, it has the makings of a nightmare."

63

SCORLOTTI understood that the commissario wanted to be alone. He was not fooled by his air of weary calm. Brunelli might despise the politics of his situation, but he hated injustice even more—especially injustice perpetrated by people whose job was to dispense it fairly.

The walk, Scorlotti dimly supposed, would lead to a resolution.

Brunelli's own thoughts were equally vague, as he stepped out of the Procuratie and began to stump angrily along the Molo. He did not exercise enough, as it was, and as a matter of course he liked to eat too well—*seppia con nero* was just the tip of the iceberg. He counted himself lucky that he could eat well, for many people in Venice had been on rations for years, ever since the arrival of the friends and the decline of the port. Sometimes his wife reminded him to be more forgiving. Hunger makes thieves, she said.

He walked, without really choosing where he went, following the invitation of a bridge or the angle of an alleyway, but the intricacy of the walk pleased him, not least because it reflected the intricacies of his own mind. The stadtmeister complained of having nowhere to ride, or to hit his stride when he wanted a walk; sometimes he had himself shipped out to the Lido for an afternoon. "I like a straight line, Brunelli, and—let us not delude ourselves—that goes for police work, too."

Brunelli knew every inch of his city, from the water and from the land. The Grand Canal curved in a lazy backward S between islands with different dialects, different loyalties, different saints, and separate traditions.

Even faces could vary from parish to parish. But Venice itself was compacted out of all these differences. Together, Brunelli sensed, they made a whole.

That explained how the city had subdued a straggling empire, fought and traded and conceded ground when pushed, and regained what it could when the opportunity arose. The money that had built Venice—the money that had paid for the bricks and stones and crockets and secret gardens, for the handsome wellheads in every *campo*, and the churches and the schools—came from anything but following the straight line. It came, Brunelli thought, as he turned into a *sotoportego* beneath a building constructed on the profit of camel trading in the Negev, from a habit of looking around the next corner, from regularly observing juxtapositions—the curve of a bridge, the redness of an old wall, and the reflection of a tiny votive niche in a canal at night. It came from a certain sort of efficiency—not the straight-lined sort, but one that could hold a thousand turnings and windings in the mind at once.

He found himself at the Rialto and crossed the bridge.

According to the stadtmeister, the Austrians had plans to fill in canals and bring a railway across the lagoon. Why not? The city was dying on its feet. Carrots were cheaper in Padua or Mestre. Lawyers were busy along the coast—but in Venice, for sure, they wanted work like everyone else.

Brunelli found himself on a bridge with a parapet—another Austrian felicity—and leaned on the wall, looking down into the green water of the canal.

64

BRUNELLI raised his eyes from the canal and let them rove across the façade of a palazzo he recognized as belonging to the Contessa d'Aspi d'Istria.

This was where Barbieri took his last ride in a gondola.

And in the palazzo next door, one Signor Brett, who came from New York and spoke Italian like a—like what? He spoke it well: in the Tuscan dialect.

Which made three turns of the alley, three pieces of the labyrinth. There were corners to Signor Brett and no straight lines.

But Brunelli knew he was innocent of murder.

"Spare a copper, my dear?"

Brunelli glanced down at the ragged figure at his feet and frowned. "You should move along."

"S'what the other policeman says," the beggar remarked. He sounded foreign—Genoese, maybe. He had pink sores in his scalp and his face was puffy.

Brunelli glanced up—and there was Vosper, standing in a doorway up the alley with his back turned.

"How long has he been here?"

"'Alf an hour, maybe less. But there ain't nobody home."

"Nobody home?"

"The gentleman in the apartment went out."

Brunelli looked at Vosper and felt a surge of irritation bordering on contempt.

"Did—did the gentleman come this way?"

"Right over the bridge."

Brunelli knew what he had to do. "If he comes back—if he comes past again—will you tell him not to go home?"

"Not to go home," the beggar repeated. "I'll let him know."

"Here's fifty," Brunelli said, fishing out a coin. He put it into the beggar's hand. "Tell him to keep away."

"Very good, your honor. I'll be here."

Brunelli turned and began to retrace his steps.

Straight lines!

Stupid people!

65

PALEWSKI walked briskly home through the alleys and switchbacks until he reached the bridge, where the beggar hissed at him.

The sound made Palewski jump.

"I didn't mean to frighten your honor," said the beggar obsequiously, touching his brow in a vague salute. "But I'm told to let you know, you're not to go back to your 'ome."

Palewski looked down with astonishment. It was the first time he had really seen the beggar, who wore a pale beard and whose eyes were half closed as if they could not bear the light. He was, with his head sores, a fairly pitiful sight.

"Not go home? What do you mean?"

The beggar shook his head and looked apologetic. "I don't exackly know, your worship, it's just like I was tole an' all."

"Told? Who told you?"

"P'liceman, sir. What's got a kindly face. 'Cos there's another one, see, hangin' about the alley now. Reckon 'e's waitin' fer ya."

Palewski's heart skipped a beat.

Why would one policeman leave a warning, while the other was waiting outside his house?

"The man you spoke to—did he give you a name? Brunelli?"

The beggar seemed to cringe. "'E didn't leave no name, sir. Big bloke, carries some weight. I wager 'e likes his vittles an' all. Tell 'im not to go 'ome, he says. Tell 'im to keep away. On account of the other nark, 'e says."

Palewski had gone very white.

"It's no good," he muttered. "I've simply got to get into that apartment."

The beggar looked interested. "If wishes was gondolas," he remarked in his reedy voice, "I'd be on the Grand Canal, instead of 'ere on this bridge all day and night." He paused. "Is it jewels, your honor? Or cash?"

Palewski ignored him and bit his nails.

Alfredo would be here within the hour. Shortly afterward they'd make the deal and he'd be on a ship, bound for Trieste; tomorrow he'd leave for Corfu, with the Bellini in his bag.

The bag now lying under his bed, containing the letters of credit.

And a policeman watching the door.

He was aware that the beggar was speaking again.

"'Cos I got an idea, your worship, 'aven't I? Worth another florin, mebbe."

"Go on," Palewski snapped.

"I'll show yer," the beggar said in a thin whisper. He put up a grimy hand and beckoned Palewski closer.

Palewski stooped lower, with barely concealed mistrust. The man was probably half cracked, rummaging through his rags, feeling for a bit of old blanket. It occurred to Palewski that at any moment he might produce a knife.

Instead, the beggar lifted a corner of the blanket.

For a moment Palewski merely stared.

If the beggar had produced a vase of roses, or an African child, Palewski could not have been more surprised.

"*You've* got it," he croaked weakly. "You've got my bag!"

"Safe *and* sound, your honor. An' what was inside, too."

"I—you—did you look inside? I mean—"

"I ain't on the razzle, your worship, if that's what you're finking. Not in my line, if you follow."

Palewski's mouth was hanging open in sheer amazement—and relief.

"Take it now if you like, your honor." The beggar ran a dirt-seamed hand across the end of his nose. *"Anything to oblige an old friend."*

Palewski leaped back, as though he had been bitten.

He glanced around wildly, but there was nobody else on the bridge. His face was ashen.

"I—I'll take the bag," he began. "How to repay you—I mean—I think you've saved my life!"

"And you've saved mine before now, too," the beggar said. He picked up the bag in both hands and settled it on his knee.

Palewski ran his hands through his hair. His eyes were starting. He bent down and stared the beggar in the face.

"You're—you can't be! It's not possible." His voice was barely a whisper. The beggar shrugged.

"I had started to think," he said, "that you might need a hand."

Palewski's legs gave way and he sat down on the stone step with a bump.

"And it seems to me," Yashim added, "that I am just in time."

66

"THE first thing we have to do," Yashim went on imperturbably, "is find somewhere safe to put you."

"The first thing I have to do," Palewski countered, breathing heavily, "is find somewhere to drink a large glass of grappa." He peered at the beggar again and looked away. "I just can't believe it, Yash. I mean, your own mother wouldn't know you." He paused. "You look horrible. What have you done to your face?"

"I dyed my eyebrows yellow to match the beard. The beard comes off."

Palewski saw why the beggar had seemed so sensitive to light: with his eyes wide open, he looked—well, still hardly like his friend of so many years.

"I could guess that much. It's your—your face that looks so different. Wrong shape."

Yashim stuck a dirty finger into his mouth and began to work around his gums. Various damp little bundles came out; Yashim flexed his jaw.

"Wadding," he said triumphantly. He reached behind his ears and removed some putty, so that they lay flat against his head. "Know me now?"

Palewski nodded. It was Yashim—but still a horrible, scabrous, sandy-bearded parody of his old friend. "Your teeth," he objected weakly.

Yashim chuckled. "I forgot the teeth," he said and picked off some flakes of wax.

"You look completely horrible."

"I feel a lot better."

"I suppose under all those rags you're beautifully dressed, too?"

"As a matter of fact, I believe I am respectable."

Yashim stood up and peeled away a few layers of grimy cloth.

"The beard stays," he said. "It takes lye and water to get it off, I think."

"I don't know about respectable," Palewski pointed out, as he surveyed his friend's familiar brown robe. "You aren't exactly going to blend in unobserved."

"That may be part of the plan," Yashim said. "Let's go."

Leaving his rags in a bundle by the bridge, Yashim led the way to the café where Palewski and Ruggerio had had breakfast several days before.

Palewski ordered grappa. The waiter glanced curiously at Yashim but seemed more interested in his ringworm than his costume.

"The worst of it, Yashim, is that . . ." He trailed off. "My God. Yashim. Yashim." Palewski shook his head. "I still don't believe it. But it's all wasted. You're too late."

Yashim cocked his head. "On the contrary. I said I was just in time."

"No, look. I'm sorry. I've found the Bellini—I'm taking it tomorrow. In fact, I'd better get back to the house. We have to catch my friend Alfredo before he meets the policeman." He leaned across the table. "I've bought the painting, Yashim. Or nearly. The sultan's Bellini! That's why I needed the bag."

"And that's why I took it," Yashim said.

Palewski nodded. "Thank God you did. Whole thing's getting complicated—I'll explain later. I'm getting out as quickly as I can. We must get you a passage on that ship tomorrow—it's only going to Corfu, I'm afraid, but needs must, all that."

He downed his grappa and sighed. "My God, Yashim. I almost died of shock."

Yashim looked grave—or as grave as was possible for a man with a false beard with his eyebrows and lashes dyed a sickly yellow.

"I'm afraid the shock's not quite over yet." He paused. "You can't hand over the money," he said quietly. "Your Bellini's a fake."

Palewski was still.

"Oh," he said coldly. "You know that, do you?"

Yashim nodded.

"The beggar business was inspired, Yashim. I'm still finding it hard to believe you're here, like this. But if I'm wrong about the Bellini, my name's not Palewski."

Yashim smiled, a trifle sadly. "Well, it's not, is it, Signor Brett?"

"Being a beggar is all very well," Palewski replied facetiously, "but I don't suppose you were lurking under the table when we looked at the painting? The chap selling it—his brother almost died as a result. Came in waving a gun and took the bullet himself. It was dark," he added. "Very nearly shot me first."

Yashim looked interested. "Ah, so that was how it was done," he murmured. "I wondered."

"Oh, come on, Yashim. A family heirloom. Probably the best thing they'd turned up since the fall of Athens."

"They?"

"The family that's selling their painting, on the quiet." It sounded thin. "You can't go around bawling your prices on the Rialto these days. The friends—the Austrians—would get to hear about it."

"How convenient."

"Convenient? Nonsense. We'll meet them tomorrow. The vendor *and* his brother—they fixed up some sort of pact, thank God. I thought the brother had died. As soon as I've got the painting, I'll ask Alfredo who they were."

Yashim gazed at his old friend. Palewski didn't like it and looked away.

"Did you go to the theater while you were here?"

Palewski looked surprised. "The theater? I think you've got the wrong end of the stick, Yash. I've been ill, I've been busy, I've been—God, I found Compston here and had to fix up a couple of courtesans to see him off, along with his Habsburg chum." He leaned back, and now that he had found his theme he discovered it was warm. "I've had policemen dunning me over two chaps who got murdered—nothing to do with me. I've had a fellow shot under my nose—I thought he'd died. I've been threatened with guns, with hanging, with cholera. I've swum the Grand Canal. Not along it, like Byron, but Byron didn't have his shoes hanging around his neck. I was even poisoned. Nasty stuff, prosecco. So no, sorry. I somehow missed the theater."

He stood up.

"Venice *is* a theater, Yashim. You fit right in, too, with your beard and eyebrows. No wonder the waiter didn't look twice. At the end of the day they probably lay him down in a box marked 'Café Characters.' I've had enough."

Yashim hadn't moved.

Palewski stared at him for a while.

He gripped the chair and sat down.

He put his head in his hands.

He said a word in Polish that Yashim didn't understand.

"Go on, then, Yash," he said at last. "What makes you believe the Bellini is a fake?"

67

S E R G E A N T Vosper was not only a methodical man, and a slow one; the aspect of police work he liked best was standing in a doorway across the street, waiting for a suspect to appear.

At the Procuratie he had to weave his way between the stadtmeister's interminable lectures and men like Brunelli, who bantered with him. When Brunelli laughed he never knew whether to be pleased or offended. Now Brunelli would be out for his scalp.

Waiting for Brett was not, on the whole, a bad way to spend an afternoon.

He came at a quarter to six, by Vosper's watch: an ugly fellow who rolled up to the front door of the palazzo and pushed it and went inside. Vosper followed.

"Signor Brett?" he called, when he heard the man's tread on the stone staircase overhead.

The man stopped.

"Who's that?"

Vosper stuck his head over the banister and looked up.

"Police."

"Who are you looking for?"

Vosper's rule was never to answer a direct question directly. "Are you Signor Brett?"

Overhead he heard a voice muttering to itself. "Brett?" It called down, "Please—is this the Ca' d'Aspi?"

"It's the Casa Manin. D'Aspi is next door."

The ugly man came down the stairs, chuckling ruefully. "Casa this,

Casa that. You'd think they'd give us better street numbers in the nine-teenth century."

Vosper nodded: it was a good point. Numbers would help police work.

"We're waiting for a Signor Brett," he said.

"Never heard of him," Alfredo said. "I'm due at the Ca' d'Aspi. Next door, you said?"

"That's right." Man was lost He wasn't the American, at any rate. "Turn left, first on the left."

"Thank you, Commissario." As he passed, the ugly man turned and lowered his voice. "What's this Brett done, then?"

"I'm not at liberty to reveal, I'm afraid, sir." Which was, when all was said and done, a shame. Vosper took precious little glory from his work, and here was a man who didn't seem to hold it against him. He inclined a little. "It could be a hanging charge," he said.

The ugly man pulled a face. "Murder?"

Vosper compressed his lips. "That's about the short and long of it, sir. Between ourselves."

Alfredo ducked his head in an admiring gesture. "Good luck to you, Commissario."

"And good luck to you, too, sir. It's left outside, and left again."

68

IN the café Yashim was beginning to explain. "Your friend Maria," he said.

Palewski raised his head. "How do you know Maria?"

"Your Alfredo—a fat, ugly man."

Palewski squirmed in his chair. "That doesn't make him a crook."

"No. But it means that he was in charge when those two thugs searched your apartment. He sent them in. They took Maria."

"Maria? What happened?"

Yashim told him. "They had her in the Fondaco dei Turchi. The old hammam."

"You found her?"

"Eventually."

"And she is—?"

"Oh, she's all right. You can see her in a moment."

"But what did they want with her?"

"They wanted to know who you were." Yashim's glance searched Palewski's face. "How good was your cover?"

Palewski chewed his lip. "I don't think I let it slip, Yashim. And it was good enough—the American collector. Why not? Apart from that meeting with Compston and his pals, no one could challenge Signor Brett."

"Brunelli?"

"No, I don't think so."

Yashim looked thoughtful. "Someone guessed. It doesn't matter now. Your Alfredo was just covering all the angles."

"I saw the painting, Yashim," Palewski protested. "The sultan."

"And you looked at it for how long? A few seconds?"

Palewski shifted uncomfortably on his seat. "Not long, I admit. But even so, the brother—"

"Precisely. It was the brother's behavior that made you believe in the painting."

Palewski put up two fingers; the waiter nodded. He remembered that evening in the boathouse and the odd conversation between Alfredo and Mario.

And Alfredo had raised his voice—behold the Bellini! It could have been a cue.

He buried his face in his hands.

"I don't know, Yashim. It's all theater—it's impossible to tell the real from the false."

"What happened that night was theater, for sure—the dark, the gun, the scramble to get away. They even made you swim."

I won't tell him about my visit to the palazzo in the morning, Palewski thought. That's when I should have known.

Something jumped into his mind, something else that had happened in the morning. But it was vague; Yashim was speaking.

Palewski pushed the thought away.

For which another man would die.

"So now, Yashim, we've got to start again?"

Yashim looked hard into Palewski's eyes. "Start again—yes, in a way. But not from scratch. I need to find out everything you know."

Palewski started. "Don't, Yashim. You make me nervous. I'll tell you what I can."

"Good. Not here, though. We need to get you somewhere safe, away from the police—and Alfredo's people, too. I know just the place. Come on."

69

NIKO likes to paint with the brushes and the little tubes of colors in Mr. Popi's studio there is good light the brushes are quite good. If you squeeze the color out of the little tube onto the board, and you do not use it all up, it will go dry like a dog turd Mr. Popi stepped on it.

Mr. Popi is cross he will give Niko TWO bottles of brandy. Brandy tastes nice it makes Niko cough. Brandy gives Niko a good, warm feeling. ONE TWO is better it lasts longer and Mr. Popi cannot come and see Niko when Niko has grrrrrrr

Mr. Popi is writing he is cross and writing

That is good he is busy he does not hurt Niko *now sting burn Niko cannot eat*

The hat is wrong Niko painted it to look like a hat he saw but Canaletto did not see this hat there are none such in all his paintings. Mr. Popi saw it Niko did not think he could BUT he saw it Mr. Popi is clever he knows what Niko is thinking maybe grrrrr Canaletto is clever.

He makes Mr. Popi soft TWO bottles. Niko must be clever like Canaletto. Mr. Popi is soft THREE times and Father was soft THREE SEVEN FIVE NINETEEN NINETEEN times where is he?

Grrr grrrr grrr

Sad Niko is sad grrrrrrrrrr Niko can curl up very small to be sad and Mr. Popi cannot tell he is not painting HA HA

He has gone out!

Out out back!

He is talking to a man

It is a strange way to talk with that strange noise in the other room Mr. Popi is not writing he is he is he is

Dancing

Niko curls up small he can see only the feet and the legs ONE TWO THREE FOUR FIVE SIX SEVEN EIGHT all moving feet and legs THUD THUD

One color that is Venetian red one is Flesh now the color is Madder it jets out like water in Canaletto's fountains which Niko can do.

Mr. Popi is putting the color everywhere with ONE foot. Niko does not like the noise it is like the pig at Christmas it made Niko small too.

Father it is all right Niko pig is dead it is all right all quiet

Mr. Popi is all right

It was his PRECIOUS BLOOD

Niko saw this man in the church he was THE DEVIL Father you are safe THE DEVIL is on the wall

He cannot hurt you

Mr. Popi cannot hurt Niko he has no skin THE DEVIL is taking it away

THE DEVIL had a hat but hat is wrong Niko can paint like Canaletto he does not have a hat

No hat Niko

Mr. Popi said no hat and Niko likes to paint with the brushes and the little tubes of colors in Mr. Popi's studio.

There is good light there.

The brushes are quite good.

70

SOUTH of the familiar brown bulk of the Frari, Palewski found himself in a region he didn't know, following Yashim as he worked his way confidently through the narrow streets. This part of Dorsoduro seemed, if anything, poorer than the rest; the large Campo Santa Margherita, which they crossed at a slant, was full of idle men, lean cats, and laundry, as if the women took in other people's washing. The women, indeed, were down by the small canal, scrubbing and rinsing their linen in the murky green water. One of them sang out as Yashim and Palewski crossed the bridge, and there was a burst of laughter.

Farther west, they reached the court where the Contarinis lived on the ground floor. Maria was there: she ran forward and hugged Palewski, lifting her bare feet from the cobbles.

"*Mio caro!* I did not think I would see you again!"

The kitchen was very dark and smelled of smoke. Signora Contarini rose ponderously from the fire, which she had been feeding with little twigs, and bobbed a curtsy.

Yashim explained Palewski's need for a billet.

"You are welcome," the signora said, with an elegant sweeping gesture of her hand.

Later, Yashim found himself watching Signora Contarini as she worked with a short knife, enthroned on a stool by the fire, slicing carrots and onions and garlic against her thumb. She had a knack of slicing the onion so that it remained whole until the last minute, when it cascaded into rings.

One by one she dropped the vegetables into a cauldron set on irons above the fire. The polished stone hearth jutted out into the room; over it, about three feet up, hung a canopy. The smoke drifted lazily upward, some of it escaping into the room to darken the beams and ceiling. The fire itself was small, and the old lady tended it carefully with a poker, now and then tucking back stray twigs and sticks.

When the water came to a boil, the signora carefully unwrapped the beef and lowered it into the cauldron with both hands. Having watched it for a few moments, she went to the table and began to sift through her stores. She shook out a bunch of parsley, folded it, and chopped it finely into a wooden bowl. She cracked a clove from a bulb of garlic, peeled it swiftly, and with little movements of her forefinger sliced it first one way and then the next, before slipping it over and paring it into fragments.

She lifted the lid of a clay jar and fished out a few capers, which she added to the sauce. From another jar she speared a pickled cucumber on the point of her knife and sliced that, too, as she had chopped the garlic.

She put her thumb over the neck of a small green bottle and shook a few drops of vinegar into the bowl. A pinch of salt, a round of pepper, and then she began to stir the mixture, adding a thin thread of oil from an earthenware flask until the sauce felt right.

"There must be something I can do to help," Yashim said. "Perhaps I could stir the polenta?"

With her eye on the sauce the signora gave an amused grunt: the Moor, stir her polenta?

"I make it *come la seta*," she said. Like silk.

She poured a jug of water into the copper standing beside the fire.

"Talk to your friend, signore."

Yashim moved away politely: he had no wish to put the eye on his hostess's polenta. Maria was sitting by the window, stitching her torn dress. She was wearing the blue bodice and patched gray skirt she had put on before she knew they would be having company.

Yashim glanced back to see the signora threading an endless stream of yellow maize from one hand. The other worked a wooden spoon in slow, firm circles. He smiled and turned his back: in Trabzon, where he was born, the women made *kuymak* in the same way.

Perhaps they worshipped the same gods, these women, as they performed the daily miracle of transforming the baser elements into silk, the rarest luxury the world could afford.

Maria raised her head from her sewing. "Some days," she said in a near whisper, "we hang an anchovy on a string, above the table. Then we each rub the anchovy on the polenta—and it tastes so good!"

Her mother leaned over the copper and examined her work. She had finished pouring the maize but she continued to stir, slowly, with her free hand on the rim of the pot as the polenta gradually stiffened.

"Maria! Fetch the board."

Maria set aside her sewing and jumped up. She took what looked like a little bench down from two pegs in the wall and set it before the fire.

Yashim watched, in spite of himself: the signora's face was rapt as she tilted the pan and the polenta glided out across the board, as smooth as yellow silk.

Maria was putting plates and forks around the table.

"Maria!" Her mother hissed and nodded to the wooden chest. There followed angry words in a thick dialect that neither Yashim nor Palewski could properly understand.

Maria blushed and cleared the table again. Then she fetched a fresh cloth from the chest and shook it out over the table.

Yashim smiled at the signora and she eyed him back, one eyebrow faintly raised. Yes, he thought, we understand each other, Moor and Venetian, in the simple duties of ceremony and propriety. The table had needed to be dressed.

The cloth sparkled, and it seemed as though the room were not the mean, low-ceilinged hovel it had been but brighter, orderly, hospitable. Even the food smelled richer.

Maria set the table. Her mother skimmed the stock.

Maria's father, a whippet-thin man who worked on the boats and had been enjoying a puff of cigar smoke with his friends in the yard, joined them with handshakes and curt welcomes.

They ate the beef sliced, on a mattress of polenta swimming with good stock, with spoonfuls of the salsa verde, in silence and appreciation. Maria's little brothers and sisters sat with uncanny stillness, having been bawled in from the neighboring alleys. Except for the oldest boy, a good-looking lad with Maria's tangle of black hair and rolled shirtsleeves, they had shaved heads and huge round eyes, which they turned on Palewski and Yashim, but particularly Yashim, as they silently spooned up their polenta.

Finally a little girl, more wriggly than the rest—she could scarcely have been more than seven, Yashim supposed—broke the silence to ask him if it was true that in Moor-land nobody had to go to church.

"I think that God would be sad," Yashim said thoughtfully, "if nobody went to thank him, now and then. For food like this, and children like yourselves, and a sunny day like today."

"Is he sad in your country, when nobody goes?"

"Not at all, signorina. Because some people do go to church, and others go to mosque, and some people go to the synagogue. So he hears people thanking him in lots of different voices, like yours, and mine, and your mother's, and our friend Palewski's here, and that makes him four times as happy."

She looked at him again, a little dubiously, and didn't reply.

And much later, when everyone else was asleep, and the two friends sat together by the embers of the fire, Yashim spoke about the calligrapher, Metin Yamaluk, and the missing book of Bellini drawings, and how his instinct had warned him that there was something wrong.

"He was a pious old man. He died with a look of terror on his face."

He told him, too, about Resid's cryptic remarks. "He knew something was going on in Venice. Something dangerous."

Palewski for his part explained about the contessa's party, and the death of Barbieri, and how Alfredo had been his last hope.

Yashim bit his cheek. "Yes—and I wonder how this Alfredo knew what you were looking for."

"Rumors, Yashim. Speculation was born on the Rialto." His chair creaked. "Everyone knows something and is sure of nothing. Except that I miss my bed," Palewski murmured, pulling the blanket up beneath his chin. In a minute he was asleep, legs outstretched, his feet on the hearth like a soldier on campaign.

Yashim took longer to settle. Palewski had sketched for him a cast of characters: some were frauds, some were dead, and some, he was sure, knew more than they were letting on.

71

THE signora was sweeping around his feet.

"You sleep like a child, signore—a big man, as you are!" she said, when Palewski opened an eye. "Well, Maria will be down presently."

Her husband had gone out, taking Yashim with him. "He rows the barges at San Luca," the signora explained. "Your friend the Moor said to tell you, signore, you should stay where you are."

The importance of staying put was not lost on Palewski: the police might still be watching his flat, and he had no wish to run into Alfredo, either.

Maria came down, yawning and pretty in a bodice none too tightly buttoned. She and Palewski shared a dish of grilled polenta, while she told him in greater detail about her ordeal.

"They were Venetians, too!" she concluded in a tone of wonder. "My mother doesn't understand it."

Yashim returned half an hour later. He was carrying several of the signora's string bags, crammed with provisions, as well as a change of linen for Palewski. He was also wearing a turban again, though nobody seemed to notice. Palewski remembered a gang of building workers he had recently seen near the Campo San Polo. They, too, had been wearing turbans—though theirs were noticeably less clean and white.

"The signora has agreed to let me cook tonight," Yashim said happily, biting into a slab of polenta. He took a yellow envelope out of his pocket. "In the meantime, you have an invitation, my old friend. I picked it up, too, from your apartment. Signor Eletro, today at twelve o'clock."

Palewski folded his arms. "I'm supposed to be in hiding, not strolling about Venice with a character out of the Arabian Nights. Who's Eletro?"

Yashim stood up. "Don't you know?" He picked up Palewski's hat and gave it to him. He presented Maria with a bow. "*Arrivederci,*" he said with a smile.

"Be careful," she said.

Yashim took his friend by the arm and steered him outside, through the yard.

Palewski pulled a surly face. "All right, Eletro's one of the dealers Ruggerio told me to approach. I sent him a card."

"What's his line?"

"How would I know, Yashim? Probably a line in plausible talk. I don't suppose he's got a Bellini in his attic."

"Probably not. But I'd like to get his measure, anyway. It might come in useful."

They settled into a gondola.

Palewski blew out his cheeks. "Frankly, Yash, I almost wish you'd never turned up. I could be miles away by now. I liked the Bellini—and the sultan would have liked it, too."

"Until he discovered it was a fake."

"If it *was* a fake," Palewski said moodily. "*I* didn't know. *He* wouldn't know. And the dealers, like Eletro or Barbieri, would probably think it was real, too."

"But what if they guessed it was fake?"

"Oh, then they'd have a crack at selling him something in the same line, and back both pictures to the hilt. And why not, dammit? It's a ridiculous affair, and everyone's happy."

Yashim frowned. "It would be false."

"False? The whole game's false. I have a picture of King Sobieski in my sitting room, Yashim. I like it. Man looks like a king."

"I know the picture," Yashim said.

"Of course you do. Fact is, it was painted twenty years after Sobieski died. It's written on the back. And I don't care!"

Yashim looked across at his old friend. They were sliding along a sequence of narrow green canals. As they burst out into the lagoon, the frail craft began to pitch.

Yashim put a hand to the gunwale.

"Lies beget lies," he said. "Until, one day, someone needs the truth."

Palewski stared out over the lagoon. "The truth."

They were too close to the heart of it now: the ineluctable mystery of human affairs, the questions of faith, doubt, and proof.

"I wouldn't want the sultan to have a fake," Palewski said finally.

They were back now in the body of Venice, sifting through its veins and ventricles. The gondolier pulled up at a tiny *campo*.

"Wait for us," Yashim said.

The *campo* was unusually deserted: it took Yashim a moment to realize that the entire left side was only an empty façade. Behind a half-opened door he saw piles of rubble and charred beams; a cat slipped by and disappeared. In the center of the narrow courtyard was a wellhead tinged with damp.

Palewski shivered beside him. "No wonder they torched it. Place looks like it never gets the sun," he remarked. "Where's Eletro?"

"It must be this side," Yashim said. "There's only one door."

The door swung open at the first push. Inside, a narrow corridor disappeared toward the back around the foot of the stairs.

"Damp. Very." Palewski pulled a face.

Yashim sniffed the air. "It's not damp," he said. "It's drains. And by the way, you can introduce me to Eletro as the pasha's servant."

"The pasha's servant?" Palewski echoed. "What's that supposed to mean?"

Yashim shrugged. "Nothing at all. Come on, he'll be waiting."

The smell was stronger on the stairs, and on the first floor landing Palewski gagged and put a handkerchief to his nose.

"Smells like gangrene," he mumbled. "Look at that."

He was pointing to a door whose jambs were black with thickly clustered flies. A fat bluebottle buzzed lazily past them and crashed into the landing window.

Yashim pulled the folds of his cloak together and approached the door: a buzzing swarm of flies rose to the ceiling and made a rush for the window. Palewski had to close his eyes as they went by, batting against his face and hat; Yashim, half twisted toward him, put his hand on the doorknob.

Yashim felt flies crawling onto his wrist.

He gave the knob a savage twist and shoved back the door to release a bar of sunshine and a thick hot guff of decay.

A swarm of flies moved in the opposite direction.

Yashim ducked instinctively, dragging his cloak over his eyes and mouth. The high, sweet reek of rotten meat caught in his throat and he stepped back onto the landing.

Palewski was at the window, rattling the knob, and then both of them were leaning out into the shade of the *campo*, choking for lungfuls of clear air.

After a few minutes Yashim covered his nose and mouth again and went back to the doorway. He strode into Popi's flat and crossed to the opposite window, which he opened.

This time it was not only the stench that made him retch.

The walls, the floor, the table, and the chairs were all caked with patches of dried blood, over which crawled thousands of glittering blue flies. Between him and the door lay only vaguely the shape of a man, so bloated and rotten had it become in the heat of the sun. Beneath its coating of flies the body was both swollen and deliquescent, melting over the floorboards as if its skin could no longer contain its molten putrefaction.

Palewski came to the door.

He threw up in the hall. He felt better, until he saw the flies crawling over his vomit.

He stood in the doorway again and gestured clumsily to the heaving corpse.

"Where's his skin?" His voice was a croak.

Yashim glanced again, gagged, averted his face, and tried to concentrate on the room. It was the room of a workingman, a tradesman. Even without the blood it needed a fresh coat of paint. A small oilcloth lay under the deal table, and a board sat on the table with something fuzzy on it, probably an old cheese. Next to it was a knife. The knife was not bloody. At the other end of the table stood a chair, paper, and a pen. The paper was spattered with blood, but it was the same paper as the letter. Nothing was written on the paper. A bottle of wine stood beneath the chair, with the cork stuck in.

Several paintings hung on the walls.

A slight breeze had set in, blowing between the sunny window in the flat and the shaded window on the stairs. Palewski crossed the room with his handkerchief to his nose and joined Yashim at the window.

"Could be Canalettos," he gasped, turning to the sunlight.

"Canalettos?"

"Those paintings. Fashionable. Last century. Painted Venetian—what, *vedute*. Pretty scenes." He coughed into his handkerchief. "He did them by the yard—fabulous technique. Seen one, seen them all."

"You mean—they look the same?" Yashim stared at the paintings for a while. "These ones are, in fact, identical."

Palewski turned to look. "So they are," he murmured. "How very extraordinary. Why, the old swindler! So that was his racket."

He turned and opened the other door, cautiously, with his face buried in the crook of his arm.

The window in here was already open. There was a smell of turpentine and oil.

"This is where he must have done them. Look."

Yashim followed him in, noticing the paints spread out on a little table daubed with slicks of green and yellow. A large canvas lay against the wall; another stood on an easel. In the corner of the room was a dirty unmade bed.

Yashim studied the canvas on the easel.

Palewski glanced at it. "Another Canaletto," he remarked carelessly.

"But not by Canaletto," Yashim reminded him. He peered at the painting, mesmerized. It was a busy picture, replete with the sights of canal life in Venice in the 1760s. Gondolas slipped across the rippled water; matrons hung out of balconies, drawing up their shopping on a string; a periwigged grandee lectured his ladies on the classical orders in front of Santa Maria della Salute; a dog barked at a beggar; a woman sat at her window, reading a letter with a happy smile.

Unlike Palewski, Yashim had never before seen such attention to detail. It was more than a realistic rendering of light in paint. It was like looking through a window. He almost believed he could jump in and come out wet, floundering in the Grand Canal.

"It makes no difference," Palewski was saying. "This man Eletro must have had a sort of brilliance—but it's all reflected. And why not? Canaletto held a mirror up to this city and painted the reflection. Very clever. Medal of honor. Eletro holds a mirror up to Canaletto. Clever, too. Medal of honor, second class."

Yashim straightened up. "Is that Eletro on the floor next door, do you think?"

"I assumed so. I don't know, now you mention it."

"No, I think it's him, too." Yashim gestured to the tangled sheets and blankets. "This is where he lived. And where he was left dead." He returned his gaze to the canvas, fascinated by the depth of perspective, the animation of the tiny figures who looked solid and real in the foreground and then dwindled into mere brushstrokes as the distance lengthened.

He moved his head back and forth, screwing up his eyes.

"It wasn't Eletro who painted this picture," he said finally. "It wasn't your Canaletto, either. But whoever it was, he did hold a mirror up to Venice. Look."

He was pointing at the canvas—not touching it. The paint was still fresh.

Palewski bent his head and looked.

"Good God!"

Yashim wasn't pointing to the foreground. He was pointing, instead, to a tiny window in a row of windows almost lost in the shade of the great church. There, in a darkened room, a man with red arms and a curious topknot could be seen grappling with a pair of bloody legs.

72

VOSPER stood stiffly in front of the stadtmeister's desk and repeated what he had said.

"The pasha's servant, sir. His very words."

The stadtmeister spread his papers across his desk, in a gesture of despair. "I have nothing about this. Nothing! And you say he was wearing a turban? My God!"

"I'm sorry, sir."

"Sorry? *Ja, ja,* we will all be sorry, Vosper. What are we to do? Tomorrow, you say?"

"That's what he told me, sir."

"Did he say how many? Any names?"

"I—I don't think so, sir. He thought I knew all about it. I assumed you had been informed."

"*Der Teufel!* I work with idiots!" The stadtmeister began opening drawers, pulling out sheaves of yellow imperial paper, all embossed with the K.u.K. double-eagle crest. "Go back, Vosper, and find this man, this pasha's servant, and bring him to me immediately. Be tactful of course. You will say that the stadtmeister wishes to run through a few items on the reception program and would be pleased to discuss them this afternoon."

Vosper's heels clicked. "If I can find him, sir."

"Find him? Of course you must find him! Isn't he staying in the American's old apartment?"

"Yes, sir. He was just moving in."

"There you are, then. And Vosper"—the stadtmeister chewed his mustache—"send Brunelli to me, right away."

73

PALEWSKI studied the picture.

"It doesn't make sense," he said. "If that's Eletro being killed—why, who would have painted such a thing? And when, Yashim?"

Yashim was at the open window. It was a twenty-foot drop into the canal below.

He turned and surveyed the room: bare walls, the little paint-splattered table, a crucifix above the bed.

He was about to go back through the door when his glance fell on the tangle of sheets and blankets on the bed.

Yashim strode over to the bed and tugged at the yellowing sheets.

For a moment he thought he had been deceived, that there was nothing there.

The man was curled up with his arms over his head, his knees drawn up to his chin, his hands clenched into bony fists.

Yashim took his arms and pulled them back, to reveal a wizened face the color of old sheets, eyes shut, the mouth dry and cracked.

There was no resistance in the curled-up figure: he was beyond strength, possibly beyond all help. His limbs peeled apart to the touch.

"We need water," Yashim said. Without hesitation he bent down and scooped the man up in his arms. "Pick up the painting."

They waded through a cloud of flies and on the landing Palewski pulled the door shut behind them. Outside in the *campo* he opened the well cover and pulled up a bucket of water. Yashim sat down and held the man against his chest, sprinkling his lips with drops from the bucket.

He took the water in his hand and ran it over the man's face.

The eyelids did not stir, but the cracked lips moved slightly.

Yashim held his hand as a scoop and let a little water trickle into the man's mouth. There was a catching sound, and the man swallowed.

"What are we going to do with him?"

Yashim looked anxious. "We'll take him to the Contarinis. Don't worry. He hasn't killed anyone. No blood on him." He glanced up. "It's you I'm worried about."

He unclasped his cloak and wrapped it around the frail skeleton.

Palewski said, "Sometimes it's the ones who seem weak, like him, who survive."

They carried him to the gondola. The gondolier started at the sight of Yashim's bundle. "What's that? It looks like a pietà," he exclaimed, crossing himself.

"Take us to Dorsoduro as fast as you can," Palewski said. "And pray, my friend, for the resurrection."

74

THE stadtmeister's atlas confirmed that Venice and the Ottoman capital, Istanbul, were separated by only four degrees of latitude. Very significant, he thought. Two Mediterranean cities—one sheltered from its direct influence by the Adriatic and the lagoon, and the other by the Sea of Marmara.

Brunelli was just the man for the job.

"Ach, Commissario," he said, as Brunelli entered. "I need your help."

"Help, sir?" Brunelli faced his chief with a dull expression. "I was under the impression that Vosper provided you with all the help you need."

"What? What?" The stadtmeister reddened. "Look, Brunelli. It is my job to organize the disposition of forces in this city to the maximum advantage of the public. Operational necessities. I mean, let us not delude ourselves, what? Sergeant Vosper is a very good man. Good man. But this crime of passion—I cannot afford to squander all my resources on such an inquiry. Sometimes, we must keep the best in reserve." He grinned, showing his yellow teeth. "Do you follow me, Brunelli? The best, in reserve. And now, I require your help."

A crime of passion—so that was it! Brunelli could hardly refrain from laughing. Vosper and the stadtmeister in pursuit of a jealous lover who sawed off a man's head and stuck it on a communion platter. The passionate Signor Brett!

The stadtmeister put his fingertips together.

"I am not quite sure how this situation has arisen," he began, "but without our knowledge some sort of visit has been arranged, to this city, by a senior functionary of the Ottoman Empire."

"A pasha in Venice, sir?" Now Brunelli did allow himself a smile.

"Not in the least comic, Brunelli. High matters of state. Not for us to question. I want you to take charge of the, ah, arrangements."

"Perhaps you could be more specific, Stadtmeister."

"If I could be more specific, Brunelli, more specific I would be!" the stadtmeister roared, growing very red. "The pasha has sent a man on ahead—he is staying in the American's apartment, and Vosper is to bring him here, to see us. We must find out what the pasha proposes to do—and how long he will stay."

"Do we know when he is to arrive, sir?"

"Yes," the stadtmeister said very quietly. "Yes, Brunelli. He's arriving from Istanbul tomorrow morning. And you will be his—liaison!"

75

YASHIM was not certain that the pitiful figure in his cloak would live to see Dorsoduro, but Palewski was right: he was still alive when they carried him into the signora's kitchen and laid him down on a pallet of straw.

The signora took one look and raised her hands. "In my house! He will bring disease to us all."

Yashim said, "He isn't ill. He's starved. Bring me some hot water and a towel. I will wash him."

To Palewski, it was an almost biblical scene: the smoky, blackened room, the emaciated figure on the pallet, and Yashim carefully wiping away the sweat and dirt.

"A little soup, signora, if you don't mind. Not too hot."

Palewski knelt to hold the man upright, while Yashim put the spoon to his lips. He swallowed, weakly.

"If it hadn't been for that appointment—" Palewski frowned and shook his head. "What happened in that room, Yashim? Who is this man?"

He looked down, into his face. The eyes were closed; he was asleep already. He looked better clean: his hair in little golden tufts, his ears surprisingly delicate and small, with three little moles on the tip; you could see the veins in his forehead.

"Scrubbed up well, at least."

Yashim rocked back on his heels. He took a small leather bag from his pocket and fished in it for a pinch of latakia tobacco, which he rolled up in a spill of rice paper. He touched the end to a brand and smoked it, in silence.

"As to that," he said finally, blowing a perfect ring into the air, "I have few ideas. I don't think he is the killer. It is possible that he painted the murder scene, in which case he may have more to tell us presently. If he recovers."

He paused and glanced at his friend. "But if he's not the killer," he began, then shook his head. "I don't like it, Palewski. It's getting—very close."

Palewski's shoulders jerked. "Close—to what?"

Yashim pointed a finger. "To you. First Barbieri, then Eletro."

"But Boschini—the man in the canal. I—I hadn't had any contact with him."

"No, you weren't given the chance." Yashim took a whiff of his tobacco.

"Do you think it's time to call it quits? Get back to Istanbul. Admit defeat." Palewski laid the man down gently on the pallet and drew Yashim's cloak up to his chin. "That painting seemed such a simple solution to my troubles, once."

Yashim nodded. "I think we should plan to stay a little longer," he said. "Someone offered a Bellini for sale. The sultan got to hear of it, at least, so I assumed that the painting was available. But you haven't heard a thing in ten days."

"No. And everyone keeps getting killed."

Yashim held up his hand. "How did the sultan pick up the rumor? Who told him?"

"I've no idea."

"Let's say it was your friend Alfredo. He created the whole scenario in order to get somebody out here—and double-cross him."

"So there never was a Bellini?"

Yashim looked puzzled. "I don't know. Someone was supposed to come to Venice. But then—why are people being killed?"

"Why do people get killed? Over money, or women."

"Or because they know too much."

Palewski started.

"Alfredo knew where to find me," he said slowly. "The day after we saw the painting he was waiting by Florian, in the piazza."

"Go on."

"I'd simply told Ruggerio to meet me there for lunch. He was there, too, at a table."

"I see. So Ruggerio told Alfredo where he could find you."

"Yes. Maybe. It might have been a coincidence."

Yashim flicked the end of his cigarette into the fire. "Perhaps. But one of them seems to have guessed something else: that you were not Signor Brett. Why else would they take Maria to be questioned?"

"Maybe the gang just wanted to be sure who they were dealing with. To be sure I could come through with the money."

"No. A courtesan deals in ducats, not thousands in silver. They took Maria because they wanted a confession. Something intimate. They already suspected who you really were."

Yashim found himself examining his friend. He saw a perfectly plausible visitor to Venice, like any other: well dressed, acceptably à la mode. Signor Brett, connoisseur!

"Are you—" He blushed. "Are you circumcised, Palewski?"

"No."

Yashim glanced away, baffled, and his eye fell on something on the floor beside Palewski's chair.

He sighed heavily. "Let me see your hat."

"My hat?"

"There." Yashim held the hat by the brim and invited Palewski to look inside.

"Well, I'm—! But I made no secret of the fact that I'd been in Istanbul."

"That's right—but casual visitors don't get their hats in Istanbul. I wouldn't buy my pantaloons in Venice, either. It isn't conclusive, of course, but it would have raised Ruggerio's suspicions."

"Suspicions of what, Yashim? I don't understand."

"That you were the man from Istanbul."

"The man from Istanbul," Palewski echoed.

"Why would it matter so much to Ruggerio that you came from Istanbul?" Yashim tapped the hat against his palm. "There could be two possibilities. Either he was expecting someone from Istanbul—and couldn't be sure if you were the one. He might have expected someone like me. Or—pah." He shook his head and murmured, *"Olmaz."*

"Impossible?" Palewski echoed.

Yashim's eyes narrowed. "No. Ruggerio could also have been confused because he *didn't* expect anyone from Istanbul."

Palewski wrinkled his nose. "It's been a trying day so far, Yashim. You're getting tangled up in a double negative, or whatever. I mean to say, you can't *not* expect someone to come from Istanbul. It may be *unlikely*, but that's not the same thing, is it? Why shouldn't Ruggerio expect someone to come from Istanbul?"

Yashim nodded and pinched his lip.

"Only one reason that I can see," he said. "Because that someone was already here."

Palewski folded his arms.

Yashim stared absently at his friend.

"In the painting. The man with the red arms. Did you notice anything else about him? Something odd?"

"Odd? I don't think so. It's very small."

Yashim was on his feet. He dragged the painting from the wall.

"When I first saw it, I had the impression that the killer was a foreigner. Not Venetian, I mean." Yashim squatted and squinted at the tiny figures. "I think I was right. Look."

Palewski frowned at the painting. "Not much to him, is there? Except, well . . ."

"Well?"

"He's shaven-headed, isn't he? Except for the sort of topknot."

"The topknot, exactly. And if I'm right, and he came from Istanbul?"

"In Istanbul," Palewski said thoughtfully, "I'd take him for a Tatar."

The Tatars were consummate horsemen from the steppe and for centuries they had been the Ottomans' closest allies. But the Russians had seized their Crimean homeland. Since then many had fled the rule of the infidel czar, settling instead in the Ottoman Empire across the sea.

"He could be one of those Crimean exiles you see around," Palewski continued. "Most of them come from the Black Sea coast, nowadays. It could be that—or a loose brushstroke."

"Our painter is nothing if not precise."

"But Venice is hardly awash with Tatars, Yashim. He'd stick out a mile." He looked at his friend. "Unless he wore a hat."

"Another hat."

Palewski stood by the fire, his hands tucked behind his back.

"Why didn't the Tatar see the man who painted him? He must have been in the same apartment."

Yashim glanced at the sleeping figure on the mattress. "But *we* didn't see him, either, did we?"

76

THE name: now the time had come. He had come for the last name.

The man shivered in the sunlight.

It was about to end. They would take their little walk again, for the last time.

The assassin a few paces behind him, like a respectful bride.

Or like a hunter, stalking its prey.

Their last walk.

The last name.

The last death.

The man blew out his lips and told himself to think of the payment. They had promised him—enough. Like Venetians they had weighed, assessed, and judged him, as though they knew his price.

The fear of death, and the hope of gold.

He wiped his mouth with the back of his hand and began to walk.

77

APART from the cauldron, and the copper she had used for polenta the night before, Signora Contarini had an iron frying pan, a milk pan, and two earthenware pots—one was tall, with a narrow mouth, the other a broad dish, as in the fable of the stork and the fox.

Yashim decided to avoid the copper: it was too much the signora's own, an altar to a household god.

He also decided, partly for the same reason, not to use her knife. The small kitchen knife that Malakian had given him, the damascene blade infernally bright even in the dim light of the signora's kitchen, felt eager and balanced. It was a link to his world, too, away from this strange city of unbelievers and canals. Yashim had spent several days in Venice, and he had been confused, much of the time, by the mix of what was familiar and what was foreign.

He poured a few handfuls of chickpeas into the tall pot, covered them in water, and pushed the pot to the back of the fireplace.

Palewski seemed to have read his thoughts. "I never told you, Yash, but Venice made me ill for a day or so."

"Ill?" Should he use the polenta board to chop onions? He thought not.

"Giddy. Dropped me off the map. When I got here I thought— Cracow. Rynek Glowny. Colors, shape of the windows, carved stone doors. Baby Gothic, I don't know—we had it more grown up. And all these churches. Nuns—even in gondolas!" He laughed. "And then—then it tilted the other way, and everything I looked at *felt* like Istanbul. Sliding about on the water, and Armenians and Greeks, and sometimes the domes, too, with their lead and their curves. So the next time I saw those nuns—they reminded me of girls in chadors, taking a caïque up the Golden Horn."

Yashim's eye fell on the table. The signora, he noticed, scrubbed it every day with lye and ashes. The signora might not notice if he used it—carefully—as a chopping board.

"Giddy," Palewski said again, as if the word pleased him. "I was looking at a beautiful Koran, in the Armenian monastery, and I felt—giddy. Only legible book in the place, as far as I could see. They got it from my old neighbor's family—the Aspis."

The man on the pallet turned his head and Yashim saw his eyes were open wide. His skin was drawn tight against the skull, but his eyes were big and dark and unafraid.

Yashim smiled. "Palewski, our friend needs water, and some soup."

He turned to his baskets. Palewski held a glass to the young man's lips and heard him drink.

The onion was green; Yashim took off its top and tail, then chopped it into halves. He sliced the halves.

"I don't know how you can think of food," Palewski remarked. "After this morning."

Yashim shrugged. He dropped a lump of butter into the cauldron and pushed it up against the fire. For a few moments he handled the cooking irons, trying to work out which did what, before he tipped the onion into the cauldron and lifted the handle onto a notch in the bar.

He admired the arrangement of irons, adding them to his stock of dreams. Yashim had always dreamed of a *yali* by the Bosphorus, with water reflected on his ceiling. Better water than here, he thought: Venice, at least in summer, stank.

He glanced across to where Palewski was feeding the man who looked like an emaciated child.

But the man will live, he thought. He knows who killed Eletro.

And I know, too.

He paused, touching the rim of the cauldron.

Not his name. Not his whereabouts. But I know what he is.

He stirred the onion with a spoon and frowned.

What I don't know yet is: *Why?*

78

B RUNELLI waited much of the afternoon for Vosper's Ottoman servant, but when he did not appear at four o'clock he decided to take another walk.

The beggar must have followed his instructions. Certainly the American had disappeared.

Giving his apartment over to a pasha's servant.

Brunelli knew one thing the stadtmeister and Vosper did not know: that Signor Brett claimed to have been in Istanbul before he arrived in Venice.

Brunelli walked on, taking turns as random as his thoughts.

He found himself on the Rialto bridge.

There was a link, he knew, between the two events: the pasha and the mysterious American.

But the American seemed to have vanished into thin air. He might have left Venice altogether. And as Signor Brett took his leave, a pasha's servant made his appearance—in exactly the same place.

Vosper, of course, had never met Brett. He couldn't identify the man he was looking for, on such an absurd charge, by sight at all.

But even Vosper, surely, couldn't have believed that Brett was a pasha's servant?

He turned a corner and reached the Zattere, with its long view of the Giudecca and the decayed wharfs, dilapidated houses, and old churches lining the waterfront.

Vosper, obviously, was capable of believing anything, but why would Brett spin him such an extraordinary story?

Brunelli stopped. He burst out laughing.

If Brett wanted to shake Vosper off his tail, what better than a lie so huge, so wildly inspired, that Vosper would be forced to swallow it whole?

If Brunelli had thought for a moment that Vosper and the stadtmeister were right, and that Brett was a suspect, he would have had no hesitation in joining them in the hunt.

But he had met the man, and he trusted his own intuition perfectly. That dimpled trollop Maria had backed him, too. Brett was crooked, somehow, but he wasn't a killer.

He had given Vosper the slip. He'd convinced the stadtmeister that the bureaucracy his paymasters were so famous for had finally become unhinged, and the sky was falling on his head.

Brunelli grinned.

He liked Brett, and he'd like to talk to him for a while.

He thought he knew where to find him, too.

79

IN the signora's frying pan Yashim fried slices of aubergine in oil. When they were brown, he took them out and laid them on a plate. He chopped tomatoes roughly and put them into the pan with a pinch of salt and sugar, stirring them from time to time.

He peeled and chopped a few cloves of garlic, which followed the onions into the cauldron. When the onions were soft, he stirred in a couple of pounds of minced lamb. The lamb had been expensive; he had to try several butchers before he found it.

The meat browned. He threw in a big pinch of cinnamon, a bunch of torn basil, and the tomatoes.

In the milk pan he melted butter and flour to make a thick roux. He added milk slowly, keeping the pan at the edge of the fire. When he had the sauce, he sprinkled it with salt and a pinch of grated nutmeg.

He scraped the meat into the flat earthenware, covered it with layers of aubergine, and poured the sauce on top.

With the moussaka ready, he rinsed off the frying pan and oiled it. When it was very hot he crushed into it a few dried peppers between the palms of his hands and cooked them until the flakes were almost black. He spooned the homemade *kirmizi biber* into a cup of flour.

"The Armenian monastery."

He spoke so quietly that Palewski, chasing flies on the windowpane with a handkerchief, couldn't be sure he'd heard properly.

"The monastery?"

"You said you were giddy. You were in the library, looking at a Koran."

"That's right. Felt peculiar."

"An old Koran?"

"No, no. Quite recent—very lovely, too."

"From the Aspi family, you said? Did you see who made it?"

"I just wanted to go home and sleep, Yashim."

"I'd like to see it," Yashim said.

"Now?"

"I think that would be best," Yashim agreed. "Wrap up. It could be cold on the water."

80

IT took them almost an hour to reach the island. The channel was marked with stakes, gaunt as gibbets in the dusk. The water was still and oily.

Palewski pulled the bell rope and they heard it jangle in the porter's lodge. After a few minutes a little window was thrust back and a face appeared.

"Who are you? It's late."

The monk spoke in Italian; Yashim answered in Armenian. "I apologize, Father. Signor Brett visited the monastery a few days ago, but he was unable to speak to Father Aristo."

"Father Aristo," the monk echoed. "He will be in the scriptorium."

He undid the bolts and let them in. When he had locked the door again he put his hands in his sleeves. "Please, follow me."

They crossed a courtyard and entered a wide passage. The sconces had just been lit. The monk opened a door softly, without knocking, and Yashim inhaled a rich and pleasantly familiar smell of old books, ink, and wood. The scriptorium was lined with shelves, lost in the gloom; a candle guttered on the broad oak table that ran down the middle of the room.

The table was bare, except where it erupted into a confusion of papers and books close to the candle, reminding Yashim of the Polish ambassador's study in Istanbul. Father Aristo's conical black hat stood on a pile of dictionaries, and Father Aristo's bald head lay on the papers. He appeared to be asleep.

The monk smiled. "Father Aristo works so hard," he whispered. Then, a little louder: "Father. Father Aristo."

"We came to see the Koran, especially," Yashim said quietly. "Perhaps we should let Father Aristo sleep?"

The monk shook his head. "He would be disappointed."

He touched the old monk's arm.

Father Aristo raised his head and looked around, blinking. His beard was magnificent and white.

"Some visitors, Father."

Father Aristo groped on the table for his spectacles and put them on carefully, tucking the arms behind his huge ears.

"I was having a nap." He had a very deep voice and a sweet smile.

Still in Armenian, Yashim introduced them both. "We wished to look at the Koran, Father."

"Ah yes, the Koran. By all means. It is very splendid. Would you like some tea?"

While the other monk went to fetch the tea, Father Aristo spread the papers in front of him.

"This is our dictionary," he explained, looking fondly at the books around him, as if their presence were a pleasant surprise. "Between English and Armenian. I have reached the fourteenth letter of our alphabet."

That left him with twenty-four to go, Yashim thought.

The monk returned with a tray and three glasses of sweet tea.

"It is a holy task, because the Armenian script is a holy script," Father Aristo said. "It has come to us unchanged, down the centuries. The first letter is *A*, for Astvats: God. The last is *K*, for Kristos. Mashtots received these letters in a dream, after years of study. It was a very good dream, my friends. These letters," he added, slowly, "have kept us together for fourteen hundred and thirty-five years."

He rose to his feet, carefully lifting the chair from the floor.

"But you have come to see the Koran. I will show it to you."

He disappeared into the gloom. He seemed to know his way around by touch, for in a few moments he returned with a large leather-bound book, which he placed on the table.

"The Muslims, too, respect their script as holy," he said. He looked at Yashim. "Is it not so?"

Yashim bowed. He lifted the cover and saw that this was, indeed, a very fine Koran, of a quality that would suit a palace or a great mosque. Inside the cover was a short inscription in Latin.

Palewski leaned over. "It says that Alvise d'Aspi presented this Koran to his friends at the Armenian Monastery of San Lazzaro in the year—" He frowned. The roman numerals MCCLXIV made no sense. "Twelve sixty-four?"

Father Aristo smiled and patted his arm. "Of course. Count d'Aspi was a good friend to us. He used the Armenian calendar, which begins in A.D. 552 in your calendar." He nodded. "There is a great deal to explain about the Armenian calendar, but you must come earlier in the day, no?" His eyes twinkled behind his spectacles. "You would say, 1816."

Yashim turned the pages. Each sura was brilliantly illuminated, according to a tradition that went back to the twelfth century, with stylized foliage crammed with animals and birds. There was no calligrapher's signature; Yashim did not expect one.

The work itself was a signature; it bore the stamp of the man who had single-handedly worked to make this beautiful book. It must have taken months, if not years. The calligrapher was Metin Yamaluk.

The endpapers were very beautiful and carefully produced. Yashim paused over them, frowning. They showed a square, and between the corners and the midway point on each line of the square ran an endless knot, forming an eight-pointed star.

Palewski pointed to the diagram. "Seen that one before. It's on the floor of the contessa's salon, I think."

"Is it?" Yashim murmured. He had seen it, too, weeks before in Yamaluk's studio in Üsküdar.

The Sand-Reckoner's diagram.

Yamaluk's Koran had been commissioned by Count d'Aspi. And Yamaluk himself had met the new sultan, to present him with an address.

"Printing!" Father Aristo sighed and gestured to the shelves. "I wonder, gentlemen, where Dante would have put the printers? Benefactors— or criminals?" He shook his head. "I hardly know."

"I knew the man who made this Koran," Yashim said.

They stood together in the candlelight, gazing down at the illuminated pages.

"Thank you, Father Aristo," Yashim said. "You've shown me exactly what I needed to see."

The old man nodded and rubbed his glasses with a fold of his soutane. They left in the dark, with the old monk's blessing.

The gondola was waiting at the gate. Palewski and Yashim climbed into the little cabin, where Yashim bent forward with a look of triumph.

"I'd like to meet your friend, the Contessa d'Aspi d'Istria," he said.

Palewski shrugged. "Maybe." He paused. "I tried to see her, too, twice. Three times. She wasn't receiving visitors. Not after Barbieri was killed."

Yashim was silent for a while. The water gurgled softly against the hull of the gondola.

"I think I know where we might find the painting, Palewski," Yashim said. "If we're not too late."

81

YASHIM sliced three onions, fine; they were red and crisp and he spread the rings onto a large white plate.

He took a big lamb's liver and prepared it carefully, removing the arteries and the tough membrane. He sliced it into strips and tossed it in the flour and *kirmizi biber*.

In the frying pan he sautéed garlic and cumin seeds. The oil was hot; before the garlic could catch he dropped in the sliced liver and turned it quickly with a wooden spoon. The meat tightened and browned; he spooned the slices out and laid them on the onion rings. He chopped some dill and parsley and sprinkled them over the dish, and then, hungry, he took a piece of liver with an onion ring and popped them into his mouth.

Venetians would have cooked the onion until it was very soft. Delicious, in its way, and sweet, but lacking the boldness of the Ottoman original, Yashim thought, as the textures and flavors burst in his mouth. His *arnavut cigeri* looked better, too.

A shame that he had found no yogurt. He sliced a lemon and laid the wedges around the plate.

He drained the chickpeas. He would cook them with onion, rice, and the remainder of the signora's delicious stock.

He made a marinade with the nigella seeds he had found at the *épicier*. They had been labeled black cumin, but Yashim knew better. He mixed them with lemon juice, crushed garlic, salt, pepper, and oregano. Into a bowl, weeping, he grated two onions. He mixed the pulp with a spoonful of salt.

He cleaned his knife and used it to slice three swordfish steaks into chunks, which he turned into the marinade. He took out a stack of vine leaves he had stripped, without much guilt, from a tendril blown over a high garden wall on his way home that morning. He washed them, softened them in the chickpea water in bunches of two or three, and dropped them into a bowl of cold water.

He squeezed the onion pulp between his hands and trickled the juice over the fish.

The signora used a long flat knife with a rounded end to smooth her polenta. Wondering if it were sacrilege he decided to use it as a skewer for the fish.

When he had wrapped each piece of fish in its vine-leaf coat, he found that the polenta knife was too blunt-ended to get through the leaves. Patiently he stuck each packet with Malakian's little knife, widened the hole, and slipped it onto the broad blade.

He drizzled what was left of the marinade over the fish and set the skewer over the embers of the fire.

He prepared the rice. When it was covered with a cloth, and steaming gently, he went outside to the well and carefully washed his hands, his face, his ears, and nose.

"When you are ready, we can eat," he announced.

82

COMMISSARIO Brunelli liked to think he'd seen everything in Venice, but when Maria brought him into her mother's kitchen he changed his mind.

"My name, signora, is Brunelli. Vittorio Brunelli." He took a deep sniff, and his chest rose. "I hope I am not disturbing you."

The candlelight, at first, made the hairs prickle at the nape of his neck. He felt it all—the light, the smells, the shadows on the faces—long before he realized what it was.

It was a feast among the poor.

He saw the turban. He saw Palewski's lean, pale face. He saw Maria, doubtful, with her jet-black hair. He saw children, shaved headed, staring at him with their big eyes, and their father, smiling, and the shadows and the black beams and the embers of the dying fire.

He advanced, unsteadily, into the room.

"Buon appetito," he said with a bow, and stumbled into a pallet on which he was scarcely surprised to see the figure of the dying Christ.

"Please, Signor Brunelli," the signora said magisterially. "Join us."

Brunelli found himself squashed onto the end of a bench with a small child on one side and Yashim on the other, and knife, fork, plate, and red wine in front of him.

The only difference between this and other feasts he could imagine was that no one seemed actually to be eating.

His nostrils twitched, and his gaze returned to the table. It was covered with a clean cloth, and on it stood several plates. He saw a mound of rice, a dish of something with raw onion, a heap of curious green packages about the size of eggs, and an earthenware dish containing something in a white sauce.

Around the table he noticed a lot of very suspicious faces.

The Brunelli name was not inscribed in the Golden Book, which had listed the aristocratic families entitled to enjoy the burdens and the rewards of government. But the blood of Venice flowed in Brunelli's veins nonetheless, the blood of men who had eaten raw horsemeat with the riders of the Crimea, nibbled thousand-year-old eggs with the Great Khan in Cathay and spice-laden stews with the Bedouin of the Persian gulf— not to mention boiled cabbage in the halls of the Polish kings.

Brunelli stretched out his hands, inspired, and delivered a grace. It was a grace he had heard said in the Ghetto, many times.

"Blessed are you, our God, Lord of the Universe, who brings forth bread from the earth."

Palewski smiled and helped the signora to the pilaff.

Brunelli picked up the vine leaves and offered them to his neighbor. Yashim took one, Brunelli another. They passed the dish along. A small child helped himself to some pilaff. Maria's father took a spoonful of liver and onions, while Maria picked up a vine-leaf parcel and bit into it. She gave a little cry of appreciation.

"It's fish! Mamma, try one!"

In a matter of moments everyone was eating and talking all at once.

Brunelli leaned across the table.

"Signor Brett," he began.

Signor Brett cut him off.

"I haven't been straight with you, Commissario, I'm afraid. Not from the start. For which I'm sorry. This is Yashim."

"Good," the big man said. "I don't like straight." He took a sip of wine. "What are you both doing, exactly?"

Palewski looked over at Yashim. "What *are* we doing, anyway?"

"Looking for justice," Yashim replied. "Justice, and a Bellini."

Brunelli raised a single eyebrow.

"Both valuable, signore. Both rare."

And Yashim smiled and told him everything they knew.

83

MUCH later, when Brunelli had gone home and the Contarini family had gone to bed, still drowsily exclaiming their surprise: Raw onion! Fish in a coat! Lasagna without pasta!—Yashim and Palewski drew closer to the fire.

"Tell me more about the contessa," Yashim suggested.

Palewski shrugged. "I haven't much to tell. Except that she's very beautiful, she fights foil, and some ancestor of hers was with Morosini in the Peloponnese. She's a surprise, Yashim. Something dangerous about her, maybe. She won't marry either, I don't know why."

He repeated the details of the family tragedy that the old lady at the Ca' d'Istria had given him.

"Her father was the last Venetian bailo in Istanbul. Hence the Koran. And she was born there, as it happens."

Yashim raised an eyebrow. "And she won't see you, you say?"

Palewski shook his head. "I'm not even sure she's there. The last time I tried no one even came to the door."

Yashim prodded the embers with a stick.

"I've got an idea," he said slowly. "Venice is a theater, you say. Perhaps the time has come to take a more theatrical approach."

"What do you mean?"

"Once, the doge married the sea."

"Napoleon burned the *bucintoro*," Palewski pointed out.

"Quite so. I wasn't imagining a return of the doge. But I've been talking to Signor Contarini. The bargee."

Palewski looked surprised. "What does Signor Contarini have to do with it?"

"Everything. Venice has been starved of entertainment for far too long. What I imagine," said Yashim, sketching his plan in the smoke from the signora's fire, "is a visit. A visit," he added, yawning, "from a lost world."

Palewski rubbed his hands across his face and stretched his feet to the fire. "I don't know what you're talking about."

"Don't worry. You'll see."

84

YASHIM was gone again the next morning when Palewski and Maria sat down to breakfast. Maria, too, had errands to perform, so Palewski spent the morning in the yard with the unemployed men, trying to penetrate their dialect and taking the occasional whiff of a very cheap cigar. An old man without teeth had been at the battle of Borodino. They shared their disappointments and capped each other's reminiscences for the entertainment of the younger men, until the signora called him in for lunch.

Yashim returned a few minutes later and sat down to a thick lentil soup with evident enjoyment.

After lunch, Yashim spoke quietly to Maria and her mother; Palewski could not quite hear what they said, but the old lady looked thoroughly dubious. Finally she burst out laughing and flipped her apron over her head to hide her bad teeth. Palewski watched Yashim give the signora some money.

Yashim came out into the yard. Palewski threw him an inquiring look.

"The signora," Yashim explained, "has agreed to spend the afternoon baking. Along with a dozen of her friends."

"Buns?"

"Buns are traditional in Istanbul. I imagine they'll be equally appreciated in Venice."

"Yashim, I'm completely confused."

"In which case," Yashim replied, smiling, "my plan is more likely to succeed."

85

IT was a Canaletto morning in Venice. The sun shone, the sky was blue, and a wind that could raise a flag was blowing in from the lagoon as a barge carrying an Austrian military band began its slow ascent of the Grand Canal. At its stern the imperial white and gold of the Habsburg empire; at its prow a small green ensign with a silver crescent moon.

A flotilla of gondolas moved in its wake, three abreast. Beneath the cover of their black felze they were almost all empty. They represented absent dignitaries of the Habsburg empire.

The Venetians were out in force. Since dawn they had been spreading from the slums of Dorsoduro, moving through the alleyways on foot, revealing the news to bakers stoking their ovens, vegetable sellers setting up their displays, lamplighters on their morning rounds. Mothers coming in for bread decided to keep their children out of school; men on their way to work stopped and discussed the business with their friends at the café door.

From Dorsoduro the news washed over San Polo and Santa Croce; by morning it had crossed the Rialto bridge into San Marco and Castello. Venice buzzed with anticipation and curiosity. At ten o'clock the balconies were full. Shutters unopened for twenty years were creaking back, and for a nominal fee people were allowed into mothballed palazzis and untenanted apartments. Rugs and hangings dangled from windows.

Ladies whose last procession on the Grand Canal had been Josephine's, in 1799, smiled at the memories it evoked. Young men drawn to the windows by the possibility of sighting, all at once, the hidden beauties of the Grand Canal, twirled their whiskers and leaned out, while girls of barely marriageable age raced to the balconies to be seen.

Behind the flotilla of gondolas came a barge, low in the water and heaped with flowers whose colors, massed in florets of red and gold, recalled the colors of the Venetian flag. A cheer went up from the crowd jostling for position on the first pontoon.

Behind it, the Ottoman barge hove into view, tricked out with hoops of greenery. Between the hoops acrobats and fire-eaters juggled with sugar buns, scorched them, then tossed them to the delighted crowds.

In an open gondola of imperial carmine, gracefully acknowledging the hoots and clamor of the crowds, followed the Ottoman pasha himself, in a swathe of red silk and under an enormous and dazzling turban.

The crowd threw their hats in the air and roared.

The procession carried on up the canal. Shortly before eleven it passed beneath the Rialto bridge, where a crowd of onlookers and market vendors laughed and blew kisses as the Venetian colors passed below.

For forty years Venetians had been fed a diet of poverty and degradation. Sullen to the last, they had watched the arrival of French troops, or Austrian generals, while the spirit of Carnevale withered. But this cavalcade was ballooning into a full-blown regatta. A cheerful retinue of skiffs and hired gondolas, passenger wherries, and rowboats milled around the pasha's slender gondola; fishermen were selling space in their heavy barche; children were running up the alleys near the canal, popping out at each pontoon. The people afloat waved to the people on land.

In years to come, old pickpockets and cutpurses would shake their heads when they recalled that morning.

The cavalcade came to a stop when it reached the Ca' d'Aspi. Only the men who rowed the leading barge, which carried the military band, pressed on, and soon the brassy strains of oom-pah-pah faded away.

Nobody moved. The cheering stopped. It was said that you could hear the water slap against the foundations of the palazzo.

On the piano nobile one solitary window was open, where the Contessa d'Aspi d'Istria stood leaning on her hands, pale and impassive. Now and then the breeze caught a strand of her fair hair and played with it, lifting it into the air, brushing it across her face, but she made no move to push it back.

Some of the gondoliers, looking up, seemed transfixed. They would have a song before the month was out, about the love of a woman for an infidel, and her years of torment, and how in the end he had come to woo her in spite of the Austrians and their cannons.

The crimson gondola slipped from the center of the procession and with a sweep of his oar the gondolier brought the boat up against the landing stage.

The pasha stood up, carrying a small box wrapped in gold paper.

The unnatural silence broke at once. Wild conjectures circulated among the crowd, which were embroidered and improved as the day wore on. Some were to say that the pasha had brought her a sultan's diadem; others that it was a gossamer handkerchief that the sultan bestowed, each night, upon the concubine destined to share his bed. It was said that the Aspis, in their days of power, had rendered the sultan a service so great he had found no way of repaying it until now, when the Aspis groaned like the rest beneath the heel of Austria. Some said it was money. Some said it was jewels. Some said it was a holy relic that the Venetians had missed when they sacked Constantinople in 1204.

A wag said it was a box of Turkish delight.

What no one could possibly have guessed was the truth, which Yashim confessed to the contessa when Antonio had shown him upstairs.

She turned reluctantly from the window.

Yashim bowed. "I must apologize, signora, for the intrusion. The box is empty."

She tucked back a strand of her hair.

"How disappointing," she said quietly. She dismissed Antonio with a wave of her hand.

When he had gone she said, "I suppose that you have come to kill me, pasha efendi, the way you killed the others."

"No, Contessa. I hope I have come to save you."

She gave a small smile. "No one can save me. It is written—surely, as an Ottoman, you know that."

She put a hand under her hair and swept it up, exposing her slender neck.

Yashim held up his empty hands.

"No bowstring, Contessa. You sent to Istanbul—and I am here."

She glanced at him, sideways, her hand slipping slowly from her neck so that her hair fell in golden sheaves.

Yashim knew more than enough about pretty girls. The sultan's harem, where he could come and go at will, was full of girls whose charms were those of any young animal. They had clear eyes, and smooth skin, and the form and figure of nymphs released into the real world, supple and glowing. Their feelings raced across their lovely faces, registering each moment of happiness or jealousy or fear with a perfectly unguarded openness. Pretty girls: you smiled to see them, like puppies chasing their own tails.

But the contessa was a woman.

"I sent to Istanbul?" She pushed off from the windowsill and crossed the room. "You seem very sure, my pasha—I don't know your name, I'm afraid."

"I am Yashim," he replied with a short bow. "I serve the sultan."

It was rather less than the truth, but it was not quite a lie.

"You sent Sultan Abdülmecid a message—you made an offer. The Bellini portrait of his ancestor."

For a moment she checked herself. "Is that what you told them? Boschini. Barbieri. And now they're dead."

And then a foil was in her hand.

"For myself, I may determine the time and the place," she said, raising the point of the foil.

There was no button on the tip.

"*Com'era, dov'era,*" she murmured. "*In guardia.*"

He saw her lift her knee, and then she was on him in a blur, a whirl of stamping feet and lifted shoulders—and a blade sparked by his ear as Yashim launched himself to the ground.

He rolled, twice, and the point of the blade skittered across the marble at his feet.

He sprang up, twisting and backing. The contessa had recovered her position: she stood with her left hand free, feet apart, breathing through parted lips. For a second he thought that the blade had snapped from the hilt, before he saw the point swing out only inches from his eyes.

As Carla lunged, Yashim whipped his head sideways and, at the same second, he took a step forward, against his instinct to pull back. They were almost beside each other, flank to flank. Yashim cracked his right arm down and felt his sleeve brush hers as she let her arm drop. She came out of it with a sweep of the foil, away from him, using the weight of the sword to bring her around.

She had her elbow back, drawing the tip of her foil away. Yashim saw it retreating through the air, like a mosquito, and flung himself into a left-hand roll.

The contessa sprang through his wake, making a diagonal pass that would deliver her at his right.

For a moment, as he raised his head, Yashim was disoriented.

Two things ran through his mind.

One was a remark about fencing he had read once in a French novel. "The art of fencing consists in two things, and two things only: to give, and not to receive."

The other was: ignore the tip and watch the feet.

The feet! Slamming both hands onto the floor, Yashim flung out one foot across the marble in an arc, hooking the contessa's feet and sweeping them from under her.

She rolled backward and sprang to her feet. Yashim was standing again. They were about six feet apart.

She rubbed her hand across her hip.

Her blue eyes glittered.

Blue eyes: Yashim raised a fist and uncoiled two fingers, the old sign to ward off the evil eye.

The contessa understood it. She began to smile.

Her smile broke into a snarl and she clapped her feet to the ground and sprang.

Yashim saw the point of her sword flying through the air.

The point!

He parried, chopping down as the blade soared toward his chest.

She must have been surprised as the tip moved: he saw her eyes travel to the point. But in a moment she was on him again, flicking the point almost effortlessly upward, toward his abdomen. He sliced down, and as the blade struck his forearm he stepped forward and sideways and felt her hair slip through the fingers of his left hand.

He almost had her.

She curvetted around again, slipping her head to one side, drawing back.

His hand was empty. The other was bleeding.

There was no edge on a foil's blade, of course: only the point could kill. But the contessa's foil moved fast enough to draw blood.

"You are confused about the rules, pasha efendi," Carla said. She had adopted her guard again.

Yashim was watching her feet.

"I follow the pattern," he said shortly. As he spoke he took a step toward her, hand spread, and then, as she turned the nails of her sword hand uppermost, he stepped back again, lightly and to one side.

She eased herself around to face him again, half turning her hand: now her nails were down.

He wondered if she would allow him to make the same maneuver twice.

He hoped so, for behind her, now slightly to her right, was the collection of weapons he had made Palewski describe, in minute detail, as they sat together in the smoke of la signora's kitchen.

And beneath him, laid out in colored marble on the floor, was the pattern he already knew.

They had been following it from the beginning. Breaking ground and giving ground, back and forth—and always to the side. An endless knot, inexorably rotating.

He needed two more points. Two more would bring him around, but the next was the hardest. The pattern was not completely regular. The next point of the pattern brought you closer in, unguarded on either side.

He raised his hand to his turban, in perplexity.

Carla didn't wait for him to finish the move.

There is an attack in fencing called the flèche: properly performed, it is the killer stroke, if any stroke may be so called. The feet come together; the body is launched; blade and body are concentrated behind the point with enormous speed and, regardless of the attacker's build, also huge strength.

Carla's flèche was properly executed. Quite suddenly she had become the arc, and the point of her foil was traveling through the air precisely as the move suggests. She was an arrow.

And Yashim, like the fatalist he never was, had time only to bow his head.

86

TWENTY years had passed since Yashim first entered the palace school. He had been a young man already, four or five years older than his companions, those inexperienced, beardless youths whose pranks and chatter had tormented him in those first few months of indifference and despair. He was admitted as a favor: his father could think of no other way to heal the terrible damage that his enemies had wreaked upon his son. Perhaps, too, he was sent away because he so forcibly reminded the old governor of his wife, Yashim's mother, the beautiful Elena.

Elena had been in the cave. She was dishonored, and then she was killed. His father's enemies had reserved for Yashim, however, a yet more exquisite torture. The act itself lasted only seconds; it involved only pain. But the bitterness of that moment would mock him all his life.

Sportively gelded by his father's enemies, Yashim had brought his pain and his despair to the palace school in Istanbul, and they had meted out unremitting discipline, constant training of body and mind. Yashim entered a world ruled by the rod, a world of hard wooden beds, floggings, cold baths, and weekly expulsions. The old eunuch who governed them was a martinet, capricious, exacting, manipulative, mildly predatory. To the least talented he was unfailingly kind, before he kicked them out. To those who showed true promise he was a scourge. Yashim did everything well, but it was three years before they discovered what he did better than anyone. Before he made himself indispensable.

At first he had resisted the regimen, scarcely capable of believing in the possibility of redemption, and doubting that there was anything left in him to redeem, as though he had already died. His spirit was indeed dead. He was surly and slow. He didn't sneer at the old teacher, or at the acres of cold calligraphy they were forced to ingest, or the games of wrestling and *gerit*. He was a cultivated young man, stronger, faster, more experienced than the others. He simply didn't care.

The old eunuch started waking him early, an hour before the other boys, in the dead watch of the night. He woke him with a crack of his silver-tipped rod across the legs. "You have less time than the others. We must make more." Sometimes he made him run. Sometimes he would recite the Koran. At night, when the other boys talked in whispers, Yashim fell asleep exhausted.

Yet slowly, without knowing why, he had found himself waking up. He learned to channel his agony of mind into the discipline imposed upon him by the old *lala* and stopped being afraid of doing well. Train the body and cultivate the mind, and the heart will follow: that was the old Ottoman precept.

Out of the myriad accomplishments he had been expected to attain, the recitals, the music and the languages, the rhetoric and algebra and deportment and logic, the horsemanship, archery, *gerit*, Yashim retained only fuzzy memories of the wrestling school.

Yet even that had perhaps been expected by the palace school. By study, after all, anyone could learn the Koran; anyone could learn to pull a bow with craft and effort. But for the men who were to direct the energies of the empire mastery of all arts was not an end, only a begin-ning. To remember a thing was nothing. What counted was the power to use it.

Yashim's knowledge of the Sand-Reckoner's diagram was scarcely available to him in thought: it was ingrained at a level of instinct.

The woven bands of an endless knot belonged to the invisible ma-chinery of his mind.

Twenty years on, in a palazzo in Venice, the instinct came alive.

87

WHEN the point of the foil, aimed at Yashim's chest—sixte, in the nec-essary jargon—touched the bulbous floret of the turban that covered his head, it released Yashim from a burden he had been carrying since early morning and allowed him, at the same time, to slide forward, holding the muslin in his hand.

With his turban skewered by the foil, Yashim sidestepped and ad-vanced, in three mildly unbalanced steps. As he moved he whirled the length of muslin around himself, as though he were striking a gong, and at his back the contessa's blade, embedded in the folds, was swept from her hands.

It struck the floor with a metallic clang and skittered, spinning, until it thudded against the wall beneath the window.

Yashim did not watch it go, as Carla did. He used the opportunity to spring and grab the pimpled leather hilt of the nearest weapon, which happened to be a Turkish scimitar.

Only then, in an effort of self-preservation, did he glance around.

To his surprise the contessa was standing hand on hip, watching him. She had made no effort to retrieve her foil.

The scimitar was firmly wired to the wall. Yashim reluctantly released his grip and dropped his hand.

The contessa smiled.

"I always seem to be meeting sabreurs," she said.

"Sabreurs?"

She gestured to the scimitar. "You conquered eastern Europe with that. The ancestor of our saber. The Hungarians adopted it, as they adopted everything else you brought to the battlefield. Hussars. Dragoons. Military bands. We fight like with like, Yashim Pasha."

"Yes," Yashim said. He stooped to retrieve a length of turban. He wound it around his bleeding hand and tore it with his teeth. "Yes, of course."

"And the saber won the battle of Waterloo," she added. "It's not in fashion now."

He wound the remainder around his head.

When he felt properly dressed he said, "I am not a pasha."

She stepped forward and rang a bell. "Coffee, Antonio." To Yashim she said, "The people of Venice seem to think you are a pasha. You gave them something they have missed for many years. In my eyes you are a pasha, even with your empty box."

Yashim thought he detected a glint of amusement—a cruel amusement—in those beautiful blue eyes. The pasha—with his empty box! Yashim, the eunuch.

"Contessa—I—" He found himself stumbling. "The Armenians' Koran. I recognized the hand."

She put her finger to her lower lip and stood there, thinking.

"You knew the pattern," she said.

"I was trained to it," Yashim replied. "And so, as it seems, were you."

88

"I'M sorry about your hand."

"I doubt it."

She laughed. "You were better than me, Yashim Pasha. I thought—I hoped I would learn something about you. Less than I imagined." She paused, lowering her lids. "You never attacked. Perhaps I should have let you take that saber."

"It was stuck to the wall," Yashim pointed out.

"But that's not it," she went on, in a fascinated voice. "You hid yourself. How did you do that?"

Yashim shrugged. "I was lucky."

"Don't condescend to me."

Yashim paused. "Perhaps I used you."

"Used me? How?"

"I'm afraid you were almost too good, Contessa. I'm no expert on foil, or fencing, but I saw how you moved your feet. The way you advanced to attack. It looked faultless. Only you didn't concentrate on your opponent."

"I hope you don't think I underestimated you."

Yashim shook his head. "That's not it. It's rather that you didn't estimate me at all. Afterward, you think I hid. I'd say—you didn't really look."

Yashim could see her blush. She bit her lip.

"You're saying that I was showing off?"

"You're conscious of your power," he said evenly. "And you are beautiful, of course."

"And beauty makes me weak."

"No. It's thinking about it that unbalanced you."

"Unbalanced me! Anything else I should know, maestro?"

He hesitated. There was, in fact, something else he had discerned about her movements: but then, he had never fought a woman before.

"Why *don't* you kill me, Yashim Pasha?"

She said it so suddenly that Yashim had no time to react.

"How can you be so sure of me?" he said.

"Ah! So sure?" She laughed again, but without merriment. "Thank you, Antonio. That is all."

She poured the coffee into two tiny luster cups. Her hand barely shook.

She picked up Yashim's cup and brought it to him, with a little bow. They were very close.

"Eletro," she said. "A man called Popi Eletro."

She sauntered back to the tray and picked up her own cup.

"Then I knew," she added, taking a sip. "Boschini was drowned. Count Barbieri was killed, leaving my house. But they were my people."

"Your people?" Yashim was confused.

"Like pashas, Yashim." She smiled. "But Eletro was one of—the *reaya*."

Sheep: the *reaya*, nonbelievers whom the sultan was bound to rule. A common man.

"And then, of course, I knew," she said. "The Fondaco dei Turchi. You can see it from this window, Yashim Pasha. Come."

A ragged cheer went up outside as she flung back the window and leaned out. The contessa raised a slender hand.

"You see that ruin? In centuries past, Yashim Pasha, the fondaco was your caravanserai in Venice, the *han* of Ottoman trade. Secure and secluded—but magnificent, of course. That's where we held the party."

Yashim looked out. The barges had gone; a few gondolas bobbed on the gentle waters of the Grand Canal. Still the people were there, crowding the pontoon almost opposite the Palazzo d'Aspi.

"Cement the union!" a gondolier suggested, his voice lost in the laughter of his friends.

Yashim withdrew his head.

"I know the fondaco," he said. "What's left of it. Someone's been using the hammam as a prison. A private prison."

She shrugged. "It wouldn't surprise me."

"The party, Contessa?"

For the first time she looked wary.

"Eletro owned the building. That's why he was there."

"Eletro?" Yashim sounded incredulous.

She shrugged lightly. "The fondaco is a ruin. And Venice is cheap."

Yashim said nothing, studying her face.

She returned his gaze. "Whatever you see, Yashim Pasha, it is not fear."

"No," he admitted.

"Boschini and Barbieri were the other players. And when Eletro was murdered, then I knew."

"But why have a party in that ruin?"

She shrugged. *"Com'era, dov'era."*

As it was, where it was. Yashim had heard that phrase before.

"I—we—wanted to pretend, for a moment, that nothing had really changed."

"We?"

"The duke and I."

"The duke?"

"The Duke of Naxos. Our guest, in Venice."

Yashim's head was spinning. "But the Duke of Naxos—" he began.

"Died three hundred years ago, yes. Joseph Nasi, a Jewish financier. Sultan Selim the Sot made him Duke of Naxos, for his assistance in the seizure of Cyprus."

"So this duke—your guest—was an impostor? And you knew it?"

She gazed at him appraisingly. She held out her hands. "Perhaps you really have come to save me," she said.

89

An old woman complained to the police that a beggar had taken up residence on her steps and wouldn't move.

He was sitting on the steps with his head on his knees. By the time Scorlotti reached him he was locked into place; only his arms had risen weirdly, like the arms of a devotee, as the rigor set in.

There wasn't a mark on him except for a dull purple flush on the back of his neck and a faint bruise over his Adam's apple. His papers, and a small amount of change, were still in his pockets.

The old woman slammed the door and turned the lock; Scorlotti heard the bolts shoot home.

He took the corpse to the mortuary in a gondola.

90

"Naxos belonged to the Venetians, until the reign of Süleyman," Yashim said slowly. "Only the Venetians appointed a Duke of Naxos, until it fell to the Ottomans. After that, there was only one. Joseph Nasi. But when Nasi died, the title would have, I don't know, lapsed."

"I suppose so." She seemed amused. "Or else—it was added to

the many titles already possessed by the man who bestowed it on Nasi."

"Sultan Selim?"

"Sultan," she intoned, closing her eyes, "padishah, lord of the two seas and the two continents, ruler of Mingrelia and Hungary, in the Crimea, Khan, and Voivode in the Danubian principalities. He was the Duke of Naxos."

"So now—" Yashim was struggling to comprehend. "The Duke of Naxos . . . ?"

She gave an equivocal shrug. "Would be the sultan. Or his son, perhaps."

"I don't believe it," Yashim said.

"Are you playing with me, Yashim Pasha?"

But Yashim could only stare.

"Fourteen times since the conquest of Istanbul, the Aspi family has provided Venice with a bailo in the city," Carla continued. "Istanbul has been our second home. One of my ancestors, Alvise d'Aspi, was the richest merchant prince in Pera—Süleyman the Magnificent went to visit him, Yashim Pasha. They were friends. My father, also Alvise, was the last bailo of the Republic. He knew Selim III well; they played music together. Can you believe that? Or have times so far changed that men do not remember?"

"I believe it," Yashim said. His mouth was dry.

She gestured to the arms on the wall behind him. "The Aspis have not been afraid to fight, either. We were not all merchants and ambassadors, Yashim Pasha. We supplied the Republic with admirals and generals, and when Venice was pressed too hard, we have helped make wars to win peace."

She turned to face him. "I am the last of the Aspis. That is—my pride, if you will. But you must believe me when I tell you that I knew the Duke of Naxos. I knew him by instinct, as if he were my own son."

Yashim's eyes traveled over the swags of weaponry, the golden cornices, the fantastical trompe l'oeil—and saw nothing.

Abdülmecid! The Duke of Naxos, Crown Prince of the throne of Osman?

The shy, retiring boy—that pale youth who had been afraid to watch his own father die—had come to Venice, in disguise!

It was impossible. No one of the Ottoman line had ever stepped beyond the borders of the empire—unless to conquer. The idea was mad! And yet . . . and yet.

Sultans disguised themselves. It had happened: incognito, they had moved through the markets and the mosques, gauging what the people said.

Incognito! In Venice at Carnevale everyone was incognito—why, incognito was a Venetian word!

And Abdülmecid enjoyed a freedom his father had never known, a freedom that would disappear on his elevation to the throne. As sultan, he would be watched every minute of the day.

Abdülmecid spoke French.

"The duke. Did he win—or lose?"

"At cards?" She looked surprised. "He played well."

"He won? Money?" Yashim had never gambled.

"I said he played well, Yashim Pasha. But Barbieri is very good—and the stakes were high."

"The party, Contessa, was arranged by you?"

"You could say I inspired it. The duke had a cicerone—I suggested it to him. He made the arrangements with Eletro."

"But why did Eletro come? He wasn't an aristocrat, as you said. He was a sort of criminal."

"He plays cards. And it was Carnevale. A period of misrule. It used to be glamorous—and very long. A long season of parties, gambling, drinking. Everyone goes masked—that's part of the fun, I suppose."

"You don't think so."

Carla shrugged. "It's tradition. As for Eletro, he merely wears a mask." She paused, remembering. "We took a gondola to the water gate. He was there already—Eletro, I mean—like a host, really. It was night, of course, and you couldn't see the state of the place beyond the candlelight. Hundreds of tiny candles, in glass jars. And the doors—they were flung back—opened onto a great stone staircase, with the candles flickering on every step. Eletro led us up—Barbieri recognized him, I think, or guessed—with a great candelabra in his hand. And it was exciting because I have been in every palazzo in Venice, I suppose, at one time or another. But I'd never been there before. So it was Venice, but not quite like Venice.

"Halfway up the stairs we all stopped. The fondaco, you know, was a Byzantine palace. Once, even the Emperor of Byzantium stayed there—and he brought six hundred and fifty priests of his Orthodox faith, too. So we stopped to look down into the courtyard. It was lit, with flambeaux. And anyway, the doors above were shut—at least, there was a great curtain across the doorway. There was a lot of incense in the air—I suppose the place didn't smell very good, after all those years of collapse—and Eletro in a grotesque mask, holding the candles in one hand over his head, and putting his fingers to his lips. So we stopped and listened.

"You couldn't hear anything at first—just the people on the stairs, and I had the duke on my arm and he—he gave it a squeeze. Then some of us heard a very faint, eerie sound—it was the scrape of a violin but very quiet—but as we listened it got gradually louder, and then other instruments fell in, and all of a sudden Eletro whisked back the curtain and there we were! The piano nobile—it's a huge room—lit by a great candelabra in the middle, and all the walls hung with muslin, and the orchestra playing in the gloom somewhere—I think from overhead."

"How many of you?"

"About a dozen, if I remember. We sat at table, and there was champagne and supper. And afterward we played cards."

"At other tables?"

"Little card tables. All set up. That's when—that's when the four men got together."

"You didn't play?"

"Not that night. The stakes were too high, Yashim Pasha. I helped the duke, a little. He was very young."

"Yes," Yashim said, thoughtfully. "Yes. I suppose he was." He paused. "And the cicerone?"

"Oh, he moved about, seeing that everything was all right."

"Who was the cicerone, Contessa?"

"One of the Barnabotti. A professional. His name is Ruggerio."

91

VOSPER caught up with the pasha's servant at the entrance to Palewski's apartment.

"Begging your pardon, signore, but the stadtmeister wants to know when it would be convenient to hold an audience with your master."

"An audience?" Yashim cocked his head. "I don't think an audience is really appropriate, Sergeant. The pasha is making a private visit."

Vosper's face lengthened. "A private visit, signore? It's—it's irregular, I should tell you. I think the stadtmeister is expecting some sort of, some kind of, ah, visit."

"I will mention it to the pasha, signore."

"You wouldn't care to come to the Procuratie yourself and explain what you've told me to the stadtmeister?"

"I'm afraid not, Sergeant. I am not at liberty to make calls. But as I told you, I will inform my master—as you may yours. Good day."

With Vosper gone, Yashim packed a small bag with Palewski's clothes and made his way back to the Dorsoduro.

"Our friend sat up and ate a bowl of soup," Paleswki said. "Like a wolf."

"Has he said anything?"

Palewski and Maria exchanged glances. "He makes—noises. I don't think it's talking," Maria said.

They found the man sitting up with a blanket wrapped around his knees. He made no effort to turn his head when they came in, but sat still and silent, staring at the fire.

Yashim came and squatted down beside him.

"It's good you've eaten," he said. "My name's Yashim."

The man did not react. Yashim took his hand and guided it to his chest. "I am Yashim," he repeated. He patted the man's hand against his chest. "Yashim. Do you understand?"

He glanced up at Palewski, who pulled a face and shrugged.

Very slowly the man's head moved around, although his eyes remained fixed for longer on the fire. Finally he looked at Yashim.

But when he opened his mouth to speak, only a sound came out—a sort of moan, from his throat. His lips hardly moved.

Yashim blinked. He smiled. He leaned toward the fire and pulled out a burning twig. With the charred end he wrote his name on the hearth. YASHIM.

He pointed to the name, and to himself.

The man hardly looked at the name. He stared for a while at the twig in Yashim's hand, then looked into his face.

Slowly, almost fearfully, he put out his hand and took the twig, glancing between it and Yashim.

His head turned toward the hearth. He leaned forward, his tongue protruding between his compressed lips.

Palewski gave a low whistle. "It's you, Yash. He's drawing a portrait of you."

Yashim knelt up and cocked his head. The man sank back on his hams and almost shyly handed him the twig again.

On the hearthstone, in a few rough strokes of charcoal, was Yashim himself, turban and mustache and—most extraordinarily—the very look of him, right down to his expression of concern.

"You're the painter!" Yashim exclaimed involuntarily. "The Canaletto painter."

The man's eyes clouded over.

Yashim smiled and shook his head. "It doesn't matter," he said and patted the man on his scrawny arm.

He stood up slowly and led Palewski to the door.

"What do you make of it?"

"Pff. I've never seen anything like it. He must have forged the Canalettos."

"Yes. Did you see how he concentrated, too? Like a child."

"That's not a child's drawing," Palewski pointed out.

"No. I think we should give him some better materials. Paper. Charcoal. Maria?"

Maria was gone for more than an hour, but when she returned the man took the paper and charcoal with whimpers of pleasure. He laid the paper on the floor and began immediately to draw, filling each sheet with sketches of the room, the window, the people, with the same lively concentration he had shown when he sketched Yashim on the hearthstone.

He drew for over an hour, but more and more slowly. And then he rolled back into his bed and went to sleep.

Yashim studied his drawings, awestruck.

"At home," he said at last, feeling the hairs prickling on the back of his neck, "we would say this man is touched by God."

"You think he can't speak—or won't?"

"I suspect that speaking is not his way. Perhaps he sees and understands things differently from us."

"What are we going to do with him?"

"Feed him. Give him strength. And we will wait and see."

"Where are you going?"

"Back to the Palazzo d'Aspi. It's not every day the contessa receives a pasha, and she's expecting me to stay. I think I will."

"I see." Palewski sounded cool. "Much as I enjoy a hearty lentil soup, Yashim, I'm beginning to chafe under the social arrangements. Can't I go back to my own apartment yet?"

He looked so cross that Yashim laughed. "I thought you got to sleep with the daughter of the house?"

"Yashim!" Palewski looked shocked. "Anyway, Maria sleeps with half her family as it is."

"I'm sorry, it won't be for long." Yashim looked serious. "Tell me, if someone loses at cards, and owes money, what does he do?"

"Shoots himself, if he's a gentleman," Palewski said. "Unless he can pay, of course."

"He can pay—but he wouldn't have the money on him. What then?"

"Then, if he's trusted enough, he'll give his creditor a note of hand."

"A note of hand? A promise to pay later, you mean?"

"Depending how often they cash up, the whole game can be notes of hand. I lose, I write you one. You stake it next time. Lots of paper, back and forth. I gave it up, years ago. Too many fellows gamble and drink at the same time. Awfully dangerous, gambling."

"Signed paper?"

"Signed, of course. Next day, when he's feeling like Marat in his bath, the unlucky gambler gets presented with all his notes for immediate payment."

"I suppose, in some cases, the signature might be worth more than the note."

"Threaten to show it to the wife, sort of thing? Happens. Depends on the company you chose."

"Or on who you are," Yashim murmured.

"You're being mysterious, Yashim."

Yashim nodded slowly. "It *is* still a mystery, my friend."

92

THE contessa received Yashim in the salon where, only that morning, she had tried to kill him. Yashim wasn't sure when she had looked more beautiful: now, in the shadowy salon, or before, with murder in her eyes. Her dress was beaded with seed pearls that shimmered mysteriously as she moved, and her hair was pinned up, revealing her slender neck.

Candles were lit on a table laid for two.

"I have thought about you all day," she said simply. "Wondering what you know."

Yashim bowed his head. "I know too little, Contessa."

"So." Her eyes sparkled. "What do you know of the pattern—our pattern?"

Yashim frowned. "I've been wondering about that myself. Today, I would have said that it is a system—the key, if you like—to a discipline of combat. Both of us used it."

"And is that all?"

"It might be—except that I have seen it elsewhere, without really seeing it at all. Yamaluk the calligrapher used it, on the binding of the Koran your people gave to the Armenian monastery. His daughter told me that it was a symbol of the infinite richness of God's creation."

"Very good. That's one meaning—the essential one, I suppose." Carla traced the line of the diagram with her foot. "Did you speak to Yamaluk efendi, in Istanbul?"

"I spoke to his daughter. Yamaluk efendi has—passed away."

"I am sorry to hear it. My father always loved his work."

"His daughter continues the tradition," Yashim said.

She looked at him again: he felt raked by those eyes.

Then she laughed quietly. "Istanbul has changed, Yashim Pasha."

He acknowledged it with a gesture. "But you, Contessa, cannot know Istanbul."

"I was born there," she retorted. "I lived there until I was three years old. Istanbul is in my blood. But Venice has changed, too." She took a breath. "This morning you mentioned Bellini."

Yashim started. "Yes."

Carla sighed. "Gentile Bellini went to Istanbul in 1479, at the sultan's invitation."

"To paint the sultan's portrait."

"The portrait was an afterthought," the contessa said, shaking her head. "The sultan commissioned it only after he'd seen what Bellini could do."

"But if Bellini wasn't sent to paint the sultan's portrait, why did he go?"

The contessa gestured to the table and took a seat.

"One of my Aspi ancestors took Bellini to Istanbul, as an unofficial ambassador. Mehmet considered himself to be a universal ruler. As the conqueror of Istanbul, he became the most powerful ruler in the Byzantine world, a world that informally included Venice." She touched her glass. "The diagram was a symbol of sovereignty that Mehmet wanted to understand. The Byzantines had woven it into their church ritual. To them it represented the union of the finite and the infinite. The worlds of God and men. For us, it also symbolized the endless round of commerce—a reminder, if you like, that everyone could share in the infinite bounty of the world. Mehmet, I suspect, saw it as a symbol of dominion: one world, one ruler, under God."

"But why Bellini? Why couldn't your ancestor have explained the diagram?"

"It's a good question. I think Gentile knew the city. He and his family had almost certainly been there under the Byzantines. The father, Jacopo, did portraits of the imperial family before the fall of Constantinople."

She raised her chin. "He wasn't political, Yashim. Not a warrior. Not a diplomat. Not a merchant, either. He simply had a gift. A near-magical ability to freeze the moving finger—time."

"Freeze it? How?"

"In paint. In pencil. He understood pattern—but he also helped to pioneer the art of portraiture. He was an adept in both worlds—the world of pattern and geometry, which is eternal, and in seeing the eternal in the things that change and are subject to time."

"I see."

"After Gentile painted Mehmet's portrait, the idea caught on—in Venice, rather than Istanbul." She lifted the glass to her lips. "But the pattern kept its meaning. A mutual inheritance from the Byzantines. An esoteric bond between our two cities."

Yashim frowned. "The sultan entered a secret compact? Through Gentile Bellini?"

Carla smiled. "Nothing so sinister, Yashim. It was simply a pattern, an interpretation, we could share. A point of contact between our two worlds."

Yashim leaned back. "And perhaps an effort to describe them, too? The links are made at various points around the square."

Carla looked very radiant in the candlelight. Her hair, pinned back, glowed against the gloom of the great dark room. Her eyes sparkled, lit by her slow smile.

"The pupil has excelled the teacher."

"But if it was essentially a symbol of peace—" Yashim hesitated.

She nodded slowly. "The pattern reconciles, Yashim. It's true. In an immutable square, those fixed and opposing points are linked and reconciled in an endless weave. *Com'era, dov'era.* East with West, Venice with Istanbul, death and life, man and woman." She gazed at him, her eyes bright. "But then came Cyprus."

Yashim remembered. It was a long time ago: in 1570, Ottoman troops had swarmed across the richest jewel in the diadem of islands that linked the Venetian empire through the eastern Mediterranean. A year later the Venetian fleet, backed by Spain, had destroyed the Ottoman navy at Lepanto.

"Cyprus—and the battle of Lepanto—changed the meaning of the symbol. It came to stand for dominion and war. After that, I suppose, both sides developed a style of combat based on the Sand-Reckoner's diagram."

Their eyes met.

"Joseph Nasi helped Sultan Selim to finance the attack on Cyprus," Yashim said. "In return, he was made Duke of Naxos."

"Go on."

"So when Abdülmecid chose the name for his disguise, he was sending some sort of signal. A hostile one."

Carla shrugged, and the shadows slid across the hollows of her shoulders. "Close. I think—not altogether hostile. Only realistic. Venice is an occupied state for now, and so our relationship with Istanbul cannot be *com'era, dov'era.*" She gave a small, secret smile. "But your new sultan has a romantic streak, too. And a certain—curiosity. That's why he came."

She touched a finger carelessly to her lips, and Yashim knew immediately what the contessa did not say.

"And the Bellini? The portrait of the Conqueror?"

Carla laughed softly.

"It was something sentimental. A link—the last link—between the Aspis and the throne of Osman."

"You didn't think—it might be something dangerous to possess?"

"It belonged to me. It was no one else's affair. Until now."

"May I see it?"

She gazed into his eyes. Yashim felt his head swim: the contessa was beautiful, but by candlelight she seemed ethereal.

"Of course," she said. "Come."

93

SHE walked ahead of him, with an aching grace, holding the candelabra in her right hand and the train of her skirt in her left.

They entered a corridor, where she paused at a door.

"This is my room," she said.

The candlelight filled the room with shadows. On one side stood a magnificent bed, with richly carved posts and hangings of figured damask. At the end of the bed was a broad, low sofa, covered in tattered silk, which Yashim guessed had come from Istanbul. The floor was covered in a soft Turkish carpet.

On the wall opposite the bed, between two full-sized portraits, hung a small curtain.

The contessa gestured to the portraits. "My parents."

Yashim's heart was thumping.

Lucia d'Istria had been a very beautiful woman. Her daughter had inherited her fair hair and even her smile, but Carla's eyes belonged to the count. They were blue, steady—and a little hard.

Yashim's own eyes flickered to the curtain.

The contessa put a hand to his shoulder. "Do you want to see it very much?"

"Yes."

"Ask me, then. Say it."

He turned his head and regarded her curiously. "I want to see the painting very much," he said.

She gave a crooked smile, reached out, and tweaked the curtain pull. "There."   '

94

YASHIM'S first feeling was one of relief, as he saw that the panel was much larger than the painting Palewski had been shown.

It stood framed in a simple band of gold, about twenty inches high and sixteen inches wide. Inside the frame was another, a painted arch that framed the portrait of the aging sultan like a window, its sill draped with heavy brown damask embroidered with pearls, florets of rubies and emeralds, and a silver threadwork crown. There were six crowns, in two columns, on either side of the frame. Mehmet was the seventh sultan.

Yashim peered up at the portrait. The arched brows, the long slender nose, and the pronounced chin were all traits he recognized: when Abdülmecid was old and sick, he too might look like this.

"Mehmet the Conqueror," he murmured.

"An English milord might pay for it," Carla said. "Or an art dealer from America, even. To them it would be—what? An old master, with a curious tale behind it. Better than the rich man's Vivarini, but scarcely equal to his Titian, or his Veronese." She tossed her head. "It deserves better."

"You want to observe the pattern, don't you? Not step out of it."

"Precisely. You are an Ottoman, Yashim. I know that. Perhaps you are not a pasha, but you are from the palace. You understand the pattern: not to explain it, maybe, but to use it. If anyone is to return the painting to Istanbul, it must be you."

"You said it was your pride to be the last of the Aspis, Contessa. What did you mean?"

"They say a good captain goes down with his ship, Yashim Pasha. So it is, with families like mine. The old families, who lived for the Republic. I took a vow—and I was not alone."

"A vow to be celibate—like a nun?"

She smiled at him. "I would say more precisely, a vow never to marry. The Austrians could take La Serenissima—but they could never take us. The blood of the Republic."

Was it true, Yashim wondered, that these old families were the blood of the Republic? They had directed its course for centuries, certainly: but where had it run? Into the sand, at last. Surely the blood of Venice flowed in the veins of the sailors who manned the ships, the oarsmen, the soldiers? Wasn't Venice as much a speechless painter, or a cheeky gondolier, as an Aspi or a Gritti? Wasn't Venice a place for the living rather than a bitter memory, frozen for all eternity?

The contessa had made a choice: but for her, perhaps, it was not too late. For Yashim, the choice was already made.

"Are you not afraid," he said gently, "that you have abandoned Venice?"

She was very still: only the candlelight caught a misting in her eyes. She shook her head. "I made a vow. And Venice will not rise again."

Their eyes met. Then:

"Yes," she answered very softly. "Yes, that is my only fear."

95

HER arms moved out to him.

"I haven't been afraid to love," the contessa said. She slipped her hands around his chest.

Yashim looked down. "I think, madame, you do not want—"

"I want, Yashim. I really want."

"I am a eunuch."

She laughed softly. "A eunuch? Why not? I'm not waiting for a man, or a woman—or a eunuch, Yashim." She smiled a secret half smile. "I'm waiting for a lover."

But later, much later, he saw the tears run down her cheeks.

"Don't stop," she breathed softly. Her face gleamed in the candlelight.

"I'm sorry," he said. "I only—"

"Shhh." She touched his head. She threw herself back in a slender arch, stabbing her fingers into the sheets, her wild golden hair flying across the pillow.

"Tell me," she said later. "Tell me how it happened."

Yashim was silent for a time. His glance moved around the room, seeing the louvered shutters against the windows, the patterned damask of the curtains around the bed, the paneled walls glimmering pearl gray, the dark spaces where the portraits hung.

"How is nothing," he said slowly. "It is done as it is done. By the knife."

He dreaded her next question: even now, after all these years, he had no complete answer. Men's motives continued to surprise him. Women's, too.

"Why?"

He shook his head. "Who knows? Whether a thing is done from duty, or desire."

Their eyes met.

"Once," she began, "I—I went to Istria. I had a son."

She said it so abruptly that Yashim blinked.

"A son," she repeated through gritted teeth.

Yashim was still.

"I was so young. So—so resolute."

"Resolute?"

"The vow I made, Yashim."

She shuddered and covered her face with her hands. "I gave him away," she said tonelessly. "I wouldn't come back to Venice with a baby. So I gave my baby away."

Yashim said nothing: there was nothing he could say.

"I have spent my life trying to forget him."

She drew up her face and stared at the wall, her fingers to her temples. "And there is not a day I do not think about him."

Her breath hissed between her teeth. "I have never told this to a soul. I wonder why I'm telling you?"

Invisible Yashim, the lover who leaves no mark.

"Perhaps I am telling you because I think you will not judge me."

"No one can judge but God."

She stood up, erect and graceful, and poured a glass of wine.

"He would be twenty-four," she said. "A little peasant boy from Istria."

"Would you—would you look for him?"

She shook her head. "I tried. Two years ago I went back to the convent where he was born. They understood, Yashim, those nuns. They understood, they prayed with me—but they couldn't help. They said—they said that my son was a blessing to a woman who had lost her child." She clenched her hands. "And I have become that woman, Yashim. Not by the will of God, but by my own. My own!"

She picked up the glass and drained it, and with a wild laugh she flung it into the fireplace.

"Why should I ever be afraid, Yashim? You can be frightened only when you have hope, and I have none."

But later she curled up to him: "I want you to take me again, *caro*."

But Yashim only shook his head and stroked her hair until she fell asleep.

Then he got up, silent and weary, and went to the room that had been prepared for him.

96

HE dreamed Palewski's dream that night: of a never-ending search beneath the stones of Venice, and each stone had to be turned, one by one, by hand. But there was nothing underneath: only earth and water. And there was a woman, wringing her hands beside him.

He could still hear her groans and cries when he woke up, in the dark, and lay there listening against his will.

Muttering a prayer for her soul. A prayer against the darkness of the night.

He rolled swiftly aside and leaped to his feet.

That scream—was it really the sound of a woman mourning?

Or the sound of danger?

After the scream, silence.

The corridor was pitch-dark. Yashim felt his way along the wall. He reached a door and passed it. The next door he opened: slatted moonlight filtered through the louvered shutters onto the four-poster bed, hung with dark drapery; the room felt huge and empty.

He was about to shut the door when a low growl made the hair stand up on the nape of his neck.

He took a step into the room, wishing he had a candle.

And a white shape launched itself through the air and slammed him back against the wall.

He felt soft hair whip across his face and hard nails dragging across his chest.

She bit him like a wild animal, on the neck, on the cheek, clawing at his chest and shoulders.

He got a hand beneath her chin and flung her back. He could taste blood on his lip.

Carla staggered back and then flung herself forward again, sobbing and biting.

Yashim grabbed her arms and tried to force them down. She whirled around from side to side, trying to break his grip, dragging him back toward the bed.

Then he was on top of her, pinning back her hands above her head. Her hips writhed under him.

She spat into his face.

Yashim shook his head. Furious, he dragged a cord from the post and doubled it around her wrists. She twisted under his grip, almost threw him off, so he shifted his weight farther up her body. Her legs thrashed the bed.

With a heave he shifted her shoulders across the bed, bringing her wrists to the bedpost. As he leaned over her to tie them back, she jerked her head, snapping at him.

She made a furious lunge at the cord with her arms, trying to move it.

With a spring Yashim was off the bed, standing close, panting.

The cord held.

Carla gasped, reaching for breath. Between gasps, she began to laugh.

Yashim closed his eyes; his chest heaved.

She thought she had won.

He felt a rush of anger: if she *had* won, then he had lost.

Let it be, he told himself. Let it be.

His breathing eased.

And something cold, and very fine, slid up beneath Yashim's ear as a voice whispered in it softly, "Thank you."

97

Seconds passed.

Yashim supposed that Carla had laughed again.

He was very still now. He felt the blade below his ear.

But just one thought ran through his mind, like a drumbeat.

Teşekkür ederim meant "thank you" in Turkish.

Yashim tensed his stomach. His shoulders bunched.

And he jackknifed. He took a step forward, his shoulders dropped, and he doubled at the waist.

He sensed, rather than felt, the blade slicing through the soft skin behind his ear.

He kicked back abruptly with one leg.

His hope was that the Tatar had lost form: killing Venetians was like liming a tree for birds.

His foot connected, but not hard: the next moment, the Tatar had a grip of his ankle. Left hand—Yashim wrenched himself forward and took a mouthful of the bed.

With both hands on the mattress he launched himself backward.

The Tatar sidestepped easily, but now Yashim was at his back. As the Tatar whipped around, Yashim flung out one fist, and then the other. The raised knuckle of his middle finger sank into the Tatar's cheek.

The Tatar had him by the scruff of his neck; Yashim felt himself choke and flailed blindly. Then the Tatar seized his waistband and with a grunt sent him crashing through the air—Yashim raised his hands and the shutters burst apart like rotten twigs.

But Yashim was already twisting as he flew: his knees doubled against the windowsill and for a second he saw the dark bulk of buildings swing upward. His head cracked against the wall—in a moment the Tatar would flip his feet through the window, and he would be gone.

Instinctively, Yashim tensed his legs. With a final effort he jerked himself upright: the Tatar was at the window.

Yashim grabbed him with both hands—but the momentum was too feeble to carry him into the room. As he fell back again he kicked out, spinning them both into space, precipitating the Tatar over and over into the air.

Only in Venice would anyone survive a two-story drop.

The Tatar smacked into the water first. Yashim seemed to pummel in on top of him and was thrashing and coughing as he came up for air.

He kicked out, in panic: the Tatar was still beneath the water.

Yashim scudded back, toward the security of the palazzo wall, and there, in the faint glow of lamplight on the water, he saw the Tatar break the surface ten yards away.

He was swimming away, up the canal.

Yashim wished he could let him go.

He wiped his mouth with his fingers and tasted blood.

With his other hand he found the knife. The knife that Malakian had given him for an asper: the cook's knife.

A knife that a hunter might carry, too, for slipping off a pelt.

The knife that was made of damascene.

Yashim kicked off from the wall and began to hunt.

98

"WONDERFUL, wonderful," Palewski murmured. He had his boots before the fire and a sheaf of drawings on his lap.

"Very good!" he said enthusiastically, holding a drawing of the cottage up before his eyes. He nodded vigorously, and his new friend chuckled and bobbed about.

Rather like having a child of one's own, Palewski thought.

"Wonderful," he said again, picking a new sketch out of the heap. "Maria, have you seen what our friend has done?"

Maria came over and leaned against his chair. Palewski felt the roundness of her breast against his cheek.

"This," he said. "And this."

Maria heaved a sigh. "Incredible! Like an angel!"

"Perhaps you'd like to sit here and look through them, Maria?"

"Yes, signore—but mamma wants the room swept and clean."

"I could sweep."

Maria laughed. A warm, happy laugh: it was the first time she'd laughed since she came home. "I think he really likes it when *you* look at his drawings."

Palewski gave her an exasperated look. "I don't think he's all that fussy, Maria."

But Maria had taken her broom and was banging it about under the table.

Palewski sighed. "But this is beautiful!" he said, to make Maria laugh again.

The odd young man nodded and gobbled and grinned.

Palewski felt a twinge of remorse. The fellow's drawings were sublime: it was only that he produced them in such volume! His tongue always at the corner of his mouth, his eyes sparkling, his hand moving freely across the page. Time after time the young man had summed up whole scenes in a few lines: the tilt of a woman's head, the atmosphere of a crowded room, the curve of a child's cheek. Several times Palewski had recognized himself, down to the outstretched legs and the fashionable width of his lapel.

Sometimes the young man drew from memory—rapid sketches of the piazza filled with people, with the Austrian bandsmen just about to play; or the view from a high window, of rooftops and the lagoon and the distant Dolomites.

"Hello!" Palewski said, sliding another picture from the sheaf. "Here's Barbieri!"

99

THE Tatar was moving away from him through the dark water. Yashim guessed that he'd been hurt in the plunge—winded, certainly.

Perhaps, too, the Tatar had lost his knife.

Perhaps the advantage had shifted to him.

The water was not especially cold, and Yashim was lightly dressed: the Tatar had several yards' start on him.

Yashim watched him swim across the mouth of a small canal; on the other side he began to move faster against the canal wall, scrabbling like a bat, using the brick foundations of the next palazzo as handholds.

Yashim plunged across the canal and followed suit. Now he could hear the man's breath and the splashes as he lunged through the water. In the moonlight he was a dark shape against the wall.

At the next corner the Tatar swiveled left and disappeared.

Yashim kicked off warily from the wall and circled the corner.

The Tatar was nowhere to be seen. The canal was a dark chasm, but as Yashim bobbed in the water a distant light flicked on and off.

Yashim was puzzled, until the moonlight picked out the faintest outline of a low crenellated barrier across the mouth of the canal. Now and then, he remembered, the authorities would close a canal for dredging.

He swam cautiously to the far side of the barrier, the knife in his hand. When he touched the rough wood he held his breath, pressing his back against the masonry wall.

Had the Tatar climbed the barrier already? Or was he on Yashim's side, waiting in the dark?

Yashim groped for the top of the thick plank. It was about eighteen inches above the surface. He slid the knife back into its pocket and in one smooth motion he hauled himself up.

The canal beyond was dredged and empty. The canal bed glinted at his feet, about ten feet below. The Tatar was nowhere to be seen.

Yashim swung his legs over the barrier and dropped down into the soft mud.

100

YASHIM inched himself gingerly along the wall: the mud was over his feet, mixed with chunks of broken bricks and stones. It churned over at every step, releasing a noxious belch of putrefaction. It occurred to Yashim that the whole city was built on rot. Sodden pilings, rotten brick, the submerged miasma of the lagoon's decay.

The canal bed was lower in the middle, a shallow V that sloped up toward the buildings on either side. It was scarcely twelve feet wide.

Overhead were the doorways that gave access to the water, too high, as Yashim judged, to reach, the walls below smooth with accumulated slime. He placed his weight against the wall. His hand skimmed across the slippery algae and he overbalanced, clawing for a moment at the stones before he slithered down into the base of the trench.

The mud was thicker here, the water up to his knees. The effort of raising one foot only drove the other deeper into the cloying ooze. Yashim swayed, hands outstretched, surprised by the clutch of the mud around his ankles.

The Tatar struck like a crocodile in the swamp, slithering upward from the water-lined trench.

He swarmed up Yashim's legs from behind, judging it well, scarcely pressing his feet to the canal floor. As Yashim sprawled the Tatar was on top of him, his hard fingers grasping for Yashim's neck, his whole weight pressing Yashim's shoulders down into the stinking trench.

Yashim barely had time to grab a lungful of air before he was facedown in the mud, his knees pressed into the thick slime. He fought an impulse to choke.

Dimly, he thought that the mud had caught him, more dimly still, that the mud might save him.

Thrusting against the splayed weight of his left leg, Yashim rifled to break the Tatar's hold. His arms swung free. He thrust himself up for air and when he splashed back into the water he took the Tatar's knees in his hands and shot himself backward, barreling like a rifle bullet between the Tatar's legs.

For centuries, the Ottoman Turks had practiced a unique form of wrestling in which two men, oiled from head to toe, grapple with each other under a blazing sun. Fierce as these contests are, they are generally friendly. Punching is not allowed.

But in Venice, in the mud, Yashim and the Tatar fought beneath a cold moon.

Yashim took the man's topknot in his fist, but as it slithered from his grasp he raised his knee sharply and drove it against his throat. The Tatar gave a gurgle, and Yashim thrashed back again, scrambling in the watery trench for purchase.

The Tatar was up to his waist in the water, kneeling: a figure of clay. Yashim reached for his knife, blessing the ignorant cook who had once bound the handle with a spiral of cord. Even in this slime his grip was sure.

The Tatar lurched to his right, trying to scramble out of the trench and up the side of the canal.

Yashim put his thumb over the top of the handle, like a stopper, and staggered toward his prey.

Sometimes the Tatar slipped and slithered back, sometimes Yashim. Once, he almost had the Tatar in his grasp, one hand around his ankle, the other stabbing blindly into the mud; then the Tatar kicked down savagely and both men skittered backward. The Tatar stopped short of the trench. He was on all fours, clambering higher, while Yashim thrashed out of the water below him.

The Tatar saw the rope first. Perhaps he had known it was there all along, a possibility of escape, hanging down in a lazy swag from a doorway high overhead.

Before Yashim could squirm out of the trench, the Tatar had made a grab for the rope. His hand slipped off, he staggered. But he regained his balance in a moment, and this time he managed to worm his forearm over the rope, using his elbow as a fulcrum, maintaining his hold by taking his other hand in a butcher's grip.

Yashim approached warily: his fixed hold gave the Tatar an advantage.

The Tatar swung from the rope like an ape, and his foot caught Yashim in the belly—not a winding blow, but enough to knock him down.

When he struggled to his feet, the Tatar was already cradling the rope, and then he was upright against the wall, standing precariously in the loop, his hands groping overhead for the lintel of the doorway.

Perhaps Yashim could have flung his knife, in the hope that it would strike its mark. Perhaps he could have struggled up the bank again, made a lunge for the assassin, forced him back into the mud, to start the whole weary, heavy, uncertain process of execution over again.

But Yashim was tired. He was weighted with mud: wet, wounded. His ear was bleeding.

By the time he reached the rope himself, the Tatar had vanished.

101

YASHIM found himself at the mouth of a narrow alley, barred by a few planks to stop pedestrians from falling into the dredged canal.

He climbed over the barrier and peered into the gloom. The usual weak light burned at the farther end of the alley. Yashim squatted and thought he could just make out the outline of muddy footprints.

At the corner he paused to scan the ground, but the footprints were by now invisible. There were at least three directions the Tatar could have taken.

Yashim leaned against the wall and tried to think.

Somewhere in this city the assassin had a safe place. Somewhere he could sleep, and eat, and leave at will, sure of attracting no attention.

He would have gone there now. Wounded and disarmed, he needed somewhere to change his clothes, wash his wounds. The Tatars were not punctilious about washing, unlike the Turks, but they would clean a bleeding cut.

Yet Venice was a poor city: and the poor are many, and have eyes.

They would see a stranger, even a careful one. Yashim had spent time in the Crimea, the Tatars' homeland. He knew how they lived in the saddle on a handful of dried meat, but the Tatar would have to draw his water from a well, out in the *campo*. That was the way Venice was built. Some cities clustered around a citadel, but Venice shaped itself around its wells.

Unless . . .

The Tatar could have found one place to draw water, unseen.

Somewhere with its own supply.

Somewhere people had lived almost isolated lives—secure, secluded, and magnificent, too.

Yashim turned to the right, and began loping back toward the Grand Canal.

102

TH E cat watched the man washing his face. He took a rag and dipped it into the water, then washed his leg.

When he was done, he took a piece of cloth and tore it into strips.

The cat tensed, arching her back. Beneath her, a covey of blind kittens groped for the warm milk.

The man tied the cloth around his leg. The cat could smell his blood.

When the man stood up, he winced but made no sound.

He stood silent, immobile, watching the window.

Watching for the dawn to break.

103

GINGERLY Yashim pushed at the door.

He felt the hinges protest against his weight, but they made no sound.

As the door swung back, Yashim stepped inside and flattened himself against the wall.

If he was wrong about the fondaco . . .

He had left the contessa tied up on her own bed.

As his eyes adjusted to the darkness he saw the first glimmer of dawn through a chink in a broken door.

After a few moments he crossed the hall, half crouching, knife in hand, making no sound in the dust on the floor.

He had been here before. The hammam where Maria had been imprisoned was on the ground floor to his left, in the back corner of the huge old building. Here the ceiling was sagging, broken laths spilling downward; the floor above was probably unsound. But the contessa had gone upstairs to Eletro's party.

Through a gap in the door he looked up at the sky. Carla had mentioned a central court, and if it was not typical of a Venetian palazzo it was just what Yashim would have expected of an Ottoman *han*. The courtyard, as far as he could see, was choked with a riot of plants—a few trees, a massive fig, and a tangle of brambles that had grown up through the paving stones. It would be surrounded by lockups, where the merchants' goods were stored, damp and very dark. The Fondaco dei Turchi was almost entirely windowless. At ground level, no windows at all. Above, only one or two small openings on either side. The Ottomans had wanted a safe cocoon—safe from thieves, safe from infidel eyes.

A perfect place to hide.

He closed his eyes and tried to picture the front of the fondaco, as he had seen it from the contessa's window. On the canal, a small quay, half built over; behind it, eight or so columned arches forming an arcade. A row of shorter columns above formed a loggia that, like the arcade beneath, ran almost the whole length of the façade, though on either side, on both floors, three or four arches had been blocked up like bastions that had lost their turrets.

In the room, or rooms, behind the loggia there would be light, but anyone in them would be invisible from the canal.

The door was stuck fast, so he groped his way through the ground-floor rooms until he reached a low opening onto the courtyard. He swung his legs over the sill and dropped down into an open arcade, heaped with broken tea chests, rotting bales, empty crates and barrels—the detritus of an abandoned trade.

He wondered where the Tatar was. He hoped he was somewhere overhead, perhaps where the contessa and her friends had played, in rooms overlooking the Grand Canal.

Cautiously he began to pick his way along the arcade, keeping to the darker shadows and using whatever cover the rubbish strewn around it could provide. At the end of the arcade he had to move into the open to reach the portico that he imagined would lead to the stairs.

He stooped and ran, swinging quickly through the archway, sliding with his back to the wall to the foot of the stairs, where he stopped to listen.

He crossed to the farther wall and began to climb the stairs, his eyes straining in the half-light.

He tried not to think that he might have got it all wrong. He concentrated instead on his instincts, telling him the assassin was waiting overhead, behind the door to the great room where the sultan himself had played cards.

He stopped and listened again.

Something the contessa had said came into his mind, but then it was gone as he reached the turn of the stairs and found himself by a row of empty windows divided by slender columns. They had stopped here, the sultan and his friends, to look at the lights in the courtyard.

There were no lights now as Yashim inched to a window, but through the trees and weeds the breaking dawn revealed bands of lighter stone across the dark paving of the court, spelling out the pattern he already knew so well.

He pulled back his head. The dark mass of the doorway lay above, but it was impossible to see whether the door was open or closed. Yashim hovered, uncertain whether to go forward or back. The door must be closed, he thought; otherwise it would be backlit, however dimly, by the gathering light on the Grand Canal.

It was a cat or, as it seemed momentarily to Yashim, the ghost of a cat, that saved his life, for as it materialized dimly and inexplicably in the doorway, Yashim finally remembered what the contessa had said.

What looked in the half-light like a closed door at the top of the stairs was only a curtain hanging in the doorway.

Yashim dropped to the floor, rolled once, and sprawled against the stairs just as the doorway erupted with a bright flash. Then he was squirming on his elbows headfirst down the stairs.

Behind him he heard the sound of a pistol being cocked.

When he twisted around the Tatar was already there, silhouetted against the breaking light, coolly looking down into the dark with the pistol in his hand.

Yashim's hand closed on something small and hard that was lying beside him on the step. It was a glass jar, big enough to hold a candle.

He threw it, and it tinkled to pieces at the Tatar's feet. Yashim pressed himself against the stairs.

The Tatar jumped back and fired again, blindly.

Two barrels, both shot.

Yashim said, "It's over now. The killing stops."

He took his knife by the point of the blade, protected by the darkness at his back, and began inching farther upright.

The Tatar cocked his head. "Resid told you that?"

"It's only the truth, my friend."

The Tatar considered this in silence.

"I was told, one more," he said at length. "I do not need to make it two."

Still the Tatar did not move. "Let me tell you something, efendi. In the old days, when my people made war, we rode west, for days and weeks, behind our chief. We rode fast, touching nothing, stopping for nothing. Seeing everything."

"I know how the Tatars fought," Yashim said, moving slowly. "I know your khan." He was almost ready.

The Tatar turned his head and spat. "Before," he said, "we had a khan. When we had ridden a long, long way, but only at the time he chose, we turned our horses east, toward home."

Yes, Yashim thought, and then the pillage began. The looted, burning villages, the piles of dead, the roped convoys of slaves.

"We were moderate," the Tatar said. "We had seen what we wanted, we took it, and we rode for home. Nothing more."

He was backing away now, moving out of the light.

"So you see, efendi," the Tatar said. "I was sent to Venice, and soon I, too, am going home."

The Tatar had gone.

Yashim sprang for the stairs. It would take the Tatar only a few moments to reload.

At the top he whipped back the curtain.

It was a huge room, empty except for a small square table and a broken chair leaning drunkenly against the back wall. It was lit by a colonnade running the whole width of the building—almost. At the farther end was an empty doorway set into a wall of planks and bulging plaster: perhaps the assassin had ducked in there. Perhaps he was already loaded, cocked, and waiting for Yashim to step inside.

As he hesitated, Yashim heard something scrape at the window, or beyond it. He glanced up. Already the first barges were making their way down the canal. Flinging himself forward, he scrambled feetfirst through the nearest window and dropped into the loggia.

Under the balcony was a lean-to, covered in broken tiles.

Beyond it was the canal.

Yashim craned forward, searching the surface of the water. A few hundred yards away, where the canal curved, he recognized the outline of the Ca' d'Aspi.

Ten minutes away. Ten minutes, running through the maze of the Venetian streets.

But for a powerful swimmer less, far less. Three hundred yards, in a direct line.

And the Tatar had a head start.

He swung himself over the balustrade, holding onto a slender column.

Beneath him was a barge stacked with firewood. It was rowed by two men, with another at the tiller, and it was moving fast.

As Yashim dropped down onto the mass of broken tiles, they began to slide.

104

HE fell awkwardly, wrenching his leg as he rolled across the cords of wood.

The tillerman gave a shout of surprise.

Yashim snatched himself upright and turned to the man who was staring at him, dumbfounded.

"It's me!" Yashim cried. "The pasha!"

A look of consternation swept across the tillerman's face.

"Tell them to keep rowing!"

The tillerman glanced at the men forward. "Row on! Row on!" he barked. "You, you don't look like the pasha," he objected simply.

Yashim scrambled to the front of the barge. His eyes swept the water. It was flat, oily, gleaming in the half dawn.

He had the advantage now, surely? The barge was moving faster than a man could swim, and it was three hundred yards to the Palazzo d'Aspi.

He peered at the shoreline, where the buildings dropped into the water. The buildings were clear, but there were freestanding mooring posts, too. Was the Tatar hiding somewhere among them?

If he were hiding, then he must have seen Yashim jump.

But he'd been swimming. He couldn't have seen.

Yashim glanced ahead, and that was when he saw a slight movement to his right. It was out of the corner of one eye, and when he looked again, there was nothing.

Only the mouth of the empty canal and the low crenellations of the caisson he'd climbed an hour or so before.

But the Tatar had slipped over it again. He'd seen him go.

Or had he?

Was it a faster way back to the Palazzo d'Aspi?

Had the Tatar seen him coming?

And if he jumped—and was wrong—would the contessa die?

Yashim scuttled back to the man at the tiller. His foot throbbed.

If he jumped, could he swim?

The mouth of the canal was only fifteen yards ahead.

Yashim stood up. He put both hands to his mouth and shouted, *"Get down on deck!"*

The tillerman looked up, mouth agape.

Yashim grabbed the tiller and swept it out of the man's hands.

Loaded with cords of beechwood from the foothills of the Dolomites, the barge heeled and swung right, driven by its own massive momentum. The portside rower staggered and vanished with a shout into the canal; his companion sprawled across the logs.

For a moment it looked as if Yashim had made the turn too soon. As the bows swung around toward the edge of the palazzo, it seemed inevitable that they would crash into the masonry wall.

But even as it tilted to the left, brushing its gunwales against the surface, the heavy barge was still making its way downstream.

Over the still and silent waters of the Grand Canal, its solid keel cracked against the caisson like a rifle shot.

The broad prow lifted out of the water, scraping up on the irregular jutting timbers, and Yashim and the tillerman were thrown forward.

For a moment the barge seemed to hang at an unnatural angle. The impact had driven the stern so low that as it slewed to port it seemed to be pressing upon a scoop of water that would at any second rush back and overwhelm it.

Clinging to the edge of the hold, Yashim glanced back. The water was like oil again—slow, gurgling, wreathing itself in coils and bubbles.

Something cracked like a rifle bolt, and the barge lurched.

The waters at the stern rushed in. They swept in beneath the rudder, picked up the barge and lifted it, and as the boat began to rise, a shudder swept its length.

The central plank of the barrier snapped in two. The weight of the barge dropped suddenly a few inches. The crossbeam beneath curved, then popped from its rabbets, and as the prow of the barge dropped through the barrier, Yashim raised his head.

He saw the Tatar, standing in the trench up to his knees, his hands in the water.

He saw him staring upward, blankly, as water began to billow across the shattered caisson.

The water jetted out on either side of the barge's keel, like two green wings, scouring the walls and then curling inward, dragging with it shattered timber that smacked against the walls like weightless wickerwork and then swirled inward, smashing down onto the trench in a thundering plume of foam and mud.

The boiling deluge rolled down to the far end of the canal, crashed against the caisson, and jetted up into the air.

Yashim gripped the edge of his plank and held on for dear life.

Very slowly, like a fat woman nudging herself into a bath, the barge creaked forward. As the backwash returned, it met a new wave of water and then, as if someone had lightly smacked its rump, the barge glided abruptly and harmlessly into the canal.

The man at the prow stood up shakily.

Yashim removed his fingers from the plank. When he looked around he saw the other rower in the water of the Grand Canal, clinging to his oar.

The tillerman looked back and then at Yashim. He was white as a sheet.

"Paolo," he said, with an exasperated jerk of his head. "Always, he misses everything."

105

YASHIM found the contessa sleeping, still braided to her bed.

He slipped the cords easily and she rolled over, still sleeping, gathering her hands to her chest. He lifted the sheets and laid them over her.

Back in his room Yashim looked at himself in a mirror. The tillerman was right: he did not look like the pasha. He looked barely human. He had lost his turban and his hair was stiff with the mud that caked his face, his neck, and his clothes. His shirt was ripped to the waist. Blood had dried down one cheek, and his eyes looked unnaturally white.

He stripped off his wet things and washed his face and hands in the bowl, turning the water a muddy gray. He wiped himself over with a damp towel, shivering, wishing that the Venetians among all their thefts and adoptions from Istanbul had chosen the hammam. He felt as though the rotting ooze of the canals had seeped into the pores of his skin, and cold, too. What he needed now was unlimited hot water and a man to knead him like fresh dough. He put on some fresh linen and dry clothes, and felt somewhat refreshed.

Back in the salon he stood for a long time at the window, watching the traffic thicken on the canal, listening to the sound of bells and thinking about the man he had killed.

106

THE bells of San Sebastiano were ringing when Signora Contarini sallied forth in her best bonnet. Her husband had willingly ceded his position on her arm to Stanislaw Palewski, who walked solemnly at her side. Behind them came Maria, holding the speechless young man by one hand and a small sister by the other. Her brother followed with two children.

The Contarinis were going to Mass.

"The mad boy should come," the signora had decided. "Why not? He's a Christian, isn't he?"

"How can you tell, signora?" Palewski replied. "He might be a Moor, like Yashim."

She shook her head vigorously. "Believe me, signore, he's a Christian. As I hope you are, signore."

The man remained quiet until they reached the church, when he began to utter small cries, patting the doorway with his hands and nodding amiably. Some of the parishioners stared, but Signora Contarini kept her chin level and swept her entourage grandly inside, where they had some difficulty in pressing the man into a pew. He seemed to want to go around and around the walls, touching everything. Only when Father Andrea entered did the man grow still, his stubbly head cocked in wonder at the motions of the priest.

As the Communion approached, the signora became a little agitated.

"He must stay with the children," she hissed.

They shuffled forward to the altar rail. Palewski knelt between Signora Contarini and Maria to receive the host.

"In nomine Patris, et filii, et spiritus sancti."

"Amen."

Palewski lifted the wafer to his mouth.

Maria nudged him. The signora was putting the wafer in her mouth, and beyond her knelt the speechless young man.

Palewski glanced sideways. The man's face was transfigured by an expression of—what, exactly? It was the expression worn by an apostle in a medieval Assumption. Amazement? Fear?

Signora Contarini's head jerked with impatience when she saw the man.

"In nomine Patris, et filii, et spiritus sancti," Father Andrea murmured, holding out the wafer.

The man reached up. He took the priest's hand in his and brought it to his cheek.

Father Andrea murmured a blessing. He made to move on, but the man seemed unwilling to let him go.

As he stooped to say something in the man's ear, Palewski saw a look of confusion cross his face. Then the color drained from his cheeks.

107

TOUSLE-haired from sleep and looking lovelier than ever, Carla entered the salon to find Yashim asleep with his forehead against the windowpane.

She gave a small cry of surprise, and Yashim opened his eyes. She was dressed in her nightgown, under a long embroidered coat whose sleeves were slashed to dangle at the elbows.

"I thought you were dead," she breathed.

"That was another man," Yashim answered, rubbing his eyes. "He came to kill you."

She took his hands. "Tell me what happened."

He told her, almost reluctantly, and when he had finished she said, "Yesterday I thought you had come to kill me, Yashim. Instead, you saved my life."

"Will you sell me the Bellini?"

"You?"

"The sultan."

She drew herself up to her full height. "The money, you understand. It's not for me."

"I didn't think so."

"No, of course not." She bent forward and kissed him, softly, on the lips. "But I wanted you to be sure. In Venice, Yashim, honor is all that's left."

Then the door opened, and two white-jacketed soldiers came in.

Behind them followed Sergeant Vosper and finally, looking stout in his uniform, the stadtmeister himself.

At the door he checked himself abruptly. "Contessa?"

He bowed and clicked his heels.

"I regret intruding upon you, Contessa, in this manner," he said, "but it is a matter of urgency."

"Urgency?"

"Indeed. You will be so kind as to give me the papers."

And he held out his hand, as if the contessa were holding them in hers.

108

"NIKOLA!"

The young man gave a birdlike cry, and then he was gobbling, and grinning, and nodding his head in an ecstasy of pleasure, patting Father Andrea's hand to his cheek.

In the midst of his astonishment, Palewski still wondered what, exactly, was the liturgical form. Could Communion be interrupted? Father Andrea seemed to have little choice: the man—Nikola—was not going to be parted easily from him.

In the end the priest solved the problem by lifting the altar rail and bringing Nikola to stand beside him like an acolyte. While he grinned and nodded, Father Andrea continued with the wafer and the wine, smiling broadly all the while.

After the service the priest and the speechless man came back to the Contarini house together, hand in hand. Commissario Brunelli was there already, telling Signor Contarini about an extraordinary accident that had occurred on the Grand Canal only that morning.

Over breakfast Nikola's story emerged.

"Nikola," the priest explained, leaning back to look at him more carefully, "is my old friend. We were in Croatia together, Nikola and I. But one day, he disappeared."

The young man pulled a long face and solemnly shook his head.

"No? Well, I expect we'll learn something about that, by and by. Everyone searched for him. In the end, we discovered that he had been seen getting into a coach, with a stranger, bound for Trieste."

The young man, Nikola, nodded again, but this time he slid from his chair and began rifling through the pictures he had drawn. He found the one he wanted and laid it on the table.

Everyone craned for a better look. It was a charcoal sketch of a man sitting in a hard chair. He was solidly built—a strong man gone to seed, one would have said—his eyes were cast down, almost modestly, looking at a picture or book on his lap.

"Yes," the priest said slowly. "That's the man. I knew it! He called himself Spoletti. From Padua."

"It's Alfredo!" Palewski cried.

Brunelli leaned forward. "You're both wrong," he said, shaking his head. "That's Popi Eletro."

109

CARLA gave a shaky laugh. "The papers? I don't understand."

The stadtmeister curled his lip. "Please don't joke with me, Contessa."

Carla's chest lifted. She half turned her head. "I have nothing whatever that belongs to you, Stadtmeister. Nothing at all."

The stadtmeister's eyes were like currants. "To me, no. But I will see to it that you get a receipt from the relevant authorities."

"Ah, the authorities." Carla took a deep breath. "But what, exactly, do the authorities seek?"

Finkel's jaw was working. "We both know exactly what you need to produce. Let us not delude ourselves, Contessa. You have a note of hand, signed by the Duke of Naxos. You also have a proscribed artwork by Gentile Bellini."

"Proscribed? What does it mean?"

"It means, Contessa, that the state has seen fit to confiscate the said work in its own interest. I hold a warrant, signed by Vienna. A certain compensation can be agreed," he added.

"A warrant! How alarming." The contessa sounded less alarmed than furious. "And when did you receive this warrant?"

The stadtmeister looked uncertain. "Receive it, Contessa? Why, I'm not sure. A week or so ago. Of course," he added, running a gauntleted hand over his whiskers, "I shall be delighted to discuss the, ah, compensation due at any time that suits you. You will find the authorities can be generous, I'm sure."

Yashim's mind was racing ahead. His curious gift for self-concealment might just allow him to get out of the salon by the end door. Beyond, he imagined, there would be a staircase to the second floor. With luck, and time, he could then come down to the contessa's room. Take the picture.

It was the contessa herself, unfortunately, who broke the spell.

"You are a witness to this insult, Yashim Pasha," she said, switching to Italian.

The stadtmeister's eyes swiveled toward the window.

"*Der Teufel!*" he muttered.

Yashim inclined his head. "I am sure the stadtmeister has no intention of insulting you, Contessa. He has done his duty, as I have done mine."

He salaamed politely. "A thousand pardons, Herr Oberst, if my presence surprises you. Allow me to introduce myself. Yashim Pasha, of the sultan's household, making a purely private visit to your city."

The stadtmeister clicked his heels, but he looked extremely wary.

"A private visit? Where's Brunelli? Vosper!"

Sergeant Vosper shuffled his feet and said nothing.

"The amiable commissario," Yashim went on, "is a credit to your office." He took a few steps into the room. "I regret that my understanding of German is only limited, but I think the contessa is mistaken if she thinks you have been insulting her. I am sure you mean nothing of the kind."

"No, no, of course not," the stadtmeister replied, sounding nettled.

"Forgive me, but it seemed to me that you were talking about a portrait—and a note."

"That's right."

"But perhaps there has been some misunderstanding," Yashim pressed on. "After all, it was for the sake of this same portrait, and the note, that I came to Venice."

The stadtmeister's face darkened.

"But that—that's not possible," he growled.

"The contessa and I made the arrangements yesterday," Yashim continued imperturbably. "At this moment, Herr Stadtmeister, the portrait is on its way to Istanbul, via Corfu—the ship left Trieste last night. Of course, I will take the matter up on my return to Istanbul. I shall speak to Pappendorf myself. If there is any need to adjudicate a claim, then you will appreciate, sir, that the Ottoman government of Sultan Abdülmecid stands by its international treaties and obligations."

The stadtmeister opened his mouth to speak, then shut it again.

"But the note!" His voice was almost a squeak.

Yashim had certain ideas about the note, which did not include a fiction of having it shipped to Istanbul.

"I had no difficulty in destroying it, Herr Stadtmeister. You may rest quite easy on that score."

The stadtmeister gaped. "Destroyed it! *Der Teufel!*"

It was Yashim's turn to look surprised. "But surely, Herr Stadtmeister, it was to our mutual advantage that the note should cease to exist?"

The stadtmeister merely gurgled.

Without the slightest attempt at a bow, he turned on his heel and left the room. Vosper shuffled off after him. Only the two soldiers clicked their heels, shouldered their rifles, and with immaculate nods toward the beautiful contessa retreated backward through the door, closing it gently behind them.

Carla turned to Yashim with an expression of amusement.

"Very neat, Yashim Pasha. Very neat, indeed."

"Oh, it was nothing," said Yashim carelessly. "I just followed the diagram, that's all."

110

HE glanced through the window in time to see the stadtmeister sitting rigid in his gondola, mopping his brow with a handkerchief. Opposite sat Vosper, his shoulders hunched.

The gondola moved off with a lazy flourish.

Had Vosper been less downcast, or the stadtmeister less rigid in defeat, they might have seen another gondola sweep up to the steps of the Palazzo d'Aspi. They would not have recognized Palewski, but they would have known the man who sat beside him.

"Palewski was right," Yashim murmured. "Venice is exactly like a theater."

"Palewski?" the contessa said. "Who is Palewski?"

Yashim smiled. "Count Palewski is the man I sent to Venice to find the Bellini. You know him as Signor Brett."

The contessa put a hand to her throat. "The lancer."

"The lancer?" Palewski was Yashim's oldest friend, but there were still things they had never discussed. "He is the Polish ambassador in Istanbul."

She nodded, beginning to understand. "Then he, too, is one of us. One of the dispossessed." She wrapped her hand around her fist. "I have been a fool."

He could hear them now on the stairs.

"I thought, at first, that he was the killer."

"Palewski? But that's—"

"Ridiculous? But he came for the Bellini, too."

"I sent him, instead of me."

Carla frowned. "You? You didn't tell him about the pattern."

"I didn't know," Yashim admitted. "It was to be a signal, wasn't it? That the palace had received your offer."

Before she could answer, Palewski and Brunelli were shown into the room.

"Commissario. Count Palewski." Carla greeted them with a slight bow.

Palewski leaped a few inches and peered at Yashim. "Not Signor Brett, eh?"

"Your Ottoman friend was very clever," the contessa said. "And I have been very foolish. I should have guessed: the Polish Legion."

Palewski inclined his head. "The lancers, Contessa. In Italy under Dabrowski. Later, the Vistula Uhlans. Lance and saber." He shrugged. "Out of fashion now, as you said."

The contessa laughed. "Only the saber. Handsome men never go out of fashion."

"Things have changed since yesterday," Yashim said. "I caught up with an assassin."

He told them of the night's events. He explained how he had broken through the dam, and how the Tatar had been swept away in a torrent of surging foam.

"This," Brunelli said wistfully, "I wish I had seen."

"He was a professional assassin. He killed three people here."

"And found them how?"

"As to that, I think somebody showed him. Somebody who signed his own death warrant as soon as the last name was released."

"Ruggerio," Brunelli said.

"He's dead?"

Brunelli nodded. "He played a foolish game, Yashim Pasha."

Yashim was silent for a while. It was Ruggerio, of course.

"He served the Duke of Naxos," Carla said.

"That's how they knew of him, perhaps. But Ruggerio and the Tatar, how did they come together? Here, in Venice."

Brunelli shrugged. "Perhaps we'll never really know."

"Perhaps not." Yashim looked thoughtful. "Perhaps not."

The contessa took a deep breath.

"I have something to give you, Yashim. Commissario, would you mind? It's not heavy, but it's a little far to reach."

They went out together, and Palewski told Yashim about Maria's priest and the way the man had recognized him.

"Yashim," he said, "you're not listening."

"I have an instinct," Yashim said slowly, "that something is going wrong."

Brunelli entered with a heavy tread. Behind him came Carla. She looked very pale.

"The painting," she said in a tone of dazed wonder. "It's gone!"

111

BEHIND the curtain, where the Bellini had hung, the slim gold frame was empty.

Yashim glanced at Carla.

She gave him a look of scorn. "So you think I'm playing with you, now? No, Yashim, you're wrong. It was mine—and now it is gone."

"We saw it here last night."

"Yes, but the Tatar! He took it, before he attacked!"

"The Tatar—" A sudden hope flickered in Yashim's breast. "In that case, it must still be here. Search the room. Look under the bed."

Brunelli and Palewski sprang to obey, but Carla didn't move. "Here in the room?" She sounded puzzled. "He took it with him, I'd imagine."

"I fought him, Carla." Yashim sounded surprised. "I'd have noticed him carrying a two-foot panel under his coat."

She sank down onto the bed.

"A two-foot panel?"

"The Bellini, Carla."

She had closed her eyes.

"I see. You were expecting a painting on wood."

Palewski nodded. "Gentile used it."

"It—it wasn't on panel anymore."

The room was still.

"I had it lifted fifteen years ago."

"Lifted? What do you mean?"

"Oh God." Carla put her hands over her face. When she pulled them down she was looking at Yashim.

"I had it transferred to canvas."

"Canvas?" Yashim echoed. "Why? How?"

"Old board doesn't last," she said wearily. "Especially not in Venice, with the damp. It warps and cracks, and the paint begins to deteriorate. Eventually there's nothing left."

"But how do you put it onto canvas?" Palewski asked. He was kneeling by the bed, and he sounded genuinely interested.

Carla waved a hand. "It's a process. Very new. Barbieri told me about it. Oh, he didn't know I had the painting. Maybe he knew, I'm not sure anymore. I took it to Florence, and they did the work. I think," she went on, sounding very controlled and looking at the ceiling, "that they glue the face to canvas, then chisel away at the panel until they get to the paint from the wrong side. Then they flip it over."

"Good God!" Palewski sounded appalled.

The contessa gave a shaky smile. "It doesn't sound good, does it? But it works. They touch it up a bit afterward, I suppose. But then it lasts."

She glanced up at Yashim, aware of the irony in her last words.

But Yashim wasn't looking at her.

He was staring at the empty space inside the frame. What he saw was not the damask that lined the walls but two men, fighting in the mud, tearing at each other's clothes, slippery as eels.

And the canvas, wrapped about the Tatar's body.

He saw the Tatar swimming back. The Tatar scrambling over the dam like an otter.

There hadn't been time to think. No time to wonder why the Tatar had chosen to go that way.

He'd simply assumed he was going back for the contessa. To murder Carla as he had murdered the others.

To finish his job.

And now in his mind's eye he saw the caisson spring, and the Tatar groping for a painting in the mud, then his look of blank incomprehension as he was swept away in a bounding deluge of timber and foaming water.

He sat down on the bed beside Carla and put his arm around her shoulders.

"The painting's gone," he said.

Brunelli blew out his cheeks in sympathy.

Carla put her hand to her head and began either to laugh or to cry; Yashim couldn't tell which. Probably both.

She turned and buried her head in Yashim's shoulder. Palewski raised an eyebrow at Brunelli.

They went out silently together, closing the door behind them.

Yashim never knew how long they sat together, rocking gently to and fro. He held his arms around her lovely waist, his face buried in her soft fair hair; she breathed on his chest with one slender arm flung around his neck.

It felt as though they might never move apart.

Yashim's thoughts revolved. He remembered Palewski talking to him in the salon.

He'd been talking about a priest.

Palewski. Yashim remembered something else he'd said, long before, about a picture he had hanging in his drawing room in Istanbul—the room Yashim had always loved, with its books, and the shabby escritoire and leaking armchairs, and the portrait of John Sobieski, King of Poland, over the sideboard.

"Carla," he murmured. "You took the duke's note of hand, didn't you? It was you."

She snuggled her head upward and he felt her blow gently onto his neck.

"I must know, Carla. Was it you?"

"I told you," she murmured. "I didn't play."

He felt her sigh against his skin.

"It wasn't a note of hand, Yashim."

He brushed back her fair curls to reveal one perfect ear, tender as a mouse's, with three little moles along the tip.

He stooped and brushed them with his lips.

"A love letter from the duke?"

He felt the muscles of her face move against his skin. She must have smiled.

"And you stuck it to the back of the picture."

"The Aspis—and the house of Osman," she whispered softly. "That letter was a final link."

"You wanted to be remembered?"

"Remembered. Honored, perhaps. Eight hundred years, Yashim, thirty generations. And now, today, there is nothing left." She moved her head back to look into his eyes. "The Republic is dead. The Aspi d'Istrias die with me. *Com'era, dov'era.* It isn't true."

"It never was."

Yashim, of all people, knew it was never true. You could never go back. You went on, shouldering the burdens of your past, and the world changed.

He brushed his lips to the perfect ear, remembering clearly what he had heard Palewski say, when he heard nothing at all.

The burdens of your past.

"Tell me, Carla, when you went to Istria to see the nuns again, looking for your son, did you have a way of recognizing him? Some mark?"

He felt her stiffen. "How did you know?"

"Three little moles," he said quietly.

She raised her head. She looked wary.

"If you want," he began slowly, "if you can, then there is something left for you, after all."

"I don't know what you mean."

"Your son."

Carla jerked her head back as if she had been bitten.

"I think your son is in Venice."

She slipped from his arms, sinking to her knees. At the side of the bed her hands went out, almost in prayer, toward Yashim.

"If you are playing with me," she said, her face contorted and in a voice that rose from her throat, "I will kill you."

Yashim shook his head. "Your son," he said, "would not hurt a fly. You will find him—" He paused. "Not *com'era, dov'era*. Not what he was, but as he is. And I can show you where."

112

MARIA slipped her arm through Palewski's.

"I hope you get back to your wolves and sleighs," she said.

"One day, perhaps." Palewski squeezed her arm.

A light breeze ruffled the waters of the Giudecca.

"I'll write," he said.

She shook her head. "Don't. I'll think of you as—as the wind. You won't be back, will you?"

"No." He coughed. "I won't be back. But I'm glad I came, Maria. I met a beautiful Venetian girl who was very brave and very generous."

He tilted back her bonnet and kissed her.

"I shan't forget." He put a little box between her hands. In it was a diamond brooch and a note from a bank in Trieste. "For your trousseau, Maria." He turned and walked up the gangplank. Yashim was waiting on the deck.

Together they leaned over the rail. The shoremen cast off. The foresail banged in the wind before the sailors aloft made it fast. Then it went taut, the ship creaked, and they began to move away from the dock.

As the gap widened, they saluted their friends. Carla was standing by Father Andrea, who had Nikola by the hand. Commissario Brunelli stood a little apart, but as they watched he offered Maria his arm; her bonnet barely reached his shoulder.

A cloud slid from the sun's face, lighting the polychrome walls of the Doges' Palace, the marble columns of the piazza. The Clock Tower across the square glowed.

Palewski raised his hand, and the dwindling figures on the *riva* waved back.

"Final curtain," he announced. The ship heeled around. They saw the mouth of the Grand Canal and the calm bulk of Santa Maria della Salute, and the wind from the mainland was in their face.

"Will you miss it?" Yashim asked at last, as the great church of San Giorgio slipped past on the starboard bow.

"Miss it?" Palewski was silent for a while. "Regret it, perhaps, a little. The way one regrets one's youth and what's passed. For a moment Venice brought it back."

He took off his hat and ran his fingers through his hair.

"I missed tea," he said. "And our Thursday dinners, Yash. I missed the muezzins, too. Venice would be better with muezzins."

"Yes. Perhaps."

"I'm looking forward to seeing Marta again."

"She will be happy to see you back."

Palewski bit his lip. "The Bellini was only an idea, Yashim. We'll have another."

"The Bellini . . ."

"You're not listening, Yashim."

Yashim nodded. "Yes," he said.

113

FOR several days Yashim kept to his cabin, but on the morning of the fourth day, as they began to thread a course between the islands of the Aegean, Palewski found him on deck.

He looked pale.

Palewski sat down beside his old friend.

"Two more days, and we'll be home." He paused. "Come on, Yashim. It was only a painting."

"It's not the painting," Yashim said.

"What, then? You rescued Maria. Saved the contessa. Young Nikola would have died without you. And your disguise—it was terrific." He peered at his friend and sighed. "But I don't know why they didn't just send you, Yashim."

Yashim was about to reply when his eye was caught by a movement on the water. "Look!" he said, pointing. "Porpoises."

There were three of them, scudding through the bright water, turning their bodies in the sunlight.

"They're watching us," Palewski exclaimed in delight.

Yashim smiled. "Strange, isn't it? These interlocking lines. Our own lives. It's in the diagram, I suppose. *Com'era, dov'era.* Nothing, in the end, moves out of the square."

"The diagram? You're speaking in riddles, Yashim."

"The Sand-Reckoner's diagram. Everyone's face is turned inward, you see, but they adopt a different background as they move. It's like a shadow sliding across a building. *Com'era, dov'era* describes a sort of ideal moment before the dance begins. Before things change."

"When someone—or something—shifts its position, it changes, too? Is that what you mean?"

"Nothing is still. Nothing remains the same—except the pattern that lies underneath."

"Hier ist die Rose, hier tanze!" Palewski murmured. He crinkled his nose. "Hegel."

Yashim went on: "Everyone belongs in the diagram. Maria, Ruggerio, Barbieri, Carla, and you. Even me." Yashim laid his thumb and forefinger on the rail. "Take Maria. She's linked to Ruggerio—it's Ruggerio who puts her in your bed. That provides you with an alibi when Barbieri turns up dead. I don't know how close you were to getting arrested then."

He put another finger down. "Alfredo, now. Taking Maria was his big mistake, but he had to find out who you were." Another finger. "Alfredo becomes Eletro, as it were. Eletro, dead. But Eletro is linked to the boy, Nikola. That's five intersections. Now it goes back to Maria. She takes Nikola to church, where he recognizes the priest."

He put his other thumb down on the rail. "Which is not the end of the story: you connect Nikola to the contessa."

"And she's linked to Ruggerio and Eletro by the game of cards in the Fondaco dei Turchi."

"Yes. Everyone's placed. Except the Austrian."

"Finkel?"

"He's the one who has no obvious connection."

He stared out over the rail. They were among the Cyclades, a group of Orthodox islands that had fallen to Venice after the sack of Constantinople in 1204. Three hundred years later, with some relief, the islands' Greek inhabitants had welcomed the Ottomans. Here and there, on the horizon, the islands' outlines shimmered in the sunlight.

Something gathered at the back of Yashim's mind.

Venice and the Ottomans: two empires locked together in trade and war, moving to a pattern reproduced all across the Mediterranean. Venetians taking possession of Byzantine strongholds. The Ottomans snapping at their heels. In the tiny Cyclades, as in mighty Cyprus.

"Patterns aren't measurements," Yashim said finally. "I've seen the

Sand-Reckoner's diagram on a sheet of paper and on the floor of the wrestling school, in Istanbul. It'll work on any scale."

"Of course."

Yashim closed his eyes. "And a pattern repeats, too." He thought of the İznik tiles he had saved from the fountain. Minute versions of a larger pattern. "The same shapes reoccur throughout. A square, for instance, is the center of a bigger square."

"Yes," Palewski agreed.

"Perhaps the diagram we've followed fits into a larger version of the same diagram? Making room for Finkel after all. Extend the connections that link everyone in Venice, and you could have a version of the diagram that includes Resid, and the sultan, too. It's like this. The Tatar should have killed Carla that night. Next morning Finkel turns up at the Ca' d'Aspi. He has been sitting on the order to remove the painting and the note."

"So why does he choose that morning to make a move?"

"Exactly. Either he thought that Carla was dead or he knew already that the Tatar had failed. Either way, there must be a link between them."

Palewski slapped a hand to the rail. "The Tatar was working for the Austrians!"

"Not quite. He was sent by Resid. But he was steered by Ruggerio, who was killed when the job was done."

"Ruggerio could have told Finkel."

Yashim nodded. "Easily. It's a diagram of possibilities, but it doesn't touch on motive, Palewski."

"Resid's motive is fairly obvious, isn't it? He sent the Tatar to destroy the evidence that the Duke of Naxos was in fact Sultan Abdülmecid. To save the sultan's honor."

"With Austrian help?"

Palewski threw up his hands. "I don't get it, Yashim. Why would the Austrians help Resid?"

Yashim bit his lip.

"There's more to it than the sultan's honor. Resid was chasing down evidence that the sultan had misbehaved in Venice. Evidence that could safeguard his own position, too."

"Blackmail? That's more like it," Palewski agreed. "But it still doesn't give the Austrians a motive."

Yashim smiled grimly. "On the contrary, it gives them every motive. What do the Austrians want from the Ottoman Empire?"

"Peace and quiet, I suppose."

"Exactly. The Austrians are overstretched. In Italy, in Poland, in Galicia. They are keeping a lid on things, but only just. Even Carla wanted the money for the cause of Venetian independence. The Austrians would like nothing better than a compliant sultan. Finkel's instructions were to get the note, but he didn't do anything until the last minute. And then, thanks to us, it was too late."

"You mean Finkel knew about the Tatar? He sat back and waited for the Tatar to do his job for him?"

"By eliminating the witnesses, one by one. Who'd ever imagine a Tatar assassin would be stalking the streets of Venice? You didn't believe it yourself, even when Nikola put him in his painting. And that gave the Austrians their alibi."

"If the Tatar got the incriminating note, Resid would have the Austrians to thank," Palewski said slowly. "If he failed, the Austrians would take it themselves. Either way, they stood to gain by cooperating with Resid." He gave a low whistle. "No wonder Resid didn't want you hunting the Bellini in Venice. He was handing control of Ottoman foreign policy to Austria."

They exchanged glances.

"This is going to be awfully hard to prove, Yashim."

"Yes."

"And it isn't over while Carla—the contessa—is still alive."

"No."

"And if Resid finds out where we've been . . ."

"Yes."

Palewski looked out to sea and sighed. "Do you know, I am missing Venice much more than I'd expected."

114

THE Bosphorus quivered in the summer heat. On the Pera shore of the Golden Horn, where once the plane had extended its grateful shade, sunlight sprang from the rubble of the broken pavement. Across the Horn the courtyards of the mosques were full; people squatted against the walls and moved lazily to and fro between the arcades and the fountains.

Outside the Topkapi Palace, Yashim stopped by a fountain whose scrolled and overhanging eaves created a welcome strip of shade. He set a book and a small parcel down on the stone bench and washed his hands and face beneath the spigot. Then he went through the main gate of the Topkapi Palace into the First Court.

There were more people here than was usual, now that the Ottoman court had moved to a new, European-style palace on the Bosphorus. They came for the dappled shade of the trees beneath which they sat cross-legged: elderly men in fezzes and pantaloons, drawing on long pipes; younger men with swathed wives, watching their children scamper through the dust.

Yashim crossed the court and reached the High Gate, where he knocked.

A sleepy halberdier opened a wicket.

"Yashim *lala*, to see the valide sultan."

Inside, the gatehouse was cool and dark. Yashim sank gratefully down onto a stone bench.

A few minutes later, another halberdier saluted him, and they went out into the glare of the Second Court. Instead of crossing to the far corner and the entrance of the harem, the halberdier took him to the central gate and then right, toward the Treasury.

He found the valide in the Baghdad Kiosk, lounging on a divan set up beneath the arches.

She smiled and raised a hand when she saw him, her bracelets tinkling like water.

"Don't look so shocked, Yashim," she said as he approached. "There are limits to our endurance."

Yashim smiled and bowed. The valide's apartments were like ovens in the heat.

"It's not the heat, Yashim. I was born to it, after all. It's the stillness. I thank the sultan, Yashim. He suggested I come here." She patted the divan. "I have no idea how he intends to rule and frankly I am too old to care. But I approve of his consideration."

The Baghdad Kiosk was one of the oldest parts of the palace, a medieval cavern open to the breeze with a view running straight up the Bosphorus.

"I'm not shocked, valide. I'm only pleased that the sultan—"

"Remembers me?" She arched an eyebrow, while Yashim shook his head. "I even sleep here sometimes," she said. "I also like the view. It makes me feel like a sultan myself."

A girl came in carrying a tray of cooling sherbet.

"Tell me about Venice," the valide said.

Yashim almost dropped his glass.

"Venice, valide?"

"Do the women still sit in their *altana* on the roofs, making their hair go yellow?"

Yashim lowered his eyes, nonplussed. The valide's vision of Venice was so different from the one he'd seen.

"I brought you something," he remembered.

She undid the parcel. Inside, carefully wrapped in tissue paper, was a pair of candlesticks. They were made of a twist of pink Murano glass, and each had a tassel of colored pendants dangling from the rim.

The valide examined them carefully. "Very pretty, Yashim."

Yashim felt satisfied; the valide was never lavish with her praise.

"I should have liked to have seen Venice," she continued. "But perhaps it is very ugly now?"

"It is beautiful, valide. But it is poor."

The valide lifted a bangled arm to the balustrade and turned her head. Her profile was still extraordinarily clear.

"Istanbul could become poor one day. Who knows?"

"I felt the same, valide," Yashim admitted. "Istanbul and Venice always ate from the one dish."

"I suppose you are right. Istanbul the master, Venice the servant—and when the master has dined, the servant clears his plate." She looked at Yashim. "Perhaps that's why the sultan came here last week. To talk about Venice."

Yashim felt himself blush. "The sultan spoke of Venice?"

The valide raised her chin. "In the olden days, Yashim, the sultans left their dominions only in time of war—to conquer. But that age is past. Abdülmecid is young, Yashim, and he has not lived in the world. He knows it. I think he regrets it, too."

But he has lived in the world more than the valide might suppose, Yashim reflected.

"He comes to me because he thinks I know Europe. I don't discourage him."

"You—have traveled, valide?"

"You *might* call it traveling, Yashim. Certainly I met some quite interesting men." A smile hovered on her lips. "I threatened the Dey of Algiers with the vengeance of the French navy. Later, I pulled his beard. I, too, was very young."

Yashim smiled. The dey had sent his captive on, to Istanbul, as a gift to the sultan. Perhaps he didn't like having his beard pulled.

"But Abdülmecid is less experienced," the valide continued. "I have encouraged him to read more French, I hope."

Yashim remembered the Dumas.

"I have brought this back, valide. Dumas's *Ali Pasha.*"

She took it with a small smile.

"I don't think it's quite right for the padishah," she said.

"No," Yashim agreed.

115

BEFORE he left the palace, Yashim crossed the Third Court and entered the imperial archives, where the vast records of the bureaucracy that had governed millions of lives for centuries were all held.

He spent an hour going through an elaborate index, waving away all offers of help until he found the volume he wanted.

A librarian disappeared into the huge stacks, crammed with volumes of correspondence and reports, ancient scrolls, imperial firmans.

"The records you're asking for are not yet bound." The librarian fluttered his hands apologetically. "They have only just been delivered."

"I'd like to see them anyway."

The librarian frowned. "It's against regulations to let out unbound records."

Yashim waited.

"You can't remove them, efendi."

"I'll examine them in front of you, if you like."

The librarian sniffed. "That won't be necessary," he said crisply.

A few moments later, Yashim was leafing through a pile of diplomatic records.

It took him twenty minutes to find what he wanted.

116

"WHERE yous been, efendi? You have a *yali* now, I thinks, like some big pasha, hey?"

Yashim smiled and shook his head. "I've been away, George."

George scratched his chest. "Is too hot here, Yashim efendi."

George grabbed a bucket and roved from piles of spinach to pyramids of tiny cucumbers, sprinkling them with cold water. When he was finished he rubbed his wet hands across his face.

"Today, you is not busy, efendi."

He caught a dozen or so tiny artichokes, one by one, and placed them on his scales. They were no bigger than his thumb.

"Some tomatoes. Some garlic. Aubergine—here." He took four long green aubergines and weighed them, too. He carefully placed everything in the basket with his huge hands and crammed a fistful of herbs— parsley, dill, rosemary—on top.

He puffed up, waved his arms, and subsided with a gesture of calm. "You cooks in the heat and eats in the cool," he bellowed, miming to suit. "Dolma. A raki. No meat."

Yashim paused on the way home to buy bread, yogurt, and olives. When he got back, the little apartment was like an oven. He threw back the windows and left the door slightly ajar to encourage a breeze.

It was only when he picked up the basket again that he noticed a small parcel by the door.

He undid the string.

Inside was his knife.

With it came a letter.

My dearest Yashim, I wished to send you a souvenir of Venice, but really, there is nothing. So I sent Antonio to find your knife, in the courtyard of the fondaco.

You saved my life, which was not important until now. Before, I had no feeling—I lost it, I suppose, when my brother died, and then my mother. Until now I knew neither joy nor tenderness, but only pain, in the way you know about. With Nikola there is pain, but it is another kind, and it is very mixed with something else. Of course I wish—but what do I wish? For nothing. I commune with an angel. Father Andrea is very good.

I am sorry to have lost the painting, because it would have been good for us to have money. About the letters, I will let the fish read them. I know—and you know—that they did exist. Which is enough.

Your loving friend,
Carla A-I

He put the letter aside and examined the knife. The binding on the grip had come loose, but the steel itself was bright and sharp. He weighed it in his hand.

"You have traveled a long way," he said aloud, "since Ammar made you."

He wiped the blade with a cloth, glad that the knife was clean.

"Ammar made you to chop vegetables," he said.

He took a board and set to work. With the knife he prepared the tiny artichokes, trimming their leaves. He chopped the tomatoes, slit the aubergines, crushed and salted the garlic cloves. The room filled with the scent of herbs.

The Tatar had been dispatched to expunge every trace of the sultan's dishonor. To kill, leaving no witnesses.

Palewski had said something on the ship, before the porpoises broke the cover of the sea, something he had put from his mind.

Resid had sent a killer and not him.

I could have done it, Yashim thought, without killing anyone. I might have retrieved the letters—and the painting, too. That is my job.

He stuffed the aubergines with tomatoes, onion, a little parsley and garlic, carefully gathering the last fragments from the board.

If the Austrians already knew about the sultan's visit, killing the witnesses was a waste. A waste of life, above all, but also a risk.

With sticky fingers he set the aubergines into a dish.

He filled an earthenware with the artichokes, drizzled them with oil, a splash of water, and a sprinkling of lemon juice.

When it was done he stuck his head out of the window and shouted, "Elvan! Elvan! Come!"

A boy levered himself out of a patch of shade and stood up, stretching.

"I am here, Yashim efendi," he called.

Upstairs, he took the dishes from Yashim and carried them down the street to the baker's shop, where the baker put them in his oven.

Yashim went to the hammam.

An attendant took his clothes and led him through to the steam room, where he spread out a towel for him on the hot slab.

Yashim lay down. The heat seeped through his limbs. His muscles relaxed.

Only his mind remained tense.

He stared upward, at the light shining through the domed ceiling, and remembered the Tatar at the top of the stairs, framed in the dawn breaking through the Byzantine windows.

Resid's assassin.

He wiped the sweat from his eyes with two hands. He went over his conversation with the valide in his mind.

He did not protest when the hammam attendant slopped over in his pattens to lead him from the slab.

He let himself be seated by the spigot of hot water and began to mechanically sluice himself from head to foot.

Seeing nothing. Hearing no one.

Until a bare foot prodded him in the ribs.

He glanced around then, surprised, through a film of steam.

For a moment he didn't recognize the young man with slicked-down hair who sat beside him on the marble floor.

"You have disobeyed me, Yashim. I find that—interesting. And unfortunate. We were getting along so well."

Yashim recognized the voice. It was Resid Pasha.

117

"DISOBEYED you?"

"I told you I would summon you when the time was right. But yesterday you visited the Old Palace. Topkapi. You spoke with the valide."

Yashim put his scoop under the flow of water and let it fill.

"We discussed a book, Resid."

"You are supposed to be in Venice, remember? The sultan ordered you to go."

"You asked me to stay, my pasha."

Resid's eyes were like gimlets. "Don't try me, Yashim. I am the slave of the padishah. His lightest wish is my command."

"There must be some mistake. Maybe I misunderstood."

"Impossible. The sultan's order was very clear. You were to go to Venice. But you are here."

"Yes, my pasha. I am here." He poured the water over his head. He rubbed a hand through his hair. "The ship docked yesterday."

"What ship?"

"The packet from Trieste."

Resid said nothing, but the scoop he was lifting stopped in midair.

"We are all slaves of the padishah, Resid."

Resid let the water trickle onto the floor. "Really, Yashim, this is so interesting." There was something gravelly in his voice, and Yashim wondered if it might be fear. "Did you—succeed?"

"I believe so, in a way."

"In what way, Yashim?" The young vizier turned his scoop gently between his fingers. "You found the painting, perhaps?"

"Yes, Resid Pasha. I did." Yashim put his scoop under the spigot and watched it fill again. "The portrait of Mehmet the Conqueror," he said, raising his voice slightly above the bubbling water. "Among other things."

"Other things?"

"Letters."

"Letters. A pity that you decided to go to Venice, after all. I warned you it was a dangerous city."

Yashim stared at Resid.

"It's not a worry, Resid Pasha. I'm safe home now, in Istanbul."

Resid filled his cupped hands with water and splashed it over his face. "I wish I could share your confidence, Yashim. One hears so often these days of accidents, if not banditry. Perhaps we should try to install more lighting, as I hear they have in Venice? Security in the city, however, is not my concern—I deal with foreign affairs."

"Curiously enough, it is those very foreign affairs of yours that give me confidence," Yashim said with a gentle smile. "One particular affair, at least."

Resid's own smile was bland and fixed. "And what—affair—might that be, Yashim *lala*?"

"One that a certain Duke of Naxos had with the Contessa d'Aspi d'Istria. As an affair, I gather, it was one-sided, and largely epistolary. Though of course I may be wrong."

Very slowly, Resid picked up the scoop. He held it in his hand, empty.

"I'm sorry to hear you say that, Yashim. At home, or abroad, my loyalty is to the sultan and to his good name."

"Even a sultan may be judged by the company he keeps, Resid."

A masseur arrived and knelt at Yashim's feet. Yashim waved him away.

"You drag the sultan into this?" Resid hissed. "I expected better of you, Yashim."

"The sultan? No. Abdülmecid wasn't a part of this." Yashim let the water patter into his open palm. "You should have let me go, Resid. Your Tatar wasn't good enough."

"My Tatar?"

"He's dead, Resid. Who was he, anyway? A relative of yours perhaps?"

"You question me?"

Yashim sighed. "Not really, no. After all, you couldn't have sent me, Resid Pasha."

"You? What could you have done?"

"A service to the sultan. That's what I do, Resid. My training. My talent. But in this case, my services were not required."

Resid said nothing.

"Last year," Yashim went on, "the sultan sent an envoy to Vienna. In Trieste he develops a slight malady, which keeps him there a few days. I've checked, Resid. The dates of his mission to Vienna are on the record."

He poured the water over his head.

"In Venice, it's Carnevale. Parties, drinking, gambling. Everyone is in disguise. The Duke of Naxos arrives. The name is cleverly chosen. It sounds faintly familiar to the Venetians—remember? But it means so little, except to the man himself. Perhaps he's thinking of Joseph Nasi, the last man to genuinely hold the title. An influential adviser to Süleyman, in his old age, and then to Selim, his son. No friend to Venice, either."

"Go on."

"The Contessa d'Aspi d'Istria draws her own conclusions. The imperious young visitor writes her a letter. Carla is a snob—she imagines that the Duke of Naxos is Abdülmecid. She's quite charmed. So, apparently, is his cicerone.

"Later on, when someone discreetly offers the Bellini portrait to the sultan through the calligrapher Metin Yamaluk, this envoy suspects it is her. He's grander now. A pasha. He has farther to fall, so he needs someone he can trust. Someone in the family. He sends a Tatar to Yamaluk, to make sure, but the calligrapher is an old man with a weak heart, and the Tatar kills him. Maybe that was an accident—I think it was."

"You only think so? Why so uncertain now, Yashim *lala*?"

"There's no evidence either way. But I think it was an accident because it was so ill omened. For you."

"For me?"

Yashim sighed. "You were the Duke of Naxos, Resid."

"And you think the omens were proved?" Resid gave a tight little laugh. "It's not over yet, Yashim *lala*. Go on."

Yashim shrugged. "Why bother? You know as well as I do that you were afraid. You were afraid that if the contessa started to negotiate with the sultan, the truth would come out. So you decided to kill her, and everyone else associated with that game of cards."

Resid gave a strange smile. "So, the contessa is dead. Thank you for that, Yashim."

Yashim cocked his head to one side. "No, Resid. She didn't die, because I stopped the killer."

"I see." Resid blinked. "The indefatigable Yashim."

"No, no. I'm very tired, Resid."

Resid leaned forward. He brought his sweating face to within a few inches of Yashim's.

"It's a new regime, Yashim *lala*," he hissed. "New men. The sultan's young, like me—but I have experience he needs. A new regime. And, Yashim, just between ourselves, I control it."

Yashim said nothing.

"Fetch me the letter," Resid burst out. "Fetch it and save your skin. Or go away and die, if you prefer." He leaned back against the marble wall. "Barbieri died. So did Eletro, and Boschini. Maybe the contessa's next, after all. And do you know? Nobody cares."

Yashim stood up. "You're right, of course. It's only Pappendorf who'll be surprised. I suppose the Austrian ambassador thought you were delivering him the sultan."

"What do you mean?"

"Ruggerio was an informer. He told the Austrians that the Duke of Naxos was Abdülmecid, so Pappendorf came to you, didn't he? With a threat to expose the sultan—and an offer of cooperation. He expected you to manage it, I suppose. Blackmail at a high level. You went along with it, of course, to avoid suspicion falling on you. You and the Austrians, together, could eradicate the evidence against the Duke of Naxos. No one would ever know he'd been to Venice at all. The Austrians would help by giving your assassin a free hand, but in return they expected to own the sultan. How surprised they'll be to discover that all they own is you."

"I control affairs," Resid said grimly.

"For how long, Resid?" Yashim asked. "Viziers come and go, don't they? Sometimes they go gracefully, with blessings, to retirement and old age. But you're too young to retire safely. You'd live too long and know too much."

"I control affairs." His voice shook.

"The Austrians might not think so, Resid. They bought a sultan. You have delivered—who? A man who bungles a simple killing even when everyone's straining to look the other way."

Yashim got to his knees. His face was set. "The palace is a little world," he said. "You wouldn't be the first vizier to forget that the people, too, have a voice. I saw them, Resid, when they gathered around the great tree. It wouldn't take much, I think, when the people learn that you sold your sultan's name to protect your own."

Resid was staring at him, his mouth open.

"The trouble with advisers is that they get things wrong. Even Joseph Nasi, I recall, got it wrong from time to time. The good thing about them is that they're dispensable.

"You, Resid, promised everyone your loyalty and your good faith. The people, with your pieties. The sultan, with loyalty. The Austrians, with a leash on the sultan. There's a diagram we both know, where the background changes as you move. But com'era, dov'era: you've disappointed even me."

A memory flashed into Yashim's mind, something Carla had said. "When it's all gone, Resid, honor is all we have left."

He stood up and walked out without looking back.

118

YASHIM returned to his apartment. Elvan had brought the dishes back from the baker's.

He peeled and chopped the cucumbers. He sprinkled them with salt, crushed two cloves of garlic, chopped them fine, and put them in a bowl with some yogurt. After a while he squeezed the water from the cucumbers and mixed them into the yogurt.

Then he washed his hands and sat silently on his divan, looking out across the rooftops of Istanbul.

119

"I brought raki," Palewski said, taking the bottle from his bag. "I wanted to feel properly home."

Yashim fetched two painted glasses and a jug of water. He set some olives on the table. He put some of the artichokes on a dish, with the aubergines, sliced. He cut the bread and left it on the board, which he put on the table with the yogurt.

Palewski poured an inch of raki into each glass and turned it milky with the water.

He handed one to Yashim. "*Prosit!*"

When they had drunk, he sat tossing an olive in his hand and looking expectantly at Yashim.

Yashim shook his head. "How's Marta?"

"I'll tell you about Marta later," Palewski said. "I want to know if you've heard anything from Resid."

Yashim lifted an artichoke to his mouth. It tasted very good.

"Yashim."

"I saw him this afternoon, at the hammam."

"So he doesn't know about Venice, then?"

"He knew when I told him."

Palewski stared. "That's a death warrant. For you and the contessa, too. Who's to say he wasn't just doing his duty, protecting the sultan's honor?"

Yashim took a sip of raki. "Me," he said. "And he knew it, too."

Palewski frowned. "You against him?"

Yashim wiped his hands on a napkin and laid it on the table. "Remember the Duke of Naxos? Carla said that the title would have reverted to the sultan on Joseph Nasi's death."

"Which is why Abdülmecid used it."

"No, Palewski. Abdülmecid wasn't the sultan then. He was only the crown prince."

"Hairsplitting, Yashim."

"Maybe. But fakery is endemic in Venice," Yashim said. "How do we know that the Duke of Naxos who came to Venice in Carnivale really *was* the sultan?"

Palewski gave an impatient shrug. "Carla recognized him, Yashim. And then—the Tatar. The murders. Covering up a youthful indiscretion."

"An indiscretion, yes," Yashim echoed. "It was committed by a man nobody really knew. He wore a mask and called himself the Duke of Naxos. It hurt me to think that the sultan could have gone drinking and gambling in Venice, Palewski." He bit his lip. "There's something else. I saw the valide today. Abdülmecid has set her up in the Baghdad Kiosk."

"Good for him."

Yashim nodded. "She mentioned how innocent he was of life, too. But that's not it. Good for him, you say? Yes. Abdülmecid might kick over the traces once in his life, but he was brought up well. An Ottoman gentleman, however young, does not pay visits in the character of an enemy. And Nasi was an implacable enemy of Venice."

Palewski was still. "You're right, Yashim. I hadn't thought of that. Whatever sultans have been in their time, they have always had, what? Form. Even Mahmut, poor fellow. He was a great bear, but you couldn't fault his manners."

He speared an artichoke. "But if the sultan wasn't masquerading as the Duke of Naxos, who was?"

"Resid Pasha."

Palewski choked, so Yashim got up to fetch him another glass of water.

"That, of course, changes everything," Palewski spluttered.

"Everything? No. The pattern doesn't change. Carla thought she recognized the duke. And Ruggerio was watching—mistakenly—the professional guide, whose gift was to assess the people he met. I think something in the way Carla behaved alerted him, too."

Palewski clouded his glass with water. "And he informed on them—to the Austrians."

"The same pattern," Yashim said. "I don't know when Resid realized the mistake. He didn't correct it. That was his conceit."

"And the Duke of Naxos was taken to be the sultan."

"Yes. Resid allowed people to believe the sultan had been to Venice."

Yashim ate a slice of aubergine.

"Only when the sultan came to the throne did Carla get Metin Yamaluk to hint to the sultan about the painting. She wanted to be discreet, for her sake and his."

"Giving him the opportunity to delicately ignore her, if he liked," Palewski said.

Yashim spread his hands. "Instead, the sultan was intrigued. He had nothing to hide. He knew nothing about the contessa. He'd never been to Venice. He simply wanted to follow up on the hint. He wanted the painting."

"And when he sent for you," Palewski reasoned, "Resid had to make a move."

"He moved fast. He stood me down."

Palewski sucked in his cheeks. "He decided to trade on what the Austrians already believed, Yashim. And sent the Tatar to eliminate all witnesses. One of his people. Resid's mother is a Tatar, too."

Yashim nodded. "He was also meant to recover the incriminating love letters Resid had sent Carla."

"Love letters? I thought we were dealing with gambling debts. A promissory note."

"So did I, until Carla told me the truth. Or the half-truth. At the time we both believed the letters had been written by the sultan."

"But—but they're gone, aren't they? With the painting?"

Yashim looked his friend in the eye. "Resid doesn't know that. He thinks I have them."

Palewski reached for the raki and poured them both another drink. "What will he do now?"

Yashim shook his head slowly. "I see no way out. We can only wait."

Palewski blew out his cheeks.

"I'm sorry, Yash. Making you think of food at a time like this. I shouldn't have come."

He began to rub his wrists, unconsciously.

"We have to eat," Yashim said. "How's Marta, then?"

Palewski regarded the ceiling thoughtfully.

"I have some rather strange news, as it happens."

"She's getting married?"

"Married?" Palewski looked astonished. "Good God, Yashim. You *are* morbid. No, thank heavens, she's not getting married. She's back in the house." He shook his head. "And she's cleared up everything. Everything. She rearranged my books."

"I saw that," Yashim confessed. "I didn't want to tell you."

"No, well, I admit I was pretty aggrieved. I'd made a pile of books on the table in the hall. Folios, some of them—a church history by Foulbert. An interesting seventeenth-century survey of the Greek islands by a Dutchman, writing in Latin, not accurate but—well, anyway, that's not important. Thing is, I'd been dropping books onto this table for weeks on my way in and out of the garden—you remember coming into the garden, when all this began?—and it's a bit dim down there."

"A bit dim. So?"

"When Marta started to shift the stack she found a letter stuck between two books. It must have been left on the table, and I didn't see it."

"A letter?"

"Propped on the mantelpiece when I got home. Arms on the fold in green ink, raised."

"Palace?"

"Invitation, Yashim. He had been there all the time. An invitation to the sultan's inaugural ball." Palewski buried his face in his glass. "Half a mind to cut it, anyway," he mumbled.

Yashim looked at him, unsmiling.

"Signor Brett would go," he said. "Signor Brett has the proper garb."

Palewski shrugged. "You know I hate that kind of thing."

"Honor of the Poles," Yashim said.

"Dishonor, more like. Bad champagne."

"The Austrian ambassador will have spoken to Karolyi by then."

"So?"

"Pappendorf's face," Yashim said.

They looked at each other over the rim of their glasses.

"Pappendorf's face!" Palewski repeated happily. "*Prosit!*"

120

THE water slapped lazily at the green weed that fringed the pilings of the bridge.

There was no tide, only the perpetual current from the north, slipping under the movement of warm water from the sea, which set up whorls and currents that the boatmen knew.

Caught between these ceaseless, shifting eddies and countercurrents, the pasha who died young described a forgotten pattern. He moved like a dervish, his limbs open and relaxed. Beneath Byzantine domes, dilapidated palaces, and tethered boats, the pasha's corpse twirled in the moonlight, unseen, his arms flung wide in a gesture of vacant resignation.

So he turned, around and around, as the moon sank behind the towers and domes.

When dawn broke, the first workmen returned to the bridge. The pasha's body had scarcely moved from the place where he went in, yards away from the deep waters of the Bosphorus on which, in her days of glory, the city had made her fortune.

Overhead, the workmen stared down into the clear water.

AUTHOR'S NOTE

Four decades after the events described in this book, Sir Henry Layard, distinguished explorer, archaeologist, and Her Britannic Majesty's Ambassador to the Sublime Porte in Istanbul, was dismissed from his office following a change of government in London.

The incoming government proposed taking a tough line with Turkey-in-Europe. Sir Henry Layard was considered to be too chummy with the Orientals.

In vexation, rather than returning to his ancestral halls (tricked out, needless to say, in Canalettos, not to mention the ruins and friezes of ancient Tyre), Sir Henry and his young wife moved to Venice, where they bought a palazzo, the Ca' Cappello, not far, in my mind at least, from the Ca' d'Aspi.

One afternoon in 1865, just as he was stepping into his gondola to return home, Sir Henry was approached by an elderly and evidently impoverished man who asked the milord to buy an old painting for five pounds.

Scarcely glancing at the painting, and determined not to be late, Sir Henry refused. He stepped into the gondola and was carried away.

On arriving home, he found the painting propped against his door.

He hung it in a special room, all on its own.

Lady Layard survived her husband by twenty-three years. She remained in Venice, very much upon her dignity as Sir Henry's widow but fond of social life nonetheless. Younger residents like Henry James knew the Palazzo Layard as the Refrigerator.

In her will she left the painting of Mehmet II, by Bellini, to the National Gallery in London.

Details about the damage to the painting, probably inflicted when it was lifted from board to canvas, and about the heavy restoration work carried out in the nineteenth century, can be obtained from the gallery. Both were considered so extensive that curators have cautiously labeled the painting *attributed to*, rather than *by*, Gentile Bellini.

It continues to travel the world; it was recently in Venice, and before that, at the turn of the century, it drew enormous crowds when it was exhibited in Istanbul.

Oddly enough, as I was writing this book, Sotheby's in London sold a smaller likeness of Mehmet II—much the same size as the picture Palewski saw at the Palazzo d'Istria—for almost half a million pounds.

It was, supposedly, a later copy of the Bellini portrait.

As for the album of his father's drawings that Gentile Bellini presented to Sultan Mehmet in 1480, there were, in fact, two. One on paper, bought from a market in Smyrna in 1823, is in the British Museum; the other, finer, album on parchment is in the Louvre.

It was discovered in the attic of a house in Guyenne, France, in 1886.

The Fondaco dei Turchi remained a ruin of sorts until 1860, when it was bought by the municipality and restored to its present condition. Following the restorers' motto, *com'era, dov'era*, every effort was made to remodel the building as a Byzantine palace of the twelfth century. Consequently, all traces of its former grandeur, as well as its decay, were efficiently erased. Clad in gray marble sheeting, and remodeled within, it is now perhaps the ugliest building on the Grand Canal.

ACKNOWLEDGMENTS

I am indebted to the enthusiasm and encouragement of my publishers around the world, and to the efforts of translators to render Yashim intellible in, I think, thirty-eight languages. To Ottar Samuelson and the team at Dinamo: *Skål!* And a special thanks to Marina Fabbri, of the Courmayeur Noir Festival.

Yashim himself could not have traveled so far, for an Ottoman investigator, without Sarah Chalfant and Charles Buchan at the Wylie Agency. Thanks to Richard Goodwin for making Yashim the Movie, now showing at www.jasongoodwin.net, a website created by my son Izaak. Emma Clark, from the Prince's School of Traditional Arts, helped me out over women calligraphers; Carlo Pescatori had us in Venice; Amr Ben Halim was responsible for a memorable recent trip to Istanbul; and Jim Perry acted as my fight coordinator. Thank you all.

I like to think of Venice as an aspect of Istanbul; part of its fabric, and much of wealth that built it, came directly from the shores of the Bosphorus. Sending Yashim there always seemed like a good idea.

My own explorations of Venice have been made with my family. Together we have tramped the streets, visited the chill reconstruction of the Fondaco dei Turchi, eaten at Florian's (though not much; the prices are steeper than in Palewski's time), chosen ice cream on the Zattere (like Maria), admired the horses, and shopped at the Rialto market.

This book is dedicated to my son Walter, who loves Venice, drawing, jokes, and Venetian ice cream—passions matched at home by his Byzantine efforts to get onto my computer and substitute for Yashim's world others more ignoble and remote.

Read on for an excerpt from

Jason Goodwin's next Investigator Yashim mystery,

An
Evil
Eye

Available in hardcover July 2010

1

IT has been such a lovely day, being all dressed up like a big bear. Furry boots. Furry hat.

"You must catch it this time, silly!"

"I will try, my precious!" The kalfa smiles at the little girl. But it is hard to catch a ball made of snow when the light is beginning to fade. The little girl knows this. It is what makes her laugh.

Later she says: "You may sit in the arbor. I am going to play."

She runs to the big tree, taking big steps in the snow, like a bear. She is a bear and can hide behind the thick black trunk. There is not as much snow on the ground here.

Peep-o! Her kalfa is sitting in the arbor, on the stone seat where they have put the cushions. Peep-o!

Silly kalfa! She is not looking. She doesn't know there is a bear so close.

The little girl glances around. The trees at the end of the harem garden are tangled and black and white with snow, and the snow between is quite fresh and smooth. She sets off, planting her fur boots into the white coverlet one after the other. Counting. The kalfa cannot see her; the tree is between them.

One step, two step, three step, four.

The trees are close. She can see between them now, into the shadows. For a bear those shadows would be a good hiding place.

The little girl stops. She turns her head and looks back with a dubious frown. Of course she cannot see her kalfa, because of the big tree. What she can see are her footprints in the snow, and for a moment she wonders how they got there, those footprints coming after her across the shrouded lawn. They have swerved from the big tree and chased after her, dark sockets running across the whiteness. They are headed right toward her. To where she is standing.

And before she can turn her head she knows that the bear is on the other side, in the shadows behind her. The little girl opens her mouth to say something, perhaps even to scream, but nothing comes out.

Later she remembers the kalfa calling, and running back toward the big tree, running too slowly like in a dream, willing her face forward, with the footprints always just a step behind her.

When the kalfa crouches down to put a shawl around her, the girl tells her about the bear.

The kalfa laughs, smoothing her hair, but her eyes go out toward the garden.

Later, much later, when the little girl hears the sound of her kalfa's soft breath rising and falling beside her on the divan, she laces her fingers together over her chest and squeezes them very hard.

Her name is Toron, and she is five. The kalfas are more than five. Maybe they are fifteen, or eighteen, years old. Together they will live in the sultan's harem forever and ever and ever.

2

YASHIM winced and gave an exclamation of surprise. "*Everything that is useful,*" he read, "*is ugly.*"

The walnut fell into the palm of his hand. He picked off the shell and dropped the nut into the mortar.

The Franks, he knew, often made their slightest opinions sound like revealed laws. For a few moments he contemplated the nutcracker in his hand, with its chased brass handles and polished iron jaws; then he let his eyes wander around the apartment, from the shelf beside the divan, with its collection of porcelain and books—were they useful? he wondered—to the stack of crocks and pans in the far corner where he cooked.

Yashim shook his head. What sad world did this Gautier inhabit, that everything useful could be described as ugly? Here at his thigh was a marble mortar, and there a kitchen knife given to him by an old Armenian trader in the bazaar. These useful things, Yashim felt, were also beautiful. When he half closed his eyes and thought about Istanbul, he thought of its lovely minarets, for calling the people to prayer. He thought of the scalloped and fluted fountains, which relieved the people's thirst. He considered the slender caïques, which bustled people across the water in all directions. Surely no one thought them ugly!

He cracked another walnut, smiling as his thoughts turned to the sultan's palace. The loveliest women that the empire could provide—would Gautier call them useless, then? Yashim was one of those rare men—if he was a man—who knew the harem for what it was: a school, an arena for ambition, a human factory geared to the production of royal heirs. Many a pasha had blessed the Circassian girls for drawing a headstrong sultan away from delicate affairs of state and into their beds. Not just their beds: the mere effort of observing the intricate etiquette of the harem quarters was enough to keep a sultan busy.

Gautier had got it the wrong way around.

Yashim placed a silken band between the pages of the book and laid it on the divan, careful not to let his oily fingers stain the green leather binding with walnut juice. The binding, and the immaculate gold tooling on the spine, revealed that it belonged to the valide, the sultan's grandmother, who shared his taste in French literature. "If half of what you have told me about Venice is true,"* she had said, "I suggest you try M. Gautier." The book was called *Mademoiselle de Maupin*, about a woman who dressed like a man and was known as a champion swordswoman.

---

* See *The Bellini Card.*

Having scattered the shells out the window, Yashim carried the mortar to his kitchen, set it on the bench, and put a small open pan on the coals. He began to pound the walnuts with a stone pestle. When the pan was hot he threw in a scattering of cumin seeds. He rattled the pan on the coals and poured the seeds into a black iron grinder. He turned the handle. Beautiful? Possibly. Useful? Certainly.

Yashim ground the cumin over the walnuts. He added a pinch of *kirmizi biber*, scorched chili flakes, which he had made in the autumn. He sprinkled the end of a dry loaf with water, then carried on pounding the walnuts. Eventually he squeezed the bread dry and crumbled it into the mortar between his fingers, along with a generous dollop of pomegranate molasses and a spoonful of tomato paste, which he kept under oil in a jar.

When the *muhammara* was finely pounded, he carefully threaded olive oil into the mix, stirring all the while. He tasted the puree, added a pinch of salt and a twist of pepper, and poured it into a bowl, which he covered with a plate and set to one side.

For the next hour he worked at his remaining mezze: a light salad of beans and anchovies mixed with slices of red onion and black olives, and another made with grated beetroot and yogurt. Finally he made soup with leeks and dill.

He was almost done when there was a knock on the door. A chaush in palace uniform stood at the top of the stairs, carrying an invitation on vermilion paper. Yashim's presence, it appeared, was required at the Beylerbeyi palace that afternoon for the announcement of a royal birth—Abdülmecid's first child since his accession.

Yashim bowed, placed a hand to his chest, and murmured, "I shall attend, *inshallah*."

Which explains why, when a second messenger from the palace arrived a few hours later, out of breath and clutching a sealed note, Yashim was no longer there.

3

ELIF bowed her head and gently touched the strings of her oud, straining to hear their tiny hum. Her face was rapt; it was also very beautiful. All the orchestra girls were beautiful—it went without saying, for they played, and lived, for the pleasure and delight of God's felicity on earth, the sultan Abdülmecid.

Satisfied with the setting of the strings, she glanced up to where Ayla was tuning her mandolin, her ear cocked to the belly of the instrument. The two girls exchanged smiles.

Smiles were the harem's petty cash, of course, like frowns and enthusiasm, frostiness and barbed remarks. A smile or a stamped foot—the harem girls passed them back and forth as minor articles of trade. Behind every gesture lay the desire to be noticed. Behind the desire to be noticed lay the hope of preferment: up the ranks of the harem girls, closer and closer to the body of the man whose life, in a way, these girls were destined to curate.

But the smile that passed between Elif and Ayla was a smile of sheer complicity.

Four hundred sequins in silver money. Two necklaces, one of onyx, one of jasper. A gilded coffeepot, three silk shawls, and a jade mouthpiece that Elif thought was more valuable than she let on.

She turned a peg a fraction and laid a finger to the string.

Now that the dust had settled and they were all ensconced in the imperial harem, it turned out to have been a good day's work. The cannons had boomed across the Bosphorus. The late sultan's women had been ordered into the carriages waiting to take them to the Old Palace. It wasn't

Elif's fault that the women took so long about it. They were too busy weeping and grabbing at the sultan's treasures, stuffing jewels down their décolletages, rolling up silver candlesticks in Persian rugs, snapping bracelets onto their wrists. You couldn't blame them, exactly. They had nothing left to look forward to now. Their master was dead and it was the turn of the new girls. Abdülmecid's girls.

Who waited as long as they could. The cannons were firing and their master, the sultan, would be returning to the palace. His palace.

What a racket there'd been: first the wailing and the keening for the departed sultan; then the smashing, and the tantrums, and the screams and the gnashing of teeth when the Chief Black Eunuch told them to pack and be off. As if they could have expected anything else! Abdülmecid's girls were horrified by the rumpus. It was so . . . so undignified. That's what Ayla had said. Elif had called it disgusting, but undignified was better.

Elif still wasn't absolutely sure who'd led the way: Hayat said it was her, but Hayat always said that sort of thing—the way she'd claimed to be the laundry kalfa, hoping the lady housekeeper would back her up in all the confusion! More likely it was one of the lady housekeepers themselves, or all of them together. As everyone said later, if they'd waited any longer they'd have found the doors off their hinges and the whole place cleaned out.

As it was, the harem was in pandemonium. Respectable matrons bawling their eyes out; little thieving Circassians minxing and mewing, with their blond ringlets all askew; somebody dragging at the curtains in a little room; bags and boxes piled pell-mell in the hallways. A girl sat on a box crying into a broken mirror. Black eunuchs moaned and bellowed commands. Elif had stuck with Ayla, who seemed to know where she was going. They ran up a long flight of stairs and burst into a room that overlooked the Bosphorus.

There was a woman in it, shoveling the contents of a small table into a bag.

They all stared at one another. Then the woman screamed.

If she'd kept her mouth shut . . . Ayla sprang at the woman and slapped her on the cheek.

"Stop that! Stop it! What are you doing with that bag?"

The woman tightened her grip on the bag. "This is mine! Get out!"

Ayla made a grab for the bag. The woman yanked it back and the table went over.

"Now look!"

Elif snatched at the woman's scarf. Ayla kept her eyes on the bag. "What's in there? What are you stealing?"

They heard running footsteps in the corridor and one of their girls put her head round the door, then withdrew it again.

The woman with the bag seemed to have trouble breathing. Her eyes bulged and her face went red. Elif gave the scarf a last savage tug and Ayla went for the bag. The woman staggered and let it go. "It's mine," she choked.

"Rubbish. If it was yours you'd have packed it by now. Go on, get out!"

They'd shoved the woman out into the corridor. She was wringing her hands, but there were two of them and there wasn't anything she could do. Ayla and Elif put their backs to the door and watched the handle rattle.

After a while they heard more people running in the corridor. The handle went still.

The two girls turned to each other and burst out laughing.

A lot of it turned out to be junk. It was pathetic what those women tried to carry off—kohl, and half-used bottles of rosewater, and little paper talismans. She'd obviously thought she could get away with the coffeepot, but even if she'd been the coffee kalfa it didn't belong to her! The rest of the stuff in the bag was almost certainly stolen, too. All that money—and she wasn't even pretty!

Elif touched her hand to her scarf. The good thing was, it hadn't gotten torn at all.

YASHIM'S KITCHEN

When not hunting down brutal killers and untangling Byzantine mysteries, Yashim can be found cooking up culinary delights in his modest kitchen. This recipe for *mücver* is suitable for entertaining sultans and eunuchs alike.

Mücver (also known as zucchini fritters)

- 2 zucchinis
- 4 tablespoons flour
- Salt
- Pepper to taste
- 4 eggs
- 1 cup milk
- 1 thick slice feta cheese
- Fresh dill
- 1 clove garlic
- 1 cup plain yogurt
- Olive oil for frying

Grate a couple of firm, fresh zucchinis into a colander. Squeeze them dry by hand, then mix them in a bowl together with four tablespoons of plain flour, a pinch of salt, and a good scratch of pepper. Beat four eggs and work them into the mix. Now add a cupful of milk, a thick slice of feta cheese, crumbled or grated, and a good bunch of fresh dill, chopped.

Stir the mix and let it stand while you crush and chop a clove of garlic with a pinch of salt and beat it into a cupful of plain yogurt.

Now heat a generous layer of olive oil in a skillet. When the oil is hot, start dropping in tablespoons of the zucchini mix, making little patties. Fry them on both sides and pile them up on some kitchen paper. When they are all crisp and done, heap them onto a plate and spoon the garlicky yogurt over them.

AUTHOR INTERVIEW

You have written a history of the Ottoman Empire, Lords of the Horizons, *as well as a travelogue of your journeys in Istanbul,* On Foot to the Golden Horn. *Was a historical mystery the next logical step? What inspired you to move now into the realm of fiction?*

For years I was scared of writing fiction: it looked to me like skating on very thin ice. What if imagination failed? What if the plot began to sag? I wrote books that clung to facts and observations like a safety rail.

When I started to write *The Janissary Tree* I had nothing more than a central character and a period in Ottoman history that had always intrigued me. I wrote for the fun of it—and it turned out *not* to be like going out on the ice. It was more like flying.

I saw that fiction could go to places that other forms shunned. Writing is about creating patterns: sentence by sentence you select the words, and page by page, chapter by chapter, you search for rhythms and echoes. A travelogue says: here, this is the place. A history tries to explain why it's like nowhere else. But in fiction your characters, their motives, and their settings link in to a more perfect and revealing pattern.

The mystery genre is wide open, I think. It's a very accommodating form, and it locks in the element of suspense that's essential to all good writing. It can be travelogue: Istanbul, for instance, is almost a character in its own right in my books. It can throw light on the way a society works in greater detail than a simple history book. History favors the winners: fiction gives the noncombatants, bystanders, and the overlooked their voice, too.

The Bellini Card is your third investigator Yashim mystery. What is it like to return to Yashim, and how has he changed as you have written about him over the course of multiple books?

I think he has more fun than he used to. Perhaps he's more relaxed now about who he is. Maybe I've got to know him better myself. He's a lonely man who battles against bitterness, and who has found a degree of consolation in friendship. The valide is alone; his friend Palewski is alone. But what they have discovered is trust.

Talk a little about your research for The Bellini Card. *What did you discover about the period and setting that you had not known before? Are there any interesting tidbits that did not make it into the book?*

I knew the Ottoman background very well; I knew about the Bellini portrait, too—or so I thought. It's evidence of a rare cultural interchange between East and West—but when you look into it, those divisions begin to look forced. The Bellini family, all painters, may well have been the court painters of the Byzantine emperors—so Mehmed the Conqueror was emphasizing continuity—and legitimacy—by getting Gentile to do his portrait. Or was he chosen by the Venetians—for the same reason?

The bizarre tale of the rediscovery of the portrait is told in the epilogue, but not its subsequent career. Its condition—overpainted, slipped from wood to canvas, all that—means that scholars now refuse to say that it is painted by Bellini: "attributed to" is their best shot. The rank of the portrait in the canon of art has been downgraded, which is why it isn't on permanent display in London—you have to look at it on Wednesday afternoons, in a basement crammed with minor and dubious works.

But just as it's being downgraded at that level, its significance as a poster boy for East-West relations has rocketed. It regularly turns up in exhibitions—and when it reached Istanbul in the early years of this century, the lines went around the block. It's the only real portrait of an Ottoman sultan.

Why the change of location this time, to Venice?

Well, why not? Venice is Istanbul's alter ego in the Mediterranean. Venice grew up under Byzantine control. Later, in 1204, the Venetians captured Constantinople themselves. The loot from the sack of the city made Venice what she is today—the Horses in St. Mark's, the treasures in the cathedral. The two cities are reflections of each other. Venice may be more Byzantine than Istanbul.

That said, I simply couldn't resist the opportunity to write about Venice in the doldrums. So much has been written about Venice, it's hard to find another thing to say, but this is the period everyone skips. The old republic had been disbanded, trade had moved away. Under foreign occupation, Venice was a slimy, stinking, moldering slum, mired in mud and poverty. My kind of town.

Now we imagine Venice to have been always beautiful and alluring: but in 1840 only a very young Ruskin seemed to have noticed what we nowadays take for granted.

Yashim is a most unusual detective—in a field where toughness and masculinity typically rule the day, he is a eunuch, a chef, an intellectual, and often has a light touch. Was this a conscious effort on your part to go against genre conventions? Talk a bit about what inspired the creation of Yashim.

At one level, Yashim simply emerged as the best candidate for the job: in Istanbul in the 1830s, only a eunuch could plausibly talk to the women secluded in their harems, attend the palace, mix with life on the street. Maybe there are too many detectives who like food, but in Yashim's case it was an obvious talent—it's a sensual world to match the one he's lost (sort of), and it's also a way of signaling to readers the kind of world we're in. We're food savvy, and the very mention of eggplant or garlic comes freighted with the spice of the eastern Mediterranean.

It's also a question of motive. Yashim belongs to his world, but he's at a tangent to it: he watches the human comedy with a certain detachment.

That's something he shares with some of the classic detectives, like Sherlock Holmes, or Philip Marlowe, or Poirot. Actually, they're eunuchs, too: it's just not acceptable to say so in 1940s LA or Victorian London.

Funnily enough, I invented Palewski just because I realized on the job that detectives need friends in order to speak their minds. And Palewski's much more the classic detective himself, in some ways. He's a loner, he drinks too much, he has a sardonic take on the world.

When writing a mystery, do you know the end before you start and plot backward from it, or does the solution reveal itself to you along the way?

I think at the speed I write. I begin with a shadowy sort of idea, an area for scrutiny, and a vague notion of the people involved, and I let the story emerge as I write. I can't always quite tell who the villain is. A lot of my plotting is derived from the Scooby-Doo school of "let's find out who he really is!" and I have sleepless nights knitting the whole thing together. But if I knew the whole plot, and the characters beforehand—and many crime writers insist on having this—then why would I write?

Talk a little about the writing life—how long does it take to craft and develop the story, and do you rely on any tricks to get the imagination going?

My nonfiction books took two, three, four years to research and write. If you're writing a series, publishers and booksellers and readers want a book a year. That's the time frame, do with it what you will. Which means, get on with it. Dig the garden, run the children to school, wash up, whatever—and then plunge in. Keeping focused is the main challenge. I dream of writer's retreats, or of a small hotel in northern France where you can have a huge sloping room and meals thrown in for a few dollars. I never get there, of course. The stories develop out of my reading. Traveler's tales, guidebooks, memoirs; for *An Evil Eye* I've been reading a lot about magic—and also some fascinating and very rare memoirs of harem life.

At low moments I'll read a few pages of Dan Brown to remind me that it's the story that counts.

What are your favorite mysteries or crime novels?

Graham Greene's *The Confidential Agent* is wreathed with atmosphere and menace, and so is Beatrix Potter's *The Tale of Samuel Whiskers*: it's a genuinely terrifying story, beautifully told (and you get the pictures, too). Raymond Chandler's plots may flounder a bit, but I don't mind. He creates a complete world that you are forced to believe in; the dialogue is razor sharp.

Have you committed any crimes yourself?

None that would earn me jail time in a liberal democracy. That doesn't stop me waking up in the night and thinking about something I really wish I hadn't done.

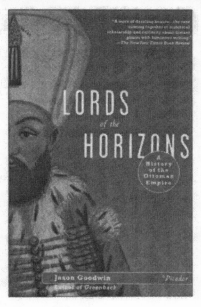

LORDS OF THE HORIZONS: A HISTORY OF THE OTTOMAN EMPIRE
BY JASON GOODWIN • ISBN-13: 978-0-312-42066-6 • ISBN-10: 0-312-42066-8
368 PAGES • $17.00

For six hundred years, the Ottoman Empire swelled and declined. Islamic, martial, civilized, and
tolerant, it advanced in three centuries from the dusty foothills of Anatolia to rule on the Danube
and the Nile; at its height, Indian rajahs and the kings of France beseeched the empire's aid. In its
last three hundred years the empire seemed ready to collapse, a prodigy of survival and decay. In
this striking evocation of the empire's power, Jason Goodwin explores how the Ottomans rose and
how, against all odds, they lingered on.

**"A work of dazzling beauty…the rare coming together of historical scholarship
and curiosity about distant places with luminous writing."**
—*THE NEW YORK TIMES BOOK REVIEW*

**"Jason Goodwin's deftly written and beguiling history of the Ottoman Empire is
particularly pertinent today when the cauldron of ancient hatred once more boils
over, but his prose would be welcome at any time."**
—*THE BOSTON GLOBE*

PICADOR
www.picadorusa.com

Made in the USA
Lexington, KY
26 April 2014